Praise for Carolyn M
Regency Brides: Daughter

"In her signature style that sucks readers st
era, Carolyn Miller crafts a story rich w.
that held me enthralled from the get-go!"

ROSEANNA M. WHITE, best-selling author of the Ladies of the
Manor and Shadows Over England series

"Carolyn Miller has quickly become one of my go-to Regency authors. I know when I pick up one of her novels, I will find myself immersed in a story with characters that keep pulling me back to the pages. . . . With a keen eye for historical detail and descriptions that transported me to the shores of England, this book was a delight."

CARA PUTMAN, author of the Hidden Justice
and Cornhusker Dreams series

"Move over, Elizabeth Bennet. Here comes Miss Hatherleigh! In true Jane Austen style, Carolyn Miller pens a delightful Regency novel filled with intrigue and a dash of danger. . . . Readers of all ages will love this fine historical romance."

MICHELLE GRIEP, Christy Award winner of the
Once Upon a Dickens Christmas series

Praise for Carolyn Miller's
Regency Brides: A Promise of Hope

"Carolyn Miller doesn't disappoint with yet another engaging Regency novel that leaves you wanting more. . . . With impeccable accuracy, witty dialogue, and seamless integration of Christian faith, Carolyn weaves a classic tale that is sure to become a permanent addition to your collection."

AMBER MILLER STOCKTON, best-selling author of
Liberty's Promise

"Fans of Christian Regency romances by Sarah Ladd, Sarah Eden, and Michelle Griep will adore Carolyn Miller's books!"

DAWN CRANDALL, award-winning author of
The Everstone Chronicles

"Carolyn Miller is witty, romantic, and heartwarming, with a gentle dose of faith-boldness, too. Layered characters and attention to historical detail make each book a great read!"

READING IS MY SUPERPOWER, blog, readingismysuperpower.org

"Readers who are looking for an English historical romance reminiscent of Jane Austen and Georgette Heyer will be delighted!"

CARRIE TURANSKY, award-winning author of *Across the Blue* and
Shine Like the Dawn

"Carolyn Miller writes with skill and grace that brings the Regency period to vivid life."

JULIANNA DEERING, author of the Drew Farthering Mysteries

"With exquisite dialogue, beautiful descriptions, and careful attention to detail, Carolyn Miller continues to draw her readers into a magnificent Regency world."

PEPPER D. BASHAM, author of the Penned in Time
and Mitchell's Crossroads series

"While many modern-day authors are able to dress their stories in an admirable reproduction, few are able to re-create the tone and essence of the era with the authenticity Carolyn Miller displays."

FICTION AFICIONADO, blog, fictionaficionadoblog.wordpress.com

Misleading
Miss Verity

REGENCY BRIDES

DAUGHTERS *of* AYNSLEY

Misleading Miss Verity

CAROLYN MILLER

Kregel
Publications

Misleading Miss Verity
© 2019 by Carolyn Miller

Published by Kregel Publications, a division of Kregel Inc., 2450 Oak Industrial
Dr. NE, Grand Rapids, MI 49505.

Scripture quotations are from the King James Version.

The persons and events portrayed in this work are the creations of the author, and
any resemblance to persons living or dead is purely coincidental.

ISBN 978-0-8254-4591-0, print
ISBN 978-0-8254-7571-9, epub

Printed in the United States of America
19 20 21 22 23 24 25 26 27 28 / 5 4 3 2 1

For Brooke

*Fellow Georgette Heyer fan and friend,
whose belief in my books helped make
dreams come true.*

❧ CHAPTER ONE

Bath, Somerset
January 1820

IT WAS THE sobbing that decided her.

The Honorable Verity Hatherleigh eased from her bed and stole across the room to the disconsolate girl whose snuffling and muffled weeping made sleep impossible. She touched her roommate on the arm. "Lucy, dear. What is wrong?"

The shrouded figure shifted, lowering the heavy blankets whose inability to stifle the sounds of sadness had perturbed Verity's slumber. Clouded moonlight streamed pale from the window, framing a plain, round face made less lovely by red eyes and blotched cheeks. "It's Papa. He . . . he's—" Lady Lucinda Wainbridge gulped, her chin quivering, a sure sign more waterworks were in the offing.

"Now, Lucy, stop, take a deep breath"—Verity waited as the older girl complied—"and tell me what has happened."

After another shaky breath, Lucinda exhaled noisily, then blew her nose with a honk reminiscent of a startled goose.

"If you don't want Miss Pelling to check in here, you might want to do that more quietly."

Lucy's eyes flashed accusingly. "You weren't here when I was telling the others."

"No, because I was in Helena's room, helping her with her French for tomorrow's examination, as you well know." Verity dashed back to her bed and pulled on her padded dressing gown. These rooms, for all the exorbitant fees paid, were never heated properly. She returned, wrapping a woolen blanket around her shoulders. "Now, what happened to your father?" Had the Earl of Retford sickened? Her heart quickened. Had he died? Poor Lucinda . . .

Lucinda shook her head. "Nothing has happened to Papa. It's what he will do."

"Which is?"

"Remove me from Haverstock's!"

This was a bad thing? "Why are you so certain he will?"

Lucinda wiped her eyes. "He's bound to as soon as Haverstock sends him the letter she found from William."

"She found it? I thought you had it well secured. Didn't you place it under the floorboard as I suggested?"

"I was going to . . ."

Lucinda's shoulders slumped, and she looked so miserable, Verity didn't have the heart to scold her roommate's folly. Dear foolish Lucy, with her silly infatuation for a squire's son of whom her fastidious parents would never approve. Many had been the confidences Lucinda had whispered, ever since Verity had been forced to leave the room she had previously shared with Helena. Many a dull evening spent listening to Lucy prattle on about William's inestimable qualities, whilst Verity strained to hear the telltale creaks in the hall that told of vigilant staff, waiting until the creaks had quite faded away before stealing across to the room which had fostered a friendship more dear than that of her family's.

Helena Chisholm was the most loyal and encouraging person Verity had ever met, filled with a zest for life and mischief that rivaled Verity's own. When Miss Haverstock had been informed about one of Verity's previous secret visits to the headmistress's study by the not-so-honorable Prudence Gaspard, Verity's separation from Helena had been swift, painful, and irrevocable. Her punishment was to be bored by Lucinda's ill-advised romance for the remaining weeks until their schooling was considered complete.

Not that Verity was against romantic attachments as such; more that with such opposites involved, this particular attachment seemed a complete and utter waste of emotions, when anyone could see it was an attachment doomed to futility and failure. Her lips twitched. Although, judging from Lucinda's descriptions of her beau, he seemed as dull as she, so perhaps they were well-matched.

"This is not funny, Verity. What am I going to do? When Papa sees what we have been writing to one another, he'll have a fit, and threaten to marry me off to old Lord Winchester. I'd rather die than marry him!" Lucinda sniffed, as another tear tracked down her face.

"What did William write that is so concerning?" Normally Lucinda shared every phrase over and over until Verity could mouth along too, but lately she had been too busy helping some of the younger girls prepare for their upcoming examinations. "Surely it cannot be so bad."

The moonlight revealed a faint blush on Lucinda's cheeks. "It was most poetic. William was describing me, you see. He said I am beautiful." She smiled a wobbly smile.

"And if he loves you, then I suppose he should." Verity nodded her affirmation, while wondering at how men could be so blind. Lucinda, beautiful? Even at her best she could only be described as somewhat attractive. Verity knew herself to hold no pretensions to beauty—her hair was too black, her eyes too pale, her eyebrows too slanted, her chin too pointed, the whole effect considered to be odd-looking rather than attractive, or so her mother said. But it had always surprised her how men could see what they wanted to see, such as the men who loved her elder sisters and openly admired their golden beauty, most recently at last month's Boxing Day Ball during which Cecy's betrothal had been announced. In Verity's mind, Helena was more attractive, her smile even brighter than the red curls that adorned her head. "Titian-haired" their drawing master had once remarked.

Lucinda sighed, reclaiming Verity's attention. "I suppose he did get a little carried away." She smiled coyly, clearly inviting Verity to enquire further.

Verity stifled the yawn. "It's very late—"

"He said my lips are like a scarlet ribbon!"

Verity blinked. Well, that *was* poetic. And rather surprising for prosy William to have thought of such a thing.

"He wrote that my hair is like a flock of goats and my neck is like a tower—"

She bit her lip to stop a smile. Surely a lovesick fool could be the only one to believe squat Lucinda held any aspirations to towers.

"But I think the part Miss Haverstock took particular exception to—"

And she whispered something about deer and breasts.

"Lucinda!" The heat of embarrassment traveled from Verity's cheeks to her toes. "I can fully understand why Miss Haverstock might take exception to these things." She paused, uncomfortably aware just how much like her mother she had sounded. She gentled her tone. "I do not think your William has much sense if he is writing to you in such an ungentlemanly manner."

"But he said it's from the Bible!"

"Yes, but the Bible isn't all true, is it?"

Lucinda stared at her. "How can you be Helena's friend and think such things?"

Verity shrugged. While she and Helena held very different opinions on matters of faith, and had even engaged in several animated discussions resulting in an agreement to disagree, their contrasting views had never marred their friendship. But that was of no matter now, nor likely to ever be of any great importance. "Where William found such words is of little consequence. What matters is that Miss Haverstock knows and will doubtless write to your father immediately, and you can be assured William will forever be banished from your company."

"But whatever will we do?"

Verity thought hard. "What gives you confidence she will act so soon?"

"She said she would write tonight! And she's like you, she always keeps her word." Lucinda's face crumpled, reminding Verity of a dropped pink handkerchief.

"Do not fret." She patted Lucinda on the shoulder. "I am sure that your father will be none the wiser." She rose, shrugged off the blanket, and exchanged her pale dressing gown for something darker.

"But—"

"Go to sleep, Lucy. I will retrieve the note and ensure any letter to your father is not incriminating."

Lucinda sagged in relief. "Thank you."

"My pleasure."

Verity spoke the truth. Nothing gave her greater pleasure than righting wrongs and seeing justice prevail. And if it allowed another adventure with Helena, all the better.

She eased open the door, quickly glancing both ways. Nobody. She closed the door gently and stole past the next room, taking care to avoid the squeaking floorboard. Her lips flattened. Nothing squeaked louder in this school than Prudence, or Gasper, as she was widely known, the moniker saying much about her unfortunate propensity for sharing what news she could about others' misdemeanors. She hurried to the room a further two doors away and crept inside.

"Helena?" She tiptoed to the bed and gently shook her friend. "Helena, wake up."

"Verity?" Helena squinted, her voice soft to not disturb her slumbering roommate. "Whatever is the matter?"

"We need to get into Haverstock's study once more."

All vestiges of sleep drained from Helena's face as she abruptly sat up. "But why?"

Verity sighed. "Lucinda's young man wrote her a letter with most salacious content."

"Lucy? But that's ridiculous."

"Ridiculous it may be, but she fears she will be forced to marry some old man and never see William again."

Helena yawned, shifted the bedcovers, and pulled on a dark tartan-patterned dressing gown. "And you must play the knight in shining armor again."

Verity grinned. "I'm afraid I must."

"Then I suppose I must as well."

A minute later they were moving quietly down the staircase at the end of the hall, not the grand central staircase, but the little one used by the maids—and sly teachers. Around them the house sighed and whispered, the building, almost as ancient as Aynsley Manor, settling into slumber. Soft snores emanated from Miss Pelling's room. Verity exhaled. Haverstock's didn't need a watchdog, not when that terrier of a teacher was on the prowl.

Down the hall came a scurrying noise. Verity shivered. She hoped tonight would not bring a repeat encounter with a rodent. Rats, with their wormlike tails and bold black eyes gave her pause like nothing else. Not even Stephen Heathcote's most absurd pranks had ever elicited so much fear.

But so far, so good.

They reached the heavy oak door to Miss Haverstock's study. All was quiet, no light spilled from underneath, so Verity grasped the door handle and turned. It clicked and swung silently open. They hurried inside, closing the door as quickly and quietly as they'd opened it. Inside, wavering moonlight cast a ghostly sheen over the detritus-laden desk: papers stacked in untidy piles, wax-spattered stubs of candles, several vases of wilting flowers, whose smell of decay wrinkled Verity's nose.

"Where do you think it might be?" Helena whispered.

Verity pointed to the escritoire. "Look for an envelope addressed to the Earl of Retford, and I'll search for the letter from William the silly goose."

Helena giggled softly then began pulling out drawers, rummaging through the compartments whilst Verity concentrated on finding the telltale blue paper William used for all his correspondence. She opened a tall cupboard where essential information was kept on students, past and present. She flicked through until she found Lucinda's file, scanning the basics: parents, county of birth, social position, her father's estimated income, a column on Lucinda's academic achievements, which was sadly short. Truly, there seemed little of real value to be gained by reading such things, especially when it felt so intrusive. Exactly why Miss Haverstock felt it necessary to keep such precise information on her students was something of a mystery, but time did not permit speculation now. She placed Lucinda's file back and picked up her own, scanning it quickly to see what had been added since last time.

"Helena, look!" she whispered. "Apparently you and I are ill-advised companions."

"What?" Helena shut the escritoire a little harder than necessary. "Show me that." She frowned, her bottom lip protruding as she read the file. "I have never understood why that woman despises you so much." Her finger jabbed the page. "She has three pages of notes about your misdemeanors, but not once has she mentioned your assisting of the junior girls. And look, there she lists your academic achievements, but no mention of your perfect marks in geography, French, nor anything about mathematics or the sciences. I don't understand her at all!"

"I believe the only science she values is that of the domestic variety, and that is something at which I will never excel."

"Not that you will ever need to, not with your income."

Verity inclined her head, acknowledging the truth of Helena's comment. Yet another reason why she valued her friend so highly; Helena did not possess one jot of jealousy. She took pleasure in Verity's good prospects as if they were her own.

"Come, we best find this letter if we are to return before dawn."

Helena yawned, as if the remark had reminded her of the late hour. "I have found nothing here. You?"

"No," Verity muttered. Where could it be? Unless she'd already posted the letter to the Earl, and included William's epistle as evidence. "She couldn't have posted it yet . . ."

"But it might be—"

"—ready to be posted!" Verity finished.

They tidied as best they could—but really, would Miss Haverstock even notice her desk had been picked over?—and moved to the small table near the front door, where a silver salver held the mail to be posted.

"*Voilà!*" Verity fished out an envelope addressed in perfect copperplate to the Earl of Retford. "Now we shall see."

They stole back to Miss Haverstock's room, closing the door and lighting a candle before carefully peeling open the paper. Inside, a second blue paper was folded neatly, the page of writing as primly precise as the penmanship lessons they'd been forced to endure under Miss Haverstock's tutelage.

Verity read it quickly, biting her lip as she read the familiar accusations.

"She is unbelievable!" Helena whispered. "How can she think you would have ever encouraged Lucinda to form such an attachment? I call it monstrous."

"I suppose it is easier to blame someone else rather than inform the earl he has a silly widgeon for a daughter."

"Yes, I imagine that must be so." Helena sighed. "But what will you do? You cannot let her tell such lies."

Verity smiled. "Of course not. But what truth do you wish the earl to know?"

Helena's eyes grew round. "Are you asking me to do what I think you are?"

"For the last time, I promise. You know there is nobody with a better hand than you."

"But what if I get caught?"

"We have not been caught so far. And don't you think that so many parents have been relieved to learn their daughters are thriving here at Haverstock's? Really, are there any parents who need to be told in long and glorious detail about their offspring's shortcomings?" Verity smiled wryly. "If they are anything like my mama, they would already be all too conscious of that."

Helena's brow furrowed. "I am sure your mama loves you."

"Perhaps. In her own special way." Verity finished mending the pen, then moved the quill and inkpot to Helena. "Now, write to the earl something that more correctly informs him as to who has been influencing his daughter."

Every tick of the wooden clock seemed to take an hour, so by that estimation almost a lifetime passed before Helena finished, and was completing the copied direction on the front. "But it must be sealed."

"And so it shall."

Whilst Helena stuffed the original letter in her dressing gown, Verity eased open the bottom drawer, pulled out the stump of wax and held it near the sputtering flame until melted crimson dropped on the parchment. With a few swift thrusts of the knife she approximated the twisted S and H that constituted the Haverstock seal, before wiping the blade on the inner hem of her gown and returning quill, wax, and ink to their rightful place.

Something clattered outside.

Verity blew out the candle, heart thumping as steps creaked near the door. She pulled Helena down and they crouched, two rabbits burrowing in the pocket of space beneath the desk.

"Is someone here?"

Verity held her breath. Miss Pelling! She was a bull terrier, persistent until she found her prey. She heard a sniff, then another. Could she smell the candle? Oh no! She placed her fingers on the still-hot wick, wincing at the burn.

The door thudded as it opened wide, hitting a crowded bookshelf behind. Beside her, Verity could feel Helena squirm. They silently shifted deeper into the leg space beneath the desk, pulling their dark gowns to cover every area of pale skin.

A sudden urge to giggle tickled Verity's chest. Whatever could they say to get out of this predicament? It was more than a little absurd, the two of them, cramped, crowded, craning their necks as they awaited their fate. Not for the first time she counted it fortunate Helena was not that much more rounded than she. Slenderness might not be to men's taste, so Mama often intoned, but it had its advantages.

Verity peered over her shoulder as the lower part of a white nightgown appeared. Her pulse thundered in her ears. Beside her she could feel Helena shaking. Was it restrained laughter or fear? Remorse bubbled up within. Tonight's episode was all Verity's doing. She did not fear punishment for herself, but Helena's attendance at Haverstock's was entirely due to her wealthy godmother's goodwill. If she should be expelled Verity could never forgive herself. She wondered for the first time exactly how one should pray.

"Little better than a pigsty," Miss Pelling muttered.

That desire to laugh swelled again. Long had she suspected Miss Haverstock's deputy as harboring such feelings, fostered by the flash of impatience Miss Pelling had exhibited on more than one occasion, but to hear it from her own lips . . .

The gown moved away. Verity exhaled silently. Then a crackling sound was followed by Miss Pelling's face!

Verity shut her eyes, waiting for the retribution, waiting for the most tremendous scold of her life, waiting—

"Drat these eyes! I cannot see a thing!"

Verity cracked open an eye and stifled a gasp. One bony hand was stretched toward her, was almost touching her shoulder! She shifted fractionally, squashing poor Helena even more in the process, until the hand withdrew, to be followed by a hard slap on the desktop, which reverberated in Verity's ears.

"I'll be back as soon as I have my pince-nez, my dear." And the scurry of feet suggested it would not be long.

After a few seconds of awkward maneuvering, Verity and Helena escaped from their hidey-hole. Verity snatched the letter from Helena's grasp. "I'll replace it while you go up the far stairs."

"But—"

"Go!"

With a quick grin Helena melted into the dark hall, while Verity stuffed William's letter in the bodice of her nightgown, and rounded the corner to the front door. She crouched behind the small table, replacing the rewritten letter with the others to be posted on the morrow. Her heart raced as she waited until she saw the white of Miss Pelling's nightgown return to the study. Quick as a flash she sped to the main stairs, slipping through the shadows, being careful to avoid the creaking steps as she neared the top.

"You there! Stop!"

Something like terror bade wings to her feet, but she forced herself to halt. Verity Hatherleigh was no coward. Neither did she want to run the risk of Helena being discovered. She turned and met Miss Pelling's angry glare.

Her face seemed pinched, all except for her nostrils, which appeared twice as large as normal. "I knew it was you! What have you got to say for yourself, young lady?"

"I am very sorry your sleep was disturbed?"

An angry hiss suggested her attempt at humor had fallen sadly flat. "Were you or were you not in Miss Haverstock's study?"

"I was."

"Yet you did not speak up when I asked you to! Why?"

"I did not want to get into trouble, Miss Pelling."

"A likely story."

"It is the truth."

A loud sniff. The pale eyes narrowed. "And can you tell me why you felt it necessary to be there?"

"She had something I needed."

"At this hour of the night?"

"She was going to dispose of it tomorrow morning."

"And this item is . . . ?" Thin brows rose.

"A letter."

"Have you got it in your possession?"

Verity sighed inwardly and withdrew the blue paper from her nightgown. Miss Pelling snatched it and whipped it open, her eyes widening as she read the brief missive from William.

Verity's thoughts ran quickly. Did Miss Pelling think it was addressed to Verity? She might well assume such a thing, for he never wrote Lucinda's name, save on the direction. Of course, if Miss Pelling turned the paper over she would realize, but if Verity pretended . . .

"Can you tell me who this William is?"

"He . . . he is a neighbor, Miss Pelling." Lucinda's neighbor, but so far she wasn't actually lying.

"And can you tell me why he finds it necessary to write in such *lurid* detail?"

"No, miss. I can only assume he is religious. It is a description from the Bible," she added helpfully.

"I know very well where it is from!" Miss Pelling drew in a deep breath. "Can you tell me why you stole it?"

"Is it stealing to retrieve your own possessions?" A philosophical argument, so not technically a lie. "I rather think it stealing for it to have been taken from my room."

"Do not—!"

"But you asked why I retrieved it." Verity gave a deep sigh. "You see, I do not want to lose his words as I have never had anyone express such admiration to me."

Which was true. It was also true that she had not met any man from whom she wanted to hear such words. Not that she wanted to be described in *quite* the same way as Lucinda preferred. But still, it would be nice if one day a gentleman could think her as alluring as a heroine in Miss Austen's work, and express similar thoughts to her. She bit her lip. Was such a thing possible? "Miss Pelling, wouldn't you like to see the words penned from your *paramour*?"

The older woman rubbed her forehead and glanced away.

Verity took a step forward. "My father would not like to be the recipient of this letter. He's not religious, you understand, and I do not imagine he should like to be burdened with such things."

"You do not, do you?"

"No. I am so terribly sorry to appear to be so underhanded—"

"Or so sorry to have been caught?"

That, too. "But I really thought it best for everyone if William's letter was not included in any correspondence to one's father." Verity put on her most pleading face. "Please, Miss Pelling, please tell me you understand?"

The teacher squinted, studying her as though Verity were an unpleasant specimen in a museum. "And the letter to your father?"

"Is undisturbed." An unwritten letter to her own papa could not be disturbed, could it?

"I agree that the, er, contents are not appropriate for a young girl to receive"—Verity held her breath—"but I can also understand your reasoning in removing unnecessary pain from your parents."

Verity nodded. "I am sure Miss Haverstock has written a full account of my misdemeanors. Anything further might result in my immediate removal from this place."

And such an event would likely result in the removal of the Viscount Aynsley's sizeable financial support, thus possibly affecting Miss Pelling's future at the Seminary, too.

"I will need to mention this to Miss Haverstock—"

"Oh, but do you think that prudent? I am sorry to say she often does not seem to make the wisest of decisions."

"Neither do you, it would appear," replied Miss Pelling tartly.

"Of course." Verity hung her head. "I have done all number of unwise things, but you do understand there has never been any malicious intent. Please, Miss Pelling, do not mention this to Miss Haverstock, as I fear she will insist on mailing William's letter, and I am sure that will not serve anyone's interests." Not Lucinda's interests, to be sure, and after tonight's little charade, definitely not Verity's, either.

Miss Pelling sighed. "Very well. I will not mention it to her."

"Oh, thank you, Miss Pelling!"

"And you may keep your letter, but I must insist you tell your young man to never write to you at this address again."

"Of course, Miss Pelling! I will ensure he never does." Verity would throttle Lucinda should he do so.

"Now go straight to bed, and catch whatever sleep you can before dawn arrives. And I will need to cancel your privileges for the next month, and shall expect you to attend to the juniors for another two weeks as punishment for such shameless behavior."

"Of course, Miss Pelling. Thank you, Miss Pelling."

Helping the younger girls was no great trial, as she suspected Miss Pelling knew.

She curtsied and ran up the stairs, quickly checked that Helena had made it back safely, then headed to her room, where Lucinda snored in blissful oblivion. After placing William's letter underneath the loose floorboard she'd suggested weeks ago, Verity stripped off her cloak, climbed into bed, dropped against the pillows, and closed her eyes.

"Verity? Is that you?"

A wave of tiredness refused her eyelids from opening. "Yes, Lucy." She yawned. "And yes, I have your letter."

"Good."

"Good night, Lucy."

"G'night, Verity. Oh, and thank you."

"You're welcome."

Verity smiled in the darkness, pulled her blankets up to her chin, and allowed the tension of the evening to slowly ebb away. Her mind drifted, wondering what the enamored William looked like, and how he could think of plain, plump Lucinda in such exalted terms. Truly the heart was a mysterious thing. She rolled to her side as her earlier thoughts resurfaced. Would she ever meet a man who caused her heart to flutter faster? Did he even exist, or was she doomed, like poor Miss Haverstock and Miss Pelling, to don the cap of spinsterhood? Her lips flattened. Somehow she didn't think Mama would permit such a thing, even if her dowry were not a very respectable fifty thousand, sure to make her one of the upcoming season's most eligible young ladies.

No, she sighed internally. She would probably marry. But would her future husband's feelings be that of ardor or mere friendly esteem? Her sisters had both found love; was that possible for her, too? And if he were someone for whom she held tender feelings, what title would he hold? For, to be sure, Papa, and especially Mama, would never allow Verity to be so unevenly yoked. She'd sensed her mother's disappointment that her sisters had settled for mere second sons, gentlemen who were unlikely to attain the high titles their brothers held. Not that she had any desire to be a marchioness or countess. Such things had never held appeal. No, other things mattered far more. Would he share her fascination for other lands? Would he enjoy the outdoors and riding? What would he look like? Where did he live? What was he doing now?

The questions continued to prod and tease, ideas swirling and shifting, until finally exhaustion dragged her into oblivion, and she lay dreaming of faraway castles and a starlit sea.

Sydney Town, New South Wales

"Stop! Thief!"

Anthony Jardine ran after the weedy youth, whose skill at dodging pedestrians and carts alike suggested this was not the first time he had fled his crime. Around him, the sound of Irish and English accents filled his ears, while January sunshine beat down as mercilessly as whips upon a convict's back, sending clouds of dust into his nose. Yet he could not give up. Newly widowed Mrs. Hetherington could scarce afford to lose her purse. He sped past a wagon piled high with skins (calf, sheep, kangaroo—the stench was appalling), then continued the chase, along George Street, following the urchin around the corner into Brown Bear Lane, whereupon he disappeared into the darkness of The Romping Horse.

His nose wrinkled as he pushed past the sweat-drenched mass of swarthy-faced laborers, of whom he suspected not a few were recently emancipated, judging from their ragged clothes and foul language.

"Has anyone seen a young lad?"

There was a jeering sound. "Ye should be ashamed of yerself, reverend!"

Anthony fought the urge to tug at his clerical collar and raised his voice. "He has stolen from a widow—"

"Cor, it's a widder now!" A woman cackled. "He gets around, this one does, worse than a bull in a paddock full of—"

"Please! Can anyone help me?"

A woman—she was hardly a lady—of indeterminate age and hair color pushed her ample bosom into his side and smiled up at him, revealing stained teeth. "I can help yer, luv."

The inn filled with raucous laughter. "Millie helps anyone for a few bob a tumble!"

Anthony's cheeks burned. "Ma'am, please, have you seen the lad?"

"Listen to him speak so fancy!" She fluttered a hand in imitation of a fan. "And so handsome, though I've never been over fond of red hair, meself."

Clearly no help was to be found here. "Excuse me." He inclined his head and shoved through the stench of smoke, cheap whiskey, and lower values. A tattered blue coat caught his eye. He maneuvered around a giant with bullock-wide shoulders and followed the urchin. The hall led past a few closed rooms—whose occupants he had no wish to disturb—stepping down to a makeshift kitchen before a propped-open door gave abrupt exit onto a small courtyard. The boy hurried to a beefy-faced man and handed him the pink purse Anthony had seen him lift from poor Clara Hetherington back on William Street.

"You there! Stop!" He stepped forward. "That money does not belong to you."

The large man looked him up and down. "I be fancyin' it don't belong to you, neither."

"A lady of my acquaintance—"

"Of yer acquaintance, eh?" The red-faced man grinned at a couple of shadows that had detached themselves from the brick-lined walls and were moving in to listen.

"From my congregation," Anthony said loudly. Technically, it wasn't his congregation—he was only the assistant curate after all—but he didn't think these people would care about the niceties of ecclesiastical management. He held out his hand. "Now, if you please?"

The shadows moved closer to the beefy man, their features wizened but eyes sharp, while the boy looked on from behind his protector's large frame.

The large man grinned unpleasantly. "And wot if I don't please?" He slipped the coins into his coat. The courtyard chilled, the sun having disappeared.

"Then . . . I shall have to report you both to the authorities."

"And how's yer gonna do that?"

Anthony glanced over his shoulder. The doorway was filled with spectators, their mouths curling as he imagined a wake of buzzards might regard a rabbit. His stomach clenched. Exactly what had they gathered to see?

"Ye may be a parson, but ye won't find much love 'ere. Yer a greedy lot, preyin' on the weak an' gullible."

Indignation dissipated, replaced by unfurling compassion—to not care about God or want to know His love? "I am sorry you feel that way."

The man shrugged. "It's nowt to me."

Anthony's oft-treacherous sense of humor begged his attention. How many times had his superiors decried the crass and difficult convicts as being "nowts"?

"Do ye be laughin' at me?" The beefy man frowned and turned to his henchmen. "I do be thinkin' he is laughin' at me."

Anthony stiffened as they nodded and murmured agreement. "Sir, I dinnae—"

"Oho, sir is it now?" He stepped forward aggressively. "Y'know what I do with them that laugh at me?"

"I was not laughing at you."

"But I thinks you was." The space between them shrank into nothing as the man's spit-flecked mouth drew closer. "And roight now, it don't matter wot anyone thinks but me."

Anthony swallowed a retort as his predicament grew in stature. Would it be cowardly to run or simply the wisest course of action? His early morning reading of the exhortation to be as bold as a lion suddenly seemed as far-fetched as the sailor stories he'd heard of fish that flew. He gritted his teeth. *Lord, give me courage!*

"I see ye might be a fool but a bold one for all that."

Anthony exhaled. Perhaps the man might be won over to reason, after all—

Crack!

Pain splintered through his cheek, piercing through to his brain as the beefy man lowered his fist. "That be for lying 'bout my Freddie, 'ere."

"But—"

Ooof!

Anthony doubled over, sucking in air as agony ricocheted through his midsection.

"And that be for being a God-botherer." The man spat and swore loudly. "We don't need none of your sort 'ere."

Anthony groaned.

"Did I asks ye to speak? Did I?" The man's eyes held a reddish glow, like an enraged boar, his mouth pulled out in an expression more snarl than smile. "Let 'im 'ave it, Jim."

At once a rain of blows fell on his back and legs. Anthony tried to defend himself, but memories of wrestling with his cousin seemed so far away, and his feeble attempts availed nothing. A thump on his skull sent him to his knees, a kick to his lower back left him gasping amidst the dirt and slurry.

He wrenched open his eyes to see dung-covered boots inches from his nose. Sour whisky fumes breathed in his face as the man bent down. "Don't ever be letting me see your ugly mug again."

Anthony lay prostrate on the dirt, unable to move, his mind slipping between awareness and dark, conscious only of dust swirling in the cold breeze and pain so immense he could almost understand those who begged to be released from this mortal coil.

His eyes closed as the first tears from heaven fell from the sky.

❧ Chapter Two

Bath, Somerset
February

VERITY LISTENED WITH half an ear as Miss Haverstock continued her spring half-term address, reiterating the prestige attached to Miss Haverstock's Select Seminary for Young Ladies. Well did Verity know there were long lists of desperate-to-be "selectees," having spied their applications whilst rifling through Miss Haverstock's study. And how often had she heard her own mama espouse the benefits of Haverstock's on her eldest two "gels," the resulting alliances ensuring Mama now took great pride in addressing said daughters as "Lady Erasmus Carstairs" and "my daughter Cecilia, affianced to the Earl of Rovingham's son." Such exalted positions had buoyed hopes for Verity. Alas—Verity's lips twisted in a wry smile—such hopes had always been doomed for disappointment, a situation only exacerbated with the shocking news of Miss Haverstock's immediate retirement, much to the consternation of various parents, if not their children.

"And now finally, may I say what a joy and delight—"

"'Finally' like in St. Peter's letter to the Philippians?" Helena murmured. "She is long-winded today."

"Her last chance to remind the parents their investment was worthwhile."

"Note she did not glance at *you* when speaking of delight at training your daughters."

No, she had not.

The indignant glare from her mother drew Verity's spine straight, her attention fixed to the front as Miss Haverstock waffled on. The withered countenance refused to meet her gaze, thus lending further weight to her suspicions that today would give as much relief to the esteemed lady as it did herself. For the restrictions and lessons had hardly dimmed her "natural vivacity," as Verity's paternal grandmother called her high spirits, instead proving more challenge than chastisement.

Verity bit back her amusement. With Miss Pelling in charge the following month it would be interesting to see if she continued with her reluctance to inform Verity's parents of her every misdemeanor. No doubt she had not yet been expelled because the seminary could scarcely countenance a failure of the third Aynsley gel, after such previous successes. She sneaked a glance at her mother, whose bitter disappointment in Verity's lack of social graces was likely to be repeated by her lack of come-out success. Her heart panged. Poor Mama. Destined for perpetual disappointment with her youngest. As Papa always said, Verity should have been born a boy. She lifted her chin, ignoring the wrinkling in her soul she always experienced when reminded of her parents' disappointment at producing no heir. It wasn't her fault she was born female.

Miss Haverstock completed her homily, encouraging the selectees and their families to partake of refreshments. Verity nudged Helena. One of the advantages of the exorbitant fees was the comparatively good assortment of refreshments on offer, at least when parents were in attendance. Helena nodded, and soon they were clutching filled teacups and small plates holding an assortment of small cakes and dainty pastries.

"Why, Helena, how thoughtful," Mrs. Chisholm said, as her daughter plied her with the offerings.

Verity offered her plate and a smile. "Mama, would you like this cup of tea?"

Lady Aynsley patted the seat beside her. "I would prefer you to sit beside me."

Verity suppressed a sigh and pretended to act like the lady she knew she would never be, smiling at trivialities, sipping delicately at the porcelain cup as her mother prosied on to Mrs. Chisholm about her two far-more-dutiful daughters. While the reverend's wife leaned in to listen, Verity gestured to the gimlet-eyed headmistress mobbed by a pack of anxious parents, and murmured to Helena, "See what happens when one devotes one's self to silly strictures?"

"Perhaps that is more the result of needing to enforce them once she met you."

"Very likely," Verity murmured, as Miss Haverstock drew near, with the air of one recently escaped from a noose.

"Ah, Lady Aynsley, Mrs. Chisholm."

"Oh, my dear Miss Haverstock! Your news has filled us with the utmost dismay."

"I know 'tis unexpected, Lady Aynsley. My sister's health, however . . ." She made a helpless gesture.

"Of course. Family must come first," Mrs. Chisholm agreed. "You shall both be in our prayers."

"Thank you."

"And while I am sorry circumstances force my leave, I'm sure Miss Pelling will lead the school admirably." The newly retired headmistress gave a thin smile that disappeared as she eyed her former students. "Helena, I wish you the best for your return to the north."

Verity bit back amusement at Miss Haverstock's refusal to say the word "Scotland," which betrayed her utter aversion to the place—a point in her favor, as far as Mother was concerned.

"And Verity." The headmistress sighed. "We can only hope for the best."

"Indeed we can." Verity smiled blandly.

The hard gaze narrowed further before Miss Haverstock turned to Lady Aynsley. "It grieves me to think Verity may not quite live up to the exalted stations of dear Caroline and Cecilia."

Verity's mother shook her head. "I know you have done your utmost."

"Yes, we have."

Verity's smile felt pasted on as Miss Haverstock continued her piercing scrutiny. While disobedience was not punishable by whipping, she had often wondered just how much pleasure it would have given the headmistress to administer the cane. Indeed, sometimes she wondered if Miss Haverstock might be better suited as a female warden for one of the convict ships she had heard about. Such places would have no hesitation in enacting corporal punishment.

She smiled wider. "Thank you, Miss Haverstock, for a lifetime of memories."

Her now-former headmistress looked at her, startled, before nodding and walking away.

Verity sighed, a sound swiftly echoed by her mother, though Mama's sounded more like a groan. "What am I to do with you?"

"What are your plans for Verity for the remainder of the school year?" Mrs. Chisholm asked.

"I'm undecided. We have a busy few months ahead, and I cannot but think a season in London would likely be of greater benefit to my girl than further education."

Verity's lips pressed together. Oh dear, no.

Mrs. Chisholm gazed thoughtfully between Verity and her mother. "You know you are most welcome to send Verity north to stay with us for the summer."

"Oh, Mama, what a wonderful idea!" Helena clapped her hands. "We could have all manner of fun! There are the horses, and we could explore the abbey nearby, and of course James would love to see you."

Verity frowned at her friend's indecorous comment. James was a pleasant fellow, but a trifle marked in his attentions whenever he had visited Helena in Bath before. She glanced at her mother, whose raised eyebrows betrayed her discontent with a mere minister's son holding such aspirations. Perhaps a little begging might be in order.

"Oh, Mama, *please*. Then you could spend time with Caroline and be there when the new baby arrives."

"Verity! Please do not speak of such things."

"But why? Surely it is not ill-bred to be excited about becoming an aunt."

"It is not ill-bred to be filled with anticipation, that is true, but it *is* ill-mannered to mention such things." Mama shifted her attention to Helena's mother. "Thank you for your kind invitation, but I'm afraid I cannot accept. We have much to attend to in these next few months, what with Cecilia's wedding, and Verity's presentation."

"Well, think it over," Mrs. Chisholm said, in that easy unruffled manner that had always appealed to Verity. "Verity is always welcome, and you may find it helpful should family matters require your presence elsewhere."

"Thank you, Mrs. Chisholm," Mama said stiffly. "I am much obliged but must decline."

Verity's spirits, which had been riding high as the crest of a wave, fell flat. How stupid to hope. Of *course* Mama would not wish to be obliged to anyone. Why, the very idea was anathema!

Her nose wrinkled. Mama's reluctance to feel obliged probably ranked as low as Verity's own desire to be presented to the King's sisters. One could only hope that poor King George III's death meant the Drawing Rooms would be canceled this year.

Too soon she bid her best friend farewell and set out for the lonely home that was Aynsley Manor, wondering, without the fizzing anticipation that had greeted her this morning, just what her future held.

Sydney Town, New South Wales

At the sound of the rattling door Anthony wrested his body into an upright position, hoping the caller would not know he had taken to resting for short periods during the day. His lips formed a mirthless smile. Resting at his age? But his body protested, the aches and pains inflicted two weeks ago weighing as heavily as the memory of the young thief's lashing yesterday. Anthony had pleaded for clemency—the lad, who could not be more than ten, had grown up in an unprincipled environment and was only following his father's orders—but the magistrate would have none of it.

"We are a civilized colony, and must strongly discourage the avarice and vice that brought so many to our shores."

Yes, a civilized colony indeed, one that might replace structures of wattle and daub with buildings of gleaming gold sandstone, but nonetheless one that locked up small children and deemed all people who spoke accented English as being rather less than acceptable. Thank God his brogue was deemed the slightly more acceptable kind, otherwise he might face the same persecution as poor Father O'Leary did, whose proclamation of truth refused to be heard by anyone other than the Papists.

By the time he shuffled to the front door, his visitor was gone, the slightly stained cream envelope under the door the only sign that Anthony had not imagined the whole thing. He gingerly bent down—the doctor said it would be another week or two before his bruised ribs fully healed—and scooped it up, his eyes adjusting in the dim light to read the neat writing:

> Mr. Anthony Jardine
> 8 Lennox Lane
> Sydney Town
> New South Wales

He smiled to himself; "8 Lennox Lane" sounded far more respectable than what it was—a row of mud and timber huts crowded together around a sewer-lined dirt lane that stank in summer and flooded misery in winter. Why the colony's senior chaplain deemed it acceptable for Anthony's use brought unanswered questions, but he had learned not to object too strenuously. Experience had proved it far more productive to just get on with things, to begin a project and then apologize, rather than wait for permission that may never come. If he'd followed protocol he would never have been granted permission for the soup kitchen that had sustained many families during the recent drought. And as for assisting the emancipists with their letters and numbers, he could hear the booming negative echo across his soul. No, Chief Chaplain Marsden might have his own ideas why

Anthony should be situated in Lennox Lane, but helping freed convicts attain learning was *not* one of them.

Anthony didn't mind, not really, for living in Lennox Lane had its advantages: he was but a short walk from the newly established Botanical Gardens, and he had grown to know his neighbors in a way that living several miles distant in a fancy house would never permit. And while the past few years he had seen things his parents would have shuddered over, births and deaths and disease and despair, he somehow felt like God was using him, a vessel of God's grace that had seen more than one heart soften to accept the message of love that still underscored the fire and brimstone so often preached from the chief chaplain's pulpit.

He shook off the unease that thoughts of Marsden always provoked and fingered the parchment in his hand. A letter from home! Perhaps Da and Ma had relented after all.

He studied the precise handwriting and knew a pang of disappointment. No, not his parents. Perhaps Amelia . . . ? Had her parents changed their mind about him?

Anticipation now curling his heart, he lowered into the lone chair, carefully slit the seal and opened the pages. Read them, disbelievingly.

No.

The letter fell from his nerveless grasp, its contents only glanced at but already engraved upon his heart. Poor David and Julia. And poor little Matthew. His eyes burned, his throat constricted. His lips compressed tightly until the initial blunt force of grief for his cousin passed, then he eased down to pick up the piece of paper.

The door rattled again, easing sunlight into the room. "Mr. Jardine!" came a stern voice. "You should nae be bending down. Ye are not full recovered yet."

Anthony coughed, the pneumonia obtained after his encounter at The Romping Horse thickening his throat once more, causing his lungs to burn.

The owner of the stern voice came into view, the blue eyes piercing as ever. Meeting John McNaughton had been another blessing from God, his practical Scots sense masking a dry sense of humor seven years in chains had not been able to break. "Why, whatever be wrong?"

He handed over the letter, watching the well-worn face stiffen for a moment as the news sunk in. "This be your cousin?"

"Aye."

There was not much Anthony had not shared, his secrets safe with the former valet, whose service to an unscrupulous London lord had resulted in a trial and punishment as severe as his master was corrupt. In the two years since their meeting, McNaughton's willingness to work for the pittance Anthony could offer and their shared heritage and humor had helped forge a bond thicker than he'd ever shared with the only family member who had wished him well on his Antipodean voyage.

David . . .

He swallowed.

As if sensing his distress, McNaughton—or Mac as Anthony referred to him in his mind—dipped his chin, years of training smoothing away his reaction. "Now that is very sad news. Very sad news indeed." He cleared his throat. "I suppose you be wanting to return for the funerals?"

"They would be over long ago."

"Of course. How foolish of me." The gaze softened. "You will be returning?"

"Yes."

Something akin to disappointment flickered in the older man's eyes, sparking an offer Anthony never thought he would make. "Would you like to return with me?"

For a second hope suffused the grizzled features but then he shook his head. "Aye, that would be grand, but I cannae afford such a thing."

Anthony nodded. As a free man, Anthony could scarcely afford the ticket to England, his savings almost as meager as when he'd arrived six years ago. A convict might receive a ticket-of-leave but could never hope to return to kith and kin half a world away, and the letter had mentioned nothing of financial provision.

"Still, I am pleased for you, Mr. Jardine."

Mr. Jardine. In the whirl of emotion since he'd first received the news and realized everything in his life had changed, he'd forgotten the most fundamental. His cousin's death meant Anthony was now the fourteenth laird of Dungally, which meant his role in this parish would be his no longer. He glanced ruefully out the window, where the shouts of the Patterson lads came loud and lively. Just when he was making some headway with hearts harder than the sunbaked soil he was forced to leave. Still, God would tend this growing flock somehow. Surely Jensen, the parson from Norwich who had traveled out with him on the *Guildford*, would not mind the extra responsibility. Or perhaps Carlton, young as he was, would rise to the challenge. Even O'Leary believed the truth . . .

At least there was no need to rush. Indeed, his lips twisted, rushing home was quite out of the question. Ships returning to England were often booked as soon as opportunity arose, as once hope-filled settlers found the harsh climate and harsher conditions of the convict colony far from their liking. He would have to rely upon the good-will of a God-fearing captain and hope the route taken would not be too protracted in order for him to assume his new responsibilities. Not that he need worry. The estate would have been empty for many months now. A few more would hurt no one.

"Sir?"

He glanced up.

"Would you like me to see when the next passage is available?"

"Yes—wait, no. Not yet." He studied the man whose concern about Anthony's sudden flight had prompted his rescue from the clutches of The Romping Horse.

How he wished he could repay such service. Not once had Mac ever alluded to that time save to say he had been sorry to be so late. His swiftness in getting Anthony to medical attention had been his saving, Dr. Jennings had said, although by that time night had settled in, along with the rain that had soaked him through, leading to the worst case of pneumonia Anthony had experienced in six years.

Lord, how can I help him? He is a friend—no, a brother—whom I cannot abandon.

His mind raced, scraping the walls of memory for any vestige of money that could secure passage for two. Would Marsden—? No. Foolish thought. The Chief Chaplain held dim views on emancipists; he would never lift a finger to help. But who else could?

"Sir?"

With a sick feeling, he gave instructions for the passage home. As soon as he was alone, he moved to the cracked window from which the lonely caw of the magpie warbled louder than the soothing birdsong he remembered from home. He tilted his face into the bright glare of early February sunshine, summer here in the Antipodes, filled with so much that was so opposite to his former world.

He lifted his chin.

He would simply pray that he could take more than just a changed perspective into his new role.

ℜ CHAPTER THREE

Aynsley Manor, Somerset
April

WAS IT POSSIBLE one could truly die of boredom?

Verity yawned, dropped the atlas with a thud, and rubbed her eyes. Last week in London for Cecy's wedding already seemed an age ago; her time at school a dusty memory. This morning's gallop had proved the only highlight of a week otherwise filled with droning duty and lectures from Mama about Verity's lack of familial responsibility and need to turn her attention to her upcoming London season.

"But what about school?" she'd asked.

"We shall see," her mother had responded, a death knell to her hopes.

Fears she might not return to finish her education had tamped down her usual exploits—what if she never saw Helena again?—but impatience still clawed within, begging escape.

A knock came at the door. "Excuse me, miss, but Lady Aynsley requests your attendance in the Blue Room."

Verity sighed, offered the maid a resigned look. "Thank you."

The maid bobbed a curtsy and Verity made her way to the blue drawing room, where Mama waited, her face pinched tighter than a pincushion. Lady Heathcote, their nearest neighbor, and mother of Sophia and Stephen, perched on a striped gold and white settee, holding a little smile and a plate with a buttered scone. This did not bode well. Verity offered her a small curtsy. "Good afternoon, Lady Heathcote. What a pleasure to see you again. How is Sophia?"

"She is very well, thank you," said Lady Heathcote, her smile widening to become reminiscent of a plump satisfied cat.

"I'm so pleased." Verity studied her, until the older woman's smugness seemed to dim, not unlike the luster from the cheap tableware Miss Haverstock always hid from parents. "What brings you here today? Did you not call yesterday?"

"Verity!"

She opened her eyes wide. "Oh, I do beg your pardon, Mother. Was I supposed to not remember Sophia's visit?"

Her mother closed her eyes briefly then gazed upwards, as if expecting help from the painted cherubs cavorting around the ceiling rose.

Except, they never did. Yesterday's visit from someone she'd once considered a friend had proved instead to be an exercise in tedium and patience, as she'd listened to Sophia's mean-spirited chatter with nothing of substance to say. Verity had resorted to her mother's oft-preferred position on a number of occasions—to no avail. Cherubs were like angels, mythical and useless.

"Please excuse my daughter, Lady Heathcote."

"I always do," their visitor murmured, as if through clenched teeth.

Verity lifted a brow, scrutinizing the older woman through narrowed eyes until their visitor was forced to look elsewhere. Then she turned to her mother. "Was there something you needed, Mama?"

"I need the truth. Is it true?"

"Please forgive my ignorance. Is what true?"

"That you were seen galloping through Aynsley earlier today?"

Verity bit back a smile, shifting her attention back to their guest. "So *that's* why you have come. I must confess I did not see you, and I was very careful to keep a lookout in case something like this should occur. Perhaps I didn't see you as I was riding so terribly fast."

"Verity," her mother uttered in awful tones.

"I must admit"—Lady Heathcote's cheeks pinked—"it was not my eyes that saw you."

"No, really? Was it dearest Sophia who saw me? She has always had my best interests at heart, hasn't she?"

Their guest twitched and fussed uncomfortably as Lady Aynsley placed her teacup down with a clatter. "We are not discussing Sophia's motivations, Verity."

"Oh, but we should. One has to wonder why she should feel the need to tell tales on others."

"It . . . it is as you said before. She has your best interests at heart."

Verity compressed her lips, head tilted as she eyed Lady Heathcote, whose scone now listed dangerously on the china plate resting on her ample lap.

"Such things are not what a proper young lady should do, my dear girl."

Her dear girl? The patronizing tone accompanying such falseness made bile rise in her throat. "Why you should take it upon yourself to come here and regale my mother about things which are no concern of yours is something indeed at which to wonder."

Lady Heathcote's face reddened. "I . . . I see it as merely my duty as a neighbor, my *Christian* duty."

"Well, my understanding, despite years of dull as ditchwater sermons at Haverstock's, is that it is a Christian's duty to love one's neighbor, not to seek division—"

"Verity! That is enough! You will apologize this instant!"

Heat pounded in her chest, forbidding speech. How dare this insufferable woman come here and stir up yet more conflict between Verity and her mother? Even now she sat smug and fat opposite, her gaze clearly triumphant as she waited.

Verity drew in a deep breath and rose. "Lady Heathcote, I hope in time you will come to realize my desire for truth and plain speaking is not vindictive, and will pardon me accordingly. I am sorry that you and Sophia prefer gossip and tattling on others, and sorrier too that today has caused such pain for my mama. Now, if you'll please excuse me."

She curtsied and departed to the sound of twin gasps, quickly followed by Lady Heathcote's high-pitched "Well, I never!"

The door closed, and the footman's wisp of a smile wiped clear when Verity glanced at him.

"Tell Edwards I will be needing Banshee directly."

His head inclined. "Very good, miss."

Quickly, before her mother could come and remonstrate, Verity raced upstairs and changed into her riding habit again, then escaped down the back stairs to the stables where freedom and solace always lay. She patted poor Bunty, the one-eyed Labrador who shadowed Edwards, the head groom, and entered the dimness within.

"Good afternoon, miss."

"Hello, Eddie. I trust she's ready?"

"Aye, but I wouldn't ride her as hard as before."

"Aye." Verity grinned.

The head groom's wide red face split into a smile. "Now don't be letting your pa hear you speak such things, not after you just returned from such a fancy school and all."

"I'll be sure to not let him."

A stable hand led Banshee to Verity, nodding as he handed over the reins.

"Thank you." She patted her pet, smoothing the chestnut's dark mane. "Are you ready for another run?"

The horse nickered, rubbing Verity's face with her nose. She laughed. "I take that as a yes."

Edwards finished checking the saddle. "She be fond of you, miss."

"At least someone is around here," Verity murmured into Banshee's pricked ears.

Edwards boosted her into the saddle, just as another footman made an appearance at the far end of the stables.

"Oh no." She nudged Banshee to the exit halfway along the long stone building.

The footman hurried toward her. "Miss, her ladyship requests you—"

"Tell her you were too late!" Verity grinned as she escaped into sunlight.

A minute later she had cleared the Manor's grounds and was heading to the Aynsley woods, where sunshine and shadows dappled patterns onto the ground. Banshee thundered across the meadow, echoing the indignation roaring in her ears. How dare Lady Heathcote presume to interfere? How dare Sophie? And why did Mama always take sides against her?

She drew in deep lungfuls of fresh air. Perhaps this ride would help clear some of the turbulent restlessness she experienced whenever her neighbors grew too assiduous in their attentions. If *only* Mother had consented to Mrs. Chisholm's invitation for Verity to spend part of the summer with Helena's family in Scotland! Her fingers clenched the reins tighter as she ducked under a low branch, Banshee's hooves continuing their steady drum. How much longer would she stay, doomed to dodging disappointed parents and unwelcome duty?

"VERITY! WHERE HAVE you been?"

Verity grimaced from her position halfway up the main stairs and turned to face her mother. She lifted a corner of her riding dress. "I would have thought it obvious, Mama."

"Don't be insolent!"

"I am sorry, Mama." Her cheeks heated, her gaze flickering to the motionless footmen in the hall. She kept her voice low. "Do you wish to discuss something?"

Her mother blinked. "I . . . er, yes." Her expression returned to its usual imperious manner. "I expect you in the Blue Room directly."

"Of course."

Verity exchanged her riding dress for the morning gown worn earlier—no need to add to the maid's washing duties. After splashing her face and smoothing her hair she hurried downstairs to the Blue Room, relief filling her as the footman closed the door. Lady Heathcote had gone.

"Verity, your behavior earlier was nothing less than scandalous!"

Verity bit her lip. Mama's ideas about what constituted scandal must surely differ from the norm. Haverstock's had in no way been isolated from society's biggest scandals; rather, it proved a hive of gossip, especially as so many well-connected selectees knew a great many things about society scandals—part of the education Miss Haverstock did not realize her seminary provided. Verity's actions were, by contrast, excessively mild. But somehow, she did not feel her mother would appreciate this being pointed out.

"You should not be so outspoken, Verity. I was embarrassed by your words."

"I am sorry, Mama, that I have caused you discomfort. But would you rather me hide behind a curtain of false nicety whilst stabbing supposed friends in the back as Sophia does?"

As her mother stared at her, Verity felt a growing certainty that her mother actually would prefer to have Sophia as a daughter, in order to play pretend with.

"You are a constant disappointment to me."

Her heart wavered. She blinked away an unaccustomed sting. "I am sorry, Mama."

"You are always sorry, but I have given up believing you will ever change."

"I know."

Her mother turned away.

The imp that always bade she speak the truth nudged open her mouth. "But if you would name me Verity . . ."

"That was your father's doing, not mine."

She stiffened. Her mother's disavowal of her name seemed to epitomize her mother's complete rejection of her very existence.

"I—"

Her mother held up a hand, precluding further speech. "I do not ask for much, Verity, only that you would not disgrace yourself, or your family. Aynsley ladies are supposed to behave as ladies, without a whiff of scandal."

Verity nodded. That was core to her mother's complaint. Disgrace reflected badly on the parent, although in this case . . . "We can always blame it on Miss Haverstock," she suggested.

"We cannot! Oh, why can't you be more like your sisters?"

Verity clamped her mouth. She loved her sisters, but had no desire to adopt their sensibilities, their fixation on matters of eternity, or their interest in whatever new and fashionable trinket the current edition of *Lady's Monthly Museum* decreed. How pointless, how utterly futile were such doings.

At least Cecy had proved this past year to have some interest in a world beyond her social standing, and Caro's scientific husband, and the impending birth of her baby, had extended her vocabulary beyond the petty concerns of the day. Her lips twisted.

Her mother sighed heavily. "Go tell Mary to pack your things."

Oh, joy! "Do I now get to return to school? I have missed Helena so much, and I cannot wait—"

"No."

Disappointment crowded her chest. Not finish her education? Granted, not all selectees returned for the final term, especially if they were to make their debut into society. Had Mama heard from the Lord Chamberlain? "Are we going to London, then? Has the date for the Drawing Rooms been announced?"

"I have decided that your behavior is not such that can be trusted to a season in London."

That was something, at least. But what, then? An idea, wondrous in its scope, lit her heart. "Am I to visit Scotland? Oh, *please,* Mama. I promise not to trouble Mrs. Chisholm. She is such a kind lady, and I promise not to get into mischief, not even if it were a month of Sundays."

"Are you quite finished?" Her mother's face was devoid of expression.

Verity nodded, heart hoping against hope, willing her mother to agree. *Please, Mama. Please!*

Her mother flicked at a piece of invisible lint on her sleeve. "You are going to your grandmother's. Now go, pack your things. I want you gone by daybreak."

"But Mama—"

"Go!"

Moisture filled her eyes and clogged her throat. She bit her bottom lip to stop her chin from quivering. To be banished like Caro had once been? Verity rose, dropping her mother a curtsy, but her mother did not see her. She had turned away long ago.

⁂

Southern Ocean

Anthony clutched the rail as he dragged in long gulps of fresh air. He rubbed a hand over his face then squinted into the distance. Nothing save the interminable blue of rocking waves met his gaze. The past weeks had seen unimagined speed, but the strong winds propelling them onward had also seen treacherous storms. He thanked God for their safety, and thanked God that the recent sightings of albatross and sea turtles suggested land was close, something his unsteady legs would appreciate. Wind whipped his cheeks, threatening to unseat his hat as he remained by the bow, where he hoped he would be out of the way of those sailors yet inclined to activity. Past days had seen sailors and passengers alike succumb to scurvy, and long hours had seen him render assistance to not a few. Thank God the signs of illness had been identified early, permitting treatment with lemon and bark. He would continue to pray and trust God for their restoration to health.

He smiled at himself. Trust? This entire trip was built on trust. Faith that God would provide passage had been rewarded with this most unique of opportunities. When word from the senior chaplain had reached the governor's ears that a young man of good family was returning to Scotland, his Excellency had requested Anthony's urgent attendance in his chambers.

He had met the governor on numerous occasions, as Macquarie was assiduous in his church attendance and promotion of godly values, but never had Anthony experienced an encounter like the last. Macquarie's recent illness had given him the appearance of great weariness, and there had been rumors he'd tendered his resignation. The great man had looked him over. Thankfully Anthony's face no longer bore a trace of the humiliation inflicted at The Romping Horse. "Jardine. Ah, I had forgotten."

"Forgotten what, sir?"

Macquarie's sudden smile took Anthony by surprise. "Nobody bends his head to the task like a true Scotchman."

"Aye, sir. My family now lives in Edinburgh, but originally hails from Dumfriesshire."

"And that is where you soon return?"

"Yes. I have recently received notice of an inheritance."

The lines around the governor's eyes seemed to soften. "News of an inheritance is often a mixed blessing."

His throat grew tight. "It is that, sir."

Macquarie nodded, his cheeks sagging in a way that suggested fatigue. "I trust I may count on you to fulfill a task for me, Jardine."

"Of course."

His eyes shadowed. Anthony's heart twisted. Was Macquarie that concerned about the rumors stemming from Commissioner Bigge's report that had the whole colony abuzz? Apparently London was not happy with the governor. "I've been given to understand you would likely not oppose postponing your return a little in order to assist in a certain matter."

Anthony inclined his head. No doubt he had Marsden to thank for giving the governor such ideas.

"I wish for you to visit Rio de Janeiro."

Anthony blinked. "But, sir, I am already booked for England."

Macquarie waved a hand. "No matter. I have secured passage for you." His brow lowered fractionally. "You will be fully recompensed, of course, as this is official duty."

That at least was some relief. Inspiration welled within and he made a further request, to which Macquarie nodded impatiently. "Yes, yes, of course. See to it, and inform my secretary."

"Thank you, sir."

Macquarie smiled. "I do not know if you are aware that I have acquaintances there." Therein followed a rather comprehensive account of Macquarie's previous visit, over a decade ago, which had seen his promise of a gift to the then-recently exiled prince of Portugal. "It never hurts for one to recommend oneself by way of a gift, especially when England and Portugal have been allies for so long, and so I wish for you to present my compliments to him, especially now he is king." His rather protuberant eyes narrowed. "You do know how to pay a compliment, do you not?"

"Of course, sir."

"Hmm." The governor looked over Anthony's humble attire and frowned. "You will need to dress more appropriately, I should think. You do have something more suitable?"

"Yes, sir." At the bottom of his trunk. Where they had remained since his arrival in Sydney years prior.

"Marsden informs me you have the capacity for social address, otherwise I'd ask one of the redcoats to do this. But they scarcely have polish, and cannot be trusted with such a mission."

"Excuse me, sir, but what exactly is the mission you wish me to undertake?"

Governor Macquarie proffered a somewhat thin smile for such a wide face. "You are to deliver my gift to the English ambassador in Brazil, and if he so wills it, to the king of Portugal himself."

It was only after they boarded that the exact nature of the gift was revealed.

Emus!

The wild flightless birds were not as plentiful in the Sydney basin as they had once been. Their meat, though tough, had proved desirous for hungry settlers, their fast legs no match for muskets and desperation. Yes, the ugly, ungainly birds with their long legs and neck, bountiful brown ostrich-like feathers, and sharp black eyes were an unusual gift. But then Governor Lachlan Macquarie was an unusual man, evident in his willingness to see past a man's flaws to his gifts.

Macquarie's first few years in office had transformed Sydney Town from a ramshackle penal colony to a well-laid town of fine buildings and public space, and had seen the elevation of former convicts into positions of influence, such as Francis Greenway, the convict who had designed the rather marvelous lighthouse at the southern entrance to Sydney Harbour. Indeed, his policies had proven of great benefit, giving the colony a confidence its origins decried, despite the rumors and speculation derived from Commissioner Bigge's reports. Wryness tweaked Anthony's lips. And after personally experiencing the governor's generosity, he could only hope his gift was received in the spirit it was given.

SEVERAL DAYS LATER, after docking in Rio de Janeiro at what must be one of the most beautiful harbors in the world, he learned just what the London-born envoy to Portugal thought.

"Why, they're hideous! Whatever was Macquarie thinking to send such a thing?"

"I believe, sir, he thought the king of Portugal might find them amusing."

Edward Thornton sniffed. "That may be so. It is hard to know at times what amuses that man."

What little Anthony had garnered from conversations since his arrival suggested that King John VI was a complex man. He had overseen the creation of many civil and cultural projects that benefited the Portuguese colony of Brazil, but was also the subject of various rumors about his marriage and health.

"He might create a menagerie," Anthony suggested. "I'm told London's menagerie has several interesting creatures, including kangaroos and emus. Perhaps the addition of animals native to other lands could prove interesting to visitors and locals alike."

"But who would see it? No, it is mad. Simply mad."

"If I may say so, sir, I believe Governor Macquarie would be most disappointed should he learn of your displeasure."

"Well, you must take care not to tell him, mustn't you?"

Anthony bit his lip. Perhaps this was one of those times when discretion might prove prudent. "I shall ensure he never hears such things from me."

"Good man." Thornton clapped him on the shoulder. "Now, remove them from my sight, and then have a spot of brandy with me. And then you can tell me how Sydney Town is doing."

"With pleasure, sir."

Somehow the invitation extended into the dinner meal, which was attended by a number of expatriates, including an English diplomat, Mr. Ramsay, whose wife seemed at least twenty years his junior. Mrs. Ramsay, with whom Anthony was seated, possessed a fair-haired prettiness that reminded him a little of Amelia, but that's where the similarity ceased. The diplomat's wife was a tightly coiled woman, her brittle laughter at odds with her soft-spoken remarks about the oppressive heat.

"Sometimes, Mr. Jardine, I simply pine for Scotland. You cannot know how envious I am of you returning home," Mrs. Ramsay said, golden ringlets dancing as she leaned forward. "I understand you head to Dumfries?"

"Aye. That be so."

She sighed. "You will not be so very far from my home at Galston."

"No, indeed." He smiled. "Merely a wee hop and a step o'er the mountain and moor."

"Perhaps I will chance to see you one day."

"You return to Scotland soon?"

"Oh, nothing is determined as yet. But I hope to before the next monsoon."

"Then I would be pleased for your visit, should you and your husband find yourself near Kirkcudbright," he said politely.

"We shall most certainly take up your kind offer," Mrs. Ramsay said, before going on to chatter about a myriad of things concerning home, but of her prattle nothing lodged in his memory save one question, asked near the end of his visit, whilst the company enjoyed the relative cool of the white stone sitting room, quietly conversing in groups of three and four.

"Mr. Jardine, please forgive me, but by your manner of address and appearance one can only wonder if there might be a young lady who is keen to see you on your return."

Anthony's cheeks heated. *Would* Amelia wish to see him? He could scarcely imagine the gentle, gracious young lady he remembered ever being bold enough to admit to such a thing.

Mr. Ramsay said softly, "Flora, *minha querida*." My dear. "Do not embarrass the young man."

"Please forgive me, Mr. Jardine. My husband always tells me I do rattle on. I suppose it must be the lack of convivial company one experiences living out here." She fluttered her fan in his direction. "But you must admit, a title and estate will attract a great deal of attention from eager mamas and those seeking a fortune."

He gazed at a tiled mosaic of blues and greens as she made inconsequential remarks to her husband. Much as he wished Amelia's parents might be persuaded to Mrs. Ramsay's point of view, so did he abhor the thought of only being approved by such materialistic values.

What should he expect, returning to the mother country, with all its hierarchal obligations and responsibilities? Returning to the parents who had practically disowned him as soon as news of his venture had leaked? Would they view him more favorably now? Would the Witherspooles receive him now he was moneyed? Living on the opposite side of the world may have been the most arduous undertaking of his life—the deprivation, the flies, the heat!—but he had also learned so much, about himself, others, God. Despite his upbringing, despite the wretched condition of so many, he had come to renewed awareness that there truly was no difference between men, neither convict nor free, English nor native, that all men were considered equal in the sight of God, that all were loved by God.

Except, he considered wryly, that awareness would be tantamount to blasphemy back home. And for some of the colony's free settlers, who considered a conviction for crime an eternal stain upon a man's character, such philosophy *was* tantamount to blasphemy. He bit back a sigh, conscious of the speculation in Mrs. Ramsay's eyes, and soon made his excuses. But still the questions lingered.

Later, when he was back in his room, as Mac helped him out of his coat—his ribs still demanding such attention necessary—he studied the servant-cum-friend. "And how was your evening?"

"Unexceptional. And yours, sir?"

"Pleasant. We ate such spiced food I thought my mouth was on fire, but also some fruits so cool and delicious I thought they might have dropped from heaven."

"From whence they were so created."

"You do well to remind me of the Scriptures."

"They have saved my life, sir."

"Aye, and mine." Anthony's grin faded. "But you know you do not need to persist with this 'sir' business?"

"How can I not, when you have provided means for me to return home?"

"How many times must I repeat: Macquarie's doing, not mine."

Mac shrugged. "You are kinder than any master I've had, and I be thinking you will be needing a valet and friend in your new role."

Anthony nodded. That was true. He would need all the friends he could find.

He considered Mac thoughtfully. Mrs. Ramsay's earlier conversation trickled through his mind. Perhaps he should see if his newly acquired rank would avail him much in the eyes of Amelia's parents. If so, well and good. But if not, did he really want to receive the fawning attention Mrs. Ramsay seemed to think likely? He frowned. No. He would much prefer to be known for his faith and character than such transient values.

Anthony shifted to the window, drawing in a deep draft of heavy, tropical-scented air. A large pink orchid glowed against glossy dark leaves, its scent subtle and alluring. Tomorrow he must see if he could track down a specimen to add to his collection of Antipodean plants, now carefully stored in his trunk. While no longer a curate, he would still be God's man, but free to pursue his other interests, and perhaps not abide by the strictures of societal expectation. And beginning afresh in a new town with unknown faces meant the only reputation he need have would be the one he would build. And if the Witherspooles rejected his suit, perhaps one day he might find a lass who placed more faith in character than rank or gold.

Chapter Four

Saltings, Devonshire
June

"VERITY! STOP YOUR dawdling and pay attention."

Verity wrenched her thoughts from yesterday's ride and fixed her eyes on her grandmother. Why Grandmama insisted on planting things herself was a mystery. Surely if one had a veritable army of gardeners, one should avail oneself of their services! But when she had voiced such thoughts, Grandmama had only looked at her blankly and said, "Why should I stop doing something I enjoy simply because I can afford to?"

How her grandmother could enjoy gardening she could barely understand. There had been many things she had not understood these past weeks. Although she supposed there was something somewhat soothing about being outside, listening to the wind rustle the treetops as summer sunshine filtered through their leaves. In the distance the sea glinted silver, the outlines of sailing ships headed to faraway lands. Her chest tightened. How she wished she could be on one of them!

"Verity!"

"Sorry, Grandmama."

Her grandmother followed her former line of vision to the sparkling sea. "Hmph."

Verity's brows rose as her grandmother muttered something. "I beg your pardon?"

Grandmama lifted the gauzy veil she always wore when gardening. "I suppose I can be grateful you at least notice such things as ships. Unlike some."

"Oh, but wouldn't you like to be on a ship like that?" Visions of exotic locales, tropical seas, and warm sands shimmered before her. "I can think of nothing I'd like more!"

"Are you in your senses, dear girl? That ship is going to the ends of the earth."

"To Scotland?"

Grandmama barked a short laugh. "Despite what your mother may say, Scotland is hardly the ends of the earth. No, unless I'm very much mistaken, that is the latest convict ship headed to the colonies."

Oh. Verity gazed out to sea, her excitement dimming, underscored with a sliver of sorrow. "Poor wretches. I suppose they deserve it."

"I'm sure they do." Grandmama slid her a sideways look. "Still want to see the ends of the earth?"

"Well, perhaps not in quite such illustrious company, although I *do* wish you'd make Mama see reason and allow me to see Helena in Scotland."

"I'm afraid you rather overestimate both my ability and your mother's capacity for reason."

Verity's giggle was quickly smothered in a sigh. "But what am I to do?"

"Learn some patience," was the tart response. "Now pass me those gardening shears."

Throughout the remainder of the week, and through the next, Verity's gnawing discontent slowly diminished as she grew accustomed to spending time with her grandmother amidst the roses of her Devonshire estate. Grandmama might be old, but at least she was not decrepit in her ways of thinking, her notions of propriety less rigid than what Verity recalled. She wondered what her grandmother would think of her surreptitious reading of newssheets last year, and the letters Cecy and she had written imploring government action on behalf of those killed at the Peterloo massacre in Manchester. Perhaps Grandmama would understand. After all, in recent times she seemed to own surprisingly enlightened views—inspired, so she said, by her long-ago friendship with Mary Wollstonecraft. She'd even commanded Mary, Verity's maid, to make her a divided skirt!

When Verity had exclaimed over such a treat, her grandmother had simply replied, "If you will spend so much time out of doors you may as well experience a degree of comfort ordinary gowns will not allow. And your modesty is quite protected, for it is not as if we ever need see people."

Indeed they had not. Grandmama seemed content with the company of her friend, Miss McNell. As interesting a conversationalist as her grandmother was—and how could she not be, having traveled to the Continent?—their social interactions were limited to the weekly obligatory excursion to church.

Verity did not mind. Saltings provided a change of scene which she explored through daily rides, until the deep disenchantment with her mother's dismissal no longer held the power to sting her to anger.

"Look at my lovely," Grandmama said, holding out a potted rose for Verity's inspection. "Dear John sent it down for me from Woburn. *Rosa spinosissima*. It's a wonderful specimen, wouldn't you agree?"

Verity touched it carefully. "*Spinosissima* for its many thorns."

"Yes, but it has the most lovely scent. I'm thinking of cultivating it as they've done at the abbey and using it for hedging." Her grandmother gazed across with another of those slanted looks. "I don't suppose you can help me?"

Verity opened her eyes wide. "And miss out on all the marvelous parties I'm forever attending?"

"Sarcasm doesn't become a lady, my dear."

Yes, but I never wanted to be a lady, Verity thought crossly.

"Now, hold this parasol while I get Perkins to dig this hole a little deeper. Perkins!"

The groundsman shoveled out several more loads of dirt, and then sprinkled in an ashy-brown mixture. Verity wrinkled her nose at the pungent tang of brine. "What *is* that?"

"Sea kelp. It makes a most excellent fertilizer, will make near anything grow, and is especially good as we have such easy access to supply." Her grandmother waved a hand toward the sea. "Now, Perkins, carefully . . . carefully!"

The rose bush dangled precariously from the gardener's hands before slipping into the freshly dug hole. After a few exhortations from Grandmama about its proper placement, Perkins finally had the plant positioned to his employer's satisfaction, and stood, wiping his brow, as Grandmama waved Verity forward to sample the aroma.

"Now, is that not the most wonderful scent? Some might prefer those newfangled French varieties but I have always preferred true British stock."

The blooms danced before her nose, wafting sweet perfume. "It *is* lovely."

Her grandmother smiled with satisfaction. "Do you know its common name?"

"I think we both know the answer to that, Grandmama."

She chuckled, apparently choosing to overlook Verity's pert reply. "It is more widely known as the Scotch rose. They grow quite wild near the sea, so I'm told."

Verity bit her lip, refusing to voice her complaint. If only she could see Helena!

Her grandmother's wheezy chuckle sounded again. "Very good, m'dear. I'm glad to see you can exhibit something of self-discipline. From the stories your mother tells, I was beginning to wonder if you held any compunctions at all."

"I am not proud of all my behavior, if that is what you are asking, Grandmama."

"Now, now, there is no need to take a miff with me. I always knew you would be a handful from the first time I saw you as a babe in arms." Her lips stretched wide in a not altogether pleasing smile. "Unlike those sisters of yours, you never were too concerned with propriety."

Verity's fingers clenched within the thick gloves Grandmama insisted she use. "Perhaps I am not so willing to be satisfied with ordinary things."

"Hence why you remain a puzzle to your mama. Yes, I know I should not speak of her so, but she and I have always been at odds."

She sighed. "Perhaps if you and I weren't so aligned in our ways of thinking it might be better. But as it is, I suspect you and I will forever remain diametrically opposed to your mother in our understanding of the world."

Verity studied her grandmother. Whatever did she mean?

"Now, Verity dear, don't wrinkle your brow like that, not unless you want to look ten years instead of only five years older than your age. I simply mean your mother seems to feel the need to maintain the illusion of politeness, yet her practice seems rarely to match. In contrast, you and I have never backed away from speaking honestly."

"Yet whenever I do so, I always manage to be in trouble."

"Simply because you lack the experience to know the how and when of it. One can maintain one's principles with a view to speaking as necessary, and not simply because one has an active mind that seeks to abolish pretense in all its forms. For some people, pretense is all they have, and to take that away means to strip away everything they hold dear. And to do that is not the mark of a lady, nor is it a quality I should wish to be displayed by any granddaughter of mine."

Verity swallowed. "Yes, Grandmama."

"Now please do not hold plain speaking against me. You know I think you are quite the best of my granddaughters, don't you? Caroline and Cecilia are rather dull creatures, although Caro proved to have more mettle than I expected. Me, I have always preferred girls of spirit, and spunk is something you have in spades, my dear. Don't lose that."

"I won't, Grandmama."

Her grandmother tilted her head, her gaze growing thoughtful as she spoke softly, almost as though to herself. "I wonder what sort of man will husband that quality most appropriately?"

A WEEK LATER Verity learned just whom her mother deemed most appropriate when she found her grandmother in the gold drawing room, her face suffused with anger. "I cannot believe it!"

"Believe what, Grandmama?"

"This is the last straw! To have raised a son so weak-minded as to go along with such schemes!"

Verity placed the basket of cut roses on the floor. "Grandmama, perhaps you should sit down." Truly her grandmother did not look well. "What is the matter?"

"What is not the matter, more like! What do you know about the Bromsgroves and a match?"

"A match?" Verity sank onto the armchair opposite. No, surely Grandmama did not mean—

"Marriage with Charles Bromsgrove, yes." She tapped a letter. "Your mother writes: 'It is to be hoped his parents have not heard about Verity's scandalous behavior and are willing to sign the marriage documents.'" She glanced up, eyes fiery in their displeasure. "Why have I not heard of this before now?"

Verity tasted a sudden nauseous sensation. "I have not heard of it, either." Charles Bromsgrove? Why, he had to be thirty-five if he were a day! She'd only met him once, when he had come for a hunting weekend. Helena had visited at the time, and they had barely paid attention to anyone else. Charles Bromsgrove was so insipid and bland she could scarcely recall his face, let alone anything he might have ever said to her. And Mama wanted her to marry *him*? How much must she hate her own daughter!

"Wasn't there some silly business about Cecilia and a match last year?"

"Apparently Cecy refused him."

"About the most sensible thing that girl ever did. I declare, your mother must think we all still live in the Dark Ages. Who are these Bromsgroves anyway?"

"I . . . I believe Mama is good friends with Mrs. Bromsgrove. They have substantial holdings in Warwickshire, ma'am."

"Warwickshire? What good thing ever came from Warwickshire? No, no granddaughter of mine will be forced to marry a farmer from Warwickshire."

A chuckle pushed past her misery. "I don't believe he is a farmer, ma'am. I think he is a distant relation to the Duke of Hartington."

"I do not care if he is the duke himself! You will not be married off like some medieval wretch."

"But what do you propose?"

Her grandmother's eyes gleamed with indignation and purpose. "What is the name of your friend in the north?"

"Helena Chisholm, ma'am. She lives in a village near Dumfries."

"That is near the border, is it not?"

"I believe so, ma'am."

"Hmm. A shame. But no matter." She drew herself up to her full height. "You will leave on a visit tomorrow."

Verity blinked. "To see Helena?"

"And to stay with her until this foolish notion of your mama's has passed. I will write to both Mrs. Chisholm and your papa immediately. Dawkins! Dawkins!"

The silver-haired butler entered and bowed. "Yes, my lady?"

"Fetch me my writing paper at once, and tell Jameson he must ready to ride to town immediately." Her face held a small smile as she glanced back at Verity. "We have a predicament of gross proportions to prevent."

The English Channel

The ship lurched deep into another rolling wave. Anthony's stomach pitched along with the swell, his earlier desire to break his fast now completely gone. Indeed, the odor from sick passengers below deck would snuff most people's desire for food. He clutched the side of the deck rails as another icy spray merged water with damp sky. The dusty streets of Rio seemed an age ago, the heat of Antipodean summer more dream than memory.

"Sir! Sir! 'Tis foolhardy to remain on deck! Ye'll be catching yer death."

"And death doesn't plague us down below?" Anthony glanced at Mac. "At least on deck I feel alive."

"But sir—"

"Mac, stop your twaddle and appreciate the good Lord's handiwork."

The older man grumbled something and stumbled away, just as a heavy sheet of seawater rained from above. Anthony laughed, his spirits unabated. This, this was adventure! Sure there were some below deck who would not agree, but he bet their prayers for deliverance were more heartfelt than usual.

His expression grew wry. This voyage had been instructive in many ways, his hours spent learning everything from sailors' tricks with ropes to fighting off a chokehold, to tending to the sick and soiled. This last activity had necessitated plentiful respites for fresh air and sunshine, even if the sunshine was currently nonexistent and the freshness of air liable to take a man's legs from under him. Ah, the joys of nearing home.

Above him came a bell's ringing, the sound of a ship sighting. Anthony peered into the gloomy gray but could see nothing. Finally, the mists parted, revealing smudges on the horizon.

He lurched inside, where the captain was sliding open the spyglass. "Can you tell which ships are which?"

"Aye, of course." The man peered through his contraption. "I believe it is the *Canada*. A convict ship."

Poor fellows. His trip on the *Guildford* had been a relatively straightforward experience, the Sydney-bound ship not as overcrowded as some. Neither had there been any problems with sickness or disease, not like some of the horror stories he had heard.

Above the howling wind outside came a thin "Land ahoy!"

Anthony glanced up at the sailor, high in the crow's nest, spyglass in hand, one arm pointing to the horizon. Along the ship's deck came a rumble of relief as sailors and passengers alike expressed thanks that the voyage would soon draw to a close. The sailors assumed a new proclivity for action. He stayed out of the way, next to Mac, whose own desire to be on dry land had resulted in the remainder of their luggage being brought from below.

"I be thinking we'll be ashore in no time, sir."

Anthony raised his brows.

Mac chuckled. "There are them that look haughty when they do that, but I'm afraid ye be not one of them. Ye possess a face that is much too good-natured for such a thing."

Before he could protest, the captain chimed in. "Aye, and a good heart. We be grateful indeed for all your help below, sir. I had not expected so many to succumb to malaise. We haven't had such a rough crossing in years."

Anthony shrugged. "I imagine there'll be not a few sailors anxious to be home."

"Aye, but beforehand, there'll be a few glad to blow their earnings on wine and women." The captain sighed. "'Tis a long voyage, I know, but I cannot say I like to see such things. Ah well, I best get on." He moved off, shouting orders at the first mate.

An hour later, the grayness had lifted to reveal Portsmouth, its fort-lined hills reminiscent of great white eyes alert for danger. Anthony's chest tightened as gratitude and anticipation mixed with the weight of his new responsibility further north.

The next minutes—or was it hours?—passed in a flurry of activity, before Anthony and Mac could finally thank the captain and crew and descend the springy gangplank to the dock.

"Thank the good Lord we be home!"

"We've a good way to go before we can safely claim that, I'm afraid."

"But when I think I never expected to see England again . . ." Mac's eyes sheened.

Anthony clamped a hand on his shoulder. "Thank the good Lord we be home."

"I do. Aye, sir, indeed I do."

Their trunks were soon loaded on a cart while Mac strode off to find The Greyhound, which the captain had promised afforded the best accommodation. Anthony gazed around him, enjoying the sensation of firm land beneath his feet, smiling as he listened to the accents of a dozen tongues, and he breathed in the atmosphere of the fishing village plumped to bustling self-importance by its naval connections.

"Hello, sir."

He turned to see a waif wearing a thin dress of pale pink smiling up at him. "Good afternoon."

She rubbed her arms, her dress doing nothing to protect her from the sharp gusts from the sea. "You look like you could do with some company."

He groaned inwardly. Did he have a sign on his head that attracted women of a certain type? But—his heart twisted with compassion— the poor mite looked like she might blow away any second. "Can I help you, miss?"

She blinked. "Uh, no. That is . . ."

"Are you sure?" He ignored the sniggers of the sailors as they hustled past and gentled his voice. "You seem cold. Have you nowhere to be?"

Her pinched face blotched pink. "I have a home."

"Yes, I'm sure you do. Why do you not return? It is too cold an afternoon for a young lady to be out dressed so."

"But . . . but—"

"Here." Anthony dug into his pocket and retrieved two coins, smiling at himself. Good thing he'd given Mac the billfold to secure their coach and accommodation. He remained a soft touch. "Go buy yourself a hot meal and maybe find something warmer to wear. And perhaps you should seek out the Mission over there." He nodded to a whitewashed building whose black-painted sign proclaimed to all the kind of lighthouse it really was. "In fact, let's go there now."

Before the girl knew where she was, he had escorted her to the door and knocked firmly, to which a white-haired elderly woman soon appeared. She looked at him, then at the girl, her countenance falling a little. "Ah, Becky. What are we going to do with you?"

"Perhaps find her a position away from so many men?" Anthony suggested.

The woman, a minister's widow he soon learned, fluttered her excuses, her tale eliciting the last of Anthony's gold. The door closed, leaving him caught between that familiar sense of helplessness at his ineffectiveness in reducing the plights of others, and prayers for the girl and the Mission which needed God's grace, too.

"There ye be!" Mac lumbered into view. "We're all set. We've rooms in Portsmouth's best hotel and the coach for London leaves right from the door tomorrow morning. And"—the blue eyes twinkled—"I've requested dinner for an hour's time."

"Good." His stomach churned with anticipation. Already this trip had provided memories for a lifetime. What would the upcoming months bring?

❧ CHAPTER FIVE

Scottish Lowlands
July

A WIDE SWEEP of silver glinting in the afternoon sun stole her attention from her book. "The sea!"

"Aye, that be the Solway Firth," said the generously sized man who had pointed out places of interest along their journey since Dalbeattie this morning. "Almost there now, lass."

"I'm so glad."

Twelve days of traveling had left Verity weary and travel sore, her sides and legs aching from the continual bumping motion of a coach and four. How anyone could journey such distances in lesser conditions she could not fathom; she was fortunate to have a grandmother willing to pay the exorbitant costs associated with the fastest means of getting Verity away.

"Because if you are not here, they cannot fetch you back and force you to marry someone in this foolish fashion," Grandmama had said that last day.

"But what if they come for me?"

"Your papa is not a complete fool, my dear. I feel sure he will see reason."

"But if he does not?"

"Then you and I will take a trip to the Continent for several months."

"Really? Oh Grandmama, I can think of nothing better!"

"Well, one hopes it need not come to that." Grandmama had smiled. "At least with you out of the way we have some time before your mother will be able to reach you."

So amidst a mixture of excitement and fear, Verity had packed her belongings and set off with her maid for the biggest adventure of her life.

The coach rounded another green hill before beginning a slow descent to the flat. On the left lay wide brown shoals of sand, parted by a gleaming river. Beyond lay a series of low hills, lightly timbered, with only a handful of whitewashed stone dwellings dotting the landscape.

Their self-appointed guide leaned back in his seat as they passed a large barn. "And this be Kirkcudbright." He pronounced it *kir-coo-bree*.

The village of Kirkcudbright nestled against the grassy hill, crowned with a dark forest of pine, the buildings stretching to a late afternoon sparkle of harbor, bobbing with fishing boats. She glanced at Mary, sitting opposite, whose face no doubt matched hers, with its widened eyes and air of excitement. She hoped Mary would remember the instructions she had given last night at the posting house. "I do not expect to need your continuous service, as I do not wish to appear out of the ordinary in any way, and the Chisholms are not wealthy. Helena shares her maid with her mother and sister, so any assistance you can offer others will be appreciated."

Mary's understanding of the situation and assurance of discretion had given a modicum of peace. But now anticipation churned afresh. What would the next weeks hold?

Verity glanced out the window again as they passed through the high street, lined with square white-stoned fishermen's cottages, with doors and window sashes painted green and blue. The horses' hooves clattered on the cobblestones as they passed a tall square-towered ruin of a castle, then a smallish church.

"That be St. Cuthbert's."

"Mr. Chisholm is the reverend there, I believe."

The large man shook his head. "Nay, he ministers in the chapel up the lane. A good man he is, despite not adhering to the Covenant."

Across the river, on a low-lying hill, another stone structure drew her attention. The large building with its pointed turrets and battlements dark with ivy looked like something from a Gothic fairy tale. Her skin prickled. She glanced at her helpful guide. "What is that place?"

His face clouded. "That be Dungally House."

"Is it occupied?"

"Nay. The laird's been gone some time now." He muttered something under his breath.

"What a shame." Verity twisted in her seat, studying its imposing features and position, where doubtless it would enjoy uninterrupted views of the sea and surrounding countryside, until the coach rounded a corner and it was lost from view.

The coach slowed then pulled into an inn, which suddenly became a hive of activity, as hostlers and servants bustled about. Minutes later, Verity was clasped in a warm hug.

"You're here!" Helena's red hair gleamed in the late rays of sun as a smile lit her face. "I still cannot believe you did not finish the term with us."

"I know."

"It feels an age since I last saw you."

"It feels an age since I first began this trip. Can you believe it was nearly two weeks ago?"

"You poor thing. Never mind, we'll soon get you rested and refreshed. Now, show us your bags and we'll have you home in no time."

After her luggage was successfully wrangled from the coach, Verity and Mary followed Helena to a waiting carriage, where a handsome, broad-shouldered young man ceased his conversation with an ostler and hurried forward. "Ah. Miss Hatherleigh. I don't suppose you remember me?"

"Hello, James."

He flashed a grin. "There. I told Helena you'd remember. See? I'm not completely forgettable."

His sister rolled her eyes, which he did not see, busy as he was looking at Verity's baggage still waiting to be stowed. "Are these *all* your things?"

Verity met his amused gaze. "I took care only to pack the essentials."

"Right. Well then, let's have you." He assisted her into the carriage, then his sister and Mary, before supervising the luggage placement on the back, while Verity and Helena shared about their respective months apart.

A minute later they were off, exiting the inn's yard back to the main road where the carriage turned across the stone bridge over the River Dee.

The big house, Dungally House, with its castellated pretensions lay ahead, beyond a thick forest of trees. Verity's heart beat faster. Might she see it again? Perhaps even visit? Oh, what tales of romance and adventure the mysterious house seemed to possess.

Before she could speculate further, the carriage pulled up outside a far more modest dwelling. "Here we are!" Helena said.

The two-storied weathered stone house stood behind a stone wall and a hedge brimming with blooms and the buzzing of drowsy bees. A couple of tall oaks leaned down, their twisting branches telling tales of climbed trees. From one branch hung a wooden swing she guessed might be used by Helena's younger siblings. The property looked friendly, without any of the hauteur of the houses she was used to visiting. Or her own.

Their arrival brought a number of auburn-haired people from all corners, people whose wide mouths and fine features would have provided clue enough that they were related, even without the distinctive hair color.

"Ah, Verity." Mrs. Chisholm drew near and held Verity's hands. "I am so glad your mother consented at last."

Verity swallowed. Exactly what her grandmother had written she had not been privy to; whether her mother even knew she had been removed from Grandmother's she had yet to ascertain. Good thing she was so far away she would not bear the repercussions—at least for some weeks—by which time she would have had any number of exciting adventures with Helena and her family. She drew in a deep breath, mind whirring for an honest response.

"I do not think anyone could be happier than I at this surprising treat, Mrs. Chisholm."

"Helena has been beside herself since your grandmother's letter came so unexpectedly. Now, I'm sorry to say the reverend is out at the moment; however, he is due to return soon." She gestured to a bright-eyed girl of fifteen, and a boy who looked to be about seven or eight. "I'm sure Helena has mentioned Frances and Benjamin over the years."

"Hello." Verity smiled.

"Miss Hatherleigh." They dipped in synchronization.

"Oh, call me Verity, please." She drew closer and said confidentially, "I always wished to have younger siblings."

"You are welcome to them, anytime."

"James, that is enough," his mother scolded, yet with affection in her eyes. "Now, Helena, please show Verity to her room."

A short time later, Verity was ensconced in her bedchamber, having reassured Mrs. Chisholm it was perfectly suitable for the daughter of a viscount.

"Mrs. Chisholm," she said earnestly, "I do not wish for you to go to any extra trouble on my behalf. Indeed, I would much prefer for people to think I am merely one of Helena's school friends, and subsequently, be treated as Helena is, with all the responsibilities she carries."

"But your mama—"

"Need know nothing, Mrs. Chisholm. She is quite distracted with my sisters at this time. If you must write, please address it to my grandmother." She smiled. "I cannot tell you how wonderful it is to be here."

Somewhat mollified, Mrs. Chisholm left, murmuring something about finding Mary appropriate accommodation, leaving Helena and Frances remaining in the room.

"I don't understand why you said that! Why should you wish to share my responsibilities? I would give anything not to have to garden, or teach Sunday school, or accompany Mama on her visits to people like old Mrs. Podmore." Helena made a face.

"Because, dear friend, I want my stay to be as easy as possible for you all. If that means sharing the load, then I will gladly do so." And if it meant she could stay longer and enjoy this last chance at freedom, all the better.

The room fell silent whilst they watched Mary finish unpacking Verity's clothes.

"You don't know how lucky you are to have a maid." Helena sighed. "Mama, Frances, and I share Fiona, and she possesses no imagination at all when it comes to dressing hair or clothes."

"How imaginative do you wish her to be? I'm assured by Mama that the wearing of five or more ostrich feathers *est sans doute pas tres chic*." Verity grinned. "I'm sure Mary would love nothing more than to dress the hair of those who actually care about their appearance. Is that not so, Mary?"

Her maid nodded. "I would be more than happy to help, Miss Chisholm, Miss Frances. It would be a pleasure to dress such beautiful hair."

"Thank you, Mary." Helena picked up the end of her red braid. "I'm sure there is nothing much you can do with this, but I'd love to look a little more stylish."

Frances giggled. "She'd love Alasdair to think her so, anyway."

"Frances Chisholm!" Helena's face had reddened. "Aren't you supposed to be helping Mrs. Cready in the kitchen?"

"I . . . er . . ."

"Leave us!"

Frances scurried away, followed by Mary's courteous exit, and Verity sank onto the bed and leaned back against the upholstered bedhead. "And who is Alasdair?" She watched in fascination as Helena refused to meet her eyes, fiddling with the sleeve of her gown, as a telltale flush traveled up her neck. "Helena?"

"Oh, he is only one of James's friends from university."

"And does he reciprocate your feelings?"

"Verity! I do not—that is, I have no . . ."

"No, it is apparent the young man holds no interest for you at all, which is why my friend is not suddenly interested in her appearance, nor does she blush at the mention of his name."

Helena giggled. "Stop! It will be different for you should a young man catch your fancy."

"I'm sure it would be." Very different; for what hope could that lead to? What would Helena say if she knew of Verity's predicament? Best not to think on that. "So tell me more about your Alasdair . . ."

Later, after a substantial dinner, during which remarks to her husband and children suggested Mrs. Chisholm wasn't yet completely immune to having a viscount's daughter in their midst, Verity joined Helena and James for a walk along the terrace.

"It's not much of a terrace, really," Helena said apologetically, "but it is nice on such nights to see the moon reflecting on the Dee."

"It is very pretty." Verity drew in a deep breath of salt-tinged air and felt her body relax for the first time in weeks. Here the whirl of familial and social expectations could not touch her.

Before her, the water reflected a golden orb, flanked by the few lights of Kirkcudbright on one side, and vast nothingness on the other. The darkness held a velvet quality, a luster thick and smooth, soothing her soul. In the distance she could hear birdsong, different from those birds in England's southwest, but their message remained the same: they were on their way home.

Home.

Her throat thickened, and she bit her bottom lip as she suddenly understood Helena's self-assurance. How could she not be confident, when she was surrounded with such family and surroundings? Each day she must know she was loved, she was wanted, treasured. Her eyes stung. This truly was a home, humble perhaps, but carved with care and grace as beautiful as the river that wove through these hills.

"Verity?" Helena moved into her vision, worry knitting her brow. "Are you quite well?"

"Of course!" She took a deep breath, pushing aside the unexpected emotions, as she motioned to the nearby hillside. "But there is something I am curious about. What is that place?"

"That is Dungally House."

"But what *is* it? I noticed it on the drive in. It seems overly grand for a quiet seaside village."

"It is the home of the lairds of Dungally."

"Not that they do any good," James muttered.

Verity studied him a moment then turned to Helena. "*Lairds* sounds a trifle feudal."

"Perhaps, but it has been that way for hundreds of years." Helena gestured to the opposite side of the river, where Kirkcudbright lights gleamed softly. "The Guthrie clan are landowners for that side of the Dee, the Irving family are lairds of Dungally for this."

"'Some have meat and cannot eat, some cannot eat that want it,'" James intoned.

"I beg your pardon?"

"It's a local saying." James snapped a stick, hurtling one piece after the other into the gloom. "Neither side have had much good fortune of late. The Guthries have had family strife over who is the rightful heir, whereas the Irvings cannot seem to find anyone to take the laird's place." He shot her a sideways glance, his face half shadowed. "Papa does not believe in curses, but there are those from the village who say until things are put aright, both families will continue to suffer."

"But how are they to be put right?"

James shrugged. "I don't know. It's just silly village talk."

"It's not just silly village talk, James," Helena said softly. "No one can deny the Irvings have seen more than their due of tragedy."

Verity studied the turrets, whose tiles glistened in the moonlight. "What happened?"

"The last laird and his wife and baby son were killed in a carriage accident over a year ago."

"How awful!"

"Aye. Then six months back a fire broke out at the western wall. Some say it was the Guthries' doing, but Papa says we shouldn't pay attention to gossip. Since then the place has sat empty."

"With nothing but the wind and wee beasties for company," James added.

Verity shivered.

"You are not scared, are you, Miss Hatherleigh?" His smile glittered. "There is no need to fear, not with me here."

Verity gazed at him steadily until his smile slipped a little.

Helena giggled. "Verity, are you disconcerting my brother with that stare of yours?"

"Thank you for your concern, James, but I shiver merely because the evening air is much cooler than what I am used to."

"Yes, of course." Helena took her arm. "Let's get inside. I'm sure you must be exhausted."

But as they moved inside, Verity could not help but cast a final glance at the brooding house next door.

Edinburgh

"I am afraid the estate is not what it once was, especially with the fire earlier this year. A sad business." The solicitor cleared his throat as he straightened the papers on his desk to preciseness. "Your Great-Uncle Irving was far more concerned with improving the house than the lands. An undertaking"—his pale blue eyes studied Anthony over his eyeglasses—"to which, I assure you, I most strenuously objected."

Anthony nodded, flattening his lips to avoid the smile. Mr. Osgood seemed the sort to object to most things.

"I'm sure you are aware that your great-uncle's tastes were, ahem, somewhat unusual."

Anthony lifted a brow.

"He had a large appetite for the exotic and the romantic, which his travels in the East and in Germany and France appeared to develop. Doubtless you will understand when you arrive." He cleared his throat. "Your cousin also was rather disinterested in the management of estate affairs, which has not helped matters, although he was scarcely in the role long enough to make a difference."

His fingers clenched; he forced his voice to be soft. "Mr. Osgood—"

"Forgive me, I mean no disrespect, certainly not in light of the most unfortunate tragedy. But still, my role is simply to account for the facts, and the lack of attention to the lands over many years cannot be disputed." He peered over his pince-nez. "I'm afraid some of the crofters have been none too happy."

Anthony shifted in his seat, which suddenly felt cramped. Days of cooped up travel and now he was stuck in a spacious, well-appointed office that still seemed too small. "Is there a steward? Any servants at all?"

Mr. Osgood consulted his notes. "It appears they were released a year ago, when the estate could not pay their wages."

Wonderful. So he had inherited a bankrupt estate, with no servants to amend matters. "Can it be sold?"

Mr. Osgood blinked. "I . . . I beg your pardon?"

"Can we sell the estate? Surely the land must be worth something."

"But it is held in family trust. Your cousin was the last of the Irvings, and his death, and that of his son, means that as the nearest male relative through your mother's side, you have inherited the estate and the roles and rights as laird. No, I'm afraid it cannot be disposed of. Indeed, it is quite out of the question."

Anthony nodded, unsurprised, nor in fact terribly disappointed. Selling would be a drastic last step. With Macquarie having arranged their tickets, Anthony still possessed some funds. And perhaps, God willing, the estate could be made to pay.

"If I may, sir, I should perhaps warn you that the name Irving is not particularly well received in those parts. News of a new laird will not be wholly welcome." Mr. Osgood leaned back in his chair. "May I enquire whether you are familiar with your family's history?"

"I know some of it," he replied cautiously.

Mr. Osgood steepled his fingers. "Are you aware of the origins of the feud between the Irvings and Guthries?"

Anthony vaguely recollected his great-uncle mentioning words to that effect at Hogmanay years ago. "Something about a castle?"

"A castle, yes, and more sadly, the widow of the laird who died not three days after being evicted by the Irvings." The solicitor shook his head. "Aye, 'tis a very bad business, that caused many a hard word to be spoken and a bloodied outcome."

Anthony listened as the solicitor regaled him of tales of raiders and religion, queens and princely pretenders, Jacobites and smugglers whose stories intertwined with those of the Irvings, thus painting a very different picture to the one portrayed in those family gatherings of long ago.

"So what you are telling me is that the Guthries have led the populace to despise the laird of Dungally?"

"Aye, that be the truth of it."

"So, not only do I possess a mortgaged estate with no servants, I also have a hostile village to appease." Anthony's lips pushed to one side. "It sounds like I will be needing nothing short of a miracle."

Mr. Osgood coughed. "Your previous occupation gives me to understand you are not wholly opposed to believing for one."

For a moment, Anthony could but stare at the wizened solicitor. Then he smiled. "You are right to remind me. Well, I obviously lack knowledge, so I am yours to advise."

As Mr. Osgood outlined numerous details and suggestions, Anthony forced himself to listen, yet his instructor's reversion to his former dryness put him in mind of lectures from both Mr. Marsden and his former professors at St. Andrews, none of whom seemed to believe he would ever amount to much.

Eventually Osgood finished and Anthony escaped outside, where the watery sunshine highlighted graying buildings he couldn't help contrast to the bright yellow sandstone adorning Sydney Town.

"Mr. Jardine, sir." Mac hurried over. "How was your appointment?"

"Enlightening." Mac didn't need to know the extent of his financial woes. "I have decided that after visiting my parents we will travel south rather than continue to Linlithgow." His visit to the Witherspooles could wait until he could ascertain the exact state of affairs. No need to give rise to hopes that might need be dashed when the truth was revealed.

He outlined a long list of errands to fulfill in the following days. "For I do not wish to wait a moment longer than necessary."

"Aye, but patience be a virtue, so they say."

"Well, I have been virtuous enough." Anthony grinned. "And so on to Dungally!"

Chapter Six

The next morning, after the best night's sleep of her life, so she assured Mrs. Chisholm, Verity breakfasted, then hurried out to the garden. By daylight the property boundaries were plainly seen, marked as they were by a low stone wall, beyond which kelp-strewn sand marked the morning's low tide. The briny scent filled her nostrils, and the breeze wisped dark strands of hair into her eyes, making her glad she had chosen to wear something warmer than Mary's first selection this morning.

"Mary, I'm afraid I shall only be needing my oldest clothes. If I am to blend in, then it is important to dress appropriately."

"But Lady Aynsley—"

"Is not here, nor do I want you to consider Mama's opinion any more than I do. Now, if you could fetch the woolen spencer, I shall be grateful."

Verity returned her attention to the Chisholm garden, noting the weeds and shrubby bushes that would have her grandmother in fits, yet she could well imagine that the rectory's inhabitants had other priorities.

She pulled out a handful of weeds, then a handful more, noting with satisfaction how much better the rose garden already looked.

"Miss Hatherleigh! Never tell me you are weeding out here."

Verity grinned at her hostess. "Very well, I will not."

"But you should not—"

"Because my mother would not approve? Mrs. Chisholm, there seems to be very little of which my mama does approve. Now, I said I wanted responsibilities like Helena, and thanks to my grandmother's recent influence, I believe it is safe to say I am a famous gardener, ma'am." She adopted a pleading expression. "Please may I?"

"If you are quite in earnest, then I suppose I must grant permission." Mrs. Chisholm's eyes twinkled. "Although I do not give my daughters leave to employ such strategies in order to get their own way."

"Then I shall try to be meek and obedient, as I do not want to be cast away."

Her hostess gave her a somewhat skeptical smile. "Now, if you simply must garden today—"

"I'm afraid I simply must."

"Then you should seek out Hoskins before you attempt too much. He is given to thinking the place would fall to rack and ruin without him."

Judging from the level of care he seemed to expend, the Chisholms would do better without him, but she nodded agreeably at her hostess.

Mary returned just then with the spencer, and Verity instructed her to see what assistance she could offer Helena and perhaps Fiona. She shrugged into the garment, immediately appreciating its warmth, before commenting to Mrs. Chisholm about the wonderful aspect the house enjoyed.

Her hostess led the way around the side of the house. "It is a lovely outlook, but I often think something closer to town would suit our needs much better."

"I cannot imagine a better view."

"You should see the outlook from next door. Ah, here he is. Mr. Hoskins, this is Miss Hatherleigh who is our guest, but who insists on lending her skills to our gardens. Isn't that wonderful?"

The elderly man's deep squint and downturned mouth suggested otherwise, but his head jerk indicated sufficient acquiescence for Mrs. Chisholm to step toward the house. "I'll send out Helena and Benjamin in a moment."

Verity nodded then turned to Hoskins, whose squint—if it was possible—had become even more pronounced. "Good morning, Hoskins."

He grunted something, which at least showed he wasn't a mute.

"I couldn't help but notice some of the roses in the garden at the front. They wouldn't happen to be Scotch roses would they?"

Shaggy brows lifted.

"My grandmother was telling me recently about Scotch roses and how they thrive along the coast, so I imagine they would grow extremely well in the gardens here."

Another head jerk. "That they do."

She moved into the outbuilding and picked up an antiquated version of the gardening shears Grandmama preferred. "I hope you won't mind if I give them a wee trim?" She smiled. "I'm sure you have things you'd much prefer to do rather than dealing with such nasty thorns."

"Aye."

She moved back to the sunlight, holding the heavy gardening implement. "I'll return these as soon as I'm done."

A final head jerk and she turned and strode to the front garden and was soon busy clipping away the rambunctious runners, wishing she had thought to bring gardening gloves from Devonshire.

Just when her arms felt like they might fall off, Helena hurried over. "I'm so sorry I took so long, but Mama and Cready were having a frightful row."

"Who is Cready?"

Helena screwed her nose. "Our cook. She bosses Mama around as though she thinks Mama is a wet goose."

"I can't imagine your mama lifting her voice let alone arguing with anyone. She seems resolutely sweet-tempered."

"She wasn't the one raising her voice. If only Papa and James had not left for the market so early . . ." Helena's gaze ran over Verity's handiwork. "I must say this all looks far neater."

"It was a little unkempt."

Helena examined Verity's hands. "Remind me to get you some gloves." Then she glanced up, her brow furrowed. "How ever did you manage to make Hoskins help you?"

"He hasn't exactly helped me—"

"He lent you his tools! Mama says he never lends his equipment. He can be almost as much of a grouch as old Cready." She glanced over her shoulder and lowered her voice. "James thinks it's because they resent us as interlopers, not being Presbyterians."

"But hasn't your family lived here for years?"

"Since Frances was a babe, but that is nothing." Helena glanced at the house next door. "People have long memories around here. Too long sometimes."

Verity experienced a prickling sensation. She gestured to the turreted house, its windows like dozens of empty eyes. "Such as the feud between the Guthries and . . . Irvings, did you say?"

"Yes."

"Surely there must be caretakers."

"If there are, they've not been seen for over a year."

"Then we could go exploring!"

Helena blinked. "What? On Dungally House grounds? We would be trespassing."

"No, only visiting. Don't you think it holds a certain fascination?"

Helena shook her head. "It is only sad."

Oh, of course. Compassion softened her voice. "Did you know the former laird and his wife?"

"Not very well. We met them, but they weren't here long, and tended to keep to themselves."

The urge to visit would not be assuaged. "But we could go see the gardens at least?"

"I suppose so. But not today. I thought you might like to meet someone."

"Who?"

And the visit to the Chisholm stables chased all thoughts of trespass far from her mind.

THE NEXT FEW days were spent with Helena and James, enjoying rides into the village and beyond. Firefly was a silver-maned mare with Arabian blood, her speed and fearlessness quite similar to Banshee. Verity was surprised at the Chisholms' stabling of her, until James had explained when they had crested Barr Hill.

"She used to belong to Lady Dungally, and after"—he shifted uncomfortably—"after it happened, the steward sold her. Papa bought her for a song, thinking Frances might use her, but Frances had a fall last April and avoids riding now."

"Poor Frances. But I can understand her reluctance. Firefly *is* spirited." She patted the silver mane. Firefly nickered, tossing her head.

"You at least seem to have the means to control her, Verity."

"Why thank you, James," she replied coolly. The past days had led to an informality between them, which would not bother her, except it had revealed a condescension in Helena's brother that made her long to prove her prowess in many areas, not just her horsemanship.

"I don't know why you sound so surprised," Helena told her brother. "I know I wrote how Verity was far and away accounted the best rider at Haverstock's."

"You mistake your writing for my interest, little sister." James glanced at Verity. "You do ride quite well, although perhaps a trifle upright, if I may say."

"You may say." Verity smiled sweetly. "Just as *I* might say you hold the reins so tightly, Lightning's bit seems to strain."

"What? No, I don't."

Helena laughed, drawing Verity's attention to a wooded section far to the east. "See the line of trees there? That marks the end of the Guthrie estate."

Her interest sparked. "The ones arguing with the Irvings?"

"Aye. You can see they have scarcely any land," James said. "One feels *so* sorry for them."

"Inheritance can be a difficult thing." Verity bit her lip. If only she had been born a boy . . .

"Well, I'm feeling chilly. Race you back to the village?"

"You will lose, sister dear." James wheeled Lightning around, grinning over his shoulder. "And so will you!"

Verity nudged Firefly. "That remains to be seen."

And to be seen, it still remained, Verity having beaten James on that encounter, and again during an impromptu race yesterday. But today's intermittent rain showers had not induced Helena to go riding, and Verity could not in all good conscience go riding alone; this wasn't exactly the protected estate where she was known as the daughter of the house. Instead, the next best option seemed to be the one that had intrigued her since her arrival.

"Helena, let's explore next door."

Benjamin, released from his morning lessons with the curate who acted as tutor, looked up from the room's corner where he was drawing. "Can I come?"

Verity exchanged glances with Helena. "I'm not sure . . ."

"Ben, it might be too damp for you. You know Mama doesn't want you catching another cold."

He looked so crestfallen Verity couldn't help say, "But if you were well wrapped up, perhaps your mama will not object."

He jumped up, face aglow. "I'll find my coat and scarf now." He raced from the drawing room.

Verity laughed, turning to Helena. "He is excited."

"He is a pain," Helena grumbled.

"He is adorable. I wish I had a younger brother."

"Not an older one?"

"No." Verity grinned. "I much prefer to be the one giving orders."

Helena's chuckle faded. "I just remembered. Mama had to go see the Lynches today. I suppose we should tell Cready."

"Why?" Verity asked.

Frances piped up from her chair, where she'd been reading poetry near the window, one of the rectory cats curled up beside her. "She always likes to know where we are, and gets very cross when she doesn't."

"Is she not the cook?"

"Cook-cum-housekeeper."

"Still, that hardly qualifies her as your guardian."

"No, but . . ." Helena looked unconvinced.

"But nothing. We will be there and back before she notices us gone, especially if Frances is so good as to say nothing, or so good as to not be found." Verity smiled at Helena's sister. "In fact, I have one of Miss Austen's books beside my bed that I am quite certain you would enjoy. And the chair next to the window in my room is *most* comfortable, as well as enjoying a lovely view . . ."

Frances rose, her face dimpling. "Thank you, Verity. I was thinking it was time for something new."

"Enjoy." Verity turned to Helena and Ben who now wore a coat and red scarf. "And if we go through the French doors here, I don't believe anyone will hear a sound."

Minutes later, they were walking along the stone wall, heeding Helena's warnings to avoid puddles whilst Benjamin kept up a constant chatter about various birds such as the windhovers he and his tutor had seen earlier in the week. Verity smiled. He really was a most intelligent boy, with a perception and interest in nature far deeper than his brother's, whose interest in the outdoors seemed limited to horses.

The gray sky appeared heavier than a blanket, but at least the rain had ceased. A breeze dampened her cheeks as she followed Helena until the stone wall met a hedge of drooping primroses. Helena stepped over the wall, onto the grassed-over river sand. By now they were well out of sight of the rectory, a mass of pine blocking views of both houses.

Helena turned. "We used to travel this way, as it is much quicker than the road. But the path is overgrown, and damp underfoot, so tread carefully."

Verity pulled her pelisse closer, the breeze from the river stronger here, the scent of brine more pronounced. From this vantage point, the boats in the harbor seemed miles away, Kirkcudbright's ruined castle tower barely discernible.

Another dozen feet and the path cut in again, and a break in the trees revealed a high white wall. Halfway along was an iron gate which Helena pushed open with a loud creak.

Verity followed her in then stilled. "Oh my goodness!"

They were in an enormous walled garden, larger than anything

Grandmama owned. Unlike Saltings, the formal paths here were matted with weeds, the shrubs long overdue for shaping. Above the garden wall appeared to be a terrace, beyond which presided the house with its turrets and battlements seemingly more severe in the iron cast of sky.

"It is remarkable, is it not?"

"More castle than house." Verity exhaled. Indeed, it held a charm similar to the castle-like dollhouse her sisters used to play with. And while certainly grand, reaching four stories high, its fairy-tale improbability kept it from possessing the ancient grandeur of Aynsley Manor or Saltings, an effect further enhanced by the state of the gardens.

"I cannot conceive how something so lovely could be allowed to fall into such a state."

Helena shrugged. "Papa said something about financial difficulties, and I suppose without a laird there is no one to care."

"So the laird is like the local squire."

"No, far more important than that. At least in this case. The Dungally family is actually connected to an ancient Irish earldom, or so Papa says."

They passed a murky round pool, centered by a stone nude in what must have once been a fountain. Verity chuckled. "I must confess I did not envisage seeing Diana in humble Kirkcudbrightshire."

"Mama says it is obscene, but James doesn't seem to mind."

Verity smiled as Benjamin made his way to the edge of the pool, chattering about frogs and newts. She listened to their burps and croaks as she climbed the set of stairs leading to the next terrace. Here a castellated stone handrail, interspersed with a series of wide, weed-strewn urns, drew the eye toward a wide bank of roses, whose ragged condition and black spot Grandmama would decry. Verity moved along the stone flagging to the first tall windows of the house. She placed her hands against the glass and peered in, but curtains shrouded her view. She stepped back. If this house was anything like her own home then the important rooms would be on the next level anyway.

She turned to face the river, whose soft glint of earlier was now shadowed by a menacing cloud.

"Verity!" Helena hurried toward her. "We should get back. It will rain again any moment."

Verity cast a final glance up at the building. Frowned. Had that curtain twitched? "Did you see that?"

Helena paused at the top of the stairs and glanced back. "See what?"

Verity pointed to the third level of windows. "I'm sure I saw something at the window."

"You're imagining things."

Just then they heard a cry and a splash.

"Benjamin!"

Verity rushed after Helena, down the tiered steps, past the overgrown roses to the pool to help drag the dripping boy onto the path. Helena unbuttoned his coat, muttering darkly as Benjamin protested.

"But I wanted to catch the newt! He's a tiny wee thing, smaller than my hand—"

"You'll catch your death if we don't get you dry soon! I should never have allowed you to come."

"Helena, that was my doing. And he can't help being a small boy with an inquisitive nature." Verity shrugged off her pelisse and wrapped it around a shivering Benjamin. "I hope you won't mind wearing this until we get you home."

"Verity! You cannot let him spoil your clothes."

Teeth chattering, he managed, "At least it is brown. Y'know the newt was this color."

Clasping his cold hand in hers, Verity hurried him to the gate as the first drops of rain pelted from above. "We cannot let him get any colder. We should hurry."

By the time they had reached the rectory grounds, the skies had well and truly opened. By the time they had entered the drawing room, Benjamin's lips held a tinge of blue, which Verity felt sure her own matched, the gown she wore having done little to cut the chill of icy rain.

"Quick." Helena guided them to the door. "Get him up to my room before—"

"Where have you been?" A formidable woman of iron-gray hair moved into the doorway, frowning, arms crossed.

"Mrs. Cready!" Helena's face paled. "We . . . we are terribly sorry—"

"But we need to get Master Benjamin up to his room immediately." Verity propelled the lad forward, noting the older woman step back. "Please see that water is heated and inform Mary I have need of her services."

The older woman stared at Verity, her pale eyes glinting with barely suppressed rage. "Don't be thinking I'll lift a finger to help that young scamp."

Not for nothing had Verity dealt with intimidating tactics all her life. Her brows rose, as she enunciated clearly, "*Now*, if you please."

The woman blinked and shifted from the doorway, allowing Helena and Verity room to maneuver Benjamin through the hall and up the stairs to his room, where they quickly divested him of his clothes and wrapped him in a blanket, much to his howling protest.

"Benjamin! Be quiet or I'll tell Mama about the rabbit you're hiding in your room," Helena snapped, which only made his cries louder.

"You can be sure I'll be telling your mother about this!"

Verity cast Mrs. Cready a baleful glance. "I didn't realize that was part of your role here." The housekeeper gasped, but any retort was interrupted by Mary's appearance.

"Ah, Mary. Please secure some hot water for a bath."

Mary bobbed a curtsy, and Verity shut the door in Mrs. Cready's face, and helped Helena convince Benjamin it would be in his best interests to get clean. "For if you don't, then how are you ever going to show me those golden eagles you mentioned before?"

Benjamin looked up at Verity, wet-lashed and miserable. "You really want to see them?"

"Of course I do."

Mary returned with cans of heated water, and Helena firmly encouraged her brother to get in the bath.

"I'm not having a bath in front of girls!"

Helena rolled her eyes. "Then use the screen."

Verity assisted Helena to drag a wooden screen in front of the bath, then waited until the sounds of splashing suggested Benjamin was at least getting wet, if not precisely clean.

"Did I ever tell you about the ospreys I've seen in Somerset?"

Her stories of wildlife managed to distract him for the remainder of his bath, and by the time he was dressed he—and Helena—were back in their usual good spirits.

"I don't know how you have the patience," Helena murmured later as they made their way downstairs.

Verity tugged at the sleeve of her fresh—dry!—gown. "I suppose I have not used it all up on a younger sibling. I find him quite delightful."

"He has his moments, I suppose, but I cannot agree my brother is delightful."

"Why ever not?" a masculine voice drawled from behind them, causing them to spin to see James's smirking face. "If Miss Hatherleigh should find your brothers delightful, I fail to understand your objections, dear sister."

"Unfortunately she was not referring to delighting in you, *dearest* brother."

"I am sure Miss Hatherleigh will revise her opinion before long." James said as he opened the drawing room door and gestured them inside.

Mrs. Chisholm hurried towards them, stripping off her gloves. "Oh, Helena! Is it true? Mrs. Cready tells me you encouraged poor Benjamin to play in the rain. You know he catches cold so easily. How could you?"

"Mama, it was not like that at all."

Verity stepped forward. "Mrs. Chisholm, I don't know what you have been told, but it was I who insisted on seeing the grounds next door. When Benjamin overheard, he desired to come, too. At that time there was no rain and he was dressed warmly in a coat and scarf. Indeed, Helena made sure he kept himself dry for as long as possible."

Mrs. Chisholm's large reproachful eyes moved from Verity to Helena. "But Mrs. Cready says he was saturated. Dripping!"

"Mama, he is seven, and insisted on catching frogs in the pond."

"But how could you let such a thing occur? I'm terribly disappointed in you."

"Perhaps, ma'am," Verity spoke up, "your disappointment should be reserved for the person who did nothing to help once we arrived back, despite seeing the need for immediate action. Helena, on the other hand, did everything Mrs. Cready did not, and ensured Benjamin was clean and dry as quick as humanly possible."

"Is this true, Helena?"

"Yes, Mama."

Mrs. Chisholm sighed. "Well, in future I would prefer Benjamin to remain here. And I really don't think you should be visiting next door. What if something should happen?"

"Like what, Mama? Do you suspect a wee beastie might have designs on our guest?" James chuckled. "Now, let me tell you about something far more interesting."

As James shared about an upcoming event called the Ridings, his excitement spreading to the others, Verity listened with half an ear, comforting herself with the fact that after today's adventures, Benjamin appeared none the worse for wear.

And below this, was a sense of relief that while Mrs. Chisholm had expressed her reservations, she had not actually forbidden future visits next door—a prospect that filled her with burning anticipation.

CHAPTER SEVEN

Dungally House
Kirkcudbrightshire, Scotland

"Sir, I MUST insist ye leave!"

"Mac, you cluck worse than a mother hen." Anthony gasped as the irritants in his nose and lungs triggered paroxysms as they were always wont to do.

"Aye, but I be the only creature looking out for yer best interests." Anthony doubled over. "But—"

"Sir, yer coughing is not helping yer weak chest any. Now out wi' ye!"

Anthony fled the stour fogging the study and leaned against the banister of the main stairs, taking careful deep breaths, thankful the creaking wood did not give way in a spectacular tumble to the tiled hall below. His ragged breathing gradually subsided, and he stumbled through hastily flung open doors to the narrow balcony abutting his bedroom. Dragging in deep lungfuls of fresh air cleared the dust from his airways. The sweet scent of roses mingling with a salty tang hung on the breeze, a scent he'd instantly enjoyed when, after a rain-delayed journey from Edinburgh, he'd finally arrived two days ago.

Mac's reaction had echoed Anthony's own, when the carriage had finally escaped the long avenue of overarching trees and the house first came into view. "I cannae believe it. Turrets!"

Turrets, indeed. Battlements, too, as if the house expected imminent attack. Inside they discovered over forty rooms, including a pink monstrosity overlooking the garden, which his new housekeeper, Mrs. Iverson, called the "Rose Saloon." He shook his head. Tangled gardens. A leaking roof. Scorch marks halfway up the western wall from an arson attempt. The telltale signs of furred inhabitants, thus necessitating the procurement of a cat or dog as soon as possible. A fine inheritance.

But what a glorious view.

He drank it in anew, uttering a heartfelt prayer of gratitude the house afforded one advantage at least. From this position he could see the sailboats gliding from Kirkcudbright's protected bay out to the mighty Solway Firth. He almost smiled. After his months at sea, he didn't envy them one jot; indeed, he would be happy to never sail again.

His gaze tracked down to the ragged walled garden below, its central pond the site of the previous afternoon's near tragedy. From his third-level position, where he'd been marveling at the views, he'd been able to do nothing, save pray and hope for the little boy's best. And thank God for the young lady—his sister, no doubt—who had the foresight to wrap him in her warm clothes. By the time he had raced down the three flights of stairs to the stone terrace, the trio was gone, leaving him puzzled as to whether the entire episode had been of his own imagination.

"Mr. Jardine, I be sorry fer botherin' ye."

Anthony turned to see his Mrs. Iverson's anxious face. "What is the matter?"

"What is not the matter, more like. The house is in such a guddle I barely ken where to start. The kitchen pump dinnae works, the chimney be that clarty I could nae see, and as for the mice . . ."

As he listened to a litany of complaints he fought the growing certainty that his solicitor had found him a housekeeper of more wind than willpower, her heavy brogue often a challenge to decipher, university days having polished such things from him. Unfortunately his slow understanding only seemed to add to her ire.

"I dinnae ken when we shall be done—"

"Mrs. Iverson." He spoke firmly. "Please do not work yourself into a swither. I have full confidence that you can make the house all it should be."

"But I cannae do it by myself!"

"Then employ some girls from the village. I know it may seem overwhelming, but I do not need everything set to rights at once. Little by little, Mrs. Iverson, one room at a time, and we will see Dungally House as it should be."

She opened her mouth. Fearing further complaint, he rushed on. "Now I will be outdoors, should anyone need me"—he raised a brow—"although I'm sure a person as capable as yourself should be able to make good decisions without constant need for my approval, should they not?"

Her cheeks reddened slightly, but she offered a nod and a curtsy and hurried away.

Anthony strode back into his room, where he retrieved a battered case from his trunk. He used a drinking glass of water to gently damp the carefully wrapped stems and stalks—they would not survive much longer without planting—but without a greenhouse, such things would not be accomplished today. After retrieving his equipment, he hurried down the small oak staircase at the end of the gallery then through a small hall, a wide door, and hastened down the stone steps toward the rose garden.

Relief at successfully evading his housekeeper filled his lungs as much as breathing in the sweet-scented air. He might be somewhat useless inside, an old chest complaint making dust removal a rather hazardous proposition, but here at least he could do something.

A quick reconnaissance yesterday had revealed several gardens of substance, as well as a walled kitchen garden, which still bore the withered stalks of the turnips and onions it once grew. The rose garden must have been beautiful once, its large rounded bed filled with the overblown mottled white of yesterday's roses.

He drew out his shears and began to snip away the dead wood, the blighted leaves, and signs of rust. Above him the aged pines sang mournfully, the wind carrying occasional traces of yesterday's rain, but he paid it no heed. He moved on to the next bush, then the next, building a satisfying pile of clippings to be burned, an endeavor that in turn would help improve the soil.

His feet squelched in the mud, and he looked at his spattered trousers and gave a rueful smile. He had purposefully worn his most shabby clothes, knowing the next few days would be ones devoted to cleaning, not entertaining. He hoped Mrs. Iverson would find a lass or two who could clean without complaint.

By the time the pine shadows were at their shortest, his pile of clippings was substantial, despite having already been twice cleared away by Mr. Iverson using a small wooden barrow he had found. Iverson's skills in outside work had been touted as a fitting complement to his wife's supposed housekeeping—the truth of which Anthony was just beginning to realize, as he rather doubted they extended much beyond carrying out the most basic (and oft-repeated) of orders. Clearly as the new laird he would be spending time attending to the needs not only of other people's lands but also of his own. Not that he minded. Better to be outside enjoying God's handiwork than in a yet-to-be-dusted library trying to bring order to the myriad accounts the solicitors had handed over. Thank God for McNaughton, whose keen eye derived joy from organizing the study and paperwork into something Anthony might comprehend.

The barrow filled once more with prickled branches, Anthony wheeled it to the growing mound that included broken discards from the house. After dusting off his gloves he moved back amongst the roses. Perhaps now wasn't the best time of year to have pruned them so severely—they looked more like gnarled twigs than rosebushes— but it stopped the rot, and wasn't that what his new role demanded? God seemed to have placed him here to prevent the estate from falling into further chaos, and though the challenge was daunting, with God's strength, he could do it. This small section of cleared garden gave hope the rest of the estate would, in time, experience order, too.

"Verity?"

Anthony glanced to his right from where the childish voice came.

"Verity! Are you in here?"

He stepped down to the stone terrace, which overlooked the walled garden below. Down by the far gate stood a boy, whose small stature belied the piercing treble of his voice, which along with his hair color, marked him indubitably as the lad from yesterday. Relief that the boy was unharmed mingled with amusement at his game. He was playing a game of hide-and-seek, and Anthony's position permitted him to see a young lass hiding behind one of the misshapen yews.

Eventually the boy moved back through the gate and away to goodness-knew-where, his slight frame eliciting no protesting whine from the gate. Still the girl remained, plucking nearby grassy weeds, while she awaited discovery. His lips twitched. He supposed he should be grateful for her efforts, despite her trespasser status.

Moving quietly, he stole down the steps, unwilling to spoil the game should the small boy return and be alerted to his presence. By now the lass had amassed a pile of weeds such as might almost require the barrow, and still she plucked away, heedless of both her gown and potential detection.

Anthony cleared his throat. "Excuse me."

"Oh!" The girl started and scrambled back behind the yew. "Get down!"

For some reason, he found himself obeying, ducking behind the hulking yew five yards from hers. He studied her as she crouched, peering through the dense foliage to see if discovery loomed. Well dressed, despite the hem of her gown being laced with mud, her dark hair twisted in a small knot, she appeared older than he first thought, her face holding a maturity neither her figure nor her actions displayed. But then, he grinned inwardly, his current behavior could scarcely denote his eight-and-twenty years. How long since he had participated in such a game?

"Excuse me, but would you be so kind as to tell me from whom we hide?"

"From Benjamin. He is seven and terribly good at finding his sisters."

She was not the lad's sister? Was she perhaps his governess? Only she seemed remarkably energetic for such a venture, and most dissimilar to the prune-like Miss Plume his sister Aileen had once endured. In an effort to regain her attention, Anthony cleared his throat.

She glanced back at him and smiled sweetly. "Can I help you?"

He blinked. "Can you help . . . ?"

"Yes. Was there something you needed?"

"I beg your pardon, but are you aware that this is private land? You are trespassing."

"Am I?" Her head tilted. "How do I know *you* are not trespassing?"

He chuckled despite himself, which was quickly stopped by her hissed "Quiet! He's coming!"

Seconds later, he heard the small boy pipe up. "Verity, if you are here, you are the winner. I'm going back to the house."

The girl smiled but stayed where she was until a fading whistle announced the boy's departure once more. She rose and dusted off her skirts.

He stood also, drawing closer to his intruder, where amidst impressions of sparkling blue eyes and glossy hair came the realization of how petite she was. He was not a tall man, and the top of her head would reach his chin.

"Why did you not say you were here?"

"And lose my hiding spot for next time?"

"You are a guileful young lass."

Her chin lifted. "I'm not so terribly young."

"You are neither so terribly old. Now, what is your name?"

"Why? Who are you?" She looked over his disreputable outdoor clothes, garments that had clearly seen better days. "Are you the gardener here?"

The gardener? He looked that grubby? But still . . . "I suppose you could say so."

"Well, excuse me for being blunt, but you keep this place in shocking disrepair."

"It is something of a shambles," he agreed mildly.

"I am surprised your employer has not released you from your duties."

"Pardon my candor, but are you always so outspoken?"

Her eyes widened, her expression growing rueful. "I'm afraid so. Mama tells me it's my besetting sin."

"Besetting sin, eh? I would perhaps think that pride or unfeeling treatment of others better qualified as a besetting sin, but then"—he lowered his head humbly—"I *am* merely a gardener."

Amusement flashed across her features. She glanced at the house. "Does this mean your employer has arrived?"

"My employer?"

"The laird," she said impatiently.

He bit back a smile. "The laird has indeed returned."

"I thought so! Helena wouldn't believe me when I suggested there was no other possible reason for so much activity after so long being vacant."

"You are very observant, Miss . . . ?" He raised his eyebrows.

Her chin rose higher. "Miss Hatherleigh."

"Miss Hatherleigh," he repeated slowly. "Now, why do you visit a garden that is not yours?"

She pointed to the dramatic view, which the white wall underscored. "How could you not appreciate that? And this garden, as unkempt as it is"—she looked at him severely—"still holds such loveliness. If I were the owner, I would ensure the gardens were maintained to maximize the vista."

"You would, would you?"

She dipped her pointed chin. "Tell me, what is he like?"

"Whom?"

"The new laird! Everyone is agog to meet him."

"Then they'll be sadly disappointed," he said wryly.

Her fine brows rose. "How can you say such a thing?"

Conscious of how his words might be construed, he said, "I . . . I mean he is an ordinary fellow. Kindhearted, some would say, but nothing terribly extraordinary or grand."

She nodded. "And what does he look like?"

"Oh, you know," he said, waving a dismissive hand, "like most of the men around here."

"But is he old? Young? Helena thinks he must be old, seeing as he is the old laird's cousin, but I don't think that means he is ancient."

"Oh, I don't know about *ancient*. But he is half decrepit, prone to hobbling about in fits of coughing."

She laughed, her amusement as uninhibited as her manners. "I do believe you are what my mai—" She coughed. "What my mama would term 'spinning a yarn.'"

"Somehow I doubt your mama would be familiar with sailor's cant, let alone have ever said such a thing."

Pink bloomed in her cheeks to charming effect.

He took compassion on her. "Rest assured, Miss Hatherleigh, the new laird is quite a bit older than you."

"Well, I would still like to meet him." She glanced up at the house.

"Whatever for?" His heart hardened a little. Was she one of the fortune hunters Mrs. Ramsay had mentioned? If so—his lips twisted—she was doomed for disappointment.

Her chin lifted. "To see if you are telling the truth."

"Ah. I see she must live up to her name, *in Veritas*."

Her brow wrinkled. "How did you know my name is Verity?"

"The young lad."

"Benjamin, of course." Her head tilted. "I suppose I must thank you for not giving me away, but I cannot help but wonder why you said nothing."

He stared at her, unable to think what imp had bade him to join the game rather than assume his responsibilities. For that matter, why did he persist in letting her think he was the gardener? Aware she was awaiting his answer, he settled for shrugging his shoulders. "I could see you were not here to destroy the grounds, but seemed to merely be idly curious."

"Idly—" She laughed. *"Touché!"*

"Familiar with fencing terms, too, I see. Most unusual for a young lady."

"And also perhaps for a garden laborer, Mr. . . . ?" Her brows rose expectantly.

All at once a thought flashed through his mind, so outlandish, so ridiculous, yet so fully formed he could barely keep a straight face. Clearly this young governess thought him but a menial laborer; would he appear so to others as well? If so, perhaps he might more easily learn the truth of the estate's problems, without the prejudice attached to his being the laird. If people accepted him for himself, then perhaps they might be more willing to overlook his family connections, and the difficulties and feud Mr. Osgood seemed so concerned about might be resolved.

His lips curved. Masquerading as a gardener might also help avoid detested social occasions, and the possibility of matchmaking mamas. In addition, it could prove an opportunity to continue God's work of liberation, to help others see beyond the immediacy of a title, estate, and all that those involved. It would not be a deception, merely an experiment, like the kind he used to conduct whilst at university, only this time on society rather than plants.

He smiled. "I answer to Jardine."

She laughed. "But of course! *Monsieur Jardine du jardin.* I suppose that makes you a true gardener?" She mock-curtsied, paced back, then grinned. "Good day, Mr. Gardener."

"Good day." He doffed his hat, and she walked away, turning once to see he still watched her, before the unkempt hedges stole her from view, and he remained wondering how to exact his plan—and how long it would be until he met the governess again.

Verity hurried away, careful to take only one peek at the gardener. Her heart thumped with excitement. The laird was back!

How fortunate the gardener was so kind. Her brow knit. He was a *most* unusual gardener, clearly someone who preferred play to work. She bit her lip. Not that she was any different, off playing games with Benjamin instead of spending time more beneficially. But she couldn't help it; leaving him with the Cready, as Helena and James referred to the housekeeper, seemed nothing short of inhumane. The woman was a tyrant, inflicting harsh and unusual punishments on poor Benjamin just because he had the effrontery to answer her tirade about Helena with a forceful "She's not like that at all! Helena always takes good care of me!"

Of course, it had reignited discussion around the breakfast table, with James and Helena exchanging dark looks and darker mutterings, to which Mr. Chisholm seemed oblivious, and Mrs. Chisholm's anxious flutterings seemed to worsen.

Only the arrival of news that Benjamin's tutor was ill and therefore unable to visit had ensured the rest of the breakfast meal had been consumed in relative peace. Verity had volunteered to teach Benjamin some basic geography, an offer gratefully received by his parents and elder siblings, all of whom had engagements in the village today. In the end she had managed perhaps an hour of tutelage before Benjamin's fidgeting precluded further studies. Only the promise of a play outside had settled him, which had led to a game of hide-and-seek, and thus to the garden—and gardener—next door.

Mr. Jardine. It was a refined-sounding name for someone who looked anything but, with his lightly tanned skin and bushy mop of dark red hair. She smiled as she stepped over the stone wall. He might lack James's height and even features—his face more honest than handsome, more good-natured than gentlemanlike—but the gardener certainly did not lack for wit, as evidenced by his easy repartee. Her smile faded. If only Charles Bromsgrove possessed a tenth of that.

"There you are!" Benjamin ran from the terrace. "I was wondering what had happened. Did you get lost?"

"No, I just found the most perfect hiding spot, and no, I am *not* revealing its location."

"Oh, but—"

"Benjamin, did you know the laird has arrived?"

His eyes widened. "You are joking!"

She shook her head. "I met his gardener, Mr. Jardine, and he mentioned it."

"How did ye meet 'im?" His little face crumpled in thought. "You weren't hiding in there, were you? I woulda seen you."

She chuckled. "You are most persistent, aren't you? But I'm afraid you are still not going to find out the most excellent hiding location." She glanced over her shoulder at the brooding house next door. "Have you ever been inside Dungally House?"

He shook his head. "Papa has. He called it *dreich*." At her raised brows he continued, "That means gloomy."

"I should like to see inside. I wonder how it might be arranged."

Benjamin's eyes lit up. "James said there was supposed to be a secret tunnel!"

Her heart skipped, even as she shook her head. "I'm sure he was just playing games with you."

"He did! 'Parently the former laird's steward said there was a passage between the House and here. Course, we looked for it, but never found it."

"Where did you look?"

"Oh, around," he said airily. "But James and Helena never found nothing, so they gave up. James reckons the man was a bletherskate."

Verity nodded. "Most likely he was. Now, how about we continue with those geography questions?"

"But—"

"You have had enough fresh air to clear your head. Come, let's find that globe and continue mapping the journey to the Antipodes."

As the small boy soon bent his head to the task of plotting the ship's voyage to the other side of the world, Verity fought to stay focused, even though every fiber of her being begged to continue the search for the tunnel abandoned so long ago.

"Verity?"

She smiled, and pointed out the coast of Brazil, all the time wondering how long it would be until she could again visit the grand house next door.

❧ Chapter Eight

Anthony finished his bowl of morning porridge, the hour not yet advanced enough for Cook to have prepared anything lavish; his needs—and pocketbook—slim enough to not demand more.

Mac appeared in the breakfast room. "Excuse me, sir? The horses are saddled."

"Very good." Anthony motioned to the sideboard. "Have you breakfasted?"

"Aye, I have, thank ye."

Minutes later they were outside Dungally's gates, riding west. Anthony was an indifferent horseman, having always considered riding more an essential than a pleasure, his family's funds not permitting a stable beyond what was strictly necessary. Nevertheless he was glad for the ride as it harnessed his thoughts away from the night's distracting, disquieting ones about the young governess. He shook his head. What kind of fool was he?

He spurred the horse across the moor, up the hill. At the crest he glanced over his shoulder to where Kirkcudbright nestled below, the high tide sheening bright.

"Sir? The first tenant is just beyond that copse." Mac gestured to a small wooded area. "The Boyds. They have complaints concerning the housing."

And not without cause, Anthony thought, as he studied the drooping thatch and broken window. Mac knocked, and seconds later the door opened to reveal a dim room, lit only by a small fire, the smell of peat permeating the cottage, tickling his nose. The wizened woman at the door peered at him.

"Good morning, Mistress Boyd," Anthony offered, doffing his cap. "My name is Jardine, and I have come to speak with you and your husband, if he might be available."

"Well, he's not," she said. She gestured to the village, a distant smudge on the horizon. "He's buried in the graveyard."

"My deepest apologies, Mrs. Boyd, I had no idea." Anthony's heart stirred with compassion. "And how are you managing—?"

"What business be that of yours?"

"This be the new laird you be speaking to," Mac snapped.

"New laird, old laird"—she shrugged—"they're all the same to me. Got nowt to do wi' any of us."

Anthony drew in a deep breath, his pity for the woman chased with exasperation that his predecessors had not viewed their responsibilities as they ought. "That may have been the case in the past, but I can assure you it is no longer." He offered a smile he hoped appeared conciliatory. "Now, McNaughton here tells me you have issue with the housing. I can see the thatching and a window need work. Is there anything else you require?"

She uttered a guttural laugh. "And what if I were to say yes? Who's going to do it, and how much will it be costing? I don't have a blessed groat left after the burying." She nodded to the house on the hill. "The Bellings check on me every day or so, drop off firewood, but I cannae repay them, save for watching their wee one when Douglas goes harvesting."

"Harvesting?" The land here by the sea was so susceptible to sea salt and wind, it seemed scarcely able to support potatoes, let alone anything more productive.

She gestured to the sea. "Sea kelp. It's what we had to do when cropping didn't work."

"You managed to crop?"

"Aye." She nodded. "We harvested corn and oats for nigh on three generations, until the mouldy blight set in and turned the crops rot-ten." A heavy sigh released. "We had to collect sea kelp, but the sea is a hungry beast, and stole more than just my John."

Again, his heart twisted with compassion. "Mrs. Boyd, I am very sorry for your loss. I assure you your roof and window will be fixed within the week."

"Thanking ye kindly, sir, but I'll believe it when I see it," she wheezed. "Folks have been promising help for years."

"Nevertheless, it shall be done." Anthony offered a small bow, which seemed to take the old lady by surprise, as she gave a flustered curtsy. "I shall be seeing you very soon." He paused. "And I would be much obliged if you would refrain from mentioning I am the laird. It seems my predecessors have not been very popular, and I wish to be known for myself rather than their lapses."

She jerked a nod and then closed the door with a slam, suggesting she did not hold much faith in his promise nor respect for his position.

But that only served to strengthen his resolve to attend to matters quickly. He scratched notes on the paper he'd brought. "Remind me when we return home to see about finding thatch and glass."

"Aye. There is that which is in the Dungally cellar," offered Mac. "I believe it was to be used for the new outbuildings."

Such as the building he'd hoped to convert into a greenhouse. His plants would have to cope without appropriate accommodation a while longer; Mrs. Boyd could not. "If we are to help the tenants then we must do so. My word is only as good as my action. And that poor woman has suffered long enough."

Mac shot him a look that could almost be described as approving. "If I may ask, just who do you see as fixing the roof? I scarcely think old Iverson able or willing."

Anthony grinned. "Why you and me, of course."

Mac snorted, shaking his head, and they got on their horses and moved to the next farm, the Bellings. A discussion with the wife provided further clarification regarding their elderly neighbor, before she freely offered her opinions about other neighbors and their various mishaps and misdemeanors, leading Anthony to make several more inscriptions. Surely if they had cropped before it could be managed again. Perhaps he could investigate improving the soil . . .

They returned to their horses and rode to the next croft, which unlike the sea-bracing others, was huddled in the lee of a hill, within sight of another. Mac murmured, "This is the one Mistress Belling said had some problems with sheep."

Anthony nodded, and before they had set foot in the yard, the door opened and a tall man with black hair and darker scowl came out. "What is it ye want?"

Mac held up a hand. "This is the new laird, Mr. Jardine—"

The man spat on the ground. "We have seen nowt of the laird since we moved 'ere fourteen years ago."

Anthony moved forward. "I have been in the role for scarcely four days, so please do not hold my tardiness against me."

The man peered at him suspiciously. "Ye be not from around 'ere."

"Aye," Anthony agreed. "I am from Dumfries."

"Well, I suppose ye cannot be blamed for that." The man spat again.

"Have some respect, man," Mac muttered.

The coal black eyes shifted back to Anthony, studying him for a long moment, before the man gave a small nod, as if satisfied, and held out his hand. "Geordie Ferguson."

"Mr. Ferguson." Anthony shook his hand with enough firmness that the man's brows rose.

"Well, a visit from the laird, at last. That's more than can be said 'bout the previous one, and the one afore that."

Again Anthony felt that pang of sorrow, both at his predecessors' lack of concern, and the crofter's acceptance of it. "I understand there is an issue regarding sheep."

Ferguson hooked a thumb at the house further up the hill. "Macdonald is a liar and a thief. He'd beat a bairn to save a groat. He be claiming my sheep as his own."

"And why would he do that?"

What followed was a lengthy list of blame and recrimination, which sounded suspiciously like the tales the Lennox Lane Patterson boys had so often told. Anthony left that house promising to look into matters, and, after extracting the man's assurance to keep his role as laird a secret, went to the neighboring Macdonalds, who, unsurprisingly, told a different story.

Anthony found the gnarled explanation all the more difficult to follow due to the heavy brogue, his slowness in understanding evidently unappreciated by the red-bearded man, whose fiery locks put his own to shame. Evidently verbosity was not a problem for this Scotsman. When his fire started anew, Anthony exchanged glances with Mac, who coughed loudly.

"If it happens again you'll need to come to Dungally House and the laird here will sort the matter out. Understand?"

The red-bearded giant grunted. "Aye."

Further visits to two more tenants left Anthony hungry and heartsore, disappointed in his predecessors' lack of care, overwhelmed by the scale of his responsibilities. Sheep stealing was the least of the problems he'd need to look into. Poverty, social division, and crop devastation were of far greater significance, requiring, in some cases, immediate attention. But how could he, a former curate with botanical leanings, possibly do what needed to be done to fulfill his lairdship to the best of his ability?

Lord, what do you want from me? I have nothing but a little learning, some compassion, and a lot of stubbornness . . .

His prayers continued as they rode back down the hill to Dungally, the hills a patchwork of vibrant greens and ochre. Clearly farming practices succeeded on the other side of the River Dee. How could he make it work here? Further conversation with Mac stuttered as he toyed with possibilities, so much that he scarcely noted the pitted drive, nor the droning exhortation of Mrs. Iverson, nor the cobweb-infested rooms still needing attention.

Somehow he'd need to keep believing this unlooked-for inheritance was a blessing from God, after all.

Verity leaned back on her heels, surveying the Chisholm garden with mixed emotions. Yes, it looked a thousand times better, but now that it was tidied, what was she to do? She had been here for just over a week, and the Chisholms were a lovely family, but truth be told, at times she had to fight the feeling that things were a little . . . dull. Yet, she scolded herself, how exciting did she need things to be? She was in a rural parish in Scotland, staying with a minister's family—hardly the place for intrigues and pirates or even the secret tunnels of which Benjamin seemed so certain. She had, of course, asked Helena and James, who had only laughed and assured her she was not missing anything, and such tales were exactly that: falsehoods.

She bit her lip. She had nothing to worry her, nothing to give rise to concern. Except this vague sense of discontent, the old restless feeling that no amount of horse riding or gardening or adventuring at school had ever yet satisfied.

"Verity?" Helena appeared around the corner of the house. "Oh, here you are. My, how much better the garden looks now!"

A glow of satisfaction warmed her chest. "I hope your parents are pleased."

"Of course they are! Papa was just saying this very hour how much more peaceful he feels whenever he gazes upon the garden now." Helena smiled. "Now, would you like to come for a ride into town with me and James?"

Verity dusted off her skirt. "Tell me, are we likely to meet Alasdair on this trip?"

"Why do you ask?"

"Only that we seem to bump into him quite often," Verity said innocently, smiling at Helena's blush.

A quick change later, and she was riding into town with James and Helena, over the bridge, past several whitewashed cottages of varying hues, but all with square-framed windows equidistant from a painted door. The last of these had an entryway with blue paint peeling away, like it had last been painted at the turn of the century.

"That is Mrs. Podmore's cottage," Helena murmured. "She's a cantankerous old busybody, with never a kind word for anyone. We're lucky she's not out front."

Verity nodded, glancing at the upper window, the curtain of which twitched. She smiled and waved.

"What are you doing?" Helena hissed.

"Being friendly." She nodded to a large, smartly dressed figure riding toward them. "Who is this?"

James snorted. "Colin Guthrie."

"Ah. Of the clan feuding with the laird?"

"Aye. This is the heir, the son of the current clan leader."

"He looks awfully pleased with himself."

James snorted again. "He shouldn't be. Word is he and his father ignore their tenants and spend money on their house and horses."

Helena murmured, "Colin went to St. Andrews with James. James likes to think they are rivals, but really, that's like comparing an eagle with an otter."

"Thank you, sister. And I suppose I am the otter?"

As his sister smiled at him, Verity said, "And yet an otter can do things an eagle cannot." She studied the horseman and said loudly, "Eagles are quite overrated."

The young man, whose thick features and florid complexion made him look ten years James's senior, narrowed his gaze, which Verity met blithely. He nodded sourly to James and Helena. "Chisholm, Miss Chisholm."

Amidst their murmured responses, he studied Verity, his gaze critical, judging from the lowered brow and downturned mouth. James made introductions then offered observations about Guthrie's horse. Verity could sense the envy and frustration of a young man whose tastes far outstripped his father's income.

Mr. Guthrie, clearly bored, turned to Verity. "Will you be staying for the Ridings, Miss Hatherleigh?"

Verity looked a question at Helena, who nodded. "It would appear so."

"You'll see some fine riding then, if I do say so myself."

"I'm sure you often say so yourself," Verity murmured, before offering her sweetest smile. "That looks to be a fine stallion." Surely the chestnut stood at sixteen hands.

"Brutus is the finest piece of horseflesh in the shire," he boasted, casting a less than surreptitious sneer at the Chisholms' mounts. "I'm sure he will carry me to the lead again at this year's Ridings."

"You aim to enter again?"

Verity glanced at James, whose stiffly voiced question echoed his erect posture.

"Why certainly. And win, of course. Why?" He peered at James. "You didn't expect to win on *that* thing, did you?"

James flushed to a color approximating his sister's hair and said nothing.

But Verity could. "Is this a race for the best riders in town?"

"And the surrounding districts. My father gives a medal to the first-place getter," Mr. Guthrie added loftily. "I have already told him to simply hand it to me."

"Pardon me, but does that not sound awfully presumptuous?" She eyed the arrogant horseman, whose cheeks now took on a mottled hue. "Surely you would not want your father accused of nepotism?"

His mouth fell open. Helena murmured, "Verity."

Verity glanced at James, whose hastily hidden grin suggested his appreciation. She returned her attention to Mr. Guthrie. "Tell me, do the Ridings truly involve the best riders, or merely those who are male?"

His eyes widened then narrowed. "You cannae say females ride better than a man."

"Why can't I?" She tilted her head. "When I know it is true?"

"Verity!" Helena hissed.

Mr. Guthrie curled his lip. "Lassies should know their place is in the home, not gallivanting around, trying to be like a man."

"Not like a man. Equal to a man."

He muttered something and drew back with wrinkled nose, as if Verity emitted a foul odor. He jerked a nod to James, before wheeling his horse around and cantering down the street, careless of a young boy whose chasing after a hoop almost saw him trampled underfoot.

"Verity! How could you?"

"Well, he seems quite unpleasant."

"Yes, but you shouldn't have goaded him." Helena's eyes were dark with reproach. "His family holds much power in these parts."

"But not against your family, surely."

Helena sighed. "They do not attend Papa's church, it is true, but their influence is such that parishioners may choose to remain home rather than attend services, or Mama may find she does not receive the best prices when shopping."

"But that is wrong!"

"Of course it's wrong," James snapped, "but then so is a lass wanting to ride in the Ridings."

"Young ladies have never done so," Helena said in an undertone. "It would be a scandal of the highest degree—"

"And what would be the point, anyway? If I can never win, then you certainly could not, even though Firefly is a good enough little mare. No," James added gloomily, "Guthrie will win, and that is all there is to be said of the matter."

The indignation that had risen so swiftly now died, replaced with sympathy for poor James. Verity exchanged glances with Helena, whose wrinkled brow suggested she held suspicions she dare not speak.

Verity offered a smile to reassure, and turned the conversation to the abbey whose ruins she had passed on the drive into Kirkcudbright.

And as the others discussed plans for a possible outing to Dundrennan Abbey, her mind was busy thinking on how it might be possible to wipe the smugness from Colin Guthrie's face, whilst proving both him and James wrong.

℟ Chapter Nine

Anthony hurried down the wide staircase overlooked by freshly dusted portraits of ancestors he had never known, nor, judging from their sour expressions, people he would have ever wanted to meet. Elaborately carved balusters speckled with muted light from the enormous stained-glass window more appropriate for a cathedral than a man's house. Clearly his housekeeper had deemed the showy hall important enough to warrant attention from the newly employed maids, as if she expected the news of his arrival to bring the curious masses. But then, Edinburgh-born, she was not to know his family's reputation would make visitors extremely unlikely.

"Mr. Jardine!"

Anthony closed his eyes as his housekeeper's high-pitched voice ceased his movements. *God, give me patience.* He turned, hoping his expression and tone conveyed pleasantness, and not his true feelings. "Yes, Mrs. Iverson?"

"Oh, I'm so glad I caught you," she puffed.

That made one of them. "Is there a problem?"

"I didn't know where you were." Her dark eyes looked at him reproachfully.

Irritation flickered within. Did she really expect him to account to her for his movements? He studied her: her reddened cheeks, a well-cushioned body that doubtless would grow less ample if she continued to pursue his whereabouts through this vast estate. Compassion

CAROLYN MILLER

chased the earlier exasperation. It wasn't her fault Osgood had recommended her to the position. His lips twitched. Although he couldn't
help wonder just how much of an estate she had kept in her previous
role . . .

As if encouraged by his almost-smile, she tilted her head at him.
"You are quite a mystery, Mr. Jardine, always scurrying off here and
there, or closeted up in the study with that McNatton fellow."

"Mr. McNaughton," he corrected gently.

She sniffed, her dislike of his valet as obvious as that which was
returned by the former convict. Mac's deftness with figures was
matched by a delight in confounding the woman's endless curiosity
through silence and an impassive countenance Anthony had often
noted—and probably could well learn from.

He swallowed a bubble of humor. What would his housekeeper
say if she knew she resided under the same roof as a man formerly
housed at His Majesty's pleasure? That revelation was something he'd
strive to avoid. "Was there something you required, Mrs. Iverson?"

"I, er, I wondered if you might prefer the salmon to the grouse this
evening. Mr. Iverson caught a very large one earlier today . . ."

"He was fishing, was he? I had wondered where he was this
morning."

She stiffened. "I am sure he was only doing so with your best interests at heart, sir."

"I am sure you are right," he agreed with a mild tone and steady
look that saw her cheeks darken. "Salmon will be fine. Now, if you'll
excuse me, I have business to attend to." He paced back. "And you
might let Iverson know there are several more piles of weeds that
might be in *his* best interests to dispose." He turned on his heel, and
escaped through the front doors.

The sharp tang of brine assaulted his nose, carried on a breeze that
suggested if Iverson did not swiftly attend to matters, Anthony's earlier pile of branches, weeds, and dead leaves would soon be scattered
far and wide. He hurried on, beneath dense foliage overspreading
the drive, an occasional faint crunch underfoot yet another sign of
an estate matter requiring attention. But the purchase and spreading

of new gravel was the least of his concerns; bad enough he preferred getting the gardens into shape more so than the house itself, and had yet to meet all his tenants, or any of his neighbors. At least the last could be put right today.

After ten minutes' brisk walking he cleared the gloom and eased open the rusting gate. A shame, really, for it would have cost a fair sum when newly installed, but years of neglect had reduced it to peeling shabbiness. Another item to add to his list, for entrusting such a task to Iverson would doubtless result in nothing more than a quick wipe and an avowal of good intent.

He turned right, heading down the hill toward the stone bridge over the Dee, past the thicket of gnarled bushes abutting a small forest of evergreen. The air now swirled with the scent of pine, and he took a deep breath, smiling as memories tugged from his childhood. Games of hide-and-seek with his sister, forays into forests of imagined hobgoblins, before removal to school had put an end to childish fantasy, and Anthony's love of learning had expanded from being out of doors to discovering truth in books. But ever had the power of nature fascinated him, although he would always prefer the sharp piney scent to the honey-mint tang of eucalypt.

The afternoon was warming. By the time his neighbors' property appeared, marked by a rock wall topped with vertical anchoring stones, a fine layer of sweat beaded his brow. When he reached the stone pillars demarcating the drive, the fine layer was itself under several more coatings of perspiration, and he was beginning to regret not driving or riding to meet his nearest neighbors in a style that might not make him appear so repugnant. He almost turned back, but questions over his visitor from two days previous had persisted, interrupting his feeble attempts at bookwork until Mac had sent him back outside to continue the garden work yesterday's visits to the tenants had interrupted.

"Hello!"

Anthony stopped, searching for the owner of the high-pitched voice.

"I'm up here."

He glanced up to see a small redheaded figure, legs dangling from the branches of a mature oak. At his feet lay a shaggy dog. "Why, hello up there."

"Are you here to see Mama and Da? They are not here, you know."

"I gathered that. I rather thought they might be at the house."

The boy blinked, then laughed. "You're funny. You say silly things like Verity does."

"Your governess?"

"Just Verity." The little boy's brow creased. "You do say funny things. Wait there."

With a swinging jump reminiscent of the monkeys he'd seen in Brazil, the little boy soon joined him at the base of the tree. "I'm Benjamin."

Anthony held out his hand, which the boy shook gravely. "Hello, Benjamin. I'm Mr. Jardine. Tell me, are you part monkey?"

The boy grinned, revealing a gap-toothed smile. "I don't think so, but I've heard old Mrs. Cready say I am."

"Perhaps she wishes she could swing from trees?"

"I'd like to see her try," the boy said, so wistfully that Anthony had to bury his chuckle with a cough.

"I was here to visit the owners, whom I assume are your parents?"

The boy nodded. "If they are out then perhaps I'll return another day."

"They're always out."

"Oh," Anthony said, nonplussed. He'd been left to his own devices? "You do not attend school?"

"I have lessons in the morning, but I don't like them much. I'd rather be outside, finding bird's nests, or badger holes, or frogs."

"Is that what you were doing the other day?"

"Pardon?"

"The other day, next door"—Anthony gestured towards his estate— "when you fell in the pond?"

The boy's eyes widened. "You saw that? Helena was so cross, but ol' Cready was crosser than a bound bear. But Verity soon stopped her," he said in a satisfied manner.

"Your Miss Verity sounds quite a formidable creature."

"Verity? She's braw. She never fusses like Frances or Helena. Mind you, Helena doesn't fuss nearly so much, but that might be 'cos I saw her making sheep's eyes at that Alasdair McConnell." His nose screwed. "I don't think I like him very much. He might be James's friend, but he pats me on the head like I'm a dog!"

This last was said in such an aggrieved tone Anthony could scarcely restrain the laughter. "I'm sure he does not think of you that way. How could he, when we both know you are more simian than canine."

"Simian?" The boy's forehead wrinkled. "I don't think I know what that means."

"Perhaps you can ask the clever Miss Verity."

Benjamin grinned. "Will you be calling round again?"

"I'm afraid I must, if I am to speak with your parents."

"You can always find them at the church. Papa is the minister, y'know."

Anthony felt a quickening of interest. The lad had said "church," not "kirk," suggesting perhaps they were not Presbyterian. "Which church is that?"

"The episky . . . the episoh—"

"The Episcopalian?"

"Yes! It always tangles my tongue," the boy added apologetically.

Anthony smiled. "It does mine, too. Well, I shall be sure to see you tomorrow, then."

Benjamin nodded, waved a farewell, and ran off after a large white butterfly, whose fluttering aeronautic display now held far greater interest for a small boy than did a slightly less-strange stranger.

When the boy disappeared behind the corner of the gray stone rectory Anthony turned and made his way back along the rutted drive, not unsatisfied with his visit's outcome. If, indeed, the lad's father was an Episcopalian minister, perhaps the family might not hold Anthony's ancestry against him. In fact, God willing, the minister might even prove convivial company. Heaven knew Mac needed Anthony to find someone else to talk to, the reticent Highlander not always amenable to Anthony's quest for lonesome-relieving conversation.

He attained the road, and headed back toward Dungally, the low-ered sun causing him to squint a little as he ascended the long rise. Far ahead, a blur on the horizon soon fractured into three distinct shapes. He lifted a hand to his forehead, shielding his gaze from the sun. Horsemen. No, he thought as they drew closer, one horseman, and two horsewomen. The trio rode swiftly, the two in the lead seem-ingly racing each other down the glen toward the road. And him.

Anthony glanced about, noting a donkey cart some way behind him, near the entrance to the reverend's house. His pulse crept higher as the riders neared. Surely they would stop their breakneck speed before reaching the road. He glanced back. The donkey cart had dis-appeared. He exhaled, and moved himself to the grassed verge, away from danger.

Neck and neck they raced, the white horse in front, then the black. Despite his earlier anxiety, Anthony couldn't help but admire the skill displayed. They came closer, the woman in blue leaning so far forward he was sure her hat would tumble off.

The rider on the chestnut in the rear appeared to urge her horse faster, in an attempt to catch the others. But it was a vain hope, as they pressed on, thundering onto the road not one hundred yards away. He scrambled atop the stone wall, thankful to see no other travelers on the road. From this position he could see the white horse was inching ahead, the rider beside applying his crop.

Above the soft sigh of pine he heard voices calling, the clatter of hooves on stone masking meaning until they were fifty yards away, forty yards, when he heard a shout of laughter.

"I told you I'd win!"

The man yelled something else that made the blue-clad girl look, and sit up and slow. "James!"

He spurred his horse on, past the girl, past Anthony. The girl shook her head, her gaze meeting Anthony's for a second.

He caught a glimpse of dark fringe and wide blue eyes, indignation turning to surprise, before the horse's momentum carried her past. Seconds later, the other girl, a redhead, rushed past.

Anthony jumped down and watched the black horse turn into his neighbor's gates, and saw the young ladies slow, look toward him, and turn their horses around.

The blue-garbed rider beamed as she drew near. "*Bonjour*, Monsieur Gardener."

He bowed slightly. "*Bonjour*, Miss Hatherleigh."

She gestured to the redhead. "This is my friend, Helena Chisholm."

"Miss Chisholm." Anthony doffed his hat. "A pleasure to make your acquaintance."

The pretty redhead smiled uncertainly. "Monsieur Gardener? But you are not French."

"*Oui, mademoiselle.*"

Verity giggled. "This is Mr. Jardine."

"Oh, the one who works for the new laird. How do you do?"

Anthony opened his mouth to correct her when Verity interrupted. "But why were you standing on the fence?"

"Yes, why?" Miss Chisholm frowned.

"Please pardon the liberty, but I was reluctant to be run down."

"Oh, we wouldn't have run you down." Verity's smile dimmed slightly as she turned to Miss Chisholm. "Although the same cannot be said for your brother. Did you know he was actually whipping poor Lightning? For a silly race!"

"He cannot stand losing, I'm afraid. And especially to a girl."

"But whipping a horse just to prove a point! I could not believe it of him." Verity turned to Anthony. "Do you ever whip poor creatures in order to prove a point?"

"I'm afraid not," he said in an apologetic tone. "I lack both creature and point."

She stared at him a moment, then laughed. "You are a tease, are you not, Mr. Gardener?"

"I fear with your persistent use of that name that it is you who teases me, Miss Hatherleigh."

She smiled, the friendly candor warming the depths of his heart, until a shout drew their attention back to the road.

"Hey!" The rider from before—presumably James—cantered towards them, a frown marring the handsome countenance. Dark hair topped a face of even features, the green eyes hardening a little as the younger man looked Anthony over. "Who are you?"

"James!" Miss Chisholm exclaimed.

Anthony stepped forward, offering his hand. "Anthony Jardine, at your service."

James ignored his hand. "Why are you talking with my sister and Miss Hatherleigh?"

"And why shouldn't he?" the redhead demanded. "Who are you to determine whom I may speak to?"

The younger man flushed. "I do not appreciate being spoken to like—"

"And I expect Mr. Jardine does not like being treated like that, either!"

Anthony said meekly, "Forgive me, Mr. Chisholm, but I do believe the ladies began talking to me. It would have been rude to say nothing, especially when I am not a mute."

"A mute?" James echoed, his deep scowl easing into mere knotted brows.

Verity grinned. "Pretending to be a mute in order to avoid unwanted conversation is something I particularly abhor."

"And something I cannot imagine you would ever partake in, Miss Hatherleigh," Anthony offered humbly.

The redhead giggled as Verity acknowledged the jest with a smile and a dip of her head.

"I must object to your overly familiar manner."

Verity sighed loudly. "James, you are becoming increasingly tiresome."

"Would you wish for me to list all the things I object to, James?" Miss Chisholm's eyes narrowed. "We could start with whipping Lightning just so you could beat Verity in a silly horse race. What would Papa have to say?"

"He didn't say much," James said grumpily. "They arrived home just before me. Mama was wondering where you both were."

Anthony bowed. "Please excuse me. I do not wish to hold anyone up."

"Not even the laird?" Verity said a sly smile.

"You work for the laird? Why is he here? Couldn't he afford to stay away?"

Anthony stilled, James's scornful expression refusing admittance to the truth. Such prejudice was reason enough to conceal his identity.

"James, you are truly the outside of enough! Leave the poor man be." Miss Chisholm smiled sympathetically at Anthony. "I'm sure you cannot help working for a living, even if it is at Dungally."

Anthony nodded meekly. "Thank you for your understanding, Miss Chisholm."

"I do hope he won't mind if we visit," Verity said, her brows rising in a way that suggested she was rarely denied. "I would love to see some more of the gardens."

"Verity!" James looked aghast. "You simply cannot—"

"Oh, but Verity, the old laird will not—"

"Object, I am sure," Anthony interrupted. "I can assure you, far from being a curmudgeonly crabbit, the new laird would enjoy knowing the grounds are being appreciated."

"Wonderful!"

Her look of delight caused a strange palpitation in his chest.

"And if it makes it more acceptable, and if the gardener has no objections"—she eyed him saucily—"you could tell him I am more than happy to help with the garden."

"Verity!"

"Oh, hush, Helena. I am not at home. Mama is scarcely going to object, is she?"

"But you cannot lower yourself to work in a garden like a servant, let alone do so unchaperoned!"

"But I will not be alone"—Verity grinned—"for you will accompany me!"

Anthony fought his own grin at the chagrin writ large on her friend's face. "Rest assured, Miss Chisholm, you are welcome to visit without fear for your safety, or concern that you will be asked to work."

"How can *you* claim to know what the laird might think?"

CAROLYN MILLER

Anthony met James's sneer squarely and said in a firm tone, "We are of the same mind regarding this. I know that he hopes to restore not only the gardens but also the relationships once broken."

James snorted. "He better start believing in miracles, then."

"You know"—Anthony smiled—"I rather believe he already does."

And with a smiled farewell and slight bow, he turned and strode back to Dungally's rusting gates, refusing to glance back at the hum of conversation, his mind spinning faster than a weaver's loom. Once safely on the drive, his steps slowed in reluctance to meeting Mrs. Iverson a second sooner than absolutely necessary. What an enlightening afternoon, he thought. But if the elder son's beliefs in any way matched the reverend's, perhaps this mending of bridges might prove more challenging than young Benjamin's words had previously given him to hope. Jumbled somewhere below that was the knowledge that one day soon he would need to admit to the truth of his identity. And deeper still lay the vague, disquieting thought that he should search his soul for a possible reason why his heart danced at the thought of having Miss Verity near.

❧ Chapter Ten

Verity glanced around the small hall. The white rough-hewn stone and small windows made the structure unlike any other church she had been in, less grand even than the old chapel Grandmama rarely used at Saltings. There was a smattering of people, townsfolk and country-reared, of which the Chisholm pew was the most full. She dared not turn around too often, wedged as she was between Helena and Benjamin, especially as she was trying to set the lad a good example. She had no desire to give Mrs. Chisholm any reason to send her home a second earlier than necessary and thereby lose this precious freedom.

Home. She exhaled silently. Grandmama's recent letter suggested Verity's whereabouts had not yet been discovered, but that she feared it would not be long until Verity's parents learned the truth. Her nose wrinkled. Best not to dwell on what that would mean; best to ignore her pending fate for as long as possible. Best to continue to pretend she was nothing more than Helena's school friend and enjoy the illusion of freedom while she could. And if that meant long rides over the moor and visits to ruined castles and abbeys, then so be it. It was far better to experience the wilds of Scotland than allow disappointment to fester within. Something about breathing fresh air and simple enjoyment with the Chisholm siblings seemed to have swept away much of her bitterness towards her parents. For how could she worry about the future when Benjamin's antics drew laughter? Here there were no demands or social obligations; in fact, she had dared to wear her divided skirt when helping in the garden, a sight at which Mrs. Chisholm had not blinked. Verity smiled to herself. Perhaps she might even try riding Firefly astride!

She shivered at the shocking thought. Helena turned, a question in her eyes to which Verity shook her head slightly, before fixing her attention to the front, as if she found Mr. Chisholm's sermon fascinating. Not that she would ever be fascinated by the Bible. Granted, Lucinda's *paramour* had found certain verses of a decidedly surprising nature, but most of what she'd heard was nothing more than the usual historical guff, pretty stories of no current relevance. Exhaustion from her journey had proved enough excuse from attendance last week; this week she could think of none.

She listened with half an ear as the sermon droned on, enough to remember a few phrases should she be asked later—a trick she had mastered years ago during dry-as-dust homilies from her mother— as her thoughts returned to their earlier contemplations. Why, the very idea of riding astride seemed even more scandalous in the quiet confines of the church! But surely it had to be more enjoyable than the sidesaddle allowed; more comfortable too, to not have one's leg hooked around the pommel. How much faster would she ride? How much easier would it be to jump? Perhaps it *could* be possible: her divided skirt would surely allow for the task, and the Chisholms did not possess a groom to object, so the main question was of borrowing a saddle. Oh, and how to actually practice. She would probably need to employ Helena's help once more . . .

As heads around her lowered, Verity closed her eyes, too. But instead of agreeing with the prayer, her mind continued to race. She would need to accomplish this without Mrs. Chisholm's knowledge, for to offend that good lady was quite out of the question—especially when it might lead to Verity being sent away. She only hoped Helena would agree. Her brow wrinkled. Her best friend had become less adventuresome since rejoining her family. Could she be trusted?

"Amen."

Verity opened her eyes to catch Helena smoothing away a smile.

"I know Papa can be long-winded," she whispered, "but you're not supposed to fall asleep."

Verity smiled weakly, and gave full attention to the recessional hymn and then joined Helena's family as they moved down the aisle. Eyes swung to her, no doubt because of her obvious newness and connection to the family. She nodded to Alasdair, smoothing down her pelisse, not the elaborately trimmed burgundy Mary had initially laid out, but a more demure dove gray, which did her complexion no good (as Mama had frequently pointed out), but it blended more with the modest attire worn by the rest of the congregation. She followed the slow procession, and was almost at the door when an extremely large man shifted, revealing the person behind. Mr. Jardine.

Her heart skipped. He wasn't looking at her, which was perhaps just as well, for it gave her full permission to gaze upon his neatly dressed, indeed, almost handsome personage. He looked most un-gardener-like today. The olive-green coat was almost severely unadorned, with none of the gilt buttons James seemed to prefer, his cravat as plain as the one worn by the older man he stood beside. But it was his expression that secured greater interest, for he wore a look of contentment that made her almost envious.

She felt a poke in her back. "Verity, why have you stopped?"

Verity's cheeks heated as Mr. Jardine finally glanced her direction and smiled.

"Oh, look," Benjamin continued, pushing past her. "Hello, Mr. Jardine."

"Hello, young Benjamin." His gaze lifted, the smile in his eyes now for her. "*Bonjour*, Miss Hatherleigh."

"*Bonjour.*" Her mouth dried as he moved closer, before Benjamin accosted him with talk about monkeys while the congregants eager for luncheon murmured complaint behind.

"Benjamin," Helena called. "We should—Oh, hello, Mr. Jardine."

"Miss Chisholm."

Verity found her tongue again. "I am surprised to see you here."

"Why?" His brow wrinkled. "Did you not expect to see a gardener in worship?"

Worship? Her heart sank a little. He spoke as though God and church mattered. Was she surrounded by people who believed in fairy tales?

The pull of congregants separated them, further opportunity for discussion lost until the huddles of conversation resumed outside in the sunshine. Helena was talking with Alasdair and his mother, Mrs. Chisholm was speaking with a group of elderly ladies, while Mr. Chisholm continued greeting people at the door. For a moment she felt an unaccountable loneliness. She pushed to her toes. Where was Mr.—?

"Are you looking for me?"

Verity whirled to see James smirking at her. "Actually, no."

"I hope you weren't looking for that gardener fellow."

"Why would you hope that?"

"If he works for the laird then he must be bad news."

"And why must those two pieces of information be synonymous?"

He stared at her, bemused, before glancing away, his brow darkening.

She followed his gaze to see Mr. Jardine talking with Mr. Chisholm at the church door. "It appears your father is not averse to talking with someone who works for the laird."

His jaw hardened. "My father is known for his overly good nature."

"A trait, it would appear, that did not pass to you."

He uttered a bark of laughter, before turning to face her, his eyes betraying something akin to contrition. "Perhaps I have judged him harshly. I suppose he cannot help it if he must work for the Irvings."

"And I suppose he cannot be held responsible for the villagers dislike of the laird?"

He chuckled again, shaking his head. "Do you always badger a fellow so?"

Verity smiled sweetly. "Only when necessary."

She glanced back and met Mr. Jardine's gaze, his smile gone, his expression one that might almost be construed as dismay. He touched the brim of his hat and turned away.

Warmth filled her cheeks as she realized what might be implied by how close James stood to her. She stepped back, peeked again at the church door.

He had gone.

⁂

Anthony slit the throat, lifted the flap with the knife point, carefully placed the wood, before tying the graft together. *Acacia dealbata* held a beautiful golden-orbed flower on feathery green leaves, but the sun-drenched conditions of its natural home were far removed from the inclement weather of southern coastal Scotland. He hoped this graft would take, although it might require something of a miracle. It was nothing less than a miracle to find that the juvenile plant had survived the journey. Perhaps that was due to his use of the metal-lined box to protect the roots, or perhaps it was their innate hardiness. Regardless, he was thankful.

After employing similar tactics on the remaining buds, he finished, replaced the bud-wood back in the wooden bucket, and moved to the vasculum, unscrewing the lid to remove the small paper envelope marked "acacia"—his contingency, in case the graft did not take. He opened it gingerly, cautious in case the tiny seeds escaped, and moved to the workbench, where he drew forth a small pot of damped dirt and placed a half dozen seeds on top, loosely covering them with soil. After a dribble of water, he moved it to the sunny patch under the window. The conditions were not ideal, but more in sympathy with the Antipodean sun than anywhere else on his property.

Next, he moved to the other vasculum and carefully unscrewed its lid. The tiny seedlings of *Grevillea acanthifolia* looked a little dry; he hoped the plants were used to arid conditions. He carefully mixed measures of loam, peat, and sand into something approximating his memories of the Sydney soil these plants had come from, before potting and placing them under glass.

After toweling his hands clean, he exited the small room he'd commissioned for his potting purposes. Perhaps one day he might afford a greenhouse, but for now, his finances had to be expended elsewhere.

He moved outside, surveying the gardens. Despite the stunted roses, the grounds were beginning to look a trifle improved. He wondered when he might receive the promised visit from the governess next door. His lips twisted ruefully. *If* he might receive said visit. For judging from the warmth he'd seen yesterday between her and young Chisholm, she would probably be too distracted to remember.

Not that he should have minded. He *should* have stayed focused on the sermon, which had proved the reverend a worthy minister of the gospel, his fervor for Scripture matched by his compassion for the unfortunate, evident by the numbers of people who had thanked him for either giving food or time this past week. Clearly he had misjudged his neighbors, their concern and kindliness such that they could never abandon young Benjamin to his own devices. Especially when the young lad was more than ably cared for by his sisters and the governess, thoughts of whom had continued to interrupt his sleep.

Not that he should be thinking on a young miss. Wasn't a man's income supposed to outweigh his dreams? Hadn't Amelia's parents made that perfectly clear? He winced. And what was he doing, abandoning all hope of sweet Amelia? Perhaps now that he was fixed in Scotland she would come around to life as the wife of a laird. Perhaps he *had* expected too much, wanting her to travel all that way, expecting her to share his passion for the lost souls of Sydney. He'd seen what that torturous voyage had wreaked on other women; never could he ask Amelia to do so.

Lord, what do you want? Should I remain single forever?

The thought stung his soul like buckshot, and for some reason, the image of his trespasser's bewitching blue eyes, glowing skin, and sharp cheekbones filled his mind.

He shook his head. "Lord, I am such a fool."

"You really should not speak so unkindly about yourself."

He spun around to see the object of his thoughts, hands on hips, grinning at him. "Miss Hatherleigh."

She gave a little curtsy. "Now, calling someone like Mrs. Cready a fool would be far more apt. That woman!"

"And who is that woman?"

"The Chisholms' housekeeper. She is abominable! You know, she had the nerve to ask me where I was going this morning."

"Perhaps she is merely concerned for your welfare."

"Not she. She is like a ferret, always listening at doors."

"I did not know ferrets were wont to do such things."

Amusement flickered in her eyes. "But I do not think she should be informing Mrs. Chisholm about the mischief her children are up to."

"Are they up to mischief?"

She stared at him. "Of course! But does that give a housekeeper the right to inform on them? I think not. Where is the loyalty?"

"Perhaps she considers her actions to be loyal to her employer."

"Only if you consider her bossy, managing ways to be a form of loyalty. She treats the family as though she is doing them a favor, when really it is the other way around."

He nodded—his encounters with the Iversons making him well able to sympathize—as she drew in a deep breath.

"Never have I met a more lovely family, so kind and generous, but I am sure Mrs. Cready is motivated by self-interest rather than benevolence. No, I do not like that woman, and am sure she detests me."

"Are you always so decided in your opinions, Miss Hatherleigh?"

"Of course! My opinions are always completely fixed and immovable." She smiled. "Except when I feel it necessary to alter them."

He chuckled. "I am glad to see the troubling housekeeper has not made you lose your sense of humor."

"Well, that is another fixed and immovable element of my life, which unfortunately tends to get me into more trouble than not."

"I have found that those without a sense of humor invariably fail to understand those fortunate enough to possess one."

"There! I knew you to be a sensible man. How can someone survive without gaining an appreciation of the absurdities of others?"

"Or even the absurdities of one's self?" he suggested.

"Ha! I see we're going to be good friends, Mr. Jardine."

As her smile widened, he was again struck by how much her face transformed with light, her smile sending a disconcerting twist to his heart. He swallowed. No, he did not need to be distracted by this bold young lady. "At the risk of sounding untoward, may I enquire if you had business here today other than suggesting that my declaration of foolishness is folly?"

"Oh, Benjamin insisted on seeing the frogs again." She gestured to the pond. "He and Frances are there while I came to ensure the laird will not mind the intrusion."

"He will not mind."

"You are sure? Helena thinks it a great imposition, while James is convinced the laird must possess a nefarious purpose in allowing such a thing."

"James is not as generously minded as yourself."

"No. Which is strange, considering his parents are so mild in their dealings with people, and Helena is the sweetest person I know."

"Your loyalty does you great credit, Miss Hatherleigh."

"As does your discernment, Mr. Jardine."

They smiled at each other, a moment of perfect accord, which caused a kind of tumbling feeling in his chest. He stepped back. Amelia. Amelia! How could he be such a cad and have forgotten her so quickly?

"Mr. Jardine, are you quite well? You look a little flushed."

"I am quite well, thank you."

"Oh good. I was hoping you might introduce the laird."

What? Oh, what a tangled web his falsehood had woven. "I must say I do not quite understand your determination to meet him."

"And I must say I do not quite understand his determination to be unmet."

"He has met some of the neighbors."

Her blue eyes widened. "Really? Who?"

He winced internally. Why must she be so persistent? "I, er, believe he has met most of the tenants, and, er, some others who live nearby."

"Well, I am pleased to hear he has condescended to visit the tenants, at least. Perhaps if the laird was more assiduous in dealing with them he might be received more favorably. I know my"—she coughed—"I know of people whose exalted positions make them quite ignorant to how anyone poorer than themselves may live."

For all her opinions, she revealed very little about her past. "Where do you come from?"

"I am sure I do not need to explain such matters to a man of science."

Heat traveled up his neck.

"Oh, you are shocked! Well, if you are referring to my home, it is south of here."

"There is not much south of here save Solway Firth."

She slanted a look up at him. "I am not Scottish, Mr. Jardine."

"No!" He mock-gasped. "Surely one so bright cannot be an English lass."

She grinned. "Now you are displaying a unfortunate propensity for prejudice. But you still have not explained. Why has the laird not met the Chisholms? As his closest neighbors I find his lack of regard rather surprising."

"I am sure the laird does not intend to cause distress; indeed, I know he wishes to alleviate it as much as possible." He smiled gently. "But is it really such a surprise for a man to want privacy?"

She searched him with such candor in her blue eyes that he felt ashamed of his deception. Why had he started this pretense? Surely this young miss was no danger to him. Except, perhaps, to his heart.

Finally she nodded. "Very well. I shall have to hope to meet him another day. I suppose considering the long-standing tension between the Irvings and Guthries, I can understand why he might not wish to advertise himself. You do him great credit to not expose his secrets."

He inclined his head, not trusting himself to further speech.

She tilted her head. Her brow wrinkled. "I wonder if he realizes such mysterious behavior only makes one speculate about his secrets."

His mouth dried. He shrugged, affecting a nonchalance he did not feel.

"Well, at least some men are honest and true." Her smile pierced him with guilt as she stepped away, glancing at him over her shoulder. "I've always abhorred liars."

And as she walked away, his heart filled with misgiving.

CHAPTER ELEVEN

"COME ON, HELENA." Verity hurried along the path woven between rushes and stones, yesterday's encounter with the Dungally gardener quickening her steps. Not that today was about seeing Mr. Jardine, she told herself sternly. Today was simply about going to help beautify the Dungally garden, even if her companions seemed rather less enthused than she at the prospect.

"Won't this be a lovely surprise for the laird?" And Mr. Jardine, she added to herself. Poor man, he was so obliging yet overworked, the grounds so extensive. "Wouldn't it be a blessing to look out and see this garden bed tidied?"

"I don't understand why *we* need to bless the laird," Frances grumbled.

"Don't you?" Helena eyed Verity with a speculative look. "I'm sure Verity has *tres bien* reasons, *non?*"

Verity's cheeks grew hot. "Was not your father speaking of the need to be kind to our neighbors just last night?"

"Wasn't he talking about old Podmore and her cat?" Benjamin asked.

Verity gently touched her bandaged wrist. "I'm sure her cat did not mean to hurt anyone."

"You don't know Mrs. Podmore," Frances said darkly. "I think she sets it on passersby deliberately."

"Well, one little mishap should not stop us helping again. Isn't that what your papa said?"

"And whom exactly are we helping again, Verity?" Helena asked, a sly expression on her face.

"The laird," Verity said firmly as she turned to the others. "Who knows, we may even get to see inside!"

"But I don't want to see inside," Frances complained.

"It must be magnificent." Verity gestured to the stone turrets. "One does not build such an edifice without ensuring an equally impressive interior."

"Well, you would know."

Verity paused and eyed her friend. Helena had spoken without rancor, but did she hold some unspoken resentment about their differing stations in life? "I have had the most wonderful stay with your family, Helena. Your parents are so warm and hospitable, and your siblings"—she smiled at Frances and Benjamin—"so much kinder than my own."

"Except when we bicker."

Verity laughed. "One must allow a certain amount of bickering between brothers and sisters, surely. Unless you wish to be counted as paragons, in which case I have no desire to know such creatures."

Benjamin grinned his gap-toothed smile. "I'm glad you're here, Verity."

"And I'm glad to be here. Now, shall we go in and help? Who knows, we might even discover the secret tunnel!"

The small boy ran through the gate with a shout, heedless of the clanking bucket and spade.

"You should not fill his head with such ideas, Verity," Helena said with an exaggerated sigh. "You know he wishes to be a pirate."

Frances giggled. "Poor Papa. Imagine a church minister with a pirate for a son."

They turned into the garden, overlooked by the imposing residence.

"It appears so empty," Frances murmured. "Why would they keep all those curtains shut? It looks so sad."

"Well at least it means nobody will notice us." Verity retied her bonnet. "Now, let's see how much we can accomplish before we are discovered."

For the next hour all was quiet save for the chirrup of birdsong and the moan of wind through the pines—and the occasional complaint from the younger two Chisholms. While Helena and Frances pulled weeds, which Benjamin placed in a pile (when he wasn't chasing frogs), Verity amused herself by using Mr. Hoskins's borrowed shears to clip away extraneous branches from the yew hedges, shaping them into forms not dissimilar to her grandmother's topiary. It was very hard work, her arms aching so, and she had soon amassed a pile of clippings that she gathered along with Benjamin's efforts, and placed in a pile she had observed Mr. Jardine use before.

She wondered if she would see him again. Her heart skipped a beat. It was nonsense, of course, for Helena to assume Verity was in any way enamored of the gardener. She wouldn't deny he was attractive, with his open countenance, laughing eyes, and his ready smile. But just because Helena was herself attached to a young man did not mean Verity need be also. Why, Mother would have a fit! A viscount's daughter and a gardener? But she also couldn't deny the hope she would see him again, and they would have the opportunity to converse in that easy way that had sprung up between them, as if no difference of age or social standing existed between them. Her heart thudded. If only her parents had selected someone like Mr. Jardine, she would happily consent to be his—

"Miss Hatherleigh?"

Verity gasped, and dropped her basket. "Mr. Jardine! We weren't expecting you!"

"I gathered as much."

He smiled, and a piercing kind of joy shafted Verity's chest. Oh, he was a charming man. Even her sisters would agree. Although he did have something like hay in his—

"Why do you have hay in your hair?"

He put a hand to his head and removed the strand, his smile turning rueful. "I thought I had removed it all." His deep green eyes twinkled. "One might ask why you have dirt on your cheek."

She placed a hand on her left cheek, but he shook his head. "It was the other, but now you are evenly matched."

"Oh." She wiped until he nodded. "I hope you do not think me so missish I cannot stand a little dirt."

"I confess to some surprise at a young lady's lack of concern."

"Come now, Mr. Jardine, I cannot believe you to be so hard on our sex." Her brows lifted. "Has someone forever stained the capabilities of all womanhood by proving herself rather more delicate than decisive?"

He stilled, before replying softly, "I have known a young lady of whom a more apt description could scarcely be imagined."

"Well, shame on her, then."

"But she could not help it. Her parents—"

"Nonsense. Backbone is not inherited, it needs to be developed, and if one's parents are overbearing then it is all the more reason for developing one." Her eyes flashed. "I cannot stand weak and simpering females who seem to believe their role is to be dependent on others."

"Perhaps not all young ladies are in a position to feel such a way."

Her brow lowered. "What do you mean?"

"Simply that there would be very, very few young ladies who would not have to feel somewhat obliged and dependent on a man, usually their father."

"But that does not make it right."

"I did not say that it was." He glanced at her clenched hands then said soothingly, "Come, Miss Hatherleigh. Do not distress yourself. I have no wish to argue with you."

Somehow his mellifluous voice eased her rippling frustration. Indeed she had experienced a similar sensation each time she had met him, as much induced by his manner as in the calmness and slight burr of his voice. Unlike some young men whose arrogance and presumption raised her hackles, Mr. Jardine possessed a restful, reassuring quality.

She breathed in. Exhaled. Unclenched her fingers. "Forgive me. I did not come here with the intention to argue."

"I am glad." His eyes smiled. "One might ask your intention, except I can see you are not alone in your endeavors. Thank you."

She shrugged, feeling an almost overwhelming desire to scrub her cheeks and remove her stupid old bonnet, but knowing that very action would only confirm Helena's earlier suspicions. Which were not correct—at all! She tilted her chin and gestured at the river. "One cannot have such a magnificent view marred by an inelegant garden, especially when it is so simple to remedy."

He inclined his head. "You are correct, of course, Miss Hatherleigh. I have simply lacked the time to attend to such matters."

"I did not mean to imply you were not working as you ought."

"But alas, the implication remains."

She stared at him, dismay stealing across her chest, until she noticed his eyes creasing with laughter. Relief escaped in a puff of air. "You possess a wicked sense of humor, sir."

"Which, alas, you concede to understand. I am sorry if you feel corrupted."

"My sense of humor was corrupted long ago. I do not hold you responsible in any way."

"I am relieved to hear it." He smiled his engaging smile. "I am in your debt, Miss Hatherleigh, for I assume I have you to thank for such thoughtfulness?" He lifted a brow, which caused another interesting twinge in Verity's upper torso.

She swallowed. Did he think her too forward? Oh, what if he were to imagine—like Helena—that Verity held a *tendre* for him? She shrugged. "It is the laird I suppose who should be thankful."

"Pray do not tell me this was contrived to meet him?"

"No!"

He laughed softly. "I am happy to hear so." His gaze turned thoughtful. "I wonder what you would say if you were to meet him?"

"As that appears extremely unlikely, I suppose you will never know."

His eyes crinkled again, and she briefly wondered how he could enjoy her bold remarks. Mother always said no young man would enjoy her idle banter.

He nodded to the other workers. "Do you think your friends are in need of refreshment?"

She followed his gaze to where Helena, Frances, and Benjamin lay on the lawn, staring up at the clouded heavens, work obviously far from their minds. She laughed. "I apologize for their lack of industry."

"Why? You are not their keeper. And it is apparent that a great deal of work has occurred today, which surely deserves a cooling drink, and perhaps some of Cook's shortbread. Would you not agree?"

"I would, as long as the laird would not mind."

"He would be a fool to not appreciate such sacrifice."

"Well, I shall tell them. We shall clear up and—"

"Please, leave it. I shall attend to it this afternoon. Tell your friends to come up for some refreshment."

"Thank you, sir." Verity grinned and raced to gather her friends, wondering why despite the heavy skies she felt sunshine pouring over her.

⁂

"And this is the library."

Anthony's visitors gazed around the book-lined walls. "It appears the laird is not terribly bookish," Verity observed, wiping off a fine trail of dust. "Or is it that his servants have not had time yet to attend to matters?"

"I'm afraid with so many other estate matters demanding time, prioritizing such things as personal comfort has yet to be acted upon."

She nodded, lips pursed. "Well, that is something to be said for him."

A warm glow filtered through his heart, one he refused to think on as he led them from the dilapidated library into the darkened Rose Room. Why Mrs. Iverson insisted the maids keep the curtains permanently drawn was a mystery. The furnishings were already faded, surely a little more sunshine would not hurt any. He strode to the window and impatiently flung open the drapes.

The young ladies gasped in unison.

From here it was a spectacular view, the Dee stretching to the sea in a silver pool. And Verity was right. The now ordered gardens (save for a few odd-shaped yews) did set off the view to perfection. "You can see how much your handiwork has improved my view."

"Your view?" Verity gazed at him, a question in her eyes.

"Uh"—he fumbled for the truth—"my room is above and shares this view."

"Oh." She returned to gaze upon the vista, while he mentally berated himself for the slip. While it was true his room did share the view—naturally the master bedchamber would possess the most exceptional vista—it was not in the servant's quarters as she obviously imagined. Inviting them inside had been fraught with potential for discovery. But how could he not? Their hard work had eased yet another burden from his shoulders. After a challenging morning rethatching Mrs. Boyd's cottage, he'd had no desire for anything save a long rest, that is until he'd seen the indomitable Miss Hatherleigh, with that endearing smudge of dirt on her cheek.

He had hoped to avoid answering any further questions, and on Benjamin's requested tour around the house had successfully eluded all servants save Cook, whose monosyllabic responses to Anthony's request for lemonade and shortbread gave no rise for suspicions that he was anything but an outdoor servant. Although, now he thought upon the matter, perhaps her immediate acceding to such requests might suggest otherwise.

Benjamin pulled on the hem of Anthony's jacket. "Are there secret passages?"

"Secret passages? I have never thought to enquire. Why do you ask?"

The second Chisholm daughter murmured, "Please do not worry about him, sir. He is always hopeful of discovering pirate treasure or, at the least, a secret lair."

"Signs of a healthy enquiring mind, Miss Frances. I, for one, am glad to know a fellow adventurer. I would not see a lad poor-spirited."

"That's just like what Verity said!"

Anthony noted the swift exchange of glances between sisters, and the way Verity's cheeks took on a pinkish tinge. Pretending not to notice, he bent to the young boy's level. "What gives you reason to believe such a thing as secret passages exist?"

Benjamin shrugged. "Just that I overheard some of the Guthrie lads talking 'bout the treasure at Dungally."

"What? You little scamp, you heard no such thing!" Helena cried.

"I did! I heard it yesterday in the village when Verity got scratched by ol' Tom, and you were all too busy fussing you didn't hear them!"

Anthony glanced at Verity. "You were hurt?"

"Oh, it was nothing. Thanks to Mrs. Chisholm I'll be right as rain in no time."

He noticed Miss Chisholm studying him intently, so he withdrew his attention, fixing it once more on the boy. "I highly doubt there is treasure lurking in the house, but I would be most interested to know if there are secret passageways."

"So we can look?"

"Of course, but if you feel the need to bang holes in the walls, I would prefer you to ask me first."

"Ask you, sir?" Verity frowned. "Why not the laird?"

He internally winced. What to say, what to say . . . "Ah, well, I'm afraid I must let you in on a little secret, Miss Hatherleigh."

Her eyes widened. "I knew it! You are—"

"The laird's steward, not just a gardener!" Helena interrupted. "And that is why you can freely guide us around the house."

"Are you, sir? I wondered if you were related to him, a nephew or some such thing," Verity said. "And wish to avoid trouble in the village while you find your way."

He blinked. Not quite what he'd intended to admit, but so near the truth, it would suffice. "You have the gist of it, ladies. Now you can understand my interest in discovering any pirate gold." He spoke quickly to divert their attention. "I cannot imagine anyone not needing to find such riches."

"Not Verity," Benjamin piped up. "James says her father is richer than Cro . . ." he frowned, "Crowy . . . Croesus—"

"Benjamin!" Helena shot him a dark look. "It is ill-mannered to speak of our guest in that manner."

The only sign that Verity had heard was the faint flush of her cheeks, intent as she was on studying the intricate plasterwork on the ceiling. Helena whispered in her brother's ear, his face filling with such comical dismay that Anthony had to turn the subject, despite renewed curiosity about the intriguing Miss Hatherleigh.

"Well, as I said earlier, if you want to hunt, I am more than happy to help you on your quest."

Benjamin's eyes lit. "Really? You mean it? Because 'parently the old laird knew of tunnels, but when James and Helena looked, they could never find anything."

"You searched?"

Helena blushed. "We searched in our house, but never trespassed here, I assure you. There was talk the Jacobites had run a tunnel between the two houses, seeing as the rectory once belonged to the laird, but then there are many silly rumors around the village."

"But not so silly perhaps, if you undertook a search?"

Her gaze dropped.

"It *is* true, Mr. Jardine, about those rumors," Frances said stoutly. "Queen Mary departed Scotland from these shores, and French ships, if not actual pirates, have cruised the Firth seeking fortune. I wouldn't be surprised if one day something came to light about their cargo."

Despite himself, Anthony felt a frisson of excitement, which he quickly tamped. He did not really need earthly treasure, although a few gold bars would certainly not be sneezed at. No, God was his provider, and he needed to remember that, despite the shining eyes of his guests, and the enthusiasm suffusing Verity's face . . .

"Mr. Jardine!"

His wince at his housekeeper's voice was not hidden quickly enough, judging from the surprise arching Verity's brows.

"Mr. Jardine, would you tell me why I found a young boy racing away up the stairs? He refused to stop when I called. Is this place to be overrun with young rascals?"

"Not overrun, Mrs. Iverson, merely visited from time to time," he murmured.

"I apologize for my brother, ma'am," Helena said. "He is a trifle excitable—"

"And it was not our intention to disturb the laird," Verity smiled.

He watched the effect of that winning smile . . . have no effect on his housekeeper.

Verity's smile faded. "I trust the laird is not too perturbed at unexpected visitors?"

"Hmph!" Mrs. Iverson's brow wrinkled as she glanced back at him. "Well, you'll have to ask him—"

"Another time," Anthony interjected. "Now, Miss Chisholm, perhaps it would be best if you could retrieve young Benjamin. I am certain he will not find what he is searching for upstairs. Mrs. Iverson, would you please escort Miss Chisholm upstairs?"

With a loud sniff, his housekeeper led Miss Chisholm from the room, leaving him with Frances and Verity.

Frances moved slowly along the wall, murmuring, "I don't think tunnels could work from upstairs, unless there are steps involved, too."

"Yes." Verity nodded. "It would be far more feasible to build a tunnel from this floor, or even the one below. Do you think, Mr. Jardine, that we could see those rooms, too?"

"Another day, perhaps, when everyone is not so tired from their morning endeavors."

"Of course." Her pleased look again elicited a curious warmth in his chest. "I look forward to it."

"As do I, Miss Hatherleigh."

And when they had gone, and Mrs. Iverson had finally left him alone, he couldn't help but tap a few walls, and count himself every kind of fool for hoping the lad's quest might prove true—and that the governess would return on the morrow.

CHAPTER TWELVE

VERITY PULLED THE covers down from her chin, but for once didn't immediately jump from bed to begin her day. Instead, she stretched languorously, yawned, and gazed past the drapes which Mary newly opened to the wide stretch of estuary gleaming silver in the morning sun. She smiled and thought back on yesterday's exploration through Dungally House. Room after cavernous room of somewhat faded décor, yet of such charm and so perfectly proportioned she had felt instantly at home.

Which was ridiculous! She was not unused to grand homes, nor was she particularly enamored of such heavy furniture. But something about the laird's house filled her with a peace she had not often encountered. Although, strangely, now she thought upon it, the Chisholms' house held it, too. Her brow furrowed. What was it? Somehow she did not feel the elderly laird could be responsible for the atmosphere of a house, especially if he had only newly arrived. Perhaps it was the effect of his steward-cum-nephew, or whatever Mr. Jardine was. Which was *what*, exactly?

"Good morning, miss. Here's your cup of chocolate."

"Thank you, Mary."

Her ruminations continued as she sipped the hot beverage whilst Mary laid out her clothes for the day. Mr. Jardine was certainly a cut above the servants Papa and Grandmama employed, his manner kindly, never obsequious, his address containing a polish his apparel did not support. She smiled. Although if appearance was the touchstone, one could hardly suppose she possessed noble lineage, which was just as she preferred. How good it was to have none of the bowing and scraping and tiresome obligations that usually accompanied the realization she was a viscount's daughter. Still, there was something altogether intriguing about the man, something that made her wish she could meet his uncle, the laird, and gain true knowledge of his nephew's ilk.

Never mind. It was enough to know he was not merely a gardener after all, and that he held a relationship with the laird which—though she didn't like to think herself proud—only engendered greater favor than if he was simply engaged in menial work.

Her heart skipped. She and Benjamin had already made plans to return today and resume their hunt for the secret tunnel. Despite earlier misgivings, she now felt sure a passage of some kind existed. Rumors didn't originate from nothing; there must have once been something to spark such gossip. *Could* it have something to do with pirates? Fanciful to be sure, but wouldn't it be lovely if there was something to be found that would prove a boon to the laird? For surely he must be a kind man, if he was so generous as to allow virtual strangers to explore his home, just on the say-so of Mr. Jardine.

She smiled over her chocolate. Mr. Jardine was all that was amiable, his understated attire suggesting he paid more attention to others than to a mirror. And he was *so* kind, and possessed *such* a good sense of humor. Her heart fluttered. And when he smiled—

"Verity?" The door opened to reveal a worried looking Helena. "Oh, there you are!"

"And there you are." Verity pushed into a sitting position against the wooden headboard. "Why, where did you think I might be?"

"When you were not in the breakfast room, I was concerned, for you are always there before me."

"Are you casting aspersions about my need for nourishment?"

"No."

"Then what?"

"I . . . er, I was worried."

"About what? As you see, I am quite comfortable, although now you have mentioned food, I must admit to being hungry. But what could possibly concern you?"

Helena bit her lip.

"Helena?"

"I . . . I was hoping you were not planning on visiting next door today, that is all."

"Why ever not?"

"Because . . . because I'm worried that you might be developing feelings for Mr. Jardine."

Verity's breath caught, and she drew back.

"I'm sorry, Verity, but you spend such a lot of time talking to him, and laughing with him, that it seems as though you are."

Embarrassment prickled her skin. "Did your mother speak of this to you?"

Helena looked uncomfortable. "She wondered why we felt it necessary to tend to the laird's garden so often."

"Because it is wrong that such a beautiful garden should be left in disarray."

"So it was a completely selfless notion of yours?"

"Yes!"

Helena lifted an eyebrow. "One you would still eagerly complete if Mr. Jardine was not in residence?"

"Of . . . course."

"Because I've seen how you look at each other, and it made me wonder—"

"I beg your pardon. How do we look at each other?"

"Like you are the only two people in the world."

Verity swallowed. "He looks at me like that?"

Helena nodded. "And whether or not you have developed feelings for him, he appears to be in danger of developing a *tendre* for you, which would not do, especially as he seems such a kindhearted man. And so I thought I should perhaps warn you, so you are not leading him to think you are only a village girl, and not the daughter of a viscount."

"And it would not do for a viscount's daughter to be enamored of any man other than the one her parents select, would it?" Verity said dryly.

Helena's eyes widened. "You *do* care for him."

"I . . ." Verity glanced away from Helena's troubled gaze to stare out the window again. Did she care for him? Well . . . yes, if she was honest. But emotions were fickle things, witness the dozens of selectees who had sighed over their drawing master's fine looks, until scandal had forced him away, and their attentions had been piqued by someone new. Just because she felt like this today did not mean she would feel like this tomorrow. And Helena was right: there could be no future, her parents had made sure of that. Perhaps it was best to resolve to treat him as an acquaintance.

Yet within, a little voice cried: how can you lose all this life and laughter? Someone who was her *friend*, who seemed to understand her in a way so few people did, someone with whom she felt such ease, even if he wasn't from her station in life. She couldn't lose that.

But . . . no. Helena was right. Verity could not be cruel, would not lead him on.

She drew in a deep breath and faced Helena. "Yes, I care for him, but only as a friend I am enjoying getting to know. But if you think it best, I will endeavor to avoid him, although I did promise Benjamin we'd visit today—"

"Frances can take him," Helena said quickly. "And I *do* think it best. We can go to the Gatehouse of Fleet for a picnic, if you like."

"Wonderful," Verity said in a flat tone. "Will Alasdair be there?"

Helena's face took on a rosy hue. "Not unless James asks him."

"James is going?"

Helena nodded, then said slowly, "You have no thought of James?"

"Only as my friend's brother," she replied stiffly. "I am not enamored of *every* man I meet."

"Oh, Verity, I did not mean to upset you, and I'm sorry if you think my questions intrusive, but I could not help wonder." Helena's brow remained furrowed. "It's only that your face lights up when he is around . . ."

"Around James?"

"No," Helena said. "Around Mr. Jardine."

And with that she offered a small smile and exited, leaving Verity to burrow under the blankets in a pathetic attempt to hide her shame.

Anthony watched the two youngest Chisholm children work their way across the room, pressing every carved panel, their excitement then disappointment a constant ebb and flow. But who was he to judge, he thought wryly, when their emotions so neatly matched his own this morning? Mac had noticed them traipsing across Dungally's lawn, which had prompted Anthony's rush to change his rough work clothes to something more respectable, only to be disappointed when he'd realized Verity was not attending them.

His question—subtly put, he commended himself—as to the health of Miss Chisholm and Miss Hatherleigh had elicited nothing more than an assurance that they were well, which had prompted a more blatant query, to which Frances had replied they were out with James.

This in turn had prompted a degree of disappointment that made him wonder if perhaps he felt a wee bit envious of the man with whom Miss Verity currently shared a roof. There could be no objection to *him*; no doubt an arrangement had been made between both sets of parents, the current stay doubtless an opportunity to solidify matters—

"Mr. Jardine, why do you look cross?"

Anthony blinked. "Do I?" He forced himself to smile. "I'm sorry, Benjamin. I was thinking of something else."

The little face peered up at him anxiously. "Then you don't mind us making lots of noise?"

"Not at all." He waved a hand. "Please continue, for I declare I am as anxious to find the treasure as you are."

"But we don't know if it's treasure."

"And we shan't know if we give up searching, shall we?"

Frances sighed. "But we have searched this room, and found nothing."

"Then we search the next."

"But that'll take ages!"

Anthony smiled at the two dusty faces. "Well, we have tomorrow, do we not? After all, we are not those who shrink back, but we press on."

"That sounds like it is from the Bible, Mr. Jardine."

"That's because it is, young Benjamin. Shall we call an end to searching for today and aim to continue tomorrow?"

Their assent and hasty exit spoke of relief, while inside he shared their anticipation that the next day might reveal something more—and might result in the attendance of Miss Hatherleigh.

He was doomed to disappointment.

The following day brought only his young visitors, and the next, squally showers. By the time Sunday arrived he felt a kind of nervousness, a sick dread he had not experienced in almost a year, not since he'd been hauled before Marsden to explain his reasoning for the Lennox Lane gathering to study the Bible. And even then, he'd been able to explain.

But this, this evident cold shoulder from the elder neighboring girls, he was hard-pressed to understand. Had he done something wrong? Said something? Appeared too eager, perhaps, for their help? Or was it—dread upon dread—that they had discovered his secret, that Verity's determination to meet the laird was problematic, because he and the laird were one and the same person? And why did he care so much for her opinion, anyway? He was a fool to care, especially when it was obvious she did not hold him in the same regard, but rather preferred the attention of young Chisholm, whom she sat next to even now, having refused to meet his gaze prior to the service. Why did he care so? What did he hope to gain from furthering this friendship? For friend she was, someone whose company brought a lift to his heart the way Amelia's smile had once done. Amelia . . .

Anthony winced, forcing his attention back to the sermon, forcing his thoughts not to stray. Mr. Chisholm spoke of grace that showed a depth of understanding Anthony had never heard from a minister before. His closing prayer was lined with understanding of the frailty of the human spirit, yet with equal conviction of the strength and power of God to help the believer conquer anything.

The recessional music played and the trickle of congregants from front to rear began. His efforts to gain the governess's attention were finally rewarded outside.

"Miss Hatherleigh!"

She stiffened, shot a quick look at her friend then finally met his gaze. "Hello, Mr. Jardine."

"What, no *bonjour* today?" He smiled.

Her blue eyes kindled in amusement, her lips lifting, as if in response, before flattening. "Not today I'm afraid."

He glanced to Miss Chisholm. "I trust you are both well?"

"Very well, thank you, sir."

"I had hoped to see you both—"

"*Both*, Mr. Jardine?" The redhead lifted a brow.

"Of course, Miss Chisholm. Your brother and sister and I have been searching for the tunnel. But unfortunately, as yet, to no avail."

"So they informed us."

"Of course." He cleared his throat. "I trust you know you are welcome any time."

"Thank you, sir." Miss Chisholm nodded, clutching her friend's arm almost as if determined to drag her away.

He bowed and watched their exit, hoping, hoping Verity would turn to meet his gaze, to offer one of those soul-lifting smiles, even just a wave.

But she did not.

ᛦ Chapter Thirteen

Verity lowered the newssheet she'd been holding and stared out the drawing room windows to the sailboats dancing beyond. What must it be like to be truly free? To have no ties to duty and roles ordained by goodness-knows-whom however many years ago? She yawned, and rubbed her eyes, blinking against a dust mote, as the deep stillness of the rectory surrounded her.

She was alone. The Chisholms were all out, attending to either parish business, in the case of Helena and her parents, or pleasure, as James and his youngest siblings attended the latest round of explorations next door. How she *longed* to be there also. But true to her word, she refused to engender feelings towards Mr. Jardine, which necessitated staying away until such feelings as she possessed were well and truly only of the mere friend variety. Which was *so* hard, especially yesterday, when everything inside her had begged to turn and smile as she'd hastened away. Pretending not to care was pure torture—but it was for the best, Helena said, and from the approving looks Helena's parents had given Verity, she supposed her flights of fancy regarding the interesting gardener had perhaps not been quite so unobserved after all.

But avoiding the treasure hunt, and without friend or even James to converse with, was rather dull. She immediately tried to repress the feeling; such a sentiment betrayed ungratefulness and a shallowness of character she had always despised. But truly, the improving nature of the Chisholms' ancient copy of the *Christian Observer* was causing an ache in her head, not unlike the one Verity always experienced in her elder sister's company. Whilst the opposite of frivolity, the articles about the virtues of domesticity couldn't help but provoke dissatisfaction at her life, or at least the meaningless nature of her existence.

Which was an unaccustomed mood, and not something to put up with any longer.

She rose, and hastened upstairs to avoid the Cready, who unfortunately had not followed the other servants into the village. Once in her room, Verity opened the wardrobe and pulled out her blue riding dress. A magnificent idea struck her. Of course! With no one around, now would be the perfect time to try. She quickly changed into suitable clothes and tiptoed down the stairs, then escaped with a rush to the stables.

"Hello, Firefly."

The horse nickered, pushing her nose into Verity's shoulder.

"I know I look a trifle odd, but it is only superficial. I am still the same." She fed the horse a lump of sugar. "Now, today we're going to try something different, so I hope you will behave."

Firefly snorted.

Verity laughed. "I'm trusting that's a yes."

She led the horse into the yard and returned to the stables, gathering Firefly's blanket, bridle, and reins, which she efficiently placed on the horse. She moved back into the storeroom, where a saddle she assumed belonged to James lay neatly on a bench. She lifted it. Almost dropped it. It was so heavy! Placing it back on the bench she then looked underneath, where a shrouded object lay. Unveiling it, she discovered another, smaller saddle, as though made for a boy not much older than Benjamin. Was it too small? After careful assessment, she dragged it out. Fortunately it was much lighter and therefore more manageable, and could be easily lifted onto Firefly's back with a minimum of fuss.

Firefly tossed her head, as if objecting to the unfamiliar weight.

"Come now, I am sure you can cope far better than I."

After checking the length of reins and that the girth was tightened sufficiently, Verity eased her left boot into the stirrup, ruing the fact she hadn't thought to supply herself with a mounting box. Firefly shifted uncertainly.

"Come on, girl." Verity waited until the mare had calmed before pushing hard with her left foot, dragging her right leg over the horse's rump, adjusting in the saddle as her booted foot found the stirrup.

Firefly nickered again, no doubt protesting the drag of material she was not used to feeling on her back. But wearing a divided skirt was necessary, although perhaps Mary could be persuaded to create another closer fitting garment for next time.

She balanced herself, the slight fear washing away under a wave of exhilaration. Sitting astride was not the shocking thing Verity had once imagined it would be. Indeed, it felt immensely liberating, like she could ride far more effectively without a stupid pommel and hooked knee slowing her down, to say nothing of the multitudinous yards of fabric construing a riding habit!

Verity patted Firefly on the neck. "Come on, girl. Let's see if it is as easy to ride as men make it appear."

Firefly slowly walked out into the yard and Verity spent a few precious minutes growing accustomed to the different roll and pitch of the horse's movements. But years of riding, and watching expert horsemen, meant she soon picked up Firefly's gait.

"Shall we see if we can go faster?"

A press of her knees saw Firefly move into a trot, another brought her almost to a canter. She straightened her seat, balancing in the stirrups until she felt greater control.

"Whoa." She patted Firefly's withers, and the horse slowed to a walk. "Now let's see how clever we can be."

Her pulse throbbed loudly as she urged the horse to the gate, where she lifted the heavy latch before encouraging Firefly to move so the gate could ease open. Then they were out, the gate was secured, and they were streaming past the kitchen window while Verity hoped—indeed, almost prayed—Mrs. Cready did not see her.

Minutes later they had escaped the drive and were cantering along the lane, near to where they had seen Mr. Jardine over a week ago.

Remorse tugged. She strove to forget him and *still* he remained in her thoughts. Would she ever be free?

In the distance she saw the indistinct shape of a horse and rider. Best they weren't seen. "Come, girl, let's see what you've got."

Firefly followed her prompts and swerved onto the glen, quickly moving into a gallop, the footfalls thudding along the heathered ground. Verity's hips and lower torso rolled, following Firefly's motion, as she leaned slightly forward. She laughed, her spirits soaring, the breeze whipping her face, wresting her hair from its chignon. Now this, *this* was riding!

She glanced over her shoulder. The rider had disappeared. She exhaled. She was safe, she was free, she was . . .

Falling!

The saddle slipped further. The ground rushed to meet her. She stretched out a hand to break her fall—

"Ow!"

Verity groaned, staring into the empty heavens, before slowly pushing herself into a sitting position. She gasped. Heat screamed through her wrist, almost as severe as the time she had nearly broken her ankle just over a year ago, on that horrible, horrible day . . .

Firefly neighed and kept running, down toward the stream and broken tree, tossing her head as if reliving the game of toss the rider. Verity collapsed back into the springy heather, staring up into the sky. Now here was a fix. If she could not collect Firefly it would soon become very apparent what she'd attempted to do, which could cause a scandal that would likely result in her being sent home. Her nose wrinkled. While she might hope Mama had almost forgotten all about her, somehow it didn't seem likely, and being reminded of Verity's deficiencies via this particular episode would not help matters. No, she must somehow return to the Chisholms' without anyone being the wiser.

"But how?" she said aloud. "I need help."

The blue skies mocked her, their empty vastness a reminder of her lack of faith.

"It's not like You exist, is it?" Verity said, appreciation of the irony of speaking so curling her lips. "But let's pretend and say You do, how would I even know You are real?"

Nothing.

Yes, just as she'd expected, nothing. She closed her eyes, feeling as though something she barely recognized as having briefly, dimly, flickered within, had now died.

Nothing. Nothing save the song of a skylark, the piping of wind over heather, the crunch of trodden grass, the hot oaty breath on her face—

"Verity?"

She opened her eyes. "Helena! What are you doing here?"

Her friend laughed and drew closer. "I might well ask you the same question! Why are you lying there, with Firefly looking like she wants to eat you?"

Verity pushed away the enquiring horse's nose, pushing herself upright. She gasped and clutched her wrist. "It's nothing," she gritted out as Helena protested. "I fell."

"You? I didn't think you ever fell." Helena's gaze shifted back to Firefly. "But why is James's old saddle—? No! Never tell me you were riding astride!"

Verity forced a smile. "I won't."

"But you could've been seen!"

"But I wasn't."

"You could've died!"

"But I didn't." Verity rose to her feet then shook off Helena's supporting hand. She clenched her teeth. When had Helena turned so prim and proper?

"You think me prim and proper?"

Verity turned, wincing anew at the hurt expression in Helena's eyes. How had she said that aloud? "I'm sorry, Helena—"

"Perhaps you might recall that we cannot all afford to be so reckless about our reputation."

Verity bit her lip as Helena collected Firefly's bridle and stomped away. She scrambled after, regret searing her heart as hot as the pain still streaking up her arm. "Helena!" She moved until she faced her friend. "Please forgive me."

The tight expression around Helena's eyes and mouth eased a fraction. "I know I can seem a little anxious at times, but our school escapades are unknown in these parts. And if I am to make a good . . ."

"A good marriage?"

Helena nodded, her cheeks tinting as she stared at her feet. "Then I cannot be known as a hoyden."

"Or even the friend of a hoyden?"

Helena looked up, a smile lurking in the corners of her mouth. "Well, that remains to be seen."

Verity grinned, hurrying to give Helena a hug. Pain spiraled through her wrist and she bit her tongue to withhold the yelp.

"You *are* hurt."

Verity clutched her wrist gingerly. "I hope it is not broken."

"You poor thing. Let's get you home and bandaged up at once."

And under Helena's solicitude and chatter about her morning visit to Mrs. Podmore, Verity felt the pain ease, and the slight frost that had recently developed in their friendship melt away.

VERITY PRESSED HER lips together, willing her expression to remain neutral as she tried to cut the roasted fowl breast into a manageable size. She glanced up to meet Frances's concerned gaze.

"What did you do?"

"I, er, fell when riding today."

"You?" James's brows rose incredulously. "Did I not hear you boast the other day of being able to ride as well as any man?"

"Have you never fallen, James?" Helena asked.

He flushed, so Verity took the opportunity to turn the conversation. "And how goes your hunt for treasure, Ben?"

His eyes lit up. "We didn't find the tunnel, but we did find a priest's hole!"

"Really?"

"It's in the Rose Room," Frances explained, "near the fireplace.

When you go inside it's like a little room, with a sliding panel so you can see into the room, but only if on tiptoe."

"I needed James to lift me," Ben confided.

"And did you enjoy today?" Verity asked James.

He shrugged a shoulder. "It was interesting, I suppose. The space was a little cramped for me, though that Jardine fellow appeared to fit well enough."

Verity nodded, stifling her chagrin at missing out on both the adventure and the chance to see their neighbor again.

Helena's sharp eyes seemed to notice her discomfort, and she turned to her father. "Papa, can you explain why priest holes would be there?"

There was a faint sigh around the dining table as Mr. Chisholm placed his knife and fork on his plate, and began to expound on the Jacobite movement of a century ago. Verity listened avidly, the minister's tales new to her ears, though judging from the glazed expressions of his offspring, not new to them.

"So the idea of a passage between Dungally House and here is not completely infeasible?"

He smiled gently at her, and for a moment she was reminded of the kindness of Mr. Jardine's expression. She blinked and mentally shook herself. Perhaps the fall had affected her brain—she must certainly be going mad!

"Infeasible, no. Improbable, yes. I can perhaps see why an important landowner might wish for an escape route from his house, but in fact he would not be that much better off than merely hiding in said priest hole until whatever unwanted visitors had gone."

"But Papa," Frances said, "here we are so much closer to the harbor—"

"And the boats for transportation so that a tunnel would make sense," Helena finished.

"But don't forget, we have searched this house completely and found not even a tiny closet, let alone a tunnel like that of which you speak."

For a moment, everyone looked around them, as if the paneled dining room walls could tell tales.

Verity rested her aching wrist on the table, the tenor of the conversation making further need for social niceties now obsolete. Soon, very soon, she would need Mary to apply some more of the poultice Mrs. Chisholm had recommended, before carefully rewrapping the bandage. She sighed, perhaps a little too loudly, as all eyes now swung to her.

"Is your wrist hurting again, my dear?" Mrs. Chisholm's eyes softened at Verity's nod. "Be sure to avoid anything too strenuous over the next few days to give your body a chance to heal."

"Yes, ma'am."

"The body is a wondrous thing, is it not?" Mr. Chisholm observed, to no one in particular. "I thank God He has created us in such marvelous fashion that measures as rest can sometimes be all we need for returning to health. Such healing seems most miraculous, do you not agree?"

Verity felt a fraud as she nodded amidst the general murmur of assent. Helena's fortuitous appearance today did not mean anything supernatural was at work. Sheer coincidence, that was all.

She returned her attention to Frances and Ben. "Well, I am glad you had such an exciting day. I'm sure if there is a tunnel, you will discover it."

"Do you mean never to visit again?" Ben appeared to droop.

Verity cast a look between Helena and her mother, ignoring the sardonic gleam in James's eyes. "I don't believe so," she said, to Ben's disappointed protest.

She concentrated on finishing her creamed potatoes, listening as the family opined about Benjamin's behavior and the laird's appreciation that Mr. Jardine had communicated today concerning the improved gardens.

The lump in her throat made ingestion difficult. She did not miss him. She did *not*!

"Helena, I don't see why you and Verity could not visit again," Mrs. Chisholm said mildly. "Provided the others are in attendance, of course."

Excitement flickered. Verity shot Helena a glance.

"I think it a fine thing to be concerned about one's neighbors," Mr. Chisholm said with a nod. "As if the laird has not enough to contend with, what with the rumors I hear in the village."

"What rumors?" Frances asked.

But Mr. Chisholm only glanced significantly at little Benjamin before shaking his head. "Go, bless our neighbor, and we'll trust God that a little kindness might go a long way to helping our village find its heart again."

Anthony glanced up at the whoop coming from the garden. Benjamin, probably Frances, James, too, if he was roped into chaperoning again. Anthony had found himself wanting to like the young man, but was only too conscious of young Chisholm's resentment, his impatience steadily growing, until that most unlikely find yesterday. For a few moments James had seemed more ally than rival—

Rival? Anthony shook his head. What was he thinking?

But he couldn't help the trickling certainty that he had lost a friendship with potential, through no fault of his own. And as much as he strove to enjoy the Chisholms' company, he longed for the return of their guest.

He had prayed about it. Asked God to take away foolish feelings he could never act upon. Asked God to rekindle his former feelings for the one who'd once held his heart. And in some ways Verity's absence had helped soothe his soul, because at least she wasn't there with her bewitching smile or enchanting laugh. For every time his neighbors visited, the ache intensified again, filling him with a sense of frustration that no amount of prayers could ease. For she was unsuitable. Wasn't she? Perhaps he should plan that visit to Linlithgow soon, and be reminded of Amelia's inestimable, far more suitable, qualities.

He resumed planting the seeds, certain the visitors would find him as they had every other time.

"*Bonjour.*"

Chest thudding, he glanced up. Echoed the smile beaming brilliantly at him. Inwardly cursed himself a fool for not responding as coolly as he ought. Called himself another fool for not caring. *"Bonjour, mademoiselle."*

She glanced around the outbuilding, its roof exposed to the elements. "I think you need new glass."

"You are observant as always, Miss Hatherleigh."

She laughed, the sound trickling joy through his heart, the hard lump in his chest of the past few days easing.

"I am happy you have returned," he offered.

The light in her face faded slightly as she glanced away, studying the clay pots he'd arranged neatly on the bench. "I am happy also," she said softly.

He wanted to ask why she had not visited, but good manners—and a certain little boy—prevented him.

"Good day, sir!" Benjamin called. "Are you coming inside?"

"Soon," Anthony assured him. "I am just speaking to your governess here."

Benjamin's face screwed up. "Governess? Verity ain't my governess."

Anthony glanced at Miss Hatherleigh, who wore a puzzled frown. "I am Helena's school friend, not Benjamin's governess."

School friend? She was still in school? A queasy kind of disgust slowly spread through him. How had he spent so much time hankering after a school miss?

"Mr. Jardine? Is something wrong?"

He forced his head to move from side to side. "No, I am quite well, thank you, Miss Hatherleigh." Why, *why* had he thought her a governess? Why had he allowed himself to hope, to imagine—No. She must be a decade younger, a preposterous age difference. No wonder she preferred to keep company with young Chisholm. He felt sick at himself, sick at his presumption.

"Don't keep him too long, Verity. Mac is nice, but I still prefer Mr. Jardine." Benjamin grinned before scampering away.

"Who is Mac?"

"My . . . er, assistant."

"In the garden?"

"No, no. He keeps . . . ahem, the laird's books and so on. An indispensable fellow, especially when one grows tired of searching every nook and cranny for a mythical tunnel and even more mythical treasure."

"Mr. Chisholm doesn't think such a thing completely unlikely."

"Well, the reverend is a good man. Perhaps he has more faith than me."

She glanced away.

"How about you, Miss Hatherleigh? Do you believe in miracles?"

He studied her, as she carelessly lifted small jars and replaced them on the bench, a small frown pleating her brow.

The space between them grew thick with the unsaid. He found himself almost wishing she would go, so he could sift his thoughts until he found something solid enough to be certain.

She lifted another jar, again in her right hand, always in her right hand. He frowned.

"Miss Hatherleigh? Are you injured?"

"I am well." She pulled down the left sleeve of her morning gown, but not before he spotted a white bandage.

"You're hurt."

She lifted a shoulder. "Just a silly riding accident. Nothing to worry about."

"But—"

"But nothing. *Au revoir, monsieur.*"

And as she turned and walked away, flashing another smile over her shoulder, he found himself wishing that his sense of duty did not demand he ignore the enchanting young visitor from next door.

Chapter Fourteen

He thought her too young.

It had been obvious from the look of shock that he'd been too slow to mask. In that moment, all thought of priest holes had fled, and her only goal was to hide her chagrin and thus escape his pity. But what did she expect? She frowned. One thing she had certainly not expected was that he would mistake her for a governess! Didn't one have to be somewhat staid and well-behaved for that? How Miss Haverstock would have laughed!

She placed the dusty *Lady's Magazine* back in the pile, wishing her wrist felt better so she might ride, weed, or play the piano—surely even embroidery would be preferable to this interminable boredom!

"Miss," the grating voice of Mrs. Cready stole Verity's attention. "There be a letter for yer."

"Thank you." A letter! Her heart raced. Was it from Grandmama? Perhaps Lucinda or one of the other selectees? Or could it be from Mama?

Verity picked up the letter the Cready had gestured to on her way back to the kitchen, heart sinking in recognition of the penmanship. She hurried away to her room where she locked the door, dropped onto the bed, and slit open the seal.

And stared as heat pounded her chest and her ears.

How *could* she?

She had hoped against hope that they might relent, had even dared whisper a prayer in her most hollow time—all to no avail. She stared at the handwriting, whose elegant script did not disguise the animosity with which it was penned.

"I have nursed a viper . . ." she read. "To have conspired with your grandmother to overturn our plans for a secure match . . . to have deliberately deceived the Chisholms, forcing them to extend hospitality for which they had no desire . . ."

Verity's hand shook. How could Mama say such things about Grandmama and Mrs. Chisholm, let alone her own daughter? Did she have no compassion? Could she not see her own part in all this? And Papa . . . Her eyes burned. How could *Papa* of all people permit such a thing?

From outside the door she heard the thump, thump, thump of feet, then a loud knock.

"Verity?" Helena's happy voice called. "Verity? Are you in there?" The doorknob twisted slightly. "Unlock the door! I need to tell you about Alasdair!"

Tamping down her emotion, she unlocked the door, forcing her lips into a semblance of a smile. "And what exciting news is that?"

Helena's chatter about meeting Alasdair down the street soon faded, replaced by a frown. "Verity? Is something the matter? Your eyes are a little pink." She clasped Verity's arm. "Are you unwell? Have you had news from home?"

"I have had news, yes."

"But nothing good, I fear." She closed the door and drew Verity to the window seat. "What has happened?"

Verity handed Helena the letter, rubbing her arms to ward off the slight chill as her friend's eyes widened. Then Helena gasped. "No! I cannot believe such a thing."

"Unfortunately disbelief in Mama's actions has never prevented their being true," Verity said. "Mama is determined to make me a lady, one way or the other."

Helena glanced up, green eyes wide. "Is this why you have been so determined to try to prove otherwise these past weeks?"

Verity met her gaze but said nothing.

"And Mr. Jardine? You care for him, knowing that it is impossible?"

A burn began in the back of her eyes. She blinked and clenched her jaw, willing away the emotion. Eventually she had enough control to affect a shrug. "It does not matter. He thinks me too young."

"Too young?"

"Apparently he thought I was Ben's governess." Her smile felt hollow. "Can you imagine that?"

"I think you would make an excellent governess," Helena said stoutly. "You've always been so smart, yet able to explain things in an interesting way. Benjie and Frances love being with you."

But it didn't change the fact that the man she wanted to impress thought she was too young.

"I'm very sorry, Verity. I understand now." Helena sighed. "And you must pardon my frankness, but I simply cannot comprehend any mother forcing her daughter into such a situation."

"That is because you have a mother who loves you."

"Verity!" Her eyes filled with shock. "You cannot say—"

"The truth? Why? I know it is difficult to comprehend when your mama is kind and seeks your best, but mine . . ." She shrugged.

"Your mother loves you."

"My mother tolerates me, on occasion," Verity corrected. "And tolerance is far from affection."

"You have known her plans all this time?"

Verity nodded, then, unable to meet the sympathy pooling in Helena's eyes, glanced out the window. Under darkening clouds, which she had learned foretold of a "mizzle" as the Chisholms called light rain, Benjamin was chatting to Hoskins who seemed to pay him no mind as he raked fresh grass cuttings. "Grandmama sent me here so Mama could not achieve things any more quickly." She laughed hollowly. "What a shame to have missed what I'm sure was a delightful *tête-à-tête* when Mama finally discovered where I was." She drew in a breath. Exhaled slowly. Forced her fingers to unclench. "I *am* concerned about what she has written to your mother. I would hate for her to be on the receiving end of Mama's rage."

Helena folded the letter and handed it back to Verity, her green eyes snapping. "Well, we shall go see her now. And I'm sure she will understand it is her duty as a Christian to keep you here, where you will be protected."

"Do you really think I need protection from Charles Bromsgrove?" she said, following Helena down the stairs.

Helena's mutter carried to her. "No, but perhaps you do from that mother." She rapped on a door and strode in without waiting for an answer. "Good, Mama, you're here. Frances, go away. Verity and I must speak with Mama urgently."

Verity slowly entered the drawing room, and saw at once from Mrs. Chisholm's face that she knew.

"Frances, I will speak with you later."

"But, Mama—"

"Later." Mrs. Chisholm gestured Verity forward as Frances shut the door. "I'm sure I can guess why you are here."

Verity bit her lip as Helena cried, "Mama, it is the most outrageous thing!"

"It is unfortunate, but not completely shocking, dear. Parents have been known to arrange marriages before."

"But Charles is ancient! I met him that time I stayed at Verity's for half term. He is nothing but a *dandy*." Helena sputtered. "Verity cannot be forced to marry him. You cannot allow it!"

Mrs. Chisholm's eyes, which had not left Verity's face since she'd entered the room, seemed to soften even more. "I'm afraid I cannot prevent it, my dear."

"But, Mama!"

"I quite understand, Mrs. Chisholm." Verity summoned a smile. "I do hope Mama was not vitriolic in her letter to you."

"It was not, perhaps, the most charitable epistle ever penned." The older woman's gaze narrowed a fraction. "May I read yours?"

Verity handed over her letter, forcing herself to stand still as emotions clashed within. Why couldn't Mama ever show one smidgen of the tenderness Mrs. Chisholm possessed? Did she dislike Verity so much? Would her parents forever resent that she was not a boy?

Worse—was Verity so completely unlovable no one could possibly hold her in esteem? Her chest tightened.

"Oh, my dear." Mrs. Chisholm stretched out a hand, catching Verity's in her own. "I am sure she did not mean to suggest you were an ungrateful wretch . . ."

"Which is why you did not ascertain that so quickly." Verity managed a laugh that sounded more like a rasping choke.

"Dear girl, I wish you could stay longer than what your mama permits, but I am forced to accede to her wishes." Mrs. Chisholm looked sadly at her. "I am tremendously sorry, however."

"Thank you, Mrs. Chisholm." The burn in her eyes begged release. Four more weeks. Only four more weeks. Then her life might as well be over.

"We shall just have to pray for a miracle, shan't we?"

And, without warning, Verity was clasped in a warm motherly hug, the likes of which she had never experienced, and of which she knew her own mother was incapable. Both facts drew emotion to trickle from her eyes. A miracle? If only she dared believe they existed.

Having spent the past twenty-four hours ruing his ill-considered reaction, from which an abundance of estate matters had failed to distract him, Anthony was filled with no small measure of relief when he spied his neighbors tripping up the garden path, for all intents and purposes looking like they had come to work in his garden.

"Mac?" he said, not moving from his window position.

"Yes, sir?"

"Could you contrive to ensure Mrs. Iverson brings refreshments within the half hour?"

"I will do my best, sir."

Their eyes met in a moment of perfect understanding. Mrs. Iverson had been unusually short-tempered in recent days, her complaints about Anthony's visitors supplanting her usual litany of household grievances.

Mac disappeared and Anthony returned to his perch at the window. Benjamin spotted him, pointing him out to Verity.

Anthony lifted a hand, fresh relief filling him as she gave a small wave. Perhaps she had forgiven his mistake, after all.

Moments later the peace of the room was interrupted by high-pitched voices.

"Good morning, ladies—and Benjamin."

"I wanted to show Verity the priest's hole." Benjamin turned to his dark-haired companion. "It's not that tricky to find once you know where to look."

"I'm sure it is not," Verity said. "But perhaps Mr. Jardine has other plans—"

"No, no, I assure you. Please." He gestured to the fireplace. "See if you can discern our medieval secret."

Moments later, with the guiding hand of the youngest Chisholm, she clicked the rosebud and the paneling next to the fireplace swung open.

"Oh, how wonderful!" She clapped her hands, glancing over her shoulder. "May I?"

"Of course."

For some reason, he felt a mite jealous of the young lad who self-importantly led the way. Anthony schooled his features to indifference, aware of the elder Miss Chisholm's scrutiny.

"Now watch your step, Verity, and your head—"

"Benjamin?" his sister said loudly. "Is it not awfully presumptuous of you to guide Verity in a task that is perhaps one that Mr. Jardine should perform?"

"Miss Chisholm, truly I do not—"

"Mr. Jardine, I am sure you do not," she said, green eyes twinkling. "But Benjamin is already giving himself airs, and if you allow him further license, I am convinced his head will swell to such a size that it will only take a gust of wind and he will be carried right across the Irish Sea."

"Helena!" protested the outraged young man. "You are meaner than Mrs. Podmore!"

She pulled him from the enclosure. "And yet somehow you still love me."

"I do not!"

"Deny it if you want, it doesn't change the fact you remain my favorite little brother."

"But I'm your only little brother!"

Anthony choked back a chuckle, meeting Verity's amused gaze before she blushed and ducked her head inside the paneled hidey-hole.

"Mr. Jardine, would you be so kind as to show Verity where the peepholes are? I'm afraid I will need to take my brother home if he insists on being obstreperous."

Anthony's brows rose, but, helpless against her determination—and his better judgment—he found himself in the priest hole with the young lady he knew was too young, yet was impossible to ignore.

"Mr. Jardine, you really do not have to do this."

He cleared his throat. "I don't mind."

She was so close, her hair tickling his nose. In the enclosed space he could hear her breathing, smell a subtle perfume, like her hair might be washed in roses. He could reach out an arm and draw her to himself—

"Now, where are the peepholes Benjamin spoke of?"

"There is a small handle"—he clasped her hand, felt heat dance between their skin, heard her indrawn breath as he lifted it to touch the wooden latch that slid open the spyholes—"here."

He swallowed. Somehow the space felt too intimate, too near. He coughed, letting go of her hand. "Can you see the room yet?"

"No, I'm too short."

How he longed to offer to lift her to see more clearly. But temptation was something he'd always fought. He wasn't about to let it win now. "If you step up there's a small ledge that might help. It's still too low for Benjamin, but Miss Chisholm could see well enough yesterday."

She pushed away, the space cooling between them. Then, "I can see! Oh, how marvelous!"

She spent the next minute exclaiming over all she could see, before stepping down, nearly colliding with him in the process. "Oh, I'm sorry, Mr. Jardine."

"Not at all."

He escaped the chamber to find his housekeeper entering the Rose Room, holding a large tray.

Her small eyes widened. "Mr. Jardine!" Her brows snapped together ferociously as Verity emerged, patting down her hair. "And just who might this be?"

Anthony fought the irritation at her presumption and exchanged glances with Verity, but was taken aback at her sparkling eyes and tilted chin.

Verity looked Mrs. Iverson over before saying in a measured voice, "Well, I *might* be the Duchess of Cornwall."

Anthony repressed a chuckle. "Or possibly the Queen of Spain."

"Or I may be a poor Liverpudlian washerwoman," Verity said in a thick accent.

"Nay." Anthony grinned, adopting a Highlands brogue. "Ye cannae be thought as dat, hen."

"Hen?" Verity's brows rose. *"Non. Je ne suis pas une poule."*

Anthony bowed. "A thousand apologies, *mademoiselle*. You are, upon closer inspection, most definitely not a hen."

"A hen?" Benjamin said, his wide-eyed gaze matched by his sisters'.

"But perhaps an Indian princess?" Verity murmured hopefully.

He chuckled, ignoring the steam he could see gathering behind his housekeeper's eyes as he addressed her sternly. "But in any case, she is my guest, and I would appreciate you treating her with a little more respect."

The bluster slowly leaked from Mrs. Iverson's expression, though her eyes remained hard as she assessed Verity. "I don't take with young ladies of quality hiding with young gentlemen."

"And neither do I," Verity said, her smile at its sweetest. "It is a good thing, then, that Mr. Jardine was merely showing me the priest hole, and not anything more sinister, would you not agree?"

Mrs. Iverson blinked once, twice, then thumped the tray down before exiting the room in high outrage.

Amid the smothered giggles of the Chisholm girls, Verity turned to him with an apologetic smile. "Somehow I do not think she believed me."

He grinned. "Somehow I find I do not really care, *querida*."

"Querida?"

"It is a Portuguese term."

She blinked. "Have you been to Portugal?"

He shook his head. "I have . . . learned a little of other languages."

"As have I. I've always been fascinated by other countries, and their customs and traditions so different from our own."

He nodded, feeling like a fraudster, as she sat and poured tea for them all as though trained by a duchess herself, all the while chattering about places she'd like to see, her animation and laughter doing much to ease his disquietude as they laughed and talked and let the tea grow cold.

But later, when his visitors had left, and he was trying to summon sufficient enthusiasm to tackle the books again, he was aware the brief interlude had left him convinced of two things: One, that the chasm growing between them had disappeared and they were once again friends. And two, that he would need to admit to the truth of his identity and past adventures before much more time ran on. For if she were to discover the truth another way, a rift would develop of such magnitude that he might as well move back to the far ends of the earth.

Permanently.

And alone.

CHAPTER FIFTEEN

"Now, VERITY, IF you would please look for this type of wool, I would be most appreciative."

"Yes, Mrs. Chisholm," Verity murmured. She exchanged glances with Helena as the reverend's wife moved away.

Helena laughed. "Your face! It is like you've never bought wool before."

"I haven't, so *help* me."

Helena pointed to several barrels holding skeins of wool. Verity frowned. There were so many different types!

Around her the little shop had come alive, buzzing with the hum of conversation, much of it to do with the upcoming Ridings and subsequent ball, which all townsfolk were expected to attend. But amidst the whispered conversations she heard reference to Guthries and Dungally House. Her ears pricked. Apparently news of the new laird had filtered in.

"But I don't understand . . ." said a round-faced lady, holding up Mrs. Chisholm.

"The Bible says 'judge not, lest we be judged,'" the reverend's wife said mildly.

The lady looked abashed at the gentle rebuke and huffed away.

"Your mother is remarkable," Verity murmured, watching Mrs. Chisholm interrupt her shopping for yet another conversation with an elderly woman. "I don't know how she has the patience. That must be the fourth time she's been stopped this morning. At this rate we'll never return."

Impatience clawed from within, yet she had said she would gladly assist Mrs. Chisholm in her duties, so keep her word she must. Even if she'd much rather be with James and Ben, searching for hidden tunnels.

"We'll be there soon enough, although Mrs. Smith can be long-winded."

"Long-winded? It looks like that woman could talk with a mouth full of porridge. I do not think I could ever be a minister's wife."

Helena laughed. "Well, I'm sure that becoming a minister's wife is not something you need worry about, for, if nothing else, such a person should have a measure of faith, should they not?"

Verity smiled, yet beneath her assumed good spirits streaked a little sadness, that perhaps she was missing something important. She returned her attention to pretending to know which skein would be best.

"Look! There he is. The new laird of Dungally!"

At the wizened woman's comment Verity joined Helena in hurrying to the window.

"Nay, I thought 'im saikless, but 'e's strang as an ox. Nowt like the thowless laird afore 'im. Worked hard, 'e did. Fixed my cottage with 'is own hands."

Verity peered out the window, but could see nobody save for the tall gray-haired man she'd seen next to Mr. Jardine at services. She leaned close to Helena. "Isn't that McNaughton? Surely he is not the laird."

"Mr. Jardine introduced him as his assistant."

Verity frowned. "If so, he seems very ordinary for a laird."

Helena giggled. "What did you expect? For him to be dressed in a big kilt and sporran?"

"Aye." Verity chuckled to cover a disquieting sense of disappointment. "I suppose the laird can't help his looks."

The older woman scowled up at her. "Ye be a fine one to talk! Sure, an' he might not be a large and bonny man, but a kinder man ye'd never meet, else my name is not Mary Boyd!"

"I beg your pardon, Mrs. Boyd. I meant to cast no aspersions—"

"Lassies are all the same. Care for nowt save a man's looks."

Heat stained her cheeks. "That is not so!"

With a loud 'hmph' and muttered "gawky Soothron" the woman waddled away.

Verity glanced at a giggling Helena. "I gather that is not a compliment?"

"No, you poor dimwitted English lass."

After giving Mrs. Chisholm her wool, Verity hurried outside to where Mr. Jardine had now joined his assistant. "*Bonjour*, Monsieur Jardine."

"*Bonjour*, Miss Hatherleigh." He smiled, his gaze warming as it touched hers, causing a fluttery feeling in her chest. "And what brings you to town today?"

"Mrs. Chisholm's wool. She's in there." Verity waved toward the little shop. "Pardon my interruption, but I couldn't help over-hear a Mrs. Boyd say she saw the laird just now. Are you here with the laird?" His smile seemed to freeze as he cast a quick glance at McNaughton. "Apparently he helped fix the thatch on her cottage."

"Did he now?"

She nodded. "I am quite surprised he would condescend to do such a thing."

"You think it condescension?"

"I know my"—parents, she was about to say—"many of good rank who would object to helping in such a menial manner."

A muscle twitched in his jaw. "Perhaps he did not consider it menial, but merely wanted to ensure the problem would be reme-died, and not put off yet again, as his predecessors apparently thought acceptable."

"Perhaps," she replied doubtfully.

"And this bothers you." He said it as more statement than question.

"No! No, indeed I think it shows a remarkable display of goodness. But he appears to be most unusual in his dealings with others."

"He is"—his eyes twinkled—"a most unusual man."

Verity gazed up at him, drawn into the depths of his gaze, as he studied her with that half smile on his face. For a moment, she cared not that they were on the village's main street nor that townsfolk were staring at them. She'd happily gaze at him for all time.

McNaughton coughed. She pulled her gaze regretfully away and turned to him. "You are not the laird, are you?"

His brows rose, and he glanced at Mr. Jardine. "Nay, lass. I am not."

"Then where is he?"

Mr. Jardine cleared his throat. "It would appear you are doomed for disappointment again, *mademoiselle*. Look, here is your friend, and the good Mrs. Chisholm. Good morning, ladies."

"Good morning," Mrs. Chisholm murmured.

"Did you see him?" Helena asked excitedly.

Verity shook her head. Why was he so hard to meet? It was almost as though Mr. Jardine did not want him to be found.

She looked up, to see his warm gaze fixed on her, as yet another couple spoke to Mrs. Chisholm. Taking his interest as invitation, Verity leaned closer. "I don't know how she manages to speak to so many people all the time."

Helena shot Verity a mischievous look. "Verity was saying how hard she would find being the wife of a minister."

"I see." His gaze cooled, as something like disappointment crossed his features.

"It is just that I have very little patience with some people," she rushed to explain. "And I could not trust myself not to blurt out the obvious."

Helena's brows rose. "I'm sure you are grateful that others are not afflicted with the same proclivity for candor."

"Perhaps." Verity's head tilted. "It would make conversation rather more pungent, do you not agree, Mr. Jardine?"

"Agree with what, Miss Hatherleigh?"

"That life would be rather more exciting if everyone were bound to tell the truth, instead of murmuring polite niceties, as I'm sure Mrs. Chisholm is right now."

His Adam's apple bobbed as he swallowed and nodded before

making a hasty departure, leaving her wondering just where his problem lay.

꙾

Anthony swung the axe, hard, merciless on another lump of wood. Shards splintered all directions, yet the thump did little to ease his soul's disquiet since this morning's ill-advised foray into the village. He bent down, threw the split shingles onto the barrow, and resumed his stance.

Another thwack of the axe sent a spray of woodchips through the woodyard. His chest grew tight, but his lungs weren't yet protesting. Another job too demanding for Iverson, yet its very physicality felt strangely satisfying for Anthony's inner tumult. What was he to do? What could he do?

Every time he saw her, he felt the tug of attraction. It wasn't enough that his brain insisted she was too young, his senses still pulled at him every time she was near, demanding he speak with her, inhale her scent—God forbid, touch her! He groaned. What could he do?

He had never been one for toying with a maid's affections. University and later church experience had taught him to bat away the few ladies eager to hurl their affections at him. Had his regard for Amelia merely stemmed from convenience? He thought back. No. He'd admired her gentleness, her goodness, her piety. His desire for marriage with her was built on mutual respect and a—misplaced—understanding that she had similar goals. His lips twisted. More fool him.

He hefted up the axe and swung again. The wood cracked loudly, dusting his bare forearms with another fine spray of wood particles. Was there any point in pursuing Miss Verity? He did not count himself a vain man, but even Mac had commented on the girl's obvious regard. He shook his head. Had he been wrong to enjoy their conversations so much? Had it given rise to hopes he should not fulfill? And if so, would admitting to his true identity only complicate matters further? Surely if she knew he was a laird, her parents would not hesitate in reeling him in. And he had no desire to be married for his inheritance. But neither did he wish to forgo what had become one of the most enjoyable friendships of his life.

He gritted his teeth and lifted the axe again. Just being with her added a lightness to his soul, a smile to his lips, just as her candor and vivacity added an unpredictable energy to his days. Somehow the drudgery of his responsibilities eased whenever he spied her. And her bright-eyed curiosity showed a sharpness of mind he could not help but appreciate. Conversation the other day had demonstrated her insight, her occasional references to running an estate showing a knowledge of estate matters that ran deep, so deep in fact it almost made him wonder—

No. He shook his head again, smiling at such fanciful notions. She was a schoolgirl. That was all. And that was all she must remain to him, regardless of foolish fancies that made him ache at night. She was but a *schoolgirl*! Of goodness knows what birth. She would never be as suitable a wife for a laird as a Scottish maid would. As Amelia would . . .

As if to reiterate his conclusions, a rumble drew through the heavy sky, followed by the first drops from above. He threw the final pieces onto the barrow and wheeled it under shelter. He glanced down at his sweat-stained shirtsleeves and shrugged. No matter. It was not as though he anticipated visitors today.

He moved to the terrace, disregarding the fine misting rain.

Peering through the mizzle he could see two figures way out in the estuary, two forms that looked remarkably like Verity and Benjamin. What were they doing out in this weather? He raced upstairs, ripping off his sweat-stained shirt and grabbing a freshly laundered one, then shrugging into a coat as he hurried down the central staircase, thankfulness nipping his heels at missing his nosy housekeeper. Two minutes later he had escaped the confines of the walled garden and was striding toward them.

"Miss Hatherleigh!"

She turned around, her balance precarious atop the rock, as the tide hurried in and sea spray drifted to her. The parasol she held appeared to be more about observing the proprieties than of any real use, her hair curling damply against her brow. She smiled, causing his heart to kick like a donkey.

He frowned to quell the emotion. "What are you doing here?"

She gestured to Benjamin. "Ben insisted on coming, much to the horror of his sisters and mother. Apparently this Scotch mist is the best time for seeing great crested newts."

He nodded, looking beyond her to where the lad foraged among the reeds. "Master Benjamin, have you found a specimen yet? If so, I would implore you to return, as it is very damp, and I would not like to see you come down with a chill."

"I've almost got 'im!"

Anthony exchanged glances with Verity before calling out again. "You would not wish to see Miss Hatherleigh catch cold?"

The red head looked up, mouth set in a mutinous line. "Verity *wanted* to come."

"But surely not to get sick?"

"Thank you for your concern, Mr. Jardine, but for some reason I never seem to get sick. Besides, how can one not enjoy the view?" She waved towards the sea. "It is so beautiful, wild, and free."

"You could be describing yourself." The words had escaped before he knew it.

She slid an upward glance at him. "Wild? Perhaps. Free? Not really. And beautiful? Now I know you jest."

He studied her. His experience might be limited, but surely this was no flirtatious device designed to harvest a compliment. Her gaze returned to the sea yet still he saw the drooping expression and the way her bottom lip protruded slightly.

In those few seconds he realized his lack of reply could be construed as silent acquiescence. He cleared his throat, as if a cold had prevented earlier response, and opened his mouth to speak, but she sighed.

"I am resigned to it, you know."

"Resigned?"

"Mama always talks about how Caroline and Cecilia received all the looks." Her glance at him was wry. "No doubt you think it vain-glorious of me to be so concerned about such matters, but she has never once said that about me."

What could he say? He watched Benjamin plunge his arm into some reeds then screw his face in disgust. The drizzle having eased, he gestured to a wooden seat positioned to capture the view. He wiped the seat dry with his handkerchief for her to seat herself and then sat beside her. "What are your sisters like?"

"Pink and white and ladylike and pretty."

"They might have their admirers, but not everyone appreciates the obvious."

Her gaze, so blue, so direct, seemed almost pleading. His chest constricted, knowing his words would be judged, yet not wanting to say something she might misinterpret. "Sometimes one can only truly appreciate beauty when in the right setting."

She nodded and refocused her attention on the sea. "Like your roses. My grandmother has banks of Scotch roses but they do not hold quite the same degree of beauty as when they grow wild here."

She had a grandmother who possessed a garden that could host *banks* of roses?

"Mr. Jardine? What is that frown for?" Her gaze returned to his, approval clearly writ in the blue depths.

His heart skipped a beat. Oh, to be worthy of such approval . . . He shook his head.

"I was thinking about the laird—"

"You surprise me."

She chuckled. "I think it quite wonderful the laird should deign to assist poor Mrs. Boyd."

"Unfortunately I had no other workers to spare."

"You . . . ? Oh, I remember. You're not only a gardener, but you help manage the estate, too."

He cleared his throat, his brain forming the words to correct her, to confess, but instead he said, "Would it be so bad if I were merely a gardener?"

Her smile grew shy. "Not to me."

But to her parents? Was that what was left unsaid? Surely they would be pleased to see their daughter contract an eligible match. But did their daughter's fancy education, and this grandmother boasting banks of roses, did this indicate they held much higher ambitions for her?

"I got 'im! Look, Verity! See his lovely crown?" Benjamin squelched through the mud, hand outstretched.

Verity pulled her cloak closer as she peered at the odd creature. "He is lovely."

"He is, isn't he, Mr. Jardine?"

"A fine specimen, indeed."

"Place him in your bucket and we'll head home, Benjie, there's a dear."

Anthony glanced at her as the lad ran off to obey.

"You have no brothers?"

Her smile froze, the light fading from her face. "No."

"I apologize if my question is intrusive. It is only that you manage the lad so well."

"Benjie is a sweet boy."

"I do not believe he would thank you for that description, Miss Hatherleigh."

She chuckled, thus encouraging him to ask, "Where does your family live?"

"In England."

"No! Dinnae tell me I've been cavorting with an English lass."

"Hardly cavorting, Mr. Jardine."

"But definitely conversing." Tension eased in his chest at the return of her smile. "Some people from the south can be rather less than approving of the Scots."

"Usually those people from the south have even less understanding than approval. I do not wish to be counted among them."

"Rest assured, Miss Hatherleigh, nobody could mistake your degree of understanding as anything but superior."

Except, of course, when it came to his real identity. But that was an explanation best saved for another day. Especially as his peripheral vision indicated the oncoming arrival of Mrs. Iverson. "If you'll excuse me, I believe I'm in for another tongue-lashing, a joy I do not wish to inflict upon you."

Her eyes flashed. "How dare she take it upon herself to treat you so?"

"A question I have pondered many a time myself. But no, put away your claws and soothe yourself. I do not need a lass to protect me."

"But—"

"Nor do I want to stay here gabbling explanations." He turned to Benjamin. "I trust you will shield your good mother from all the excitement such a creature can bring. Remember not all ladies possess the intestinal fortitude of Miss Hatherleigh here."

"Verity is full of spunk."

"Indeed"—his gaze met hers—"Miss Hatherleigh is a true out-and-outer."

Warmth kindled in those blue eyes, spearing him with guilt as he remembered his former misgivings. He cleared his throat. "You must go, before questions are asked that might prove difficult to answer."

"Oh! Very well, then."

Her frown wrinkled his ease, and he watched her departure before turning to meet his housekeeper's expression. But before she could go on the attack, he murmured quickly, quietly, "Mrs. Iverson, I assume there is a good reason why you have left your duties to keep me from mine."

"Your duties, sir?" One eyebrow hitched as she looked at him askance.

"Mrs. Iverson, I am growing increasingly tired of your constant interference." Her mouth sagged. "Now, please, no more checking up on me, or I will be forced to recommend you work elsewhere."

"But, Mr. Jar—"

"Good day!"

And he strode off to his potting room and closed the door with a loud bang.

CHAPTER SIXTEEN

TWO EVENINGS LATER, Verity sat in the Chisholms' dining room, exhaustion from the day's hard ride curbing her participation in the conversation.

"And how is your wrist, Verity?"

"It has held up well enough." She plastered on a smile, glad Mr. Jardine was not here so she need not hide from his all-too-observant eyes and uncanny insight. It wasn't as though it was aching; that would doubtless come when the numbness wore off. Today's ride along the Dee to Castle Douglas, a distance of almost ten miles, had been a great test, her wrist holding up surprisingly well, her leg muscles less so.

The long trip had proved to be about more than mere sightseeing, Helena and Alasdair in a world of their own, the affection they shared obvious, making Verity's heart prick with envy, and her acceptance of a raced return against James easy. She had won, surprisingly. James's heavier weight was no match for Firefly's stamina and speed, and her win had not put him in a good mood. Helena's insistence that Alasdair stay for dinner had proved a welcome break in the tension that clung to James like a dark cloud.

She focused again on the conversation, which now revolved around the selection of the leader of the Ridings. James and Alasdair grew quite animated, whilst the elder Chisholms discussed other matters, and Helena cast shy glances at her beau. James was adamant he held a chance, whilst his sisters held his chance at rather less than naught.

"Surely it won't be you!" Frances scoffed.

"I don't see why not," James flushed. "I have as much right to lead as anyone."

"But your horse . . ."

At her brother's scowl Frances returned her attention to her meal.

Helena murmured, "It is a shame Firefly is too small for you."

"Everything is a shame," James muttered, attacking his potatoes. "No good horse, no money for a new one."

Verity turned to Alasdair. "How is the leader selected?"

"There is a race in several weeks, of which the winner is declared the lead rider. It is supposed to be for a previously unselected young, single man who rides well, meant to represent the men who fought against the English."

James sighed. "Guthrie was leader last year but the Guthries have been known to alter rules on occasion. And he threatened he'd get his father to make him lead rider."

"How can he do that? Nobody can guarantee who will win a race."

"You can if you have enough gold to grease enough palms."

"Steady now," said Alasdair. "Don't be making accusations that cannae be supported."

James snorted. "We all know it's how he won last year."

"How so?" Verity asked.

"Colin got some of his friends to ride and cut off the main contenders," Alasdair said, gesturing to James and himself. "That meant us two."

"Really?" Heat filled her chest. "That hardly seems fair."

"Fair?" James snorted. "Guthrie doesn't know the meaning of the word."

"He cheated?" A quick glance at Frances revealed her nod.

Alasdair shrugged. "But knowing that doesn't mean anything will change."

"Guthries are always about Guthries," James muttered.

Helena leaned close to murmur, "Sir Donald Guthrie is the chief marshal."

"Guthries may cheat, but it doesn't help them," Alasdair said. "There is still contention over the heir."

Verity looked a question, to which he continued.

"Colin's father was the previous squire's cousin, but another cousin in England, an earl, has previously contested the will."

"They have spent a fortune fighting this other cousin."

"'He who is greedy of gain troubleth his own house,'" intoned Mr. Chisholm. "Like those who hunt for smugglers' treasure in nonexistent tunnels."

"Smugglers?" asked Benjamin, wide-eyed.

James made an impatient gesture. "I'm sure we'll know more about the lead rider after the masquerade next Friday night."

"A masquerade?" Verity said. "That sounds interesting."

Helena pouted. "For everyone except us."

"The masquerade is no place for innocent young ladies," James said sternly, although Verity thought she caught a wistful expression in Alasdair's eyes.

She was glad he had accepted the Chisholms' invitation to dinner, giving more opportunity to observe the man who had captured Helena's heart. Granted, he might not be the man she would have selected to woo her dearest friend, but he was amiable, he spoke with less arrogance than she expected from a friend of James, and most importantly, his eyes held a soft light whenever he glanced at Helena. Perhaps they would do well together.

"Miss Hatherleigh?"

Verity's mind raced. What had they been speaking of? "I'm afraid I still do not understand why the Ridings are of such importance."

Mr. Chisholm leaned back in his chair and cleared his throat. "The ride-outs stem from the declaration of the royal burgh of Kirkcudbrightshire, and the checking on the boundaries."

"Oh. So it's nothing to do with English and Scottish conflicts?"

James eyed her. "'Tis more about protecting the boundaries from the English, than any of their atrocities against good Scottish folk."

She nodded, focusing instead on his father. "And are there actual rides?"

"Aye. There are actually two main rides. Whilst the boundary checking stems from history, there is also a race to determine the herald, the symbolic leader as it were."

"And this is what you don't want Colin Guthrie to be?"

James jerked a nod, as Alasdair explained, "Whoever wins the race is counted a symbolic leader in the town, too."

"James would be by far the best candidate, certainly far better than Colin, for he at least holds principles."

"And where is this race held?"

Helena eyed her oddly as she replied, "It begins in the midst of town, in St. Cuthbert's street then travels up Barr Hill, then along the ridge to join St. Mary Street, before finally ending at the Castle."

"So it is part endurance ride?"

"It's a distance of twelve miles."

Verity nodded, refusing to meet Helena's eyes while her mind whirred through possibilities of how best to ensure a Guthrie loss. If only she could obtain a better horse for James . . . Her lips twisted. The funds Grandmama had blessed Verity with at the start of her trip might just stretch to such a purchase, but such a gesture would never be accepted. What could she do?

As the conversation swirled around her, an idea sparked, an idea so outlandish her skin tingled. Should she?

Purpose firmed. Verity tilted her chin. Mr. Jardine might think her young and naïve, but perhaps this would show people not to dismiss her so easily, after all.

The continued damp weather had made further visits to tenant properties less than pleasant, and the cheerlessness of his housekeeper, whose offense had resulted in an icy silence these past two days, had once again encouraged him to work with his plants.

He carefully watered the tiny seedlings from a fortnight ago, making notes in his ledger about the seedlings and grafts. How wonderful it would be to see Dungally bloom with botanical samples from the other side of the world. Others had planted specimens from the Himalaya, the rhododendron and camellia, but he had heard of very few who had planted Antipodean varieties.

A shout from outside stole his attention. Pleasure jolted within as he spied his visitors. He wiped his hands on a towel and moved to the door of his potting room.

"Good afternoon, Miss Hatherleigh, Miss Frances, Master Benjamin. I am pleased to see that neither of you are the worse for your recent newt-collecting."

Verity drew closer, the action eliciting a wrenching sensation as he inhaled the sweet perfume of roses, and murmured, "We are here because of tunnels."

"And treasure!" Benjamin said, looking around the space with interest. "I think this is exactly the sort of place a smuggler might use."

Anthony raised an eyebrow. "Smugglers, is it now?"

"I'm afraid so," Frances said apologetically as Benjamin began tapping on the walls. "Papa mentioned something last night."

"I'm sorry to disappoint you, lad, but this outbuilding is only of the most crude design." He took hold of a flimsy section of wood. "I suspect it has only been here for perhaps a dozen years, no more. I'm afraid there would not be any chance of Jacobite hidey-holes in that time."

"But what about smugglers? Surely—"

"Nor smugglers, either," Verity said firmly.

"See? I told you," Frances said with an unladylike eye roll.

Verity sent him a rueful look. "Now, Mr. Jardine appears quite busy, so shall we see if there are any frogs in the pond?"

The small boy pouted. "You just want to talk to him all by yourself." She colored. "I . . ."

"Benjamin, if you can't hold your tongue that'll be the last time you visit here," Frances said, giving him a shake.

"Oh, but Frances—"

"No, Verity. He is far too opinionated for one so young." She turned to her brother. "Now, you need to apologize to Verity or else we're going home without any time for frogs."

He offered Verity a chastened look. "Sorry."

"Never mind," Verity said. "Shall we go look for frogs?"

"You can stay," Frances said, dragging her brother to the door. "You have entertained this wretch long enough." Her lips lifted, a teasing look chasing her consternation. "Besides, I'm sure you would prefer the chance for real conversation rather than a silly boy's prattle, would you not?"

Anthony's cheeks heated at the knowing glance Frances slipped him.

Before further comment could be made, she had dragged Benjamin away, his reluctance fading noticeably as they hurried towards the pond.

"I . . . I should go, too," Verity offered. "I do not want to be in your way. You appear busy."

The awkwardness induced by Frances's sly words compounded by Verity's obvious reluctance to go stilled his tongue. What could he say? He did not want her to leave, for if she left, how could he explain himself, let alone ever master these feelings provoked in her presence?

"What is it you do here?" she asked, peering at the pots lined up on the bench.

"I am collecting seed."

She gently touched a dark, flat pod shaped like a horn. "I have never seen such a thing."

"Because it is from New South Wales."

Her eyes widened. "You have been there?" At his nod a litany of questions were fired at him, necessitating his admittance to the truth of his time in the Antipodes. Yes, he had spent time there. Yes, he had enjoyed his dual roles as assistant curate and unofficial botanist. Yes, he had journeyed across several seas, and seen exotic lands. As weight fell from his shoulders, he derived not a little amount of pleasure from her obvious excitement, as she gazed upon him with an expression of something akin to hero worship.

"Oh, Mr. Jardine, I cannot believe you never mentioned this before! Why, if I had ever been to the Antipodes, I'd be sure to introduce the fact into every conversation I had for the next ten years!"

"A topic that might grow a little dull after a while, perhaps, and would surely ward off potential conversationalists."

"Benefit indeed!"

He chuckled.

"So did you see the natives? Are they truly as dark skinned as people say?"

He nodded. "The Aboriginals are very dark, and very knowledgeable about the plants and animals."

"Which surely makes sense, as they would have lived there far longer than the English. I'm sure they'd have a wealth of information to share, if only the colonists had ears to hear, which, for some reason, I feel sure they do not. People in power rarely listen to those without."

"Indeed."

What a practical view she held. Such common sense, as though she felt sorry for the Aborigines, displaced by the convict colony so arrogantly dispatched from the opposite side of the world, almost as though she believed the original inhabitants held as much value as her people. He studied her as she peered closer at the other seedpods and dried flowers carefully laid upon blotting paper in order to capture every wispy seed, noting the delicate swirl of her ear, the delicate lines of her throat.

"I envy you, Mr. Jardine."

Her lids lifted as she gazed up at him, revealing such unbridled admiration he felt the tips of his ears heat. To cover his confusion, he gestured to the freshly watered pots. "These here are acacias, which develop feathery leaves and bright yellow puffs of flowers. They are often called wattle because the settlers used them for building wattle and daub houses." He gestured to the second set of seeds from the vasculum. "These are the seeds of another plant I hope to propagate, a small bush of spindly leaves with a striking red flower that looks rather brush-like, hence its common name 'Bottlebrush.'" He moved to another paper-lined container and carefully withdrew a dried specimen. The vibrant holly red had faded a little, but the distinctive shape remained. He glanced at his visitor, whose gaze was fixed on his sample.

"Why did you bring it back?"

"I suppose it is my scientific nature, wanting to see if such things can grow here."

She touched it gently. "It is quite wonderful, and very different to anything I've seen."

"The flora is quite remarkable, as is the fauna. Have you heard of the hopping marsupial called a kangaroo?"

"I have heard of such creatures. Have you seen one?"

"Yes. Ingenious creations, capable of bounding faster than a horse."

She sighed. "How I would love to see such things!"

Something stirred across his soul. Was she someone who would not mind the great journey and could envisage life there? Everything about her spoke of her zest for adventure . . .

Except—his spirits drooped—was his life not now here? "I believe they have a hopping kangaroo at the Exeter 'Change."

"I must visit one day. My sister told me about the tricks of the elephant." Her expression grew wistful.

"Ever since I was a young lad I've always loved creation, and marveled at God's design."

"I'm afraid I cannot see how God can take any credit. Surely life is more a matter of coincidence and chance than design."

He blinked.

"Come now, Mr. Jardine. Surely you, a man of science who has traveled to the far reaches of the earth, cannot believe in the existence of an invisible being?"

Nausea rippled through his gut. Did she truly not believe? *Lord, touch her heart.*

He cleared his throat. "On the contrary, Miss Hatherleigh. As a man of science I have not seen anything to give reason to believe otherwise."

"You believe in fairy tales?"

"I believe in the truth of the Bible."

She uttered an unladylike snort and shook her head.

His thoughts raced. What could he say that might touch a hardened heart? He gestured to the trees through the windows. "Do you really believe all of nature is the product of random chance? Do you never stop to think how wondrous it is that such a tiny kernel can contain the spark of life? That, once planted, each seed can perfectly replicate itself and produce new life? To me that suggests order and design, and that a divine plan is at work. I believe we are surrounded by God's handiwork."

"If that is so, then He is not terribly handy sometimes."

"I beg your pardon?"

She shrugged. "He gets things wrong."

"Miss Hatherleigh, I must disa—"

"It is true. My parents have often said I should have been born a boy."

His heart wrenched. Poor lass. "I'm sure they did not mean to suggest such a thing."

"Oh, I'm sure they did. Oh, please do not look at me like that, Mr. Jardine. It cannot be helped. Only it does make me question whether this God of yours—if indeed, He even exists—can be held responsible for so many good things when clearly He gets some things quite wrong."

He said softly, "Do you believe yourself a mistake?"

Her face blanched.

"Miss Hatherleigh?"

She averted her gaze and stepped back. "I . . . I am sorry for intruding upon your time."

"Please, forgive me if I have upset you. I assure you, that was not my intention."

She shook her head, her gaze fixed on his waistcoat button. "Excuse me." And with a whirl of skirts, she disappeared.

He chased her outside, but what she lacked in height she more than made up for in speed. He reached the top of the stairs as she called to Benjamin and Frances, then hastened down the steps to where his bewildered neighbors stood watching as Verity exited the gate.

"Hello, Mr. Jardine."

"Er, hello, Benjamin." Anthony forced his steps to slow, forced his attention to the small boy. "How is the frog expedition going?"

He held up a small bucket. "I found two. See how different they are? This one is spotted all over, but this one is almost completely dark." He frowned. "Why are you chasing Verity?"

"I, er"—he glanced apologetically at Frances—"I was not chasing her, only she seemed upset all of a sudden, and I was unsure of the reason."

"We best return, too." She picked up Benjamin's discarded coat. "Come on, Ben. I have no desire to offer Cready an explanation without Verity's support."

As her brother grumbled, Anthony lowered his voice. "Will you send my apologies? I did not mean to give offense."

"I am sure you did not. But perhaps you could come, too?"

Anthony opened his mouth to speak.

"Mr. Jardine!"

He fought the flicker of annoyance as his housekeeper's piercing call sounded again. "It appears I must leave that for another day."

Frances giggled. "I hope you are not in trouble with the laird."

Anthony grimaced theatrically and waved farewell as the two youngest Chisholms exited the gate and he turned to his red-faced housekeeper, who puffed and huffed toward him.

In trouble with the laird? No.

But troubled within his heart? Most definitely.

CHAPTER SEVENTEEN

A MISTAKE?

Verity collapsed onto her bed, his words ringing in her ears. A mistake. Finally the inner restlessness had a name, the endless quest for acceptance and significance stemming from that whispered conversation of her parents she'd overheard so many years ago.

She was a mistake.

Verity blinked away heat, gulped past the thickness clogging her throat. Was this why she had fought so many times against the bounds of propriety? Why she sought justice for others, as some echo of what she longed for personally, but knew she could never have?

Said like that it made sense at last.

She'd long known she was different, and in past weeks, whether on her solitary morning rides when she practiced riding astride, or when spending time with the younger Chisholms, had been aware of disquiet within. No matter the conversations with Helena and her family, no matter the sense of exultation when she'd managed to stay upright as Firefly leaped across the stream, still the feeling wrinkled her soul, like a badly stitched hem on an undergarment, which made the overdress skew. She'd felt a little skewed. Perhaps it was the knowledge that she had less than three weeks remaining before she would be returned to Somerset. Perhaps it was a kind of loneliness now that Helena, besotted by her beau, had a new interest. Although she still included Verity as much as ever, Verity could not help but feel on the outer side of the bubble that was the enamored couple.

But it wasn't mere loneliness, or fears about her future. Not now Mr. Jardine had exposed the truth she had never wanted to see. The conviction that she, the daughter of a viscount, the heiress to a fortune of fifty thousand pounds, was, in fact, a mistake.

She *was* a mistake. She should have been born a boy. Maybe her mother would have loved her if Papa had an heir.

As it was, the estate was going to have to go to a distant cousin, unless Charles Bromsgrove was willing to take his name. Charles. Weak, namby-pamby, boring old Charles. How could she ever be satisfied with someone like Charles, when she now knew men like Mr. Jardine existed in the world?

Why she still cared when he'd spoken so bluntly to her she did not know, yet she did. But she, who had always prided herself on speaking truth, could not really fault Mr. Jardine for speaking honestly. And in some deep part of her heart, she was glad he was prepared to do so; such was a mark of true friendship, was it not? He would certainly not meet her parents' approval, but she could not imagine anyone nicer, or more interesting, or who caused her heart to thump most erratically whenever he smiled . . .

She bit down on her bottom lip to stop its quiver.

There was a tap on the door. Verity swiped at an errant tear. "Yes?"

Helena entered. "Verity, the most amazing thing!"

Verity pinned on a smile. "Is it something to do with your Alasdair?"

"How did you know?"

"Only that *amazing* and *Alasdair* seem to occur in regular context as far as you are concerned." She patted the bed beside her. "Come, tell me."

"His parents are coming tonight for dinner!"

"Things must be progressing nicely if that is so."

"Oh, I hope so."

As Helena chattered on, Verity couldn't help but wonder what it would be like to have parents like the Chisholms, so open and willing to support their daughter and provide assurance of their love. Helena was most certainly not a mistake.

"Verity?"

She blinked. "I am sorry, Helena. What did you say?"

"I must go see if Mama needs my help before getting dressed for tonight."

"Alasdair will love you even if you wear sackcloth and ashes."

"But his parents might not." With a giggle and a wave, Helena exited, leaving Verity to resume her dark, eddying thoughts, and wonder if the man she admired might ever win approval from her parents. And wonder if she might ever win the same.

Lord, what do I do?

Anthony stared out the window as the voices droned and his mind whirled.

"For it is the duty of the laird to administer justice . . ."

He studied the swaying trees outside. Why had someone chosen this room to be the study? While it faced the front drive, he could not see the view of the Dee, which held far greater appeal these days. It wasn't as if anyone interesting ever visited via the front anyway, apart from this long delayed visit from the two crofters, whose dispute over sheep had finally led them to seek an audience with the laird today. No, the only visitors that sparked interest held a far more relaxed attitude when visiting their neighbor, although this was now the third day since his careless comment had sent her running, and demands from tenants and solicitors and bankers had still prevented his apol—

"Mr. Jardine?"

Anthony returned his attention to the two crofters, whose matching frowns and body language suggested their dislike was not merely with each other. "I am sorry, but I don't fully understand. You want me to feed all the sheep until the matter of ownership is resolved?"

"Aye," said Angus McDonald.

"That be so," echoed Geordie Ferguson.

"And if you do not resolve the ownership?"

McDonald shrugged. "You have more grass than we do."

"That be so," affirmed Ferguson.

But if they foisted all their sheep on his land . . .

Lord, what do I do?

He waited, listening for the still, small voice as the ruddy-faced giants eyed him. Eventually verses about King Solomon floated into memory.

He cleared his throat. "Gentlemen, your reluctance to separate the sheep into two flocks confounds me." He held up a hand to halt their protest. "While I can understand your desire to see your sheep feasting on my gardens, I admit to having some reservations. Now although I do not pretend to be an expert on livestock, a solution to your dilemma does present itself. As you are aware, there are many in the surrounding district who, if not precisely starving, would doubtless appreciate a good meal of mutton, and this is where your sheep come in."

He watched with satisfaction as their eyes widened and mouths gaped.

"I am sure we do not need to kill them all at once, merely one at a time until my steward has determined there be no remaining hungry mouths in the district. This way we'll be sure to alleviate the problem of grazing and be serving the community in a most magnanimous way. Why, you could almost consider it a tithe unto the Lord, seeing as you'll be blessing so many of the poor and needy."

"I consider it more like highway robbery," growled McDonald.

"Aye, that be so!" harrumphed Ferguson.

"You do not approve? Well, perhaps you can come up with another solution."

The two men exchanged looks. "I be thinking we can."

With a steely glint in their eyes, they touched their forelocks and exited the room none too quietly. In fact, Anthony was almost positive he heard the words "touched in his upper works" bandied about.

His lips pushed to one side. At least he had solved one problem of his lairdship, and thus provided something of amusement in an otherwise trying day.

"I see those two rascals have finally gone."

Anthony nodded to McNaughton. "And not before time. Where was I going to find room for two hundred sheep?"

His steward nodded wisely. "Seemed you were inspired."

"Perhaps I was."

He settled back in his chair, taking a moment to enjoy the rare pleasure of getting something right, before returning his attention to Mr. Osgood's latest correspondence. According to the solicitor's epistle, the estate finances had ceased their slow leak. Indeed, he seemed cautiously optimistic that estate matters might be getting back on the right track. Of course, it had helped that many of the tenants' problems had managed to be sorted out with minimal expenditure, save for Anthony's own sweat and hours. Replacing glass and thatch from stores lying in Dungally's grounds was easy; so easy, in fact, he wondered why David had not thought to do so himself. Had his cousin been *that* distracted by his obligations to his wife and child? Perhaps some ladies were more insistent than others on having their husband's full and undivided attention. His lips twisted. Perhaps it was a good thing he was not so entangled. He could well see Amelia holding such expectations, if she ever deigned to remove to the wilds of southwest Scotland, away from the delights of living near Edinburgh.

His spirit grew heavier, matching the unrelenting rain outside. Why was it that thoughts of Amelia always led to feelings of burden, whereas thoughts of the young lady next door made him smile? But she was so young, so lacking faith, so . . . completely unsuitable.

He shook his head at the folly of such thinking and returned his attention to the problem at hand, namely, how to make the land more profitable. Osgood had recommended on more than one occasion selling some of the land in order to improve income. But that was hardly reasonable for the crofters whose families had farmed there for generations. And he would not, he *could* not, employ the tactics of those landowners further north whose method of achieving estate profitability was to clear off surplus tenants in order to raise sheep. Why, the very thought was inhumane! Sheep before people? No.

But something needed to be done or else the crofters would need to leave. What could he do?

Lord?

Words spoken on his initial tenant visit flickered through his mind. Soil improvement . . .

He pushed back his chair and went down the hall.

"Mr. Jardine?"

He ignored his housekeeper and strode outside, down to the estuary, out to the section where young Benjamin had been seeking frogs. Surely if frogs could survive here, there had to be sufficient living matter for them to do so. And the sufficient living matter was what was needed by the farmers to improve their soil.

He picked up a handful of kelp. The thick, leathery folds emitted a pungent tang of brine, but deep within lay life-giving properties that sustained marine animals, and might just help sustain estate animals also. He tore a leathery flap in two, squinting as he studied the tiny segments. Really he should have his glass to see things in greater depth, but regardless . . . How amazing was God to have created such things!

He hurried to the cellars where Mac was finishing inventory. "We are going to conduct another experiment, my friend."

Mac's gray brows rose.

"Kelp is rich in minerals long leached from the soil. If we can find a way of mixing the two, surely it can only be for the betterment of the land."

Mac slowly nodded. "Aye. My family has used seaweed up north for some time now, but you might have a job of it. People round here make a tidy profit selling it in Glasgow for soap and glassmaking."

"Surely providing food is of greater worth than making soap."

"I be thinking, as Wesley said, that some might prefer cleanliness ahead of godliness."

Ideas sparked and fizzed within. "The crofters before were concerned about the poor production from their land. If we were to demonstrate improved soil then surely it would help convince them to try cropping again."

Anthony hurried to his potting room, noting with satisfaction the row of pots lined up against the window, which contained his Antipodean experiment. His experiment, carefully recorded, was already bearing results, the tiny feathery seedlings having grown to a measurable state in recent days. So if that could work . . .

He hauled out several more pots, half filling each with a varying layer of soil he had retrieved from the overrun kitchen garden. That soil, already rich in organic matter, had hosted his seedlings, so it stood to reason that when mixed with kelp it should prove even more productive. Using a knife, he cut the kelp he'd collected before into tiny pieces. Several of these he put aside; the rest he placed into a mortar and crushed with a pestle. Briny juice stained the gray bowl brown, while the pungent odor caused him to sneeze. Ah, the joys of being laird.

He studied his pots. The first would be his control sample, without kelp. He placed the strips of cut kelp into the second of the pots, leaving it atop the soil. He scooped a portion of crushed kelp into the third, again not mixing it. The fourth, fifth, and sixth pots he varied the proportion of crushed kelp to soil, mixing it in thoroughly each time. He stepped back, wiped his hands on a towel, then carefully labeled and recorded his plans in his ledger.

"Sir?"

"Ah, Mac." Anthony explained his plans. "But I suspect it would be better to leave the kelp time to break down, which is why I've crushed it, to simulate that. But I am hopeful kelp will prove the estate's salvation."

"*Kelp* prove salvation, sir?"

"Yes, well, we both know God is our salvation, but we can thank Him for creating such a resource. Now, I plan to plant potato tubers and corn seed into them and we will see if there is any improvement."

And, God willing, there would be.

THE FOLLOWING DAY brought renewed focus; amazing what a restful night's sleep could accomplish. After spending time reading in

Psalms, he'd tackled the bookkeeping, making notes about wages and expenses against his ever-dwindling supply of funds. Good thing God was his heavenly provider, for Anthony had little provision left of his own.

He prayed as he escaped his study for the potting shed. *Lord, another miracle wouldn't go astray . . .*

With Iverson off to freshly plough the kitchen garden, Anthony elected to sharpen the scythe, so there be no cause for Iverson to slacken his efforts this afternoon. He had finished adjusting the blade when a slight cough stole his attention.

"Mac. What can I help you with?"

"Sir, I just wanted to check there was nothing you required from the village."

"You're going now?"

"To collect the dog, yes."

Ah. The Aberdeen terrier from a local elderly gentleman who could no longer care for it, or so Mr. Chisholm had advised several weeks ago. He could only hope—and pray—this would finally solve Mrs. Iverson's complaints about mice.

"I cannot think of anything else, thank you." He coughed, bracing himself against the wall, then dropping his hand as he noted Mac's look of concern.

"Pardon my saying, sir, but ye seem a wee bit tired from all the helping ye do. I think you needs be careful about working overly much—"

"Mac, I'm neither an old man nor a babe. I am well able to handle my responsibilities, especially with someone so reliable to lean on. Now, tell me what you think about harvesting. I know it's early days, but I was thinking . . ."

He swapped thoughts with McNaughton, and had plunged into a deep conversation about the merits of the modern harvesting techniques used in Sydney compared with some of the more traditional ones, when the familiar call of "Mr. Jardine!" screeched again.

He bit back a sigh, met McNaughton's amused gaze, and turned to his puffing housekeeper. "What is it, Mrs. Iverson?"

"You have a visitor, sir!" she gasped.

His heart kicked. She had forgiven him! He fought a smile, strove for nonchalance. "Someone looking for tunnels?"

She wiped her brow. "Looking for—? No, no. A young lady. Come, you must hurry!"

His excitement faded, his brows lowering. Mrs. Iverson would never urge him to see Miss Hatherleigh; quite the contrary. In fact, on the few occasions when Verity had not found him, his house-keeper appeared to have taken a very long time to announce his next-door neighbor's arrival. But if not Verity, then—?

His heart thudded afresh as he strode up the multitude of steps. Could Amelia truly have come? No. Visiting without invitation was not her style. He hurried inside, up to his bedchamber to cleanse his hands at the washstand. As he raced down the central staircase, he caught a glimpse of a coach through the stained glass. A coach? He pushed open the door to the Rose Room. Who—?

"Ah, Mr. Jardine at last. I was beginning to wonder if I'd see you again."

He stared into the pretty face, framed with golden curls and wearing a coquettish smile. "Mrs. Ramsay!"

Sea air scraped her cheeks as Verity trudged the rock-strewn path between Dungally House and the rectory. She had been reluctant to visit these past three days. Had not wanted to see him after he told her she was a mistake; had not known what to say. Her lips twisted. To do Mr. Jardine justice, he hadn't actually said she *was* a mistake. His error had only been one of delivery, probing her secret wound with his bluntness, asking if she believed herself so.

The conviction that she was a mistake pressed on her soul like a finger on a bruise. But this morning she had sensed the need to visit again, to prove to him that she was not offended. Besides, she had long despised moroseness, and these past days had sought to hide her pain with a smile, to distract herself with her secret rides, geography lessons with Ben, and visiting with Mrs. Chisholm and Helena. She'd give no reason for anyone to mistrust her feelings, to suspect what lived deep in her heart.

Except Mr. Jardine seemed to have suspected.

She blinked away the burn in her eyes and shook her head at herself, entering the gate in the white wall before moving slowly through the garden to stand beside the now flowing Diana-adorned fountain. She might be thought a failure, a mistake, by some, but at least there were certain things she could regard with pride. Perhaps some of the yews were a little crooked—although, she peered closer, it appeared they had miraculously been trimmed more evenly—but if she hadn't coerced the others to help, then Dungally's gardens would still be in a sorry state.

And really, she thought, moving to the top of the steps to the terrace, who wouldn't want to gaze over beautiful gardens such as these every day of their life? The laird *should* be appreciative, even if Mr. Jardine had needed to reshape some of her attempts to cut yew trees. At least she'd tried to help. He should be thankful for her efforts!

She drank in the view. Far away in the distance a boat slipped through sparkling blue. Envy tugged. How lucky were the current—and future—inhabitants of Dungally House. If only . . .

A high-pitched giggle crept past the corner of the house. Verity's brows rose. That didn't sound like Helena, and she'd just left Frances back in the morning room of the rectory. There was no way she could have beaten Verity here. Then who—?

She crept to the side and peeked. No one.

Seconds later the screechy sound came again. She frowned. Was the mysterious female—for surely no lady could be responsible for making such a noise—one of the laird's friends? Her heart skipped. Did this mean she might finally see him?

She hurried down the side of the house, thankful for once that the laird employed few servants. Though it might mean extra work for Mr. Jardine, at least there was less chance of being outed as a spy. She paused, bare hands splayed against the sun-warmed stone as she strained to hear the voices. Still indistinct, but one was definitely female, the other voice deeper, smooth as satin, like . . . Mr. Jardine's? What?

Slowly she peered around the corner.

At first she could see nothing, the voices suggesting they might be in the great doorway, then a figure moved into view. A voluptuous figure, dressed in a blue pelisse—one she recognized as the latest crack—the woman's golden head smiling up at Mr. Jardine. A servant, one she didn't recognize, glanced her way. Verity ducked back, mind whirling.

She should go. She should return to the rectory. Find something useful and productive to fill her time. She *really* should go—

Except she had to know who the woman was.

Leaving her position against the wall, she stole across the lawn to the rose bed, its blooms tickling her with rich scents, their spindly branches not a very effective screen, but a screen nonetheless. She had to know. Who *was* that woman?

Verity peered through the branches, eyes greedy for him. From here she could see Mr. Jardine, dressed somewhat casually for such a well-dressed visitor, but carrying himself with unconscious grace and his usual ease of manner. His hair, dark in the shadowed recesses of the building, held its usual disarray, which made her wonder how often he'd pushed his hand through it today, and whether he would appreciate a wife who might smooth it down for him, or even cut it for him, even if she might not do so perfectly, thus necessitating him to fix it later . . .

She gulped.

The woman tinkled laughter then placed a hand on Mr. Jardine's arm.

Heat surged through Verity's chest. How *dare* she? Mr. Jardine moved slightly, putting greater distance between himself and the lady. As well he should, Verity thought indignantly. How could the woman—for she was certainly no lady—not realize her behavior was indecent? That Mr. Jardine possessed a warm, attractive manner and his face held a charm could not be denied, but ladies did not simply throw themselves at a man!

But perhaps Mr. Jardine—so good, so kindhearted—was as blind as her former schoolmate Lucy's young man, and could only see some lovesick fantasy.

Her hands clenched, as something hot slashed her heart again.

He should be *hers!*

She exhaled. How ridiculous! Especially as she was as good as engaged to another, and her parents would have fits. But there it was. It was like the curtains had parted, revealing the truth. Something about Mr. Jardine made her mouth dry and her heart thump and her brain not function quite as it ought. And despite her circumstances, and the hints from Helena and her mother, she could not shake this feeling that Mr. Jardine was meant to be hers. *Hers!*

Caught in the maelstrom of emotion, she smiled bitterly at herself. People did not really belong to others, despite Mama's thoughts about servants and their indebtedness to masters. But still, existing deep within her was this jolt of recognition that he, Mr. Jardine, humble gardener though he may be, was intended by the universe to be with her, and she with him. And judging from that look in his eyes she caught sometimes, he might believe it, too.

The woman's heinous laughter screeched again. How *could* Mr. Jardine prefer that kind of woman? Was it simply because the lady was older? Did she share his faith?

Verity ground her teeth. How could she share his faith if she did not know what to believe? If Papa's view on life was not correct and God truly did exist, as the Chisholms and Mr. Jardine believed, then was she doomed to an eternity in hell for her unbelief? A kind of yearning for something true, something solid to stand on, yawned before her. What if she and Papa *were* wrong?

She parted the branches, muffling an exclamation as a thorn bit her hand.

The woman moved, appeared to gaze directly at her. Verity lifted her chin and met her look squarely, whereupon the woman smiled wider and murmured something to Mr. Jardine, who turned her direction.

Verity ducked down, shame at being caught spying lending wings to her feet as she raced, hunchback-like, down the grassy verge to the stone steps. From somewhere behind she heard the sound of carriage wheels crunching over gravel, but she ignored it, running through the garden and out the gate, dragging in hasty breaths of the salty tang as she hurried to the rectory stables. Her heart wrenched, tipping between hot guilt at being caught, nausea that Mr. Jardine would prove less than what she'd imagined, and disgust at herself for running away—that was *twice* now she had run away. Why? She was no coward! She brushed away tears.

She shook her head. Forget it. Forget him. She would show him!

❦ CHAPTER EIGHTEEN

FLORA RAMSAY LEANED down from the carriage window. "And that elfin creature? Your *paramour*, perhaps?"

Anthony gulped, his cheeks heating. "She is but a friend."

"Oho, a friend, who does not like you speaking with other ladies." Her smile widened. "She seems a little young. Not quite the worthy I imagined you would select."

No. That worthy lived in Linlithgow. He cleared his throat and said stiffly, "I have done nothing to secure her affections."

She laughed her annoying high-pitched laugh. "But you need do nothing, dear Jardine. Your charm lies in the fact you do not realize just how charming you can be." She flashed another smile. "Now, I hope you will visit me one day. Perhaps when you possess a wife, if that makes you more comfortable?"

He wished to tug at his cravat that had tightened considerably. Was he that transparent? "Please extend my good wishes to your husband, Mrs. Ramsay."

"Gerald? He forfeited his right to know what I do when he refused to accompany me home." Her eyes flashed, her chin quivered.

Having no wish to become embroiled in her marriage difficulties, he said hastily, "I wish you good travels, madam."

"And I wish you good hunting, Mr. Jardine." She uttered a laugh without much mirth and commanded the coachman to drive on.

Anthony forced himself to enact the role of a good host with his feet planted on the steps of the portico as the carriage rumbled away.

Of all the times for Flora Ramsay to visit. He shook his head. What had Verity thought? His lips twisted. It was very apparent what she'd thought, her shock writ as large on her face as her running away proved. His heart wrenched. Poor lass. But perhaps it was for the best. She was not for him, no matter how much this attraction swirled between them.

He exhaled heavily. *Lord, she does not believe, so this cannae be from you. Forgive me for my nonsense.*

The sounds of the carriage faded, the air grew still, quiet. But within he still felt tightly coiled, his heart a mess of conflicted emotions, frustration knotting his fingers. The heaviness gathered, reminders of responsibilities—to his tenants, to Dungally, to his parents, to Amelia!—crept in, pushing hard against his chest, pounding in his temples.

"Enough!" He called back into the hall. "I'm going for a walk."

Without waiting for an answer, he set off. Gritted his teeth. This was *not* in the hopes of seeing any neighbors. *Not* with the intention of explaining Mrs. Ramsay's visit. Why should he explain himself? No, this was just a chance to clear his head, to find a quiet space where he might be able to hear the Lord's voice, and hopefully experience some peace instead of this incessant restlessness.

He strode through the oaks lining the drive, their overarching branches filtering light, filtering warmth. He thrust his hands in the pockets of his coat. By the time he'd cleared the trees' gloom the sky had darkened, its heaviness reflecting his soul. At the gates he turned firmly left, up the hill, following the estate boundary.

As he walked, a fine mist damped his face, the clouds merging to blur the crest of the hill with white. A fine Scotch mizzle, indeed.

He trudged on.

What was he to do? This attraction refused to die. Should he get away? But how could he leave Dungally? There was still so much to do. The weight of his responsibilities bore down again. He studied the pasture, imagining it filled with the vibrant greens of flourishing crops as existed on the Guthrie land. Would the kelp idea work? Should he follow Mac's ideas about diversification, and plant potatoes and turnips as well as oats, seek to establish dairy as well as sheep? If Dungally could develop, then there would be work for his tenants, which could only bless and prosper them all. And wasn't a blessing what he felt God had called him to be?

Somehow his feet led him to the tenant house he had first visited weeks ago.

Mrs. Boyd opened the door before he had time to knock. "Mr. Jardine! I 'twas nae expectin' a visit from you today."

"I wanted to check you are keeping warmer, now the roof and window are fixed."

"Aye, it be so." She peered behind him. "But where is your horse? Never be telling me you walked all this way from the big house."

"Aye, it be so." He managed a smile.

A pinkish tinge, that on any lesser personage might almost be considered a blush, filled her cheeks. "Why you be a rapscallion, for all ye are a laird. Now, lad, would ye be caring for a wee bite? I've made oatcakes."

His demur was overridden by her insistence. "Now, perhaps ye can tell me why you've been out. Estate troubles, is it?"

Her curious beady eyes elicited the truth. "I've been thinking on how best to improve the lands. I'm making enquiries about the use of kelp."

"Kelp?" She sighed. "Well, ye can try, but I don't much like yer chances."

"Unfortunately we seem to be running low on those."

She snorted. "Do I not see you attend services? Do ye not believe in this God to whom ye pray? Or does He not hear ye because ye do without the Catechism and instead pray those fancy English prayers?"

Anthony murmured something conciliatory then resumed nibbling on a dry oatcake. The rain pattered lightly against the window, making him doubly glad he'd sought to mend it when he had. The rain . . .

Would Verity be safely back inside, or had she gone for a ride? He hoped she was—

"I be thinking ye got something else on yer mind, lad." She peered over the top of her saucer. "A lass, p'raps?"

Heat flushed his cheeks.

She cackled. "I knew it! A man with such braw looks cannae be ignored for long."

"I don't think so," he said firmly.

"Nonsense! Modesty nae become ye when it's an obvious lie. I heard a lass say so just the other day." She sniffed. "A gawky lass she was, prancing about, wantin' to know about the laird. Why when she was Soothron, I dinnae."

His heart jumped. Verity! He forced his fingers to unclench. "What did you say?"

"I gave her what for, that's what I did. Snirtlin' the laird was plain! I told her she needed eyes in her head."

"She thought me plain?" His voice sounded strange, but perhaps that was the odd ache in his heart.

"Not like she's brinkie!"

His soul protested; he thought Verity quite comely, indeed.

"Braisant, I call it."

He downed the remaining oatcake with difficulty. "She is young."

"Well, we don't want prood ones round 'ere."

"I am sure she means no harm."

But when she continued to harangue poor Verity, and his ability to control his rising temper became increasingly difficult, he pushed back his chair. "Thank you, but I must go."

"But it be bucketing down! 'Tis foolishness to be out in this dreich."

"Nevertheless, I must not stay." He forced a smile. "Thank you for your kind hospitality."

He farewelled Mrs. Boyd and moved back down her goat track of a drive, back toward home.

Rain sloshed around the base of his boots, his shirt stuck to his back, and he soon started thinking his need to escape Mrs. Boyd's house had been foolishly premature. But to listen to more of Verity's faults was unfathomable. Even if she did think him plain . . .

His lips twisted wryly. He'd never accounted himself a vain man, but the English girl's comments had cut deeper than he cared to admit.

About halfway down the rise, he saw a rider. He watched, marveling at the grace and speed with which she rode: sailing over hedges, thundering across the heath, posture fixed, determined, as if to escape the devil himself. But why did she travel without an escort? His brow knit.

The rider turned, coming toward him. He caught a glimpse of a dark fringe of hair and pointed chin. He stepped towards her. "Miss Hatherleigh?"

She slowed, straightened, the blue eyes he remembered as always being filled with light now red-rimmed. Was she unwell? Had she been crying? What a far cry from the joyous creature he had encountered on this same stretch of road previously.

"Good afternoon, Mr. Jardine."

His mind raced, desperate to avoid mentioning the earlier incident, to not embarrass her. "Is it not a trifle damp to be out riding?"

"One could say the same about your walking, sir."

"Ah, but I'm a Scot. If we heeded every wee mizzle we'd never venture anywhere."

She nodded, her gaze shuttered, before nudging the horse as if to leave.

"Miss Hatherleigh, please. Do you attend services tomorrow?"

"One can hardly be permitted otherwise when staying in a minister's house."

"Do you see nothing of worth or benefit for yourself?"

Her gaze finally met his, hurt shining in the blue depths. "I don't know what I want anymore."

And before he could ask her meaning she turned and galloped away, leaving him feeling even more miserable than before.

CHAPTER NINETEEN

"MAMA WILL NEVER agree! She will simply say we are too young to attend."

"Helena, I never knew you to be so poor-spirited before. Are you so quick to forget Miss Haverstock's favorite play? Surely you cannot so quickly forget your namesake's words 'Our remedies oft in ourselves do lie.' No obstacle is too great to be insurmountable."

Helena laughed. "I do not know why you should be so set on attending a country rout, but if you must, I suppose we must."

"The mark of a true friend indeed."

"Besides, I would quite like to see you shake this mood you've been in since last Saturday. I noticed you scarcely exchanged two words with Mr. Jardine yesterday at services."

"I did not think you had time to notice, not with Alasdair's mother commanding your attention."

Helena blushed. "Her invitation to luncheon *was* unexpected, I must admit. But we are not talking of me, but you. Are you sure nothing is the matter?"

"Quite sure," Verity's smile became fixed. So her efforts to hide her disappointment had not been completely successful. Mr. Jardine might have made his choice; she'd obviously been mistaken in her assumptions, and could not hold it against him. Regardless, she would simply need to work harder, dredge up even more enthusiasm to compensate. "Let's find your mother."

They found Mrs. Chisholm listening to her firstborn in the drawing room. She looked up with an unmistakable air of relief. "Ah, Helena, Verity. We have just been discussing the Ridings."

"Really, Mama? I *am* surprised."

At James's flush, Verity spoke. "I'm sure the inclement weather is disappointing, but I suppose it does mean your horse will be rested for the race."

"Very well rested," he muttered.

"And it may clear, mightn't it?" Verity turned to Mrs. Chisholm. "I hope it does at least in time for the masque."

"Oh dear me, yes," said Mrs. Chisholm. "Those evenings are hard enough without rain being involved."

"Yes. It's such a shame you won't be in attendance, sister dear." James's gaze moved to Verity. "Although I would like the opportunity to dance with you, Miss Hatherleigh."

Verity forced a smile to her lips. Perhaps this was her way in. She turned to Mrs. Chisholm. "Must such an opportunity be forgone? I have never seen such a charming village event and would dearly love to."

"I'm afraid it is not quite the thing for young girls to attend."

"Oh, but Mama, if you and Papa attend, surely it cannot be so bad."

"Helena, your father and I attend only because his position demands such a thing. I have often found masked merriments have proved an opportunity to dance with danger."

Verity's chest thumped. To dance with danger? The night sounded even more enticing!

"We would be well protected by your chaperonage, Mrs. Chisholm," Verity murmured, before looking at James. "And your escort, of course."

"But I can't help feel it would be something your mother would frown on."

Verity's smile grew strained. There were a great many things her mother frowned upon.

Mrs. Chisholm offered a sympathetic look. "You do understand, don't you, my dear?"

Verity swallowed. "I understand."

"Mrs. Cready will be here, and the children, of course."

Helena's face held comical dismay. "She is not going?"

"Of course not. She despises these events, says they are little more than an opportunity for wickedness to prevail."

"Surely she does not say such things to you." Verity frowned. "Not when the minister attends."

Mrs. Chisholm sighed. "I believe there are not many who meet with Mrs. Cready's high standards."

"Then why keep her on?"

"Verity!"

Mrs. Chisholm looked from her daughter to Verity. "I'm afraid to lose her would cause more trouble than it's worth."

"But—"

"Come, Verity," Helena said, dragging her away. "Please don't cause Mama anxiety over the Cready," she murmured, once safely back in Helena's room, with the door firmly shut against eager ears. "She finds her very trying."

"But I do not understand why she remains. Surely giving unsatisfactory service is grounds for dismissal."

Helena sighed. "I'm afraid Mama and Papa do not see her service as such, and Papa has such a soft heart, he could not bear to turn someone away who has lived here so long. I understand Mama's decision is upsetting, but we expected as much, did we not?"

"We did, but it is not upsetting."

"Not upsetting?"

Verity smiled. "I did not say I would not go, only that I understood that my mother would not wish me to attend."

Helena's eyes widened. "But is that not the same thing? I know you do not wish to lie, but surely this is deception."

"Do you wish to remain home on Friday night?"

Helena's mouth pressed together.

"I thought not."

"But a masquerade requires costumes! How would we ever find something suitable at this late stage?"

"Come, where is your sense of adventure? Surely we can improvise. Your mama, what does she dress as?"

"I . . . I don't know."

Verity bit back an impatient reply and hurried back to Mrs. Chisholm. Verity's offer of Mary's assistance was accepted gratefully, her mild enquiry regarding costumes eliciting the confession that the reverend and she did not intend to dress up, although the reverend would condescend to them both wearing masks.

"Which is a shame, as when we lived in Glasgow in our younger days, we often attended revels of various kinds." Mrs. Chisholm sighed wistfully. "I used to enjoy dressing up. My sister and I used to wear real Venetian masks, along with our French ballgowns, although I suppose they were a little too saucy in hindsight. However, I had a delightful shepherdess costume, which I did not feel *entirely* out of character for one married to a minister."

"Do you still have them?" Verity asked.

"Oh, they are sure to be around here somewhere." Mrs. Chisholm's brow creased. "In fact, it probably would be good to find those masks again."

"I can help you," Verity said. "In fact, I believe I have a shawl which might suit you admirably."

At Mrs. Chisholm's fluttered acceptance, Verity and Helena spent a most enjoyable afternoon looking at and laughing over clothes, almost to the point of forgetting their purpose, until Helena mentioned it again later that night.

"I suppose we could wear Mama's old costumes, although the bodice is a little low . . ."

"Only for a buxom lass, and as neither of us are, it should fit well with a fichu or scarf. Just think! Your mama even has the wigs to match!"

Helena bit her lip. "But if we were found out—"

"It is a masquerade. How will anyone know if we do attend?"

"But Cready will—"

"Not if we are indisposed." Verity smiled. "Remember that time with Miss Pelling?"

Helena's lips stretched into a reluctant smile. "But what if she returns to your room to see how you fare?"

"I will keep it locked and feign sleep."

"And what about me?"

Verity thought a moment. "If I retire early, then perhaps you remain reading below for a short while, then complain of being bored and retire to read in bed, too. In which time we can both get dressed and escape out the window."

"But it is so high!"

Verity smiled. "I have a plan."

Anthony looked up from the letter he had been reading and glanced at the window, the pattering rain a steady accompaniment to his morning's dealings with lawyers, creditors, and other more pleasant tasks. The floor-length windows emitted only thin light, but while the heavy brocade curtains might warm the room slightly, he found their tattered state so depressing he flung them open whenever he needed to work in this room. He drew a bone handled letter knife through another envelope, the address penned by an unfamiliar, though definitely feminine, hand. Read the short epistle, examined the invitation.

A whining sound drew his attention down to where a black terrier gazed up at him.

"Ah, Dougal." Anthony rubbed between the pointed ears. "Want my attention, do you?"

The dog uttered a short bark, eliciting Anthony's smile.

"Can't find any more mice, is that it?" Although he found that hard to believe. But at least the complaints about mice from the maids and housekeeper had reduced in recent days. Dougal was proving to be worth his weight in meaty bones.

The dog sniffed, and without further ado, padded from the room, no doubt off to find another rodent.

Anthony's attention returned to his correspondence, and he tapped the letter against the side of the elaborately carved desk. Gilt inlaid and glass topped, upon which sat a pair of candlesticks, the desk was doubtless another of his great-uncle's acquisitions. His uncle had certainly held eclectic tastes, his eye for value questionable, as in the dragon-festooned tinplate candelabrum he'd discovered Mrs. Iverson polishing in the dining room. Her assurances it was silver only ceased when he showed her the lack of a silversmith's mark, and it had been swiftly bundled into a sack along with several other monstrosities. Why the twelfth laird felt such an ugly thing worth keeping Anthony would never know. But then, there were so many things that left him at a loss, such as whether he should accept this invitation. Should he?

It would be nice to forgo some of his responsibilities that ate into every available jot of time. If it wasn't the building requiring attention, it was tenants; if not money shortfall, then drama with his servants. One of the maids had quit yesterday, her hysterical outpourings about Mrs. Iverson such that he'd had to bring her in for questioning, whereupon he learned about his housekeeper's bullying. Poor girl. He had severely reprimanded Mrs. Iverson, who had apologized—gruffly—but the lass was insistent she'd not work for her "bein' such a crabbit as she is!"

And Anthony could scarcely blame her. Indeed, it would take a lady of formidable character to dampen his housekeeper's overbearing manner. Yet he'd seen Verity do it . . .

Groaning, he returned his attention to the invitation. Mrs. Ramsay requested his attendance at a small house party in several weeks, culminating in a ball. Well, he certainly had no desire to attend the house party, but perhaps it would be nice to meet others in similar positions, to glean from their experience. He laid it aside, turning his attention back to the other matters requiring decisions.

The myriad of activities demanded by his duties provided some level of distraction, although the familiar sense of restlessness continued. He'd hoped the walk on Saturday would help. It hadn't. He'd tried to pray it away at services, but the small measure of peace he'd found had vanished the moment he'd spotted Verity outside; or perhaps more accurately, his jolt of anticipation had dissipated when he'd realized she was maintaining a polite distance. His lips pursed. It was probably for the best, but still, the loss of her bright chatter and laughter had made the days drag. He glanced outside as the steady patter of rain on glass continued. So she still hadn't forgiven him.

AFTER ANOTHER FRUITLESS night's sleep, and with no sign of the weather improving, Anthony decided to visit the neighboring property. Perhaps he could somehow explain Mrs. Ramsay's unexpected visit.

He knocked on the door, which was soon answered by a wide-faced housekeeper who looked him up and down. "Yairs?"

"Good afternoon. I was wondering if Miss Hatherleigh might spare me a few moments of her time."

"And whom might ye be?"

"Mr. Jardine, from next door."

Her eyes narrowed, then she nodded, and shut the door in his face.

He smiled wryly, taking cover under the thin sliver of protection offered by the sloping doorway. No wonder she looked at him askance, coming here with his muddied boots and spattered coat. Was this just a fool's errand?

The door opened. He looked up and met Verity's shocked face. "Good afternoon."

"Mr. Jardine! Come in, please. I cannot believe you've been made to wait outside on such a wet day." She shot the housekeeper a baleful look. "I'm sure Mrs. Chisholm would not like to know a guest has been made to wait in such horrid conditions." She glanced at him before sternly eyeing the older woman. "A pot of tea and some cake might help Mr. Jardine feel more the thing, thank you, Mrs. Cready."

The woman's lips flattened. "Yes, miss."

Verity nodded regally, then returned her attention to him, her expression much warmer than on recent encounters.

Obeying her gesture to the door, he murmured, "Miss Hatherleigh, I do not wish to trouble the staff—"

"But I do," she whispered, and closed the door firmly to the kitchen. "Mrs. Cready is rather too nice in her opinion of how this establishment should be run, and bosses poor Mrs. Chisholm continuously. I've made it a personal mission to remind her of her duties to the family so they receive the respect and attention they deserve. So thank you for providing another opportunity to do so."

"You're welcome."

She smiled, and a trace of the old ease flowed between them once more, releasing a snarl in his heart. Perhaps she might understand, after all. She opened another door, which led to a cozy sitting room. A fire crackled warmth into the room crowded with furniture and more than a few people, including several female Chisholm family members, a sleeping dog, and two cats.

"Here is Mr. Jardine," Verity proclaimed, "come to rescue us from complete boredom."

"Truly a knight in shining armor!"

He smiled. "I'm afraid you rather overstate things, Miss Frances."

"Good afternoon, Mr. Jardine," said Mrs. Chisholm. "Please come, take a seat."

"I apologize for my attire, Mrs. Chisholm. I did not expect to see you all."

"Only one of us perhaps?" The older lady's eyes twinkled. "Come. Sit down. Don't worry about your apparel."

"Besides, you are no worse than James when he comes in after a day's ride," said Helena.

"And we much prefer to see you than he," added Frances. "His conversation is rather limited these days."

He glanced at Verity as Mrs. Chisholm hushed her younger daughter. "I'm afraid I have really only come to ensure you have not suffered any ill effects after your ride in the rain."

"I am quite well, thank you, as no doubt you saw at services," Verity replied.

"Please forgive me, but you did not seem completely yourself."

"Do you think me missish, sir? I assure you, I am not in the habit of swooning."

"Missish is one of the last words I would choose to describe *you*, Miss Hatherleigh."

She met his gaze, and he read the interest, the disappointment, the hope flickering in her eyes until he had to look away. This was a foolish action, to be sure. It could only fuel speculation, both for her and for the Chisholms. Sudden fury at his weakness in visiting made him rise. "So if you are well, I will leave you." He winced internally, his voice sounded harsher than he meant.

"Oh, but sir—" Her face drooped.

"You cannot leave now, Mr. Jardine. Not when we finally have hope that this day will not be a complete waste," said Helena.

The door was opened and the fat housekeeper waddled in to deposit a large tray of tea, cake, and biscuits. His belly grumbled at the sweet buttery scent.

"I fear that despite Mr. Jardine's wishes to be elsewhere, his stomach, at least, wishes to stay," murmured Verity.

He studied her, until a smothered cough drew his attention to his hostess, who insisted he remain, and with whom he managed to exchange polite conversation, whilst the young ladies resumed their game of cards, and he wondered how to drop the information he'd come to give.

After tasting a meltingly good piece of shortbread, he cleared his throat. "I wish my housekeeper had this recipe."

"*Your* housekeeper?"

"I'm afraid Mrs. Iverson remains convinced her mother's recipe is the only one. Hers sadly lacks lightness." He glanced at Verity, whose frown indicated she had not been distracted one whit. He returned his attention to Mrs. Chisholm. "We had an unexpected visitor at Dungally the other day. This would've been far preferable to serve guests."

At his hostess's murmured enquiry, he continued, studiously avoiding Verity's gaze. "Yes, her visit was most unexpected, especially as I'd only met her once. She is the wife of a diplomat I met on my return from the Antipodes. I'm afraid her visit caused some confusion." He sneaked a peek at Verity. She was biting her bottom lip, though her eyes remained fixed on the splayed cards in her hand.

"What brought her to visit?" This from Helena. "I did not think— oh, forgive me. I mean . . ."

"I did not think she would remember such a humble personage as myself, that is true. But it seems she was returning to her home, and Dungally is on the way."

"And do you expect to see her again?"

"I have no intention to." Now he did glance at Verity.

Two spots of color rode high on her cheeks. She placed a card down, looked up, met his eyes, and smiled. Warmth suffused his chest, peace filling his soul for the first time in what felt like weeks.

"Would you care to join us for cards?"

Helena's query drew his attention, his quick assent drawing sly smiles between the sisters, but he cared not. It seemed an age since he'd experienced such a warm familial circle.

An hour passed, two, as the conversation and laughter and restored relationship continued to soothe his soul, and the rain quietened to gentleness, before ceasing altogether. During a lull in an otherwise spirited game of whist, movement was heard without, and soon the door opened to reveal an extremely damp James.

He nodded to his mother's greeting, ignoring Verity and his sisters as he frowned at Anthony. "What are you doing here?"

Anthony met his gaze squarely. "I was invited."

"But you're sitting in my seat."

"James, you were not here two hours ago," replied his sister with a roll of her eyes.

"Two hours? You've been playing card for hours?"

"Not quite," said Verity. "Mr. Jardine has also been eating biscuits, drinking tea, and telling the most interesting stories of his time in the Antipodes."

Anthony's heart warmed at her look of congeniality. Her smiling approval almost made him forget the scowling young man standing in front of him. Almost, but not quite.

"I'm afraid it is time for my departure." Anthony's gaze slid to where Verity watched him, with something like wistfulness on her face. "I am glad to see you looking better."

"Thank you for coming."

He nodded, and turned to his hostess. "Thank you for a most entertaining afternoon."

"Not at all. It is you who has so thoroughly entertained us. I had no idea what an emu looked like, and now after your stories, I believe I have no desire to ever encounter one."

He smiled, bowed, and exited.

A minute later he was striding up the hill when a voice called. "Mr. Jardine!"

He turned to see Verity chasing after him, holding a small basket. "Seeing as you enjoyed the biscuits . . ." She thrust the basket to him. "There are enough for the laird and Mac, too."

"You are very good, Miss Hatherleigh."

Her eyes sparkled. "Now that is something rarely said."

He was lost for a moment, his hands filled with basket, staring at the pink-and-white complexion christened with raindrops from trees above. How he wished to wipe away the moisture, touch her cheek, touch her lips . . .

He stepped back. "Thank you again, Miss Hatherleigh."

Her face dimmed a little. "See you soon?"

"Yes."

And as her face grew radiant, he cursed himself for the feeling of gladness coursing through him that she would wish to see him again soon.

CHAPTER TWENTY

"OH, YOU ARE such helpful girls."

Verity exchanged glances with a guilty-looking Helena. "It is of no consequence, Mrs. Chisholm," she sang out, shifting the basket of weeds.

And it wasn't. She held no compunctions about helping, not if it permitted opportunity for tomorrow's masquerade. She inhaled deeply, drinking in the scents of lavender and damp earth, smiling as a pale blue butterfly fluttered past her face. Had it also enjoyed transforming from chrysalis to freedom? Anticipation throbbed. Tomorrow!

"Verity!" Helena hissed.

She glanced up. Mrs. Cready had replaced Mrs. Chisholm at the window, her beady eyes boring into them. Verity turned to wink at Helena, before pitching forward and gasping.

"Verity!" Helena's voice held a trace of real worry, despite their previously concocted plans. "Are you unwell?"

Verity opened her eyes, her swift upward glance taking in the housekeeper's frown. "It's nothing," she said, loud enough to be heard at the window. "Only you know how my monthly affects me." She clutched her waist for emphasis.

Helena hurried closer, her features straining to not smile. "Do you need to go inside?"

"No, no. I shall be well enough presently." In a lower voice she added, "Stop smiling, for heaven's sake."

Helena patted her shoulder then looked at the window. "Mrs. Cready! Could you tell Mary that Miss Hatherleigh may be needing a posset for her lady's troubles?"

Verity peeked up to see Cready give a curt nod and move away. She straightened and gestured to the ladder. "Now let's shift it against the wall and we shall be right as rain for our escape tonight."

Helena sighed as they struggled to move it under the window. "I don't think Cready will be that easy to fool."

"I do. The sooner she is put in her place the better."

"Yes, but—Quick! Here comes James."

Verity stepped away from the ladder but not quick enough as James strode forward.

"I'm surprised to seeing you both working in such a manner." He glanced from Verity to the ladder. "Might I enquire why you have need of a ladder?"

"No," said Helena.

"Yes," Verity replied.

"So which is it?" He gazed between them. "And why should there be mystery over such a thing?"

"There is no mystery." Verity shrugged. "I merely require a ladder to remove a piece of ivy that has been tapping against my window." It was not a lie. The ivy in question had caused some distracting sounds during the storm two nights ago.

"But why not remove it by simply opening your window?" His eyes narrowed. "Why the need for you to do it at all? Why not get Hoskins to remove it for you?"

"Because"—she adopted a tone she'd use to explain things to a small child—"he would not know precisely which piece of ivy it would be. And there is no use merely removing a leaf as it would quickly grow back and the whole process would need repeating."

"I see." His attention shifted to the top of the ladder. "It is quite high. Are you sure you are able to manage such a feat?"

Helena's giggle subsided after another warning look. No, James did not need to know just what exploits Verity and his sister had got up to at Haverstock's.

Verity offered her sweetest smile. "James, your concern is admirable, your condescension less so. Do you really think me incapable of climbing?"

"Yes." His arms crossed.

"But, Verity, what about—" Helena gestured to the window.

"If she returns we'll think of something." She wiped her hands on the apron she had knelt on then grasped the sides of the ladder. "James, I don't suppose you wish to be chivalrous?"

"As you have so rightly pointed out, I would not know which branch you found so offensive. Besides, you would still be searching for an opportunity to show yourself equal to me."

"But I am equal to you," she muttered beneath her breath. "Very well," she said louder. "We shall see."

She stepped up one rung, then another, working slowly to not make it look like she was used to this sort of thing, but not so slow he might think her afraid. Seven rungs, eight rungs, nine. She was past the lower story windows now, the ivy against which the ladder leaned pushing through the ladder's rungs.

"Dizzy yet?" came the voice from below.

"No. It is quite exhilarating," she shot back.

She climbed on, thankful for her divided skirt that allowed such activity without harming her modesty.

Fourteen, fifteen, sixteen rungs. She paused, steadied her footing before leaning to tear at the offending branches of ivy. She dropped them far below, then shifted her head, taking in the harbor and glimpses of the restored garden of next door. She pushed to her tiptoes, but no Mr. Jardine came into view. She turned to face the siblings below. "The view is quite lovely."

"You should come down now," called Helena.

Verity sighed. Why was Helena so goosish? Was this the result of her brother's domineering ways, or was she cowed by that Cready creature? Whatever, it was not to be tolerated. She placed a foot firmly on the lower rung. Then stepped lower again.

Suddenly her foot slipped and she was sliding down, down, down. Heart pounding, she grasped the sides. Pain shot through her hand.

She let go. And then was falling! A rush of too much air. She closed her eyes, heard a scream—

Oooff!

Arms clasped her, warm, secure. She opened her eyes.

James grinned down at her. "See? I knew you couldn't do it."

"What?" She tried to wriggle free but his arms pinned her tighter.

"Ladies will always need gentlemen, because we are stronger and more brave."

"You count yourself a gentleman, do you?" Verity spluttered. "Put me down!"

"Yes, James. I hardly think—" Helena's voice broke off as Mr. Jardine rounded the corner. "Oh, er, good afternoon."

His gaze shifted from Helena to Verity. He blinked. Almost seemed to draw back. "I appear to be interrupting. Please excuse—"

"You are not!" Verity elbowed James and he released her to an unceremonious tumble on the grass.

Mr. Jardine hurried forward, offering his hand to help her stand. "Are you hurt?"

"No." She grasped his hand, gazing into concerned green eyes, edged with what—confusion? Disappointment? Her cheeks heated.

His gaze fell to her mud-spattered hand. "But you are injured." He turned her hand palm up, his fingers warm and caressing. "You have a great splinter."

"A great splinter, but not a very good one, I fear."

His lips curled up in one corner. "At least it appears to be straightforward to remove, although it is hard to tell." His eyebrows rose ever so slightly.

"I've been gardening," she confessed.

"I did not know gardening involved scaling great heights." He looked enquiringly from her to James.

Her cheeks grew hotter. "I did not intend to fall."

"One rarely does." He smiled.

She responded in kind. There was something immeasurably easy about being with Mr. Jardine. And now that all had been explained about his unexpected visitor, she could not wait to show him just how grown up she could be.

He pressed her hand and she couldn't withhold the wince. "May I?"

She nodded, gritting her teeth as he pulled the offending ladder particle from her hand, quickly stemming the trickle of blood with his thumb. She was conscious of his nearness, his breath ruffling her hair, his scent of earth, fresh cut grass, mixed with something reminiscent of spiced oranges. Her heart beat faster. Yet although he still held her hand, his attention remained respectful, as though she was precious and fragile, not merely weak and subservient, as James apparently believed.

She drew in a breath. "Th-thank you, Mr. Jardine."

He smiled, causing her insides to flutter, and opened his mouth to speak—

"Where is my thanks?" James's scowl grew pronounced. "I rescued you, after all."

Mr. Jardine released her hand and stepped away. Instantly she felt colder. She pushed past the resentment at James's tone and managed a thank-you that didn't sound completely lacking in gratitude.

He harrumphed, picked up the ladder, resting it against the wall in precisely the same position, grumbling, "I'll get Hoskins to put this away later."

Verity shot Helena a glance. "Oh, but—"

"Hoskins seemed rather busy earlier, James," Helena said. "We really shouldn't disturb him."

"I can move it for you."

Before Verity could think of a suitable response, Mr. Jardine had shouldered the ladder and was moving toward the shed. "I passed him on my way in." His hair glinted fire-golden in the sun as he nodded to the Chisholm siblings, then to Verity. "I'm glad you were not injured."

And before she could echo Helena's goodbye, he had gone.

"Seems your gardening fellow knows when he should make himself scarce."

She bit her lip, tightness filling her chest, as Helena replied, "Apparently he also knows how to make himself useful."

"Unlike me?" James glared. "I'll have you know if I had not happened to be here, Verity would have been injured with far more than a splinter. I saved her life."

"Thank you, James. Your heroism does you great credit," Verity managed. "But if you don't mind, I think I'll go inside and see about a bandage for my hand."

And with Helena's comforting arm around her shoulders, they went inside where her hand was soon fussed over, and she began to plot how to retrieve the ladder Mr. Jardine had so thoughtfully put away.

Something like a hard knot coiled in his chest. Seeing her, clasped by another man, had made him almost want to punch the man.

Which wasn't good. Was not appropriate for a man of God at all. But neither was the feeling he'd experienced when he held her hand, as though fire had kindled between them. Standing so close to her, he couldn't help but notice the way her eyelashes curled outward at the sides, pulling his attention towards the blueness of her eyes, as guileless as the sunny Antipodean skies he'd left behind. His heart skipped a beat. The way she'd looked at him, like he was the true hero, made him feel a little breathless, even now.

Which wasn't wise. Was not good at all. He should not entertain such thoughts, not when her lack of faith meant she would forever stay beyond his reach. Not when she was so many years his junior. Not when he still needed to finally clear matters with Amelia. Not when he still needed to own his true identity, and stop misleading Miss Verity—and the village.

Mr. Hoskins's grumbled thanks repeated in his ear, along with words about the evening festivities in the village.

"I don't be holding with masked evenings and all, but it's always been the way to celebrate the start of the Ridings, just as important as the ball that closes the day."

Something within his heart tugged, urging Anthony to go. Was this a way to learn more about these people he now lived amongst? If he were masked and dressed in costume, there could be no prejudice about the laird. And if . . . others . . . attended, he might ascertain something of where their affections truly lay.

He hurried home, pondering his disguise.

❧ Chapter Twenty-One

The rooms held a kaleidoscope of color, the kilts of a dozen different clans giving clues to their masked owners. Mr. and Mrs. Chisholm had chosen to sit in the supper room, nearer the delicacies already set out, necessitating that Verity and Helena remain at the opposite end of the ballroom to prevent their discovery. Clad in Mrs. Chisholm's white wigs, with their faces heavily powdered and masks firmly tied, Verity thought she and Helena looked more disguised than most. James was not too hard to pick out, his swagger and braying laugh causing Helena's eyes to roll and Verity to shake her head.

"Look!" She nudged Helena's arm. "Isn't that your Alasdair?"

The white powder could not hide Helena's blush. "He is as much my Alasdair as Mr. Jardine is yours."

Verity's chest tightened. "Mr. Jardine and I are but friends."

"Who happen to gaze at each other like Adam must have first regarded Eve."

"Helena!"

"Well, it's true. You look upon each other with something like fascination."

Her heart thrilled. He regarded her that way? "Well, I do find him interesting."

When Helena didn't reply, Verity turned to see her friend gazing at her with a sad smile. "But you do know anything more than friends is impossible. Don't you?"

218

But none of her other friends had ever made her feel like this! She kept the smile painted on, striving for a lightness of tone. "Of course! Mama would have apoplexy." She forced her lips to smile wider. "So do not trouble yourself over me. Look, here comes your Alasdair. Let's see if we can make him ask you to dance. Remember Haverstock's fluttering fan?" Verity fluttered her eyelashes at Helena until she laughed.

"Stop! You make me think of Bessie when you do that."

"Bessie?"

"Our cow."

Verity laughed, the sound drawing more than one head to turn their way.

But not one, it would seem, that might be Mr. Jardine's. Her heart plunged. His attendance tonight had been a futile hope, after all.

Alasdair bowed, offering a greeting to them both before claiming Helena's hand as they conversed quietly. The music for the first dance began. From her place in the shadows, Verity watched the first group of dancers take to the floor.

A stir drew her attention to the door. Amidst the muted greens and reds, a golden robe shimmered under the candlelight. A hush came across the room as the figure walked into the room, dressed in a resplendent copper vest and white turban. A thrill rippled through her. An Indian!

But . . . not someone from the Subcontinent. Her gaze directed to his face, mostly covered with a bronze mask, apart from his lower jaw, whose tanned, ginger-flecked appearance couldn't hide his Celtic heritage.

The man scanned the room, seemingly oblivious to the stares and murmurs his entrance had provoked. Without further thought to discovery, she rose from her hiding place, her eyes fixed on him, until his gaze met hers. Her breath caught, her skin tingled, her heart beat strangely.

His mouth twitched and he nodded once, as if satisfied, then moved toward her, a hundred eyes following his progress across the room.

"I should have known."

She jumped, and turned, striving for nonchalance as she saw the scowling owner of the hissed words. "Good evening, James."

He snorted, and glanced at Helena who cowered behind Alasdair. "I don't suppose this was *your* idea."

Helena, to her credit, merely lifted her chin and glared at her brother. "You are not responsible for us."

"But when Mama and Papa find out—"

"Oh, don't tell them, please!"

"Not before I get the chance to dance with your sister," Alasdair said, smiling at Helena appreciatively.

Verity stepped forward, drawing James's attention to herself once again. "Come now, James. You wouldn't want anything to interrupt your special night, would you?"

His scowl eased. "I suppose not."

"And your mother and father need not know, I promise."

"How? Are you about to leave?"

"Ah . . ." Verity stifled a smile and Helena grinned over her shoulder as she moved, arm in arm with Alasdair, to the far end of the room from where their parents watched proceedings. A quick glance past her friend revealed the Indian had disappeared. Oh . . .

James turned and grimaced. "I swear she has never been this ill-behaved before."

"Is it so ill-behaved to want to dance?"

He cut her a sideways glance. "I suppose this has nothing to do with you."

"*Moi?*"

He shook his head and sighed. "I suppose if I were to leave you alone you would only find more mischief."

"Of course not!" Only, she *really* wanted to learn who the Indian was.

"Come on." He grasped her arm.

"But—"

"If you and Helena want to stay, you will stay where I can keep an eye on you." He moved her with not a little force to join the set where Helena and Alasdair stood waiting with six other couples.

Verity craned her neck. The Indian was still nowhere to be seen.

Frustration balled in her chest. She swallowed, forcing her lips to maintain a smile as she pretended interest in the steps of another unfamiliar Highland dance. Who was he? For a moment she'd thought him to be Mr. Jardine, but Mr. Jardine always held an easy countenance, whereas the Indian held a stern, unsmiling visage. Why was he so somber? And why, at that moment when their gazes connected, had she suddenly felt a spark of recognition that left her feeling most unlike herself? She drew in a deep breath, exhaled, and glanced up to see James watching her narrowly.

He stepped forward, bowed slightly, then lightly clasped her hands as they prepared to follow the previous couple down the line. "You are behaving most peculiarly."

"Perhaps it is the effect of the company."

"Would you like to return home now?"

She narrowed her gaze to approximate his. "Would you like to tell Alasdair he must cease from attending Helena?" She nodded to where Helena and Alasdair laughed softly, eyes only on each other.

James's brow puckered, a familiar sight throughout the remainder of the dance whenever he noticed his sister.

As the music died away, the general hubbub and mingling of bodies made it easy for Verity to shift to the shadowed recesses of the room. James's attention was captured by several other young men she presumed to also be in the running for the lead rider role. She glanced around, pushing to her toes. Still no sign of the Indian. Again she felt the pang of disappointment.

"Would ye be searching for me by any chance?"

She turned, recoiling from the unfamiliar man's leer and stench. "I beg your pardon?"

He stepped closer, his black mask unable to hide his bold, dark gaze and yellowed teeth. "You look ready for a dance."

She lifted her chin, fixing him with a haughty eye she had seen her mother use many a time. "I assure you I am not."

"Hoity-toity!" He glanced over his shoulder at two men, dressed equally poor in kilts and black masks that did nothing to hide their stubble. "I thought all Frenchies were nothing but whores."

Verity's insides froze as she resisted the urge to tug up her low neckline. Tonight's costume had been a mistake. And if these men were leering after her, they would likely do the same to poor Helena. She inched away. "If you'll excuse me . . ."

"Not so fast!" A hand shot out and grabbed her elbow.

Fear drummed through her veins. Candlelight did not penetrate far into the darkness of this corner, the man's grasp held such strength he could easily drag her away, and the girth of his friends would prevent others noticing. But if she screamed, Helena would be in trouble. "Please, sir—"

"Oh, it's a please and a sir, is it now? 'Membering our manners, are we?" He leaned closer, his hot breath prickling her face.

"Unhand the lady."

Verity's gaze swung from her assailant to the bronze-masked newcomer. The Indian!

The man tightened his grip. "She's dancing with me."

"I think not." The Indian's voice was low, tight, yet holding a trace of a burr, triggering a memory that dissipated almost as soon as it occurred.

"No?"

"Not when she is promised to me." He held out a hand that she took, pulling her elbow from the lecher's grasp as she stepped closer to her rescuer. The Indian bowed. "I am sorry I could not get here sooner."

"Th-that is all right."

"Shall we?" He moved her further away from the reach of the other man, placing his body between them. "I looked for you everywhere."

He had? Or was he just saying this to protect her further? "I . . . I looked for you, too."

"I'm glad." His smile flashed, rippling the edges of memory.

She stared at him. Was it—?

"Wait! Ye cannot just take her."

The Indian murmured, "Keep walking toward the others. I'll be there momentarily."

He released her and she walked back to the more brightly lit area, where the couples swung around as the musicians played another loud Scottish reel. She rubbed her arms, wishing the action would warm her more quickly. Was that truly—?

"There you are!" The exasperation in James's voice was further reinforced through his crossed arms. "I thought you knew not to wander off."

Somehow she found her voice. "*I* wasn't the one who got talking."

"Well, er . . . it was important." His brows knit. "Are you quite well? You seem a trifle out of sorts. You know there are unsavory fellows here that might not behave as respectably as one should."

Verity nodded. She knew that now. She glanced around. "Where is Helena?"

"Dancing with Alasdair. Again. I told her I'd take you both home after this."

"But . . ." She hadn't had a chance to dance with the Indian yet!

"But what? Surely I have been more than lenient with you both."

Lenient? What right did he have to assume she—or Helena, for that matter—required his leniency? She pushed down the irritation. "I did not think you wished to miss the big announcement."

He waved a dismissive hand. "That won't be for another hour, at least."

"Mademoiselle."

Verity turned to see the bowed head of the Indian. She dropped a small curtsy, heartbeat thrumming. His eyes met hers. Again that shiver of recognition.

"Your smile gives me hope that you have not entirely forgotten our dance."

"Who are you?" James demanded.

The Indian's eyes twinkled behind his mask. "That is a question best answered at midnight, I believe."

"It's a question best answered now if you wish to dance with this young lady." James hooked a thumb at her.

"Is this what the young lady also requires?"

"No," Verity said. He had protected her, and she trusted him. She turned to James. "He is a friend."

"Verity," James hissed, pulling her to one side, seemingly having forgotten the prior need to maintain anonymity. "Have you taken leave of all your senses? We don't know who he is."

"Yet he now knows who *I* am, thanks to you."

James had the grace to look somewhat abashed. "I didn't think," he muttered.

Her patience with officious men tonight had run completely dry. "That is not without precedence. Now, I want to dance with him, and if you make a scene, I'm afraid I will have to make a bigger one."

Whilst he remained glowering, she snatched her arm away and turned to the Indian, whose quickly smoothed smile suggested her *tête-à-tête* with James had not gone completely unnoticed. "Sir, that dance?"

He inclined his head. "At once, *mademoiselle*."

He drew her to the bottom of the nearest set, where his magnificent attire once again drew fascinated gazes. The "milkmaid" next to Verity murmured, "Have you discovered his identity?"

Verity shook her head, although she had a fairly good idea . . .

She studied her partner as he joined the other men in clapping while one couple moved down the center of the two lines. The Indian was not as short as the man on his right, whose balding head suggested he might be the farrier the Chisholms had employed the other day. Neither was he as tall as James, who hadn't moved since she had left him, and whose glower had attracted more than one curious glance. His robes suggested broad shoulders and a trim girth, but the mask and turban hid everything save the fact that his smile was sweet and came often.

He turned to face her, his lips tilting slowly, causing hers to lift in response, and summoning a fluttery sensation in her midsection.

The milkmaid and farrier bowed to each other then joined hands, moving to the head of the lines whilst the remaining couples clapped. Then it was their turn.

The Indian stepped forward, his gaze fixed on her, a small smile in place as he bowed to her curtsy. He held her hands gently, his smooth guidance past the other couples in stark contrast to her previous partner's clumsy or overly forceful efforts. She drew in a deep breath to calm her racing pulse, only to inhale something spicy. Her heart beat even faster.

At the head of the lines, he released her. Instantly her gloved fingers missed his.

She studied him, noting his intent perusal, his soft smile. Her heartbeat quickened.

The music changed and now the couples formed into quartets. The Indian moved closer and she took advantage of his nearness to inhale his scent. She *had* to know for certain . . .

Verity cleared her throat. "I trust you enjoyed a pleasant voyage."

"How did—?"

"Your journey from the Subcontinent." She gestured to his finery. "I assume you did not walk."

"You assume correctly." He laughed, low and merry. "And may I enquire about you, *mademoiselle*? I imagine it was not easy these past years, caught in the midst of war."

"You imagine correctly, *monsieur*." Her spirits danced as lightly as her feet. Imagine to have met a man who shared her delight in silly banter.

The music continued. A shout of laughter drew her attention to where Helena twirled in Alasdair's arms. A pang of envy hit her. If only she could be free to marry whomever she chose!

"*Mademoiselle?* You wear a troubled look. I apologize for my dancing."

"Oh no, sir. You dance very well."

"I feared my lack of practice had given cause for disgust."

"It is not that."

"Perhaps it is your brother?"

"My brother?" She followed his glance at James, whose scowl only seemed to intensify. She sighed. "He is not my brother."

"Your cousin, perhaps? I ask only because I assumed he must be a relative, as he affects such interest in you."

"Too much interest, it appears."

"Ah."

The dance moved into a pattern and it was some time before they could speak again.

"*Mademoiselle?*"

"*Oui?*"

"I confess myself to be somewhat alarmed. Your cousin continues to stare most unhappily in our direction."

"He is not my cousin, *monsieur.*"

"I assume him to be too young to be your father."

She laughed. "I am eighteen, sir."

His eyes flashed, his smile fading slightly as he inclined his head. "You appear older."

She laughed to herself. If only Mother could hear such things. She'd always complained that Verity's lack of concern with her appearance only reinforced her childish behavior. A true lady, Mother always proclaimed, took care of her appearance, and took care to not appear like a hoyden, and *never* gave rise to scandal.

She tossed her head back, feeling the pins holding her wig in place give way a little. Oh no. She stilled, one hand clasped to her head. "Excuse me for a moment."

The Indian's brow knit. "But of course."

He escorted her to a seat on the side, turning to face the whirling dancers, thus shielding her discreetly as she quickly adjusted her wig into place. Regret gnawed her heart. Soon she must go. Or if James found her, she would be forced to leave. He would doubtless have few scruples in pulling Helena away from Alasdair, either.

"*Monsieur?* You may turn around. I trust I am not so disheveled, *non?*"

His gaze traced her hair and face, dipping briefly to her lips before returning to her eyes. "You are quite lovely." As if startled by his admission, his smile faded and he stepped back. "Perhaps I should find your chaperone—"

"Please don't! I have so many questions—"

"Questions I cannot answer, I'm afraid."

"Nonsense. People are not hiding their true selves so much now." She gestured to where a couple had both removed their masks.

"I cannot be so bold."

"But surely—"

"You should not wish to be so bold, either, *mademoiselle*. Not when you are so young." His voice held—regret? He bowed and turned away.

"But there is something I must know!"

"You will remain doomed for disappointment, I'm afraid."

"Have you ever been to India?"

He blinked. His mouth opened, closed. Behind his mask she could see the questions in his eyes. Eventually he said, in a voice much less accented than before, "Why do you ask?"

"I have always longed to see the world, and would dearly love to speak with someone who has traveled further than Portsmouth."

He drew closer. "You are *not* from across the Channel? I am all astonishment."

Verity laughed, relief filling her at the returning flash of his grin. "You astonish easily, it would seem."

His head inclined, he took another step back. "Good night"—and then softly—*"minha querida."*

She *was* right! "Mr. Jardine?"

He stilled.

"It is you, is it not?" She rose hurriedly, stepping closer until she heard his breath catch. "Tell me the truth."

His head bowed. "I cannot lie to you, Miss Hatherleigh."

"I did not think you would come."

"I was not sure you would attend, either. I confess I am a little surprised that you received Mrs. Chisholm's consent."

Her cheeks grew hot. "Mrs. Chisholm doesn't really know."

"You astound me."

"But James does. You know, the one not old enough to be my father?"

He chuckled. "The one who is still not happy to see you here with me." His smile turned rueful. "He has never liked me."

"He doesn't like the laird, more like."

His eyes flashed behind the mask. "I am sorry to hear it."

"Well, let's not talk about him." She smiled. "You have a most wonderful disguise."

"Thank you. I found it among my great-uncle's things. Mac told me I had enough tan to not appear downright ridiculous."

"Your great-uncle must have traveled to India, then."

He inclined his head. "I believe he visited the Orient as well."

"Travel must run in your family. How I envy you." She sighed. "Well, I knew I recognized something about you. But your voice sounded so formal and deep, you had me quite fooled. But that is what a masquerade is for, is it not?" Her smile stretched, her heart aglow. Surely he could not be completely immune to her to say she was lovely. Unless . . . "When did you know it was me?"

"From the first moment."

"So you meant what you said before? That I"—her smile grew— "look pretty?"

He stared at her a moment before shaking his head.

Disappointment at his answer crashed over her, surprising in its intensity. "No?"

"I didn't say you looked pretty, but that you are lovely."

Oh . . .

At the expression in his eyes, the pensive twist to his lips, warmth cascaded through her. But he still seemed determined to leave, as if her presence made him uncomfortable. But she had to have him stay. She laid a hand on his arm.

"Please, would you tell me something about your travels? All this time in Scotland has given me renewed appreciation for warmer climes."

She held her breath as he continued to study her intently. Finally he sighed. "What is it you wish to know?"

A million questions wanted to burst from her. But she could see Mrs. Chisholm was moving in their direction. "Could we talk outside?"

"I . . . I do not think that is wise."

"Please? If we stay here, James will only get more cross."

"Whereas if we go outside, you think he'll be better pleased?"

Mrs. Chisholm was closer still! Verity tugged his hand, urging him to follow. Moments later they were outside the assembly room, along with half a dozen couples, the night air cooling the embarrassment from her cheeks. She moved to the terrace, whose stone balustrade protected from the water sloshing far below. Above, the sky was pricked with a thousand stars, adding dim light to that of the glowing lantern at the door.

She turned to face him. "You went to Brazil, did you not?"

"Yes. To Rio de Janeiro. That is on the east—"

"The east coast, yes, I know." At his raised brow she hurried on. "I might not have always been a well-behaved scholar, but I did enjoy geographical studies."

"I see."

"And you know some Portuguese?" At his wrinkled brow she prompted him. "You have called me *querida* several times now. What does it mean?"

His gaze dropped, his cheeks reddening. He opened his mouth to speak—

"Well, I widnae pick seeing you here again."

The voice sounded like slurry to her ear. She shrank back as the man from before drew close, his face as menacing as before, the scent of liquor still heavy on his breath.

"I thought ye had learnt yer lesson last time."

Last time? What had happened that had taken him so long to return earlier? Had Mr. Jardine hidden bruises as well as his identity? She touched his arm. "Sir, please don't—"

Mr. Jardine shook off her hand, gaze fixed on the bully. "Leave the lass be. Your contention is with me."

The brute's sneer grew uglier. "I cannae." And with a snarl and a swing, he thumped him in the chest.

Mr. Jardine gasped, tottering on his feet, mask askew.

"Stop!" Verity rushed forward. "Please don't hurt—"

"Stay back," he growled, pulling off his mask. "Apparently this gollumpus does not always need his friends to back up his boasts with their fists."

The kilted man's unmasked face mottled red. "Now who be haverin!" He swung again.

Mr. Jardine stepped aside, then in a flash grabbed the brute's hand, jerking him close, twisting one arm against the brute's throat and pinning the other behind him in a chokehold. "Ye best be learning respect for young ladies. Now, dinnae show your face around here again." He pushed the gurgling captive to the floor.

The brute muttered a foul curse, scrambled to his feet, and slunk into the night.

Around them the other couples clapped and cheered, "Good riddance to 'im."

Verity placed her hand on her heart as she slowly exhaled. This was the second time tonight Mr. Jardine had saved her from peril. "Thank you."

He shrugged, dusting off his robes and straightening his turban. "He should not trouble you again, I hope."

"I hate to think you were injured."

He gave a wry grin. "I had the wind knocked out of me, but only for a moment."

"What can I do to repay you?"

A bawdy cackle came from the woman dressed as a shepherdess. "Give 'im a kiss, hen!"

"Miss Hatherleigh, you do not . . . you should not . . ."

But in that moment everything within demanded she did. She drew as close as she dared, pushed to her toes, and moved to brush her lips against his cheek. Somehow, in that precise moment, Mr. Jardine moved, so instead of tanned cheek she encountered warm lips.

Fire swept through her senses, tingling each nerve ending. After a moment's shock, she felt his lips soften, his hands trace her cheekbones, before settling behind her shoulders. Oh, the sweetness! She sighed, leaning in to him, allowing his arms to support her as the kiss deepened. The fluttering became more demanding, heat pooled inside, insisting on more—

He pulled away and grasped her shoulders gently, his chest heaving. "You should not have done that."

Before she'd realized what was happening, he had swept her inside, virtually thrusting her at James, then stalked off.

Her mind was awhirl, the sensations of his kiss cocooning her. She ignored James's recriminations, ignored Helena's upraised brows, ignored the speeches and cooling air as the memory of that kiss warmed her with shivers of delight.

Perhaps proper young ladies did not kiss young men. But oh, she was so glad she had!

❧ Chapter Twenty-Two

He had to get away.

Anthony stared at the confusion of papers on his desk, papers demanding attention he could not give. Since arriving home last night, he had struggled to keep a thought straight in his head. What had he been playing at? For a lass. A lass barely out of school. And worse, one who didn't share his faith. Guilt seared his brain, his heart, his dreams. Yet amidst his self-disgust lay some twisted kind of pleasure at the memory of her kiss. He closed his eyes, remembering. The softness of her lips. The scent of her. The sigh she'd made as she'd nestled closer. His heart hammered, remembering how close he'd wanted her. His eyes snapped open. She could never be his. She was too young, lacked belief, and heaven knew what her ancestry was. And with her impetuosity, she'd never make a proper wife for a laird.

Wife?

He *had* to get away.

"Mac!"

His friend appeared, Dougal scampering at his heels. "I am leaving for Edinburgh."

"Certainly. When shall I begin packing?"

"Now."

Mac's brows pushed upwards. "This be sudden."

"Yes, well, it cannot be helped." He might receive a visit from his

CAROLYN MILLER

neighbors any hour now; it was best to be away before that happened, best to clear his head, get some reason into his heart and brain. "I need you to stay here and look after things. I'll travel faster by myself. I have some business to attend to, and while I'm there I may look in on my parents, and perhaps the Witherspooles."

"The Witherspooles?"

"Miss Amelia's parents. I should have visited them long ago." But now he had to. *Had* to. Had to get Verity out of his thoughts, out of his heart, before this attraction deepened. Had to see if Amelia retained any thought of him. Honor demanded he deal with his past before indulging in fantasies about the future.

"Pardon me, sir, but I do not think this wise. Won't such a visit give rise to certain expectations?"

"You mean Miss Witherspoole will think I come with an offer? Well, it is time I looked to the future."

Mac's brows rose.

"You think she will not understand?"

"I think someone else will not."

Verity.

Mac sighed. "What shall I say should Miss—that is, should any of the young people ask after you?"

"Say what you will."

The wise blue eyes blinked, before a look of sadness shadowed his features. "Very well, then."

"Don't look at me like I'm a heartless rogue. I'm doing this because, because . . ."

"Yes?"

"Because it has to be done," he snapped. Cowardly, but far safer than having her around, when he might be tempted to forget his principles and beg her to marry him, or worse, carry her off to the nearest blacksmith willing to perform the vows.

Mac bowed. "As you wish, sir."

Anthony gritted his teeth and turned away. This wasn't what he wished, but he cared not.

Honor demanded he get away.

The conviction with which she'd greeted Saturday morning—that Mr. Jardine would come to see her, that their kiss had meant something to him, that perhaps he might even feel inclined to speak to the Chisholms, might even rescue her from her hopeless predicament!— had slowly trickled to uncertainty, before withering into misgiving the Sunday following, when Mr. Jardine did not appear at services.

She had tried to speak to Mr. McNaughton, but by the time she made it outside he had disappeared, and the McConnells had scooped up the entire Chisholm clan, plus Verity, to a special luncheon to announce the betrothal of Helena and Alasdair.

Of course she was thrilled. Of *course* she was. It was just . . . no matter how much she wanted to fully enter into her friend's joy, she was conscious of a slight pull of concern, an undercurrent of something that felt like remorse. Regret, even.

Had she appeared too forward? The question plagued her at night, during the day. Her thoughts tossed and swirled between exhilaration at the kiss and hot shame at her actions, which always brought heat to her face, and, if in company, an enquiry as to why she looked so flushed.

Yes, she had behaved shamelessly.

Yes, he had behaved as a gentleman ought.

But she had seen the warm desire in his eyes, had known the delight of his arms around her, had felt the pressure of his lips against hers, a returned pressure that suggested he hadn't completely disliked the encounter.

On Monday, she was finally able to escape the talk of weddings and Ridings and hurry next door. Surely he'd be there—perhaps he was ill! Regardless, Mr. McNaughton would likely know his whereabouts, and if not, she could always ask the laird. She knocked on the heavy front door and waited.

Cobwebs arched across the carved stone lintel, evidence that the laird needed more servants, or at least some that cared. She beat the brass knocker again. *Thud. Thud. Thud.*

The house looked so quiet. Too quiet. The drapes were drawn. Her heart constricted. Was anyone home? Surely he hadn't left?

Eventually there was the sound of movement from within and the door inched open.

She smiled at Mr. McNaughton's weather-beaten face. "Good morning. I had wondered if anyone was here. It seemed everyone had gone."

In his silence, something rankled, something was not quite right. She pressed on.

"I was wondering if I could speak to Mr. Jardine, please."

It seemed his eyes were lit with compassion before he shook his head. "I'm afraid not, miss."

"Is he sick? I noticed he was not at services yesterday, and I wondered—"

"He is not sick."

"Oh. Well, that is good news. But I have something of great importance to discuss with him. I promise it will take but a few minutes—"

"He is not here."

"Oh. Well, when he returns can you tell him that if he could spare a moment to come to the rectory I'd be very grateful?"

He shifted uncomfortably. "I'm sorry, miss, but he has gone."

"Gone?"

"Aye. I do not know when to expect his return."

"I beg your pardon?"

His expression grew troubled. "He came home Friday night most perturbed, and first thing on Saturday declared his immediate intention to travel."

Her heart knotted. No . . .

"I don't mind confessing to a wee feeling of concern. He's been quite moody-like lately, up and down like a wee lass, happy as a bird one day then in the dismals the next." He shook his head. "I've never known 'im to be so."

She stared at him. Mr. McNaughton's unusual verbosity could be describing her own emotions of the past weeks.

"I know the estate was troublin' him some, but I dinnae ken he would up and leave his responsibilities. Most unlike 'im. He said nowt to ye?"

She shook her head, aware of something large and heavy in her throat. In a voice most unlike her own she asked, "Did he say where he was going?"

"He dinnae tell me much." He sighed, his gaze past her shoulder, like he awaited Mr. Jardine's return. "He has kin near Edinburgh, and a—" He stopped.

"And a what?"

He refused to meet her eyes. "There be a young lady."

A young lady? Nausea slid through her stomach. She missed the next part of his ramblings. How could he kiss her while having a sweetheart?

"—and his solicitors be there, too."

"Wait. He has a solicitor?"

His gaze shifted to fix on her again. "Of course he does."

"But . . ." She shook her head. Everything felt topsy-turvy, every-thing felt wrong. She needed something true and real to fix things into place. "I'm sorry. Surely he must have said something to the laird. If I could speak to him—"

"Who must have said?"

"Mr. Jardine! He could not disappear without letting the laird know." Why, her father would be extremely vexed if his estate man-ager left without so much as a by-your-leave! She spoke slowly so Mr. McNaughton could understand. "Is the laird in? May I speak with him?"

His brow wrinkled, his troubled eyes seeming to soften with com-passion. "I'm sorry, miss. I thought ye knew by now."

"Knew what?"

"Mr. Jardine is the laird of Dungally."

She stared at him. Had he taken leave of his senses? "No, he is not." As he nodded, she said louder, "No, he is the laird's *steward*. He said he was related to the laird—"

"Aye, to the previous one. But the title passed to him when his cousin died. I suppose I am his steward."

"No." A dizzying sensation washed through her. She put a hand on the stone archway. It felt gritty, cool to the touch. "No! Where is the laird? He will know!"

"Miss, I told ye, Mr. Jardine be the laird, and he is not here."

She shook her head. "I don't believe you."

"McNaughton?" A shrill voice preceded the housekeeper's beaky visage. She looked Verity up and down. "What seems to be the matter?"

He shot Verity an apologetic look. "Miss Hatherleigh wishes to speak with the laird."

Mrs. Iverson turned to Verity. "Mr. Jardine is away at present."

Was she deaf, too? "But I wish to speak with the *laird*."

"But I just told you, the master is away. We do not know when he shall return. He was most abrupt-like."

Suddenly Verity could not stand listening to them anymore. Mr. McNaughton's words could be attributed to loyalty, but the house-keeper's seemed to hold the ring of truth. She put a hand to her head. "I'm sorry, could I trouble you for a glass of water?"

With a huff, Mrs. Iverson bustled away. As soon as she was out of earshot, Verity said, "I'm sorry, but I really need to know," and pushed past Mr. McNaughton. Disregarding his objections, she raced up the stairs to the room at the end she remembered Benjamin saying belonged to the laird. Ignoring the scruples of entering a gentleman's room she pushed open the door and instantly the scent of spiced oranges, the scent she associated with Mr. Jardine, met her. She inhaled. No. *No!* It didn't mean anything. Perhaps the laird simply shared a preference for the same scent.

She glanced around. From its grand position overlooking the grounds and adjacent rooms and enormous four-poster bed it was obvious this was no mere servant's, or even steward's, room. It was tidy, but it was apparent its occupant had departed suddenly, the cupboard door was ajar. She raced over, pulled it open. Out tumbled the bronze mask.

No . . .

"Miss Hatherleigh."

She turned, met the servant's grave expression. "It *is* true?"

"Aye, lass. I told him no good would come of this, but he insisted he wanted to be known for himself, not judged for his position or title."

A worthy idea, one she could not condemn him for. But still . . .

"He lied to me."

His eyes seemed to hold understanding.

"And you do not know how long he will be gone?"

"I cannot say."

"Cannot or will not?"

"I know not, miss."

He had left! Without saying goodbye! And he had a young lady?

Her heart writhed afresh. Her bottom lip trembled. Tears made a sudden, stinging appearance. She blinked hard. Sniffed. Turned to the open window so he would not see the rebel moisture trickling from the corner of her eye. She angrily swiped it away.

"I'm very sorry, miss."

For some reason, his sympathy only made her struggle for self-control that much harder. She grasped the stone window casement to support herself. It felt cold and unwavering, just as she knew Mr. Jardine's decision now to be.

"I thought—" She swallowed. Pride refused further utterance. The view of the sea blurred.

"Ah, lass."

She bit her lip, but still the sob escaped. She tilted her chin, drew air through clogged nostrils, fighting desperately for self-control.

"There, there. I told him you'd be disappointed."

Disappointed? Disappointment was placing second to Prudence Gaspard in geography. This felt like a cataclysmic failure of the universe, like the sun had disappeared, never to return.

She exhaled a shaky breath, forced her bottom lip to stop quivering. Wiped her cheeks, lifted her chin. She was not Mama's daughter for naught. "I'm terribly sorry."

"As am I. I told him it was unwise to go."

And still he'd gone. How much must he want to avoid her? "I meant for breaking down just now."

"I know what you meant," he replied gently.

Somehow she forced her lips to return his small smile. Somehow she managed to make a farewell, to slump out the door, down the path, out the gate, only to collapse into the carved wooden seat where she had sat with Mr. Jard—no, the laird!—a week ago.

How *could* he have lied? Had he been laughing at them all this time? How could she have not known? She, who prided herself on her intellect had been blind—blind!—to his true identity. And he had left because of her. For really, what other reason could have made him turn tail other than her brazen kiss?

But how could he have done that when he had a sweetheart? The very idea was reprehensible!

Revulsion swept over her, curdling her stomach. She retched, clutching her midsection, then placed her head in her hands, dragging in deep breaths, vaguely aware of a dog barking somewhere. After some time she felt steadier, calmer, the whirl of thoughts slowing until she could think more rationally.

This must be why he had hesitated. Why he had seemed disappointed when he'd learned of her age, her lack of faith. It wasn't so much disappointment in her, but in himself, that he could be attracted to someone when he knew his affection should be reserved elsewhere.

For in spite of it all, she knew now he must have held her in some level of regard, else why disappear so suddenly?

For some reason that thought filled her eyes anew.

They *had* shared a good friendship. He was inherently a good man, his deception not masking evil intent. Indeed, it was not dissimilar to her not wanting to be judged as a viscount's daughter. She couldn't fault him for that. And, now she thought about it, he had been careful in his references to the laird. If only she'd had eyes to see!

She'd been such a fool! She brushed a hand over her burning eyes.

A fool. A pushy, blind, self-deluded fool. If only she had been more meek and ladylike, his feelings might have blossomed into something greater, and she might be the recipient of his heart. Instead, her brazenness had only reminded him of his obligations elsewhere.

She was rejected, a failure, always making mistakes . . .

A mistake. She was a mistake.

The weight in her chest pushed up, out, the heat spilling from her eyes.

If only he loved her enough to return!

❦ CHAPTER TWENTY-THREE

Linlithgow

AMELIA WITHERSPOOLE WAS all that was amiable, all that was pious, all that was appropriate, all that was . . . dull.

Anthony's gaze trickled around the chintz-filled drawing room, struggling to fix his attention as she conversed in a meek voice with her parents. His parents and sister glanced at him approvingly, their manner more animated than he remembered. He dredged up a smile as Mrs. Witherspoole turned to him.

"And Anthony, your recent good fortune means you will settle in Scotland permanently?"

"Oh, yes," replied his mother. "Although Kirkcudbright is a wee bit far for my liking."

Which doubtless accounted for her lack of a visit. He pushed aside the negativity, focused on his hostess. "My cousin's demise I do not consider good fortune."

"Oh! I did not mean—"

"I am sure you did not."

"Neither"—his gaze slid to his parents—"do I believe my role as laird will require permanent fixture at Dungally."

"Oh, that is good news." His sister smiled. "See Amelia? You need not live in that forsaken part of the world forever."

Amelia's placid eyes turned to him, searing guilt within. "I am glad. I would miss my family very much."

Her parents smiled benignly, their objections to his suit seven years ago apparently forgotten. His surprise at Amelia's unmarried state had almost been eclipsed by their pleased, indeed eager, acceptance to his request for a visit.

Aileen had long wanted Amelia as a sister; his sister's childhood friend had also been his parents' choice. But Anthony's calling, his thirst for adventure, had weighed against him at the final reckoning, and before he could utter the fateful words he'd found himself reeling, as if from a precipice.

He had not always appreciated Aileen's continued interest in advancing the match, communicated in her letters that had taken months to reach him in Sydney Town. But as a new widow, he supposed she wished for everyone to achieve the blessed matrimonial state she had experienced only too briefly with her naval husband. And thoughts of Amelia *had* slid into his awareness from time to time, as he wondered whether choosing to serve God amongst the godless was better than being with someone who might serve as a pattern for a Dresden china figurine.

But now . . .

He studied her. Amelia's soft golden beauty had not changed in the intervening years. In fact, he could see her aging to approximate her mother's complacent prettiness. If he were a wagering man, he'd safely bet the entirety of the Dungally estates that Amelia would never give cause for concern. She would never ride unchaperoned. Would never visit a single man's establishment. Would never boldly kiss a man.

His stomach tightened.

"And you have quite given up any desire for ministry?"

Anthony glanced at Mr. Witherspoole. Opened his mouth—

"I'm sure you won't mind my saying that it seems to have been quite a foolish notion, in retrospect."

Anthony blinked. "Sir, I cannot agree."

"But, Son—"

"No, Da. I do not regret my time in New South Wales. I would do it again tomorrow, if I could."

"But Anthony," Aileen murmured, "you could have had a career in law here." She glanced at Amelia. "Perhaps even have a family by now."

His cheeks heated, his gaze shifted to Mr. Witherspoole. "Sir, my time abroad taught me many things I would not have learned if I had stayed, not least of which was my understanding of our heavenly Father's great love for all mankind. To see men whom others considered the scourge of the empire, women whose chief trade I dare not mention in front of ladies—"

His sister gasped; Amelia's face blanched. He hurried on.

"To be in a position where I could offer these people hope in Jesus Christ is something I can never regret."

"That is enough, Anthony. You need not embarrass us with any more plain speaking."

"You would prefer the truth to be hedged about, perhaps? Mama, the Bible is unmistakable—"

"Thank you, you have made your position very clear."

But had he? He shifted forward. "I am not so sure, Mr. Witherspoole. I would not want anyone under any illusions." Anthony shifted his attention to Amelia. "I have often wondered what would have happened if I had proposed and you had said yes. I cannot believe you so"—*missish*, the imp in his head whispered—"so unable to cope as was implied. And even now, my role as laird is not one of ease and comfort. My great-uncle did himself and his tenants a great disservice by not taking greater interest in the well-being of the estate. As it is, it will take a number of years before the Dungally fortunes are turned around, and I can be in a position to offer anything more than the bare necessities."

He saw the horrified faces; the petulant twist to Amelia's lips. He wondered at the words spewing forth, but it seemed as though the weights shackling him for so long had fallen away, and he was freed to speak more honestly with his family than he'd ever thought possible.

"You must pardon my bluntness, but I would not have you suffer under misapprehension. I feel that God has put me in a position to once again be used as His instrument to help others, not perhaps, as obviously as in a church minister's role, but still to show His mercy and grace to others from all walks of life."

He took a breath, noticing again the tight faces of disapproval—and the disparity in ages between the married couples. Mr. Witherspoole had to be at least fifteen years his wife's senior. "And for this role I need a helpmeet, a partner, someone who will not find such duties arduous, but someone who will share my enthusiasm for the task entrusted to me, and would not say no should the opportunity to minister abroad arise again."

"Anthony! You cannot mean it."

"I am sorry you do not believe me, Mother, but it is true."

True.

The word rang out like a ship's bell, ushering his soul into safe harbor. Truth was what he yearned for, above social niceties, above inoffensive manners. In trying to walk the line between the legacy of his predecessors and the pain of the past, he had forgotten his first duty as a believer was to love his Lord, and to share the truth of God's love with others. And how could they believe him when he had hidden his true identity?

Regrets gnawed anew, even as he made his excuses, made his farewells, knowing this would be the last time he was invited to the Witherspooles. But he cared not. Truth burned in his soul. And the sooner he returned to share—to own—that truth the better.

"Verity? Why are you sitting out here? It is so cold!"

The words seem to come from a place far away. She had cried so much it was like her head was stuffed full of cotton. She could barely hear, barely breathe. Her eyes and nose must be very red indeed.

"Verity?" Helena moved into her line of vision, blocking the view of the Dee. She crouched down, touched her hands. "Your fingers are so cold. How long have you been sitting here? We've been getting worried."

Verity blinked. The emotion subsided. Words finally formed in her brain. She gulped. Opened her mouth. Closed it. Swallowed again. "Mr. Jardine."

Helena frowned. "Yes?"

"He . . . he's gone."

"What?"

"Mr. Jardine has gone away. To Edinburgh. To see—" She choked. "To see his *sweetheart*."

"What? No, you cannot be serious. He is sweet on . . ." Helena's words trailed away. "Come on, Verity, let's go inside—"

"Did you know he is the laird?"

"What? You cannot be well." Helena placed an arm around her shoulders, half pulled, half pushed her into a standing position. "Come along, let's get you warm. You are not making sense."

"He *is* the laird. I saw his room."

"How did—? No, never mind. You can tell me when we get back. Now, mind this rock . . ."

Verity followed, grateful for Helena's directions, her mind in a kind of blurred fog as they walked the path she'd trod so many times before, back to the rectory.

"I'm sure when we get back and you're thinking more clearly, things will make sense."

A dry chuckle burst from her throat. "All this time, I never knew." Her breath caught on a sob. "I'm such a fool."

"You are not a fool!" Helena's eyes sheened. "Don't say such things. Now look, we're almost there. Let's get you upstairs and you can tell me all about it."

Verity managed a small smile at Ben's demanding of where she had been, thankful for Helena's snapped request that he leave poor Verity alone and tell Cready to make a fresh pot of tea.

Once safely ensconced in her room, warmly dressed in a thick robe, Verity told her tale, to Helena's increasingly widened eyes. "No! I cannot believe it."

"Both Mr. McNaughton and Mrs. Iverson are sure. And I could see no sight of him. He has left."

"But to go without saying goodbye . . ." Helena's red curls bounced as she shook her head. "I cannot believe it of him."

"I can."

And Verity told her why.

"You kissed him?"

Verity nodded miserably. The best moment of her life. The worst moment of her life.

"Did people see you?"

She shrugged. "There were couples out there doing the same . . ."

"But if your parents found out, he'd be forced to marry you!" Helena's green eyes were enormous. "He *should* be here, asking for your hand, otherwise he is no gentleman."

A beat. "But I kissed him first."

Helena gazed at her with something like fascinated horror. "I . . . I don't know what to say."

Verity shrugged, lying back on her bed, staring up at the carved plaster ceiling. She, too, had run out of words.

THAT NIGHT AT dinner, news of the laird's identity and disappearance seemed to top even that of the upcoming Ridings and wedding. Verity was very thankful Helena had decided not to share the news of his sweetheart, although James cast more than one suspicious glance her way.

"Well, I call it very poor of 'im," declared Ben. "He was always so nice."

"I'm sure he is still nice," said Frances, with a worried look at Verity. "You didn't know?"

Verity shook her head, forking in more potato to avoid contributing to the conversation. She hadn't eaten this much at a meal in years.

"Papa, did you know Mr. Jardine was the laird?" Helena asked. At his nod, she cried, "Why didn't you say so?"

He placed his knife on the rim of his plate. "He asked me not to."

"So all this time you've known and not said anything?" Frances said. "Didn't you know Ver—I mean, we were all quite desperate to learn his identity?"

Mr. Chisholm turned his mild gaze to her. "I did not know it was of such importance."

Verity forced her lips up, forced in another mouthful of mashed neeps.

As his children kept up their demand for answers, he lifted a hand. "I respected his reasoning. You must admit that people have been quick to judge the Irving family over the years, often without cause." He cast a less-than-surreptitious glance at his eldest, who reddened. "I did not blame him for wanting to foster relationships without the past coloring people's perception of him. He knew that people tend to judge others on their outward appearance, but God looks at the heart. Indeed, he seems to have a very enlightened understanding of how God loves people, believing we are all equal in God's sight. I understand he was up front with his tenants, he was honest with me—"

"So it's only us he lied to," James sneered. "Typical of an Irving, even if his name is Jardine."

"And with that attitude, can you blame him?"

At his father's mild comment, James looked abashed.

"Do you think that is even his real name?" Frances wondered. "Or those stories he told us about going to New South Wales and Brazil. Do you think they are true?"

Suddenly Verity could not stand the cacophony of conjecture. She pushed away her plate. "Please excuse me. I'm rather tired."

The looks of sympathy mingled with speculation almost proved her undoing. Somehow she made it to her room without breaking down. Without calling for Mary's assistance, she toed off her slippers, climbed into bed, blew out the candle, and huddled down into the darkness.

The cold, lonely darkness.

The conversation from the dining room swirled around her. The laird. Lies. Mistakes. Judgment. Equality. God . . .

She frowned. What had Mr. Chisholm said? Something about people judging by outward appearance, but God saw a person's heart?

Did God see her? If He really was real, could He see her heart?

She gulped, but a giant lump seemed to have lodged in her throat. If God did see her heart, then He would see how cracked it was, fractured with disillusionment, disappointment, and rejection. She was a fool, a failure, a mistake, unloved by her parents, unloved by the only man she had cared for. Ergo, Verity Hatherleigh was unlovable.

But—a stubborn thought persisted—did *God* see her that way? Mr. Chisholm's sermons had often mentioned God's love; his words tonight about people being equal also suggested God did not consider a person's status as determining whether God loved them or not. If that was so, then did God love her?

Her chest grew tight. Was that truly how God saw people? Equal? Equally loved?

The thought felt shocking, running counter to generations of hereditary rank and obligation. But if it were so, perhaps it gave reason for the kindness Mr. Jardine had shown to so many. It might also explain Mr. Jardine's actions in wanting to be known for himself, to not be measured by others' shortcomings. She couldn't really blame him. She did not wish to be treated differently just because she was a viscount's daughter.

But if God really did see people as equal, regardless of title or wealth or circumstance, and belief in Him made people kinder and more accepting, then perhaps He was someone she did want to know more about. Especially if He could see into the messy confusion that was her heart and bring some hope and healing.

She sucked in a deep breath. Exhaled. Swallowed.

"God? Can you help me?"

❦ Chapter Twenty-Four

Somehow between dinner and dawn she had gathered enough scattered wits to resemble her usual buoyant self, enough to laugh off her previous night's malaise as the beginnings of a cold. This was greeted with suspicion from the older siblings, but fortunately they were either too polite or too distracted with the nearing Ridings to question otherwise. Underneath, however, was a trickling suspicion of her own, that her prayer last night had not gone completely unanswered; she had felt a sense of assurance, a measure of peace when she'd gone to sleep last night. Which would make the second time this perhaps-not-so-mythical God of the Chisholms had helped her, after her request to the heavens following her tumble . . .

She shook it off, trying to pay attention as Helena shared.

"It's the funniest thing, although a little sad, too," Helena said. "There is a feral cat that roams the alleys of town, and Mrs. Podmore is always complaining about it, that it interrupts her sleep with all its yowling and carrying on. Anyway, last night when it started again, she went outside with the heavy walking stick Gordon used to use when tramping. She saw a black shape against the back wall and gave it a few hard whacks and the creature screeched and scurried away. But this morning, when she was getting Gordon's breakfast, they noticed that Tom, their cat, was missing." Helena shook her head. "Seems the black shape was their own cat."

"Poor Mrs. Podmore."

"I suppose she deserves some sympathy, but she has always been very cross with all of us."

Verity nodded. "What is being done to search for it?"

Helena's eyes opened wide. "Tell me you are not thinking of searching. You don't even like cats!"

"No, but I can't help feeling sorry for it and for them. It wasn't the cat's fault that it was mistakenly hit."

"I suppose not."

And Verity couldn't help but feel like a search for the missing cat would help fill the hours and distract her this morning. "Let's go on a cat hunting expedition."

Helena groaned. Frances sighed. Ben met her gaze with a grin.

An hour later they were knocking on the Podmores' cottage door.

"I don't know why we always fall in with your schemes," Frances grumbled.

"I'm not exactly sure, either," Verity said. "But it is appreciated."

The door opened; their explanation met with suspicion that was soon replaced by widened eyes. "Well, if ye do that, I be mightily grateful, for that cat may be a nuisance, but he's all Gordon seems to care about. Ye know one of the grand-nieces gave 'im to us when he was just a wee kitten, nearly two years ago, and she'd be plenty upset if we cannae account for 'im."

"I'm sure. Now, Mrs. Podmore, does Tom have any preferred hiding places?"

The church bell struck the eleventh hour as she and Ben were still searching. They had split up, and Verity was growing weary, increasingly muddy, and not entirely sure this had been her best idea. But hunting for a cat along the riverbank, with a boy who preferred hunting amphibians and reptiles to felines had proved effective distraction from other, less tangible problems.

"Verity!" Frances waved. "We found him!"

They clambered up the stone steps and hurried to where Frances stood.

"You'll never believe it, but he appeared just as normal for his morning milk."

"What?" Ben's brow wrinkled. "Tom isn't dead, then?"

"Apparently she didn't whack hard enough," Frances said with a giggle.

"Well, I'm so glad for their sakes." Verity motioned Ben back to the Podmore cottage, where they met the recalcitrant pet weaving around its owner's legs. Despite now possessing a decided limp, the cat seemed quite content. Verity's lips twisted. Would that all blows could be so easily forgotten.

Mrs. Podmore nodded her appreciation. "Thank ye fer lookin'. Much obliged."

The bright chatter of the others helped distract her thoughts as they headed back to the rectory, heavy clouds soon hurrying their steps. The first splashes from the sky fell as they entered through the side door.

"Looks like you might need to forgo the ride, Verity. Would you care to play cards instead?"

And have to endure the politely unsaid speculation in various Chisholm eyes for an hour? "No, thank you. I think I might visit with Ben in the stables."

He at least would not look at her pityingly, or talk of weddings, or Friday's ride, for which, as announced at last week's masquerade, this year's winner was to receive a lordly sum of ten pounds prize money.

"Would you like me to come, too?" Helena asked.

Verity shook her head. "Do you hear that rain? I'm sure you'll be far more comfortable inside. No, really. Don't get up. Ben and I will be quite content."

And so she now stood in the stables, listening to Benjamin prattle on about spiders and their remarkable web-spinning abilities, which apparently Mr. Jardine had told him about, and wishing the rain was not *quite* so heavy as to prohibit her ride. She gazed at the floor, tracing the large, hay-strewn stones with the tip of her boot. She kicked aside some hay. Glanced down. Frowned. Were the stones carved?

She glanced at Ben. He was whittling as he chattered, oblivious to her disinterest as he continued to spout his knowledge about various insects. So she pushed aside more hay. The stones were rounded, into a complete circle. She moved to the bench and picked up a hoof pick. Bent down and dug into the crevice. It *was* carved. But why? She scuffed away the center of the circle, digging away at what must be decades-old dirt and other things she dare not contemplate, until a small groove appeared, together with a small brass ring.

"Verity? What are you doing?"

Verity eased back on her heels. "Cleaning the stable floor?"

Ben's chuckle rang off the stones.

"Do you know what this is?" She pointed to the brass ring. "Could it be an old well?"

His knife dropped with a clatter. "No. Our well is out the back." His eyes widened. "You found it! You found it, didn't you?"

"I have certainly found something," she said cautiously. She bent down, wiped the ring with the hem of her skirt, clasped it firmly, and pulled with all her might.

To no avail.

She squatted and tried again, arms straining, back paining—

"Let me have a go!"

"Really, Ben, you cannot possibly think you might be stronger than I."

But apparently he held as much presumption as his brother. He strained and huffed to no purpose. "I can't do it," he wheezed. "We shall need to get James to help."

For a moment she debated whether there was any other way of finding help instead of asking James, with his likely desire to take over. Mr. Hoskins? She sighed. "Go tell James."

He ran off, returning a short while with all his siblings. James made a great show of flexing his muscles as he squatted down, clasped the ring, straining at the heavy stones—

Before it finally shifted.

"You did it!" Benjamin peered into the dark crescent that had appeared until Helena yanked him back with a warning to be careful.

With muttered threats of doom should this prove to only be a blocked up well, James heaved the weighty cover to one side. Verity joined the siblings in gazing into the dark cavern.

The outside gloom made it hard to see, prompting Frances and Helena to run inside for lamps, amid exhortations to not let Ben get too close to the edge. They reappeared and James lit a lantern, then carefully lowered it by rope into the murky depths.

"There are steps!" Ben whooped. "It must be the tunnel."

"Sometimes wells can hold steps, in case people fall in. Remember when old Gilroy McLeod went missing? He'd fallen through the cracked timbers and couldn't get out, so he—"

"Thank you, Frances. That's enough. We don't want Ben thinking on such things," Helena said firmly. "But we do need to be careful. We don't know how deep it is. What if there is water at the bottom?"

Verity picked up a hard clod of earth. "Let's find out. If there is water, we'll hear it."

She dropped it in. There was a soft thud, no splash.

"Then it mustn't be a well—"

"But James, it might be dried up!"

He snorted. "I'm going down."

Slowly he descended, one hand on the side for balance, the other holding the lantern. "It smells pretty musty." He sneezed. "I'm nearly at the bottom—by jingo, there *is* a tunnel! High enough to walk through—"

"Wait! I'm coming, too," said Verity.

"Me, too!"

"But Benjie, you're too young."

"No, I'm not. I'm seven years old!"

"Shouldn't someone stay here in case Mama wonders where we are?"

"Are you offering, Frances?"

Silence.

Soon they had all joined James at the bottom, he and Helena holding lanterns, Verity holding Ben's hand.

"I don't like holding Frances's and Helena's hands, they always squeeze too tight," Ben whispered. "But I don't mind holding *your* hand, Verity."

The tunnel was arched with stones that glinted dully in the

lamplight, revealing a fine patina of furry green moss, interspersed occasionally with clefts as if prepared to hold a rush candle. "Someone has gone to a lot of trouble."

"It has to be the Jacobite tunnel."

"D'you think there's treasure?"

Verity chuckled. She well understood Ben's enthusiasm. "I suppose we'll find out."

James led the way, the flame flickering great shadows on the walls. Despite his protests about his sisters' squeezed hands, Verity noticed Ben was not averse to squeezing *hers* tightly. The air felt moist, cool, the air not as stale as she might have supposed. A few patches of water puddled on the ground.

"There must be some way of getting in. Look!" James pointed to the telltale signs of rodent droppings.

Verity shivered. Suddenly the tunnel felt too small, the adventure less exciting than before.

"I don't like this. What if there is a cave-in and we're all killed?"

"Frances!"

"Mama and Papa would be heartbroken. I want to go back."

"Me, too," whispered Ben.

"Well, I don't," said James. "Verity and I can go on while you three head back."

The siblings quickly agreed, leaving James and Verity to trek on.

"I've counted at least twenty paces," he said. "What distance do you think lies between the stables and Dungally?"

"Eighty? Ninety?"

"That's what I thought. Where do you suppose the end to be?"

"Mr. . . ." She swallowed. "Mr. Jardine said if a tunnel did exist it would need to come from the first floor. There—" How to explain her visit to his room? "There was no evidence of anything in the bedrooms, according to Ben."

"Hmph. He's so inquisitive, I'm sure he'd know."

Thirty paces. Thirty-one.

"Y'know, I'm sorry things turned out so badly between you two," he said gruffly.

Tears pricked her eyes. She blinked them away. "There was never anything between us."

He snorted. "Sure, and I'm a goamless wee bairn."

"No, really. He never did or said anything but what was right and proper."

Apart from the kiss. Which she had initiated. A sudden pang hit her. Had he only returned her kiss because he felt sorry for her?

Forty-five, forty-six.

"Maybe you couldn't see what any fool could, but he liked you. His face lit up whenever you talked with him, and he was never as cheerful when it was only us."

Fifty, fifty-one.

"I swear sometimes he seemed almost jealous of me," he added smugly.

"Well, he's gone now, so there's no need to talk of it anymore."

James stopped, the loss of momentum pitching Verity forward. He held the lantern up so she could see the concern in his face. "He didn't hurt you?"

Verity forced herself to maintain eye contact, to speak calmly. "Not in any way."

"Are you sure? For if he did, I'd hunt him down—"

She laughed and patted him on the arm. "You are kind, James, but there is nothing for which he can be faulted. Any hurt is to my pride, and I'm sure that is not such a bad thing, seeing as I seem to possess more than my fair share."

He chuckled, peering closely, before nodding as if satisfied. "Well, if ever you want me to call him out, just say the word."

"I want nothing save for you to be considerate to him. He is not to be held responsible for the actions of his predecessors." She thought on the times he'd appeared with hay in his hair, obviously just coming from fixing someone's property, but not wanting to sound off about his good deeds. "Indeed, he has personally seen to the restoration of various tenant houses and property. I think he is really trying to make a difference."

"But why has he gone so suddenly?"

She could only shrug.

He pursed his lips, then held the lantern forward again. Far away a gray shape scuttled away. She gasped.

"Scared of rats?"

Verity breathed in. Out. Swallowed. "They are not my favorite creatures."

He didn't snigger, for which she was grateful, only placed her hand on his arm, in a brotherly way.

The human contact comforted her, the feel of sinew and warmth and protectiveness. For some reason it reminded her of the care shown by Mr. Jardine. Her eyes blurred again.

"Careful!" James steadied her. "Now, that's about eighty. We have to be close to the end."

Don't think about the rats. Don't think about the rats . . .

A few more paces and the lantern revealed a wall. A series of crude steps, like the gnarled stumps of witch's teeth, protruded from the bricks.

"Looks like we're there. Now, I'll go up—"

"Will the stones hold you? They might be a little fragile."

"And here was I thinking you were so much more sensible about these things. You're not turning missish are you? Where's your spirit of adventure?"

"I have plenty of spirit, thank you, just a lack of interest in seeing you fall and be injured."

He placed a foot on the first broken "tooth." Frowned. "I *think* it will hold."

"Let me." She pulled him away, placing one booted foot on the gnarled stone. Pushed up, with one hand on his shoulder for balance. "It holds me. Give me the lantern."

When he protested, she snatched it from him. Pushed up again. "I find it hard to believe it was ever used. It must be near impossible to descend, especially in a hurry." Her hand found something smooth, long, vertical. "I found something like the side rails of a ladder. Here"—she handed the lantern back—"I can't hold this and pull myself up." She pressed upwards, and higher still, taking only a brief moment to look down and see James's handsome face cast into satyr-like shapes from the flickering flame. Her hair, her hands pushed through cobwebs. She grimaced, climbing higher, higher, until the stone rail stopped and her head bumped the stone ceiling. She frowned. Touched it again with her fingers. It felt warm.

"James! I think I know where it is."

"Where?"

"Hold the lantern closer to the bricks. Don't you think they seem similar to the ones in the fireplace in the Rose Room? You know, the one with the priest hole?" She placed out a hand and felt a vertical wooden surface. "I think this connects."

"But we didn't find anything."

"We weren't searching for anything more. But you know what this means?"

"We'll need to return to the Rose Room and find a latch to see if they connect." He sighed. "I wish we could go now to be sure."

"Why don't you? There is a little ledge up here I can sit upon. I'll be quite safe. If you hurry back and tell Ben, he'll be sure to twist Mr. McNaughton's arm to get inside."

"Are you sure? Should I leave the lantern?"

The thought of the furred creatures made her "yes" louder than usual.

"Well, if you're sure . . ." His voice sounded uncertain.

"I'm sure. Now go. And hurry!"

"Yes, ma'am."

And with a grin and a salute he was gone, the sound of his footsteps fading.

Leaving her with the flicker of light far below.

With the creatures of nightmares far below . . .

"No!" Speaking aloud provided reassurance. "They are down there, not here. I have no need to fear." She breathed in, calming her rapid pulse. "Do not think about that, but how to get out."

She reached out to the wooden surface, trying to gauge with the flat of her palm its dimensions. "Probably a foot wide, and maybe"—she stretched as high as she could—"at least four feet high." She thought back to the priest's hole. The wall next to the chimney breast could easily accommodate something of those proportions. But there'd have to be a mechanism to slide it open. Surely there'd be one from this side as well as inside the house . . .

Splinters rammed her fingers as she felt down the sides, searching, searching for the elusive lever.

Suddenly a clatter came below. The flame flickered out.

Verity's breath caught in her chest. Nobody was there. Nobody! It was only—she heard a scurrying sound—only a rat! She sucked in air. Exhaled loudly. She was safe. It couldn't climb.

Could it?

The old fear stole in, pressing heavy against her soul. The rustle and scurry of rodents, the helplessness as tiny feet scraped over her . . . Would she ever forget? Ever conquer the fear?

Memories surged in.

Stephen Heathcote's smirked dare. Her instant acceptance; well might his sister Sophia be called goosish, but Verity would rather *die* than be so labeled. The clandestine ride in the early morning of Caroline's wedding. She'd known she should be a good girl for once, but the dress Mama had chosen was simply horrible, so ugly, itchy, and stiff. She hadn't wanted to put it on a second sooner than necessary. Escaping the maids hadn't been as hard as saddling Banshee. But she'd managed. Enjoyed an all too brief ride, until the too-tall hedge. The fall. The ache in her arm. The sudden knowledge she would be late, and in trouble yet again . . .

She remembered the long limp home. The relief upon sighting the house. Then the loud crack, the sudden tumble down into a long-abandoned ice house. Splintering pain in her ankle. She couldn't move! Couldn't stand! Mama would be furious! The sounds in the dim, cool bricked corners. The realization that the creatures in the corners were unlike the sweet pet mice she'd secretly kept in the stables; these ones had red eyes and sharp, yellow teeth . . .

Verity shuddered.

Her calls for help had been ignored, and exhaustion meant she'd eventually succumbed to sleep. Then when she'd woken . . .

Her skin prickled anew.

She'd woken to see the creatures climbing over her, nipping at her clothes, burying under her dress. They'd told her later it was the strength of her screams and sobs that had finally drawn the servants' attention.

She remembered the sobbing most of all. The tears she'd not shed since, until yesterday. That, and the high-pitched screech of Mama, a screech so loud the villagers must have heard it, followed by a plethora of abuse.

Ungrateful, reckless girl. Foolish, selfish creature. Wicked, wretched mistake.

The scuttling, rustling sound below grew louder. Her throat thickened. Lungs grew tight. Something suspiciously like a whimper leapt from her chest.

"God?"

The words escaped as a whisper, prickling the darkness, prickling her skin. But in the echo of that whisper she felt assurance. She wasn't alone.

Verity wiped her cheeks. Her arms ached, her back was sore, the only reason her legs were not cramping was surely due to her many hours of horse riding. But here in the weighty darkness, she suddenly *knew* she wasn't alone.

God was here.

God was *here*.

She shivered.

It seemed so strange to be thinking God might notice her. It seemed so strange to be thinking of God at all! The best-intentioned sermons had not done so. Haverstock's chapel services had not, either. Yet here she was, reflecting that the One she'd always thought but an invisible mythical being might not be so mythical, after all.

Was that why she was here in Scotland? Had she been brought here as part of that divine plan Mr. Jardine believed existed in nature? What if her being here was not a matter of chance and coincidence? What if being here was not only to escape her mother's wishes, but also to find peace with God? After the past few weeks, she was prepared to accept God's existence. But friendship with Him, the kind Helena and the Chisholms and Mr. Jardine thought possible, seemed to enjoy . . . Could God really want friendship with her, too?

Mr. Chisholm's comments from last night resurfaced: "People tend to judge others on their outward appearance, but God looks at the heart . . . God loves people . . . we are all equal in God's sight."

Was it true that God regarded all people equally? Her parents didn't. They judged others according to their title and wealth—or lack thereof. But if God did not care about such things, then did this also mean God did not compare her goodness—or lack of—to others? That while she might not be as good as, say, Mrs. Chisholm, God might still desire her to be His friend?

She was not meek and pliable. She was not sweet and humble. She possessed fire and spunk that Grandmama might applaud but so many others openly deplored. God couldn't want her, too.

Could He?

"God?"

A trace of hope licked her heart, underlining her voice as it echoed in the stone chamber.

"Do You want me?"

A verse flickered into memory, one she'd heard quoted in weekly chapel services at Haverstock's, something about God loving the whole world that whosoever believed should not perish but should have eternal life . . .

If that were true, then surely as Verity was part of the whole world God must love her, too. And *whosoever* must mean everyone. Anyone. Even her.

"God, do You love me?"

Something seemed to echo deep within, like a voice she could not hear, whispering affirmation.

Her pulse increased. Was she mad to think God answered? Oh, how her sisters would laugh to think she heard from God! But perhaps she would be mad to ignore Him still . . .

For if *God* loved her, despite her mistakes—despite her feeling like

CAROLYN MILLER

she *was* a mistake—then surely it did not matter if others did not love her. Even if her parents did not. Even if Mr. Jardine did not.

Her eyes welled, and she sucked in a musty-laden breath. Exhaled.

"I'm sorry for thinking myself so clever. I'm sorry for ignoring You for so long." Her whispered words resounded in the darkness. "I know I'm filled with mistakes, filled with . . . sin."

Her various misdemeanors rolled before her, a roll call of her shame. She might have had good intentions, but how often had stubborn pride led her to deceive? So many times she had fallen short of the promise of her name. How blind had she been?

The promise of the verse stole through her recriminations. She licked salt-tinged lips, swallowed the lump in her throat. "But You say whoever believes in You shall not perish but will have eternal life. I . . . I do not know much, but I believe You are real."

Something Helena had said months ago drifted into her mind.

"I . . . I ask Your forgiveness. I want eternal life. Help me to trust You."

She held her breath, wondering what would happen. For a second, there was nothing. Then . . .

Warmth, unlike anything she'd ever experienced before, swelled in her chest and spread outwards, through her cramped legs to her toes, down her aching arms to her fingers, leaving every part of her tingling. Something that felt like peace, glorious, wonderful peace, surged through her soul, her mind, her heart, flooding her with assurance, leaving the shadowy stains of her past washed away, cleansed. Through the tumult of emotion came fresh clarity: she was *not* a mistake, she was unique, she was forgiven, she was loved.

Assurance. Forgiveness. Love.

Tears spilled from her eyes, and she laughed at herself, the sound echoing against the stones. How ridiculous to be crying at such a moment! But the emotions could not be contained. Gladness, deep, deep gladness, filled her heart, spilled from her mouth, as she sat, heart and mind whirling in the wonder of grace.

She exhaled. "Thank You, God."

Minutes passed. Rare contentment filled her chest. Come what

261

may, she was not alone. God's presence was near. She could trust Him. And she *would* trust Him.

She would trust Him in this last week of freedom.

She would trust Him with her future.

She would trust Him with her heart.

After thinking, praying, wondering, and waiting for what felt an age, there came a scratching sound, a banging sound, new noises, like voices far away. "Hello?"

She craned her neck, looked up over her shoulder. A sliver of light enlarged.

"Verity?"

"Oh, thank goodness!"

A minute more of thuds and wrenched wood and the light loomed larger. Then she saw James's face, then his hand, and he pulled her up into the paneled priest hole, then out into the Rose Room in a cloud of dust and coughs.

"Oh, thank you!" Verity exclaimed, wiping the strands of cobwebs from her skin, smiling at her rescuers, as Helena and her siblings smothered her in hugs. How dear they were to her! "I'm so *very* glad to see you."

"We're so very glad you're safe!"

Beyond James's shoulder the housekeeper's face wrinkled in disapproval, and she gave a loud sniff. "Destroying the laird's house while he's away. I've never knew such a hoyden!"

Verity lifted her chin. Smiled. "Thank you."

Mrs. Iverson began a long tirade, which ceased when Mr. McNaughton said that the laird had been just as keen to find the tunnel, and would doubtless be most appreciative to the young people.

A small dog hurried in, adding his furious barks to the noise.

"Oh! Who is this?"

"This here be Dougal," Mac said. "The master's new dog."

"Hello, Dougal." Verity held out her hand for the dog to sniff, which he did, and followed with a friendly lick, then dismissed her with a bark and trotted from the room.

Ben and his siblings continued to proffer questions, Verity answering as best she could, keeping her peace, a small smile on her face, the recent glory still so real it was like nothing could touch her. She answered mechanically while covertly studying James. He'd proved himself so kind today, so thoughtful. What could she do to help him? *Lord?*

Her earlier ruminations coalesced into renewed purpose. God considered men and women equal. He had no interest in men's pride. God had gifted Verity with specific skills and aptitudes, like adventurousness, and horsemanship, and stubbornness, and compassion.

She met Mrs. Iverson's frown and smiled wider. And if that meant behaving like a hoyden she would certainly do so. She had nothing left to lose.

CHAPTER TWENTY-FIVE

"VERITY! YOU WOULDN'T!"

"And why not?" Verity flashed a smile at Helena then smoothed her hair flat as she gazed at herself critically in the mirror. "I'm sure no one would know I was a girl."

"But whatever would you wear?"

"Do you think James—?"

"No!"

"—has some clothes he has outgrown? Perhaps your mama stores them for Benjamin's future use."

Helena stared with rounded eyes. "But you cannot! It would be utterly scandalous!"

"Only if I am discovered. Which I won't be, not with your help."

"But I . . . I do not know if I want to help you, Verity."

"Would you not like to see James beat horrid Colin? To see the arrogant beaten at their own game?"

"Well, yes, but that is only if you *do* beat them. And as soon as they discover your true identity, you will be banished—"

"I am leaving next week anyway. Besides, they will not discover my true sex, not unless something calamitous occurs. And you know I have a most careful seat."

"But you fell trying to ride astride!"

"That was long ago."

"But dressing as a boy is so improper!"

"Come, Helena. You know the worst that will happen is that I will end up somewhat mud-spattered. There is nothing to fear. Just think of it as a form of masquerade."

"But if Mama finds out—"

"I will take all the blame. You know that your mama loves you dearly, and will certainly be quite justified in blaming your madcap friend."

"But why do you wish to do this?"

"Because your brother has proved quite kind, and I would like to help him. Just think, with the prize money he might be able to buy himself a new horse! Besides, I am sick and tired of being thought inferior to males, and it is high time they were taught a lesson. Now, where might your mother store James's old clothes?"

An hour later they had returned to the room, and Verity quickly dressed in the riding attire Helena had reluctantly retrieved. She pulled her braids tight, flattening them to fit under the long linen neckcloth she tied around her neck.

"What do you think?"

"I think it is scandalous, but if you insist on wearing it . . ." Helena sighed, moving to adjust the folds. "He would not like me saying so, but I have helped James tie his neckcloth many a time. There." She stepped back, frowning. "Put your hat and coat on."

Verity shrugged into the coat, whose padded shoulders would not reveal her slight frame too closely. She plonked the beaver hat on, and struck a pose.

Helena giggled. "I still cannot abide seeing you in a pair of breeches, but I must admit, you do look quite fetching."

"It helps to not possess your bosom."

"Verity!"

"What? You must know that you possess a far more feminine face and figure than I."

Helena blushed. "But to speak of such things—"

"Is something at which only missish young ladies balk. And we are not such simpletons, are we?"

Helena sighed. "I suppose not."

Verity glanced at herself before pulling out a scarf. "I think if I can cover my mouth . . ."

"And not speak? Yes, that will be important to maintain the disguise. But will it be possible?"

Verity chuckled. "That remains to be seen."

Helena's laughter dissolved once more. "Oh, but there will be fireworks indeed if you are discovered!"

"Then I shall endeavor to do my best not to be."

<hr />

"Sir! It is good to have you returned."

"Thank you. It is good to be back."

Very good. His business had gone sufficiently well; his other matters, not so easily. It had been good to escape, but he was now extremely weary, his body carrying every bump of the past one hundred miles.

"I trust everything went satisfactorily?"

"Satisfactorily enough."

More he wouldn't say, couldn't say, until he'd sorted things within his own heart. He coughed. "How are things here?"

"Well enough. There have been no issues with the tenants."

"Good." But Mac's gaze held a tinge of trouble. "What is it?"

"It is the other matter, though. I'm afraid your identity is now known." Mac quickly filled him in.

The regrets that had hurried him home gnawed afresh. "I should have told them."

"Yes."

He sighed. Recrimination swirled. He shook it away. "Can you tell me why the village is abuzz?"

"It's the day of the Ridings, sir." Mac cleared his throat. "Not knowing you planned to return today, I allowed some of the young people to sit on the rooftop terrace to view the race."

"Very good."

Much as he wanted to ascend immediately, he forced himself to attend to Mac's accounting, to scratch an ecstatic Dougal behind the ears, to listen to Mrs. Iverson's discourse concerning his lairdly duties. It would not do to appear too eager.

"And sir, you'll never guess what Mr. Iverson discovered in the cellar. Whiskey! Ten great casks in a little room down there. Very good whiskey, too, he said."

"If you like the taste of turpentine," Mac murmured, forcing Anthony to conceal a smile.

When he finally escaped Mrs. Iverson's ramblings he jogged up the circular staircase to the rooftop terrace. He was wheezing when he opened the door. Three red heads lowered their spyglasses and turned to him.

"Mr. Jardine! You are back!"

"Good day, Miss Chisholm, Frances, Ben." He coughed, bracing himself on the stone wall.

"James and Alasdair are racing," Benjamin said. "We wanted to see them, and this is the best place from which to see the race. We asked Mac and he said the laird, I mean, you wouldn't mind."

"Of course I don't."

Three pairs of green eyes looked accusingly at him.

"I am sorry for not telling you earlier. I wanted time to be known for myself and not as the laird."

"And now you're known as a fraudster," Helena muttered, turning away.

"Miss Chisholm, I—"

"I do not think it was a very good trick to play," Frances continued. "Verity got very upset when she realized you'd lied to us all."

A twinge crossed his chest. "I am very sorry. It was never my intention to hurt anyone."

"No?"

"Miss Chisholm, I *am* sorry—"

"Oh, look! You can see them!" Benjamin's cry took them closer to the parapet. He held his spyglass with one hand, and with the other pointed to the ridge. "Look, there is James! Lightning is only three horses from the lead."

Anthony thanked God for the distraction, though he knew he still needed to make amends. He watched as the horses traded places, pushing to the lead, dropping behind, the eagerness of the others infectious.

"This is exciting watching from here. Normally we only see them flash past but to see them stretch out at this distance is splendid!" Frances said, peering through her spyglass. "We are quite passionate about stopping the English invasion, as you can see."

The English invasion. He nodded. His heart had been under siege for weeks now, thanks to a certain English maid.

As Frances and Ben exchanged views, Anthony murmured to Helena, "Where is your friend?"

She glanced sideways at him, a sudden speculative look, which caused his face to warm. "Do you possibly refer to Verity?"

He inclined his head.

Helena bit her lip.

"It is just that I expected to see her interested in the horse racing."

"Oh, she is," Frances interrupted. "But she was so disgusted at the race being only for men, she decided to go out riding, too."

Helena turned away, a little smile on her face.

Anthony saw the little smile, saw how she strained to watch the riders. His attention returned to the riders, but from this distance he could distinguish little. "Who is in the lead?"

"Guthrie." Ben squinted. "No wait, James—"

"The rider on the piebald is approaching fast. Who is that?" Frances wondered.

Anthony slid a glance at Helena. Her smile stretched. He looked back at the riders. The brown and white horse, the slight figure . . . His heart thumped uncomfortably hard in his chest. "Where did you say Miss Hatherleigh was?"

Her cheeks reddened. "Riding."

Dawning suspicion kept his voice low. "Do you mean to say she races with them?"

"I mean to say nothing." She pressed her lips together and lifted her chin, refusing to look at him, in a manner reminiscent of her friend.

His heart hitched. Verity was racing with the men? "But what if she's hurt? She could die."

Helena turned to look at him quickly. "You mustn't look like that. She will be safe." But her voice held an element of doubt.

"How could you let her?" He wanted to shake her. To shake Verity!

"Have you ever tried to stop her from doing what she wants?" Helena asked, in a wry tone. "Besides, she means no harm. Here." She passed him the spyglass.

Lord, keep her safe. Breath suspended as he watched the piebald draw nearer to the two leaders, angling closer to the others in a display of skilled horsemanship. He coughed again.

"Which one is she?"

Just as he'd suspected she pointed to the leading group of three, who had achieved a small break from the pack. "The piebald."

Where had she obtained such a mount? He watched as the horses sailed over a low hedge, one, two, three. From this distance there was nothing to distinguish the third horseman as a horsewoman. "She is a capital rider."

"Oh, she has excellent bottom. Oh!" She glanced at him, pink tinting her cheeks. "James often says that of Verity's riding, that she holds her seat very well. And she doesn't have much fear."

"Apparently not."

He continued to watch as the riders raced along the ridge. Gradually his own fear subsided, replaced with grudging admiration. "I don't understand. How did she get away with it?"

"James's old clothes."

"Surely James did not consent to such a thing."

She flushed and angled away, moving to join her siblings' loud chatter.

His chest tightened as the horses approached another steep climb. "God help her."

"Come on, Firefly," Verity urged as the little mare cantered up the slope. Just one more pass and they would be onto the straight, toward the town hall and the waiting spectators. The little mare was panting, her breath coming in heavy bursts. "Let's show those boys what we are capable of."

As if in response to her plea, Firefly appeared to find renewed energy, and surged behind Lightning, inching closer, closer to the proud colt's flying tail. Verity pulled the scarf lower to draw in fresh air. Guthrie was still leading by a slim margin, but his stallion was tiring. If she could cut him off . . .

The path was muddy, but Firefly's steps were sure as Verity swung close, rounding the corner with less than an inch to spare. There! Guthrie's chestnut stallion heaved hot breath as she urged Firefly past, steering her slightly to the right, forcing the stallion's stride to shorten, three footfalls instead of four. As she moved, James pushed into the space she'd created, pushing, pushing, as they passed from the wood to rejoin the road. Now, to ensure he kept the lead . . .

Hooves clattered along the cobblestones as they neared the church. Spectators lined the road, their cheers and calls a cacophony of sound, their faces blurring as Verity sped past. She could not let anyone think she had run less than her best . . .

Fifty yards, forty-five, forty.

From the corner of her eyes she saw a smudge of chestnut. No! If Colin overtook her now, he might just win.

"Come on, Firefly!"

She ducked lower, making her body as small as possible to reduce resistance from the wind. They inched ahead. "Come on, James!" she called.

She saw his attention waver, saw him glance her direction, saw him falter, saw Guthrie's stallion loom into view—

"Hurry!" she screamed.

Twenty yards, fifteen. Verity pressed her knees into Firefly's sides. "Come on, girl!"

Ten yards, five. The finish line was a blur of people. Gunfire cracked, announcing the winner.

James had won by a whisker.

Breath heaving, she slowed to a canter, to a trot, past the cheering crowds, blood still thumping in her ears. This part of the plan had always been a little hazy. She glanced over her shoulder. James and Colin had stopped just past the finish line, Colin's face darker than a thundercloud. She bit her lip. Whilst glad to see him get his comeuppance, she did not imagine he would be terribly pleased to learn she was the one responsible for slowing his pace and ensuring his third position. She steered Firefly past the hands reaching to pat her on the back, looking vainly for Helena. Where should she go? The raucous crowds made escape impossible.

"Good riding, laddie."

Verity nodded, smiling under the readjusted muffler. What would the man say if she lowered the scarf to reveal she was a lassie?

"Go on back. They be awardin' the prize. Sir Donald don't look none too happy, but he needs still award the money. 'Tis only fair."

More voices added to the chorus, forcing her to turn and maneuver Firefly through the crowd. She did not wish to appear a spoilsport, but what would happen should she be discovered?

"James Chisholm is the winner."

Amidst the loud cheer she leaned across and shook his hand. She tugged the scarf down a fraction, coughed, aiming to speak in as deep a tone as possible. "Congratulations, James."

Caught in the maelstrom of adulation, he shook her outstretched hand blindly, before his eyes finally rested on her, widening in shock. "You?"

She smiled, returned the scarf into position, glanced at the red-headed arbiter, and urged Firefly through the jostling crowds and raced away. Within minutes she had returned to the rectory, then began the wild scramble to wash the worst of the mud from poor Firefly's coat, divest herself of male clothes, and hurry into a morning gown before stuffing the male attire under her bed. She flew out the door and ran down the road to the village's still-teeming throngs.

Anxious to keep from James's sight—or capture the attention of anyone who might recognize the second-place getter—she skirted the crowd until she noticed Helena, hand over brow, obviously searching. Behind her were Frances and Ben.

"Helena!"

Within seconds they were laughing. "Oh, if only you could let them know how well you had done!" Helena said in an undertone.

"Everyone is looking for the rider who came second," Ben said. "Did you see him?"

"No," Verity said exchanging glances with Helena, "I didn't see *him*."

Frances looked at her, brow puckered. Looked back at Helena. Her eyes rounded. "No!"

"Look, there's James!" Ben pushed past the crowd, his sturdy legs soon carrying him from view. They moved to a quieter spot, where they could see his bright head weaving through the crowds.

Helena turned, the amusement in her eyes draining away, as worry knit her brow. "Verity, there is something you should—"

"There you are!"

She glanced up and met James's narrow-eyed, flat-lipped glare, incongruous among the cheering crowd. "Why, hello, James." She smiled. "I believe congratulations are in order?"

"You are incorrigible!" he hissed, shaking his head. He managed a stiff smile as another congratulatory remark was tossed his way. Then was led away by Alasdair into the crush of well-wishers.

"Oh dear," Helena murmured. "Seems my brother is not quite as enamored with you as before."

"A burden I will cheerfully carry." They turned towards home, the servants and a few elderly farmers ahead on the stone bridge.

"Verity, did you really ride Firefly today?"

Verity met Frances's concerned gaze. "I took her out for a bit of a run."

"No, I mean did you ride her in the race?"

"Frances! Did you not know? Only males are permitted to ride. Surely you could not imagine my involvement in such a thing. Why, the very idea is scandalous!"

Frances eyed her for a moment then chuckled. "I did not recognize Firefly for the longest time."

"Well, she did get a little muddy today."

"You made her look piebald."

"She certainly needed a good wash when I got back."

"But your clothes!"

At the clatter of hooves, they turned to see James leading Lightning, nodding as he was congratulated by a few stragglers. Mr. and Mrs. Chisholm walked a little way behind.

"James proved unwittingly helpful, there," Helena said, glancing up at her older sibling.

He did not return her smile, his eyes fixed on Verity. "I suppose you think you're very clever."

"Only moderately, I assure you."

He snorted. "I didn't expect you to go to such lengths to prove a point."

"And what point is that?"

"I suppose you think a little mud and a set of clothes will make you equal, but I can assure you it does not."

"And I can assure you I do not think it is outward appearance that ensures we are equal, but more the inner character and accomplishments that prove we are."

He whipped a nearby bush with his riding crop. "In that case your character proves you to be shameless."

"And yours prove you to be a poor winner."

"Only because you nearly killed me on the water jump!"

"I did not! It was the merest tap, and it wouldn't have happened if you had been watching where you should be traveling instead of watching me."

"You might have got yourself killed!"

"James!" Helena put up a hand. "You are aware others can hear you."

"Oh, and I suppose it was you who helped Verity find clothes. Wait!" He frowned. "Surely they weren't *my* clothes that you dressed her in?"

Helena smiled sweetly. "How else was I supposed to find something so easy at hand?"

"How dare—"

"Calm yourself, James. It was only your castoffs, the ones saved for Benjamin."

"Well, that makes everything acceptable, then," he said sarcastically before scowling at his sister. "What do you think Alasdair will say when he finds out you are so incorrigible?"

Helena blanched, and Verity hastened to say, "He will only find out if you tell him."

James snorted again. "Don't you think it is already known? Irvin Hargreaves heard you, as no doubt did a dozen other people at the finish line."

Verity bit her lip. Mr. Hargreaves, the race official, who possessed a thatch of red hair and an unforgiving posture . . .

"James, please don't tell Mama," Helena pleaded.

"If he does, I will bear all responsibility, Helena. You need not worry."

"But what if Alasdair finds out? Or worse, his parents? They will never think me suitable."

"And with actions like this, you prove yourself not!"

As Helena's face crumpled, Verity glared at James. "Don't be ridiculous. Anyone who overlooks Helena's sweet kindness is not worthy of her." Verity bit down hard on her bottom inside lip, working to gentle her voice as Mr. and Mrs. Chisholm drew near. "And if necessary, I will go and explain things to Alasdair's parents and anyone else who cares, to prove today's undertaking was all my own doing and you are not to be held responsible for any of it."

"Th-thank you." Helena caught Ben by the arm as he raced past. "Stop!"

"Ow!" he cried out as he wriggled to be free.

"We really should return, for Verity there is something you simply must—"

"Verity, wasn't that the most fun ever?" Ben chattered. "But I sure would like to know who the mysterious rider was. Did you hear?

They don't know who the person who came second is, so they're calling him the mystery rider. The Guthries are livid. Colin says whoever it is nearly knocked him down! I woulda liked to have seen that, wouldn't you?"

Verity fought a smile. "I'm sure that would be a sight to behold."

"I'll say! But I think James should be pretty glad the mystery rider was there, otherwise he might not have won. What do you think?"

She refused to look at his seething brother. "I'm sure he would have held his own."

"I don't know. I heard Lachlan's da say Guthrie was a sure thing! Hey, Verity, did you know Mr. Jardine has returned?"

She stumbled. "I beg your pardon?"

"He returned home this morning. We saw him when we were on top of the tower. You can see for miles up there! He didn't seem very well, he was coughing a lot. Ouch, Verity, you're squeezing my hand!"

"I . . . I'm sorry, Ben."

Further words she could not say. Like Moses, only parting a group of people, the laird stood at the Chisholms' drive, his gaze fixed on her. Her mouth dried. She might have courage enough for a wild horse race, but oh, if only she were brave enough to run away now!

Chapter Twenty-Six

Anthony saw the first moment she noticed him. Saw the blood drain from her face. Saw the reluctance as Benjamin almost dragged her forward in his hurry to say hello.

"Mr. Jardine! Mr. Jardine! Did you know James won?"

"I gathered as much from the noise I heard earlier." Anthony smiled at him, before looking at the winner. "Congratulations, James."

James nodded in answer, shooting Verity a scathing look before disappearing into the stables with his horse.

"I would have imagined he'd be a little happier," he said mildly. "It seems an important occasion. I certainly did not anticipate returning to such excitement."

"I'm afraid such excitement must be forgiven. Imagine, my son, lead rider," Mr. Chisholm said, pride suffusing his features. "Well, well."

"And who would want a dull and dreary life?" Verity muttered.

Anthony shot her a searching look. But before he could ask her meaning, Mrs. Chisholm had motioned him to her side.

"Mr. Jardine, welcome back. You must come and take tea with us, and tell us all about your time away."

He glanced between them. "I have no wish to intrude."

"Oh, there will be plenty of time to prepare for tonight's ball."

"Ball?"

"Have you forgotten? It's held at the Guthries to celebrate the selection of the lead rider. Such a special night in the village. Everyone over the age of sixteen is expected. The ball doesn't begin until after sunset, though, to allow enough time for the riders to rest before putting on their finery. So, you see, that allows plenty of time to hear about your time in Edinburgh before any of us need start dressing."

Perhaps this could be his way of explaining his actions. "Thank you."

Minutes later he was in the drawing room, sipping tea, trying to ignore the hurt in his heart at Verity's studied avoidance. Not once had she looked him directly in the face. Did she remember their last encounter? Was she thinking on his misrepresentation about being the laird? Was she troubled about Amelia? Or was she simply concerned about the ramifications of today's escapade, should the truth about the identity of the second-place getter become known?

"And I believe you visited your parents," Mrs. Chisholm said. "How are they?"

"Well, but getting on in years."

"Have they no wish to see Dungally?"

"They have no wish to travel beyond Edinburgh, and have never understood those who wish for more." He took another sip of tea, snuck a look at Verity. She sat poised on the edge of the sofa, head bowed, as if listening intently.

"And your business?"

"My solicitor is quite taken with the plans we have for the estate. It seems there are others who are also investigating the benefits of improving soil for better cropping."

Frustration rose like bile in his throat. Soil? Cropping? Why was he talking of this when he should be speaking of what truly mattered? What could he say to explain himself?

"I"—he coughed—"I had reason to see an old friend from university days. My sister and I spent quite some time with the Witherspoole family when growing up."

Verity exchanged glances with Helena, who said, "I did not know you had a sister, sir."

"Aileen is younger than I. She got married at eighteen. Amelia is her best friend." He placed the cup on the small table with a clatter.

"Amelia and I were quite fond of each other until I felt the call to minister in New South Wales. I'm afraid she and her family could not quite understand such a notion, and let me know in unmistakable fashion."

"Pardon me, but what call did you serve?"

"The call of God to share the good news of the gospel. I was a curate in the Church of England." He sighed. "My parents have never understood why I did not seek service in the Kirk, and stay in Scotland, and neither could the Witherspooles. I confess I'd put off seeing them on my return, but can now say I'm very glad that I did."

"Why is that, Mr. Jardine?" said Helena.

"Because it confirmed to me that anything I once felt has since died. I'm afraid Miss Witherspoole and I would never have suited. She is too quiet and retiring, preferring her own comforts above the needs of others. I cannot offer her a life like that."

Mr. Chisholm murmured agreement, but Anthony barely paid attention, too conscious of the girl who had stilled at his words.

Verity finally met his gaze. "Does not our Lord command us to care for our neighbors?"

His breath hitched. "*Our* Lord, Miss Hatherleigh?"

She nodded, her gaze wrapped in his. "I have learned a great deal in the time you have been away, not least of which is how our heavenly Father regards His children."

"You now believe?"

"Yes." And the peace in her eyes affirmed her words.

Joy exploded through his chest. "I am so *very* glad."

"I . . . I cannot help but give thanks for the fact that He loves us, and does not regard us as mistakes."

"No one who truly knows you, Miss Hatherleigh, could ever think of you as such," he said softly.

She smiled at last, her smile curling warmth into the corners of his heart.

Oh, to know her thoughts towards him, to know whether she too dreamed about their kiss. "I would be very happy to hear more of your discoveries—"

"Oh, Mr. Jardine! Did you hear? I discovered the tunnel!" Ben cried, sliding a glance at Verity. "Well, Verity and I did. Oh, and James. Anyway, it comes out at the priest's hole! Do you want me to show you? We could go now, if you've finished. Come on, sir!"

And before he knew it, the small boy had him by the hand and was dragging him to the stables, while thoughts of Verity and tunnels and faith left Anthony in a whirl of exhilaration. She believed! Such things as her age and station no longer seemed of consequence; both would matter less with time.

Finally, there was nothing to stop them.

"She is a good girl, I believe."

Verity stopped outside the drawing room's open door, and continued buttoning her pelisse, her movements quiet so as not to attract attention. Mr. and Mrs. Chisholm could not be talking about her. She should be upstairs finishing getting dressed for tonight's ball, but the room had felt as constricting as her future. And her heart still felt too full, too conflicted, so she planned a walk outside in the cool evening air, something she would have few chances more to do. She'd be forced to return in five days. Just five days!

"Of course, I'd much rather she end up with a good Scottish lad. And he'd do so nicely for her, even if he is a wee bit older. It's my belief an older husband would rein in some of the wilder excesses I believe she's been prone to in the past." A sigh came from the room. "But Lady Aynsley has always had rather lofty ideas about rank and titles and the like."

She stilled. They *were* talking about her.

"I will miss her when she goes."

Verity's throat closed. Her mother's latest letter had said Papa's man would collect her soon, but how could she leave? How could she exchange this freedom for the binds of matrimony to a man she cared not for? She knew she should trust God, but how could she cope?

She eased open the side door and hurried outside, walking in the shadowed recesses provided by the trees to the path and down to the estuary and the wooden seat with the glorious view.

The sky held touches of lilac, lavender, and faraway golden plumes, as though a phoenix had traversed the earth, trailing gold, and now flew across the Irish Sea. In the distance, Benjamin searched the shoreline. Beyond the bay, half a dozen gulls were silhouetted, fleeing the onset of dark as they headed to the light.

Lord, help me trust You.

A strange kind of peace settled upon her soul as she drank in the glory of the sunset. She inhaled the briny tang as the cooling air whisked dark tendrils into her face. She gazed up, up at the radiant orb, wishing for the hundredth time for one more miracle: that she might stay. If only she could stay here forever.

"Bon soir, mademoiselle."

She glanced up, lips curving. "Somehow I knew you would come."

Mr. Jardine's brow lifted, but the easy smile he always wore upon seeing her didn't falter. "How so?"

She gestured to the dying rays of sunlight. "I knew you would appreciate this as I."

"It is lovely," he agreed, gaze fixed on her.

Heat seemed to shimmer from deep within. She knew her face had to be quite pink. "Did you like the tunnel, sir?"

"It is a remarkable piece of workmanship. Benjamin was telling me how you stayed in the tunnel whilst the others were figuring how to access it from above. Were you not scared?"

"Yes. I have always hated the dark."

"You surprise me."

"Well, actually, I don't mind the dark. It's the creatures that live in it that I loathe."

"Ah, so the indomitable Miss Verity possesses an Achilles' heel."

"You think me indomitable?"

"I think you all that is stalwart and strong." He smiled. "Do not frown. I merely try to compliment you. Would that more people were so."

She ducked her head. She didn't feel very strong right now; her emotions felt rather wobbly and weak. Would he finally admit the reason for his deception? Would he finally explain why he'd left?

"Now, I must confess to an overwhelming desire to know about your journey to faith. May I?"

At her nod, he joined her on the wooden seat; near, but not beyond propriety. She shared about her experience in the tunnel, her conversation with Mr. Chisholm afterwards, the joy Helena had exhibited when Verity finally told her about her belief.

"I am so very pleased for you, Miss Hatherleigh."

"I am, too. I feel this sense of assurance now, that no matter what happens in the future, God is going to help me."

"Something to be thankful for, indeed."

She noticed his hand, tanned, scarred, yet possessing the fingers of a scholar, gently relax. What would his fingers feel like in hers? She gazed up, noting his profile also held the look of contentment, his hair glinting softly in the light, his nose slightly bent, like it may have been broken, his lips holding a firmness, a promise . . .

Her breath caught.

He turned. Those lips curved. "You are enjoying the view?"

Words refused utterance. She could only nod.

"It is enough to make one wish for an artist, do you not agree?"

She nodded again. Oh, if only she'd known such a man existed she would have paid more attention in art lessons!

His lips stretched wider. "What is the matter, my dear Miss Verity?" Oh, he made her name sound so treasured! "You appear as though struck dumb by a visiting angel."

No, the heaven-sent creature sat beside her still.

As his gaze became concerned, she shook her head, making a desperate effort to clear her throat, to swallow, to speak.

He had to tell her. The heaviness of his unsaid explanation grew every day, weighting his soul until even his prayers felt like they were not lifting past the ornate ceiling of his bedroom.

"Miss Hatherleigh?"

She turned, flashed a smile that appeared to him to contain a little less than its usual diamond brilliance. "Yes, Mr. Jardine?"

He coughed.

Her brow puckered. "Mr. Jardine? Is something the matter?"

The concern in her eyes made his heart thump. He licked his bottom lip. "Miss Hatherleigh, I—"

"Verity! Verity! Look what I found!"

At Benjamin's shouted call, her gaze wavered. Anthony picked up her hands, reclaiming her attention. He had to say this, had to speak the truth, had to speak it *now*. "Miss Hatherleigh, Verity . . ." Her cheeks pinked, soft light filling her eyes. "I needed to confess something long ago. I am—"

"Not merely a gardener? I have known this for some time, sir."

"I know, but—"

"Verity!" Benjamin appeared. "Oh, hello, Mr. Jardine. I was just looking for another newt. The other one ran away, or else the Cready found it. But I reckon she woulda told Ma about it if she had, don't you?"

"I, er—"

"I like your new doggie. He doesn't bark too much, does he? Hey, did you know you have a pair of owls nesting? Mr. Jardine, why are you holding Verity's hands? Are you sweethearts?"

"Benjamin!" Verity tried to pull her hands away, but Anthony gripped them more firmly.

"I am trying to have a serious conversation with Miss Hatherleigh here, which your presence makes something of a challenge."

Benjamin cocked his head but didn't move. "But why are you holding hands? I don't think Mama would like that, not unless you are going to marry—"

"Benjamin!" Verity's cheeks were now bright red. "Be a good boy and go home. I'm sure they are wondering where you are."

He frowned, but scuttled off in the direction of the rectory, looking over his shoulder at them.

Verity gazed up at Anthony, wry amusement playing around her lips. "I'm afraid he is not especially mindful of others, but then, he is only seven."

"And he does seem to possess a protective streak to rival his brother's. Miss Hatherleigh, there is something I simply must say before we are interrupted again."

Her smile grew, her silvery blue eyes alight with stars. "Yes, Mr. Jardine?"

He opened his mouth.

I am the laird.

The words wouldn't come. He cleared his throat. Tried again. "I am . . ."

But try as he might, still they wouldn't come, no doubt hampered by weeks of lying by omission. *Lord, forgive me.* He wiped his heated brow, and repossessed her hands.

"Miss Hatherleigh"—he drew in a breath—"I am the laird." He continued in a rush. "I am very sorry that I did not tell you my true identity before. I know what you thought, that I was working for him. I did not mean to hurt anyone, not seeing this as a deception with intent to hurt—"

"But you lied to me." Her eyes, always the window to her soul, showed her disappointment and confusion.

He pressed her hands gently. "Please forgive me. I should have said something sooner, but my little subterfuge soon got out of hand. When I first met you and you assumed I was the gardener, well in truth, I was. I was so new to my role it seemed hard to see myself as anything but a gardener. I have always enjoyed working with plants, and when I arrived here the amount of work to be done was so overwhelming I had to get involved."

"And that was why I was so happy to help you."

"The amazing Miss Hatherleigh." He smiled at her. "Compassionate, decisive, loyal, always willing to help others." He raised a brow. "Even if at times her method of helping might be considered scandalous?"

"You know about today?" At his nod, her cheeks pinked. "Did Helena tell you?"

"She did not need to. I must congratulate you on such a remarkable disguise."

"I was only trying to help James. I don't think he really understands that, and just resents me. But Colin Guthrie is an arrogant cheat, and I can never abide such people."

"Your sense of justice is admirable."

"My means to accomplishing it less so?"

"I did not say that."

"You did not need to." She sighed. "I only hope the Chisholms will not be embarrassed by my conduct. They have been so kind to me."

"Their generosity is appreciated by many."

"I know. And I *am* trying to be more genteel, sir."

"The surprising Miss Hatherleigh."

"Not all bad surprises, I hope."

"Not at all." He smiled, releasing her hand to retrieve the article in his pocket. "Speaking of surprises, I have not had the chance to tell you of Mrs. Iverson's discovery when I was away. Unlike the tinplate candelabrum she insisted on polishing, this is of real value." He pulled out the silver spur rowel, holding it lightly in his hand.

"It is beautiful." She gently touched the six-pointed star.

"My great-uncle was a man of diverse tastes. You know of his taste for the exotic, with his Indian attire. His taste for tinplate dragons I could not appreciate, so we've left those particular items in a box in the library. But these"—he placed it in her hand—"he had several copies of the family crest formed in silver. This spinning spur reminds me of you, your horse riding, too, how you are always moving from strength to strength."

"Oh, Mr. Jardine—"

"Please, keep it." He closed her hand over the pendant. "Your generosity in helping others should not go unrewarded. Especially when the true champion of today's event went unacknowledged, if I'm not mistaken?"

"Oh, but sir, surely there's someone who deserves this more than me."

"I know of none." He coughed to clear the burn in his lungs. "I shall always be in your debt. Nobody had demonstrated such solicitude, such fortitude, when I have behaved so abominably. I'm sorry," he added hoarsely.

"I forgive you."

"I'm sorry for not behaving in a gentleman-like manner that last evening."

"I cannot hold that against you, seeing as I have scarcely acted as a lady."

Her bottom lip protruded, and he wondered if—when—she might permit his kiss again.

She glanced down at the pendant, then back at him. "You are sure I may keep this?"

"Absolutely. As sure as I hope to dance with you later tonight at the Guthrie ball."

"As the laird?"

"Yes." He gently pressed her fingers. "Please say you will condescend to dance with me."

"I'd like nothing more."

And her soft thanks and smile and sheening eyes filled his heart with hope again.

✺ Chapter Twenty-Seven

"Sir, I really must protest!"

Anthony ignored his henchman and tugged down his waistcoat, fluffed up the cravat, and stared critically at himself in the mirror. The suit he'd worn last in Rio still fit. The arms and shoulders felt a little tight, although perhaps that was the effect of so much labor in recent weeks. He peered at his new haircut, the shorter style more Londonish than Scottish Lowlands, making a great change from his usual unruly mop. Good, yet not terribly dandified. He hoped she was impressed.

"Sir, you are not well enough."

"Mac—" Anthony cleared his throat, cleared away the annoying tickle that had edged his voice with unwanted growl. "I am not a wee bairn, and I *am* going to this assembly. Everyone above the age of sixteen will be there. Have you not told me enough times to admit to being laird? Tonight I shall declare it from the rooftops." And if everything went according to plan, he might shout another special something very soon. Hence the need to make sure his dress was as faultless as possible. Tonight must be as perfect as could be.

"I agree it is well past time for disclosing your identity, but could you not do it in a less immoderate manner? Your cough seems to only worsen, and I expect you will be running great risk of fever if you attend a cold and drafty hall."

"The vigorous nature of the village dancing will doubtless ensure we shan't be cold for long." That, among other things. The few times he had held Verity in his arms had been most wonderful; their kiss exquisite torture. Tonight he hoped to feel her lips on his again. He shivered.

"Sir, you are trembling. I must insist you forgo this evening's festivities and rest."

Anthony met his friend's frown. "Thank you for your concern, but your worry is unnecessary. I am going, and everything will be fine. Now hurry and finish getting dressed yourself. I do not want to miss a moment."

With a loud sigh, Mac exited, leaving Anthony to contemplate the evening, a small smile tilting his lips as he finally dared dream about his future.

Finally there were no more disguises. No pretense. He was neither a gardener nor an Indian. He was the laird of Dungally. Someone whose God-inspired heart for others meant he would strive to seek their benefit above his own. Would forever seek to bless and provide for his loved ones, no matter what price he must pay. And now, with no hindrance of the past, he was ready to declare himself in more ways than one. Now that he knew there remained no disparity of faith, after tonight, he would leave no doubt about his heart. She would have no call to question his intentions again.

Ignoring the burn in his chest he hurried down the central stairs and out into the crisp night air.

The chilly welcome given to Verity at the door to the Guthries' manor was almost tropical compared to the reception within. Verity glanced around, heart sinking as she encountered glares and angry glances that cut away as soon as she looked in their direction. Oh no. Apparently word had got around that the Chisholms' English visitor was somehow involved in today's Ridings. She waited beside Mrs. Chisholm as Helena's hand was instantly sought by Alasdair, but nobody approached her, though there seemed a superfluity of male dancers. Her lips curved wryly. So, she was *persona non grata*. Perhaps it was just as well she was leaving soon.

She noticed a young man whisper behind a cupped hand as he eyed her. She shivered, glanced away. Did he think her involvement in today's race signaled that she possessed a loose character? Oh, if only Mr. Jardine were here!

"Verity." Mrs. Chisholm peered at her. "Why are you not dancing?"

Verity bit her lip. Well she knew the reason, but admitting it to such a kind soul as her hostess was quite another matter.

"There, there, dear." Mrs. Chisholm patted her arm. "I'm sure James will want to dance with you."

Verity felt sure he would not. Still, she retained her smile, which felt as artificial as the spray of roses in the bosom of Lady Guthrie, whose high color suggested she had been imbibing of the punch a little too freely.

Mrs. Chisholm motioned to James who left his conversation, strode over, and bent his ear to his mother. A quick hard glance at Verity, some further whispered conversation, and he was at Verity's side.

"Miss Hatherleigh," he said through gritted teeth, "may I have the honor of the next dance?"

Verity accepted his outstretched hand, and moved to the closest set where the lines were forming. "Thank you for asking me, James," she murmured humbly.

He glanced at her, the harsh lines around his eyes and mouth softening. "I'll have you know it was not me who said anything."

She nodded. "I suspect it was Mr. Hargreaves. He seems to be speaking to a lot of people tonight."

James followed her glance to where the race steward was busy whispering to a huddle of locals. He frowned. "Well, we can't let a few old cankers dampen the evening. Let's show them you don't give a toss."

Verity followed his lead, relief at his willingness to make amends tugging forth a smile. At least by dancing with the lead rider she would no longer be considered completely beyond the pale. And she could take courage that she looked well. Mary and Fiona had worked wonders, fixing her hair and cinching the stays so tight that she now possessed something of a woman's shape.

"Oh, miss, your waist is so tiny!" Fiona had gasped. "You look very ladylike now."

"I think you exaggerate. Slightly more ladylike, perhaps." Verity had smiled, her gaze flickering to her neckline where the spur rowel pendant rested. Was it too much? Her pitiful lack of curve had never attracted a second glance, and suddenly the thought that men might judge her on her appearance made her feel slightly sick and soiled within. But if employing such feminine wiles helped a certain laird realize she was not a little girl, then surely it was for the best.

But perhaps dancing in front of so many hard faces was not the wisest of actions.

She looked up at James. "I'm sorry that my actions today upset you. You know I was only trying to help, don't you?"

"I suppose I do."

Tension eased within her heart. "It is quite ridiculous, is it not, to think an act of bravery should be so thoroughly maligned?"

He gave a reluctant chuckle. "You really are gifted at being incorrigible. I wish him good luck whomever your future husband is."

Her smile froze. James didn't know. Surely it was only a matter of days now—possibly even mere hours!—until Papa's man arrived to take her home. Then this dream would end.

"What?" James peered closely. "Why do you look upset?"

She swallowed. Shook her head slightly.

A stir came from the entrance to the hall. She followed the gazes and caught her breath.

Mr. Jardine! Only he seemed more laird-like than ever tonight. Dressed in a coat and breeches her sisters' husbands would not fill so well, he looked polished, handsome, assured. Surely if her parents could see him as such they would not think him *quite* so far beneath her? A desperate prayer rose from her heart as she begged God for such a miracle. Tonight he wore a new confidence, nodding, sharing a quick word with many of the locals, all the while his eyes were searching, searching . . .

He saw her. Stilled. Smiled.

All at once all eyes turned her direction. She cared not. She dropped James's hands, murmured an excuse and moved toward him.

"Good evening, sir."

"Good evening, Miss Hatherleigh." He bowed to her curtsy. "May I say how lovely you look tonight?"

"You may."

He chuckled, and the old familiarity rose again, chasing away this newfound shy awkwardness.

"And may I say you look very handsome. One would not expect a gardener to look quite so dashing. Nor with such a lovely haircut."

"I was hoping to look more distinguished tonight. So you approve of the hair? Another of Mac's secret talents, for which I am most grateful, otherwise I would have been forced to submit to a haircut from Mrs. Iverson. She, poor lady, is laid up with a bad cold, so Mac was forced to try his hand. Not too *ton*-like for you?"

Her mouth dried. *Ton*-like? With all the revelations of late, had Mr. Jardine learned of her father's position in society? She swallowed. "You look very fine."

He smiled, deep into her eyes. She shivered within.

"Ah, today's champion, good evening." Mr. Jardine bowed to James. "I am sorry if my arrival has interrupted your dance."

"No matter." James slid Verity a sly look. "You will doubtless be aware that Miss Hatherleigh does very little that does not suit her."

"James!"

He chuckled, stepping back to avoid another peck of her fan. "If I may leave her in your capable hands, I will endeavor to learn if any other young ladies here tonight require my attention."

He strode through the throngs, leaving them in the middle of the dance floor. They joined the nearest set for a country dance Verity knew well, which allowed her to focus on Mr. Jardine and not her steps, to relish being with him as they moved and dipped and swayed.

In all too short a time the music concluded, they exchanged curtsy and bow, and moved off the dance floor.

"Come." Mr. Jardine placed her hand on his arm. "Let us find somewhere quieter to talk."

Heart thrilling, she smiled at Helena, standing with Alasdair, and they moved into a shadowed alcove. From the window they could see the river, a lone fishing boat's lamp heading into port.

"I am very glad you came, sir."

"As am I." He possessed her hands. "I'm so pleased to see you wearing the spur rowel."

Dare she tell him she never planned to take it off?

He gently squeezed her hands, and in that moment, his smile lighting her heart, his hands holding hers, everything was finally right and perfect in her world.

"Mr. Jardine!" The voice held a sneer, a judgment.

Anthony pulled back. Blinked. Colin Guthrie stood before him.

"Of course." The scowl—held in check at the door earlier only by the arrival of the next guests—grew pronounced. "I might have known the laird would be cavorting with the doxy!"

Verity gasped. Anthony gently pushed her away, his voice low. "How dare you?"

Guthrie laughed, a nasal-inflected laugh without humor. "I dare because *she* dared first." He peered past Anthony's shoulder. "Is it true? Do you deny riding today?"

"No." Her chin lifted proudly. "Nor do I deny the tremendous satisfaction it gave me to beat you."

"Only because you resorted to cheap tricks!"

"And you would have us believe you have never resorted to such things?"

Anthony suppressed a smile. "Verity—"

"I am glad you did not win, as I'm sure many others are also. You are a coward hiding behind bullies and not a worthy recipient of any honor this village should bestow."

His eyes flashed. "And you are a jade—"

Thwack!

Anthony shook out his stinging fist, which had somehow connected with Guthrie's face all by itself. "Do not disrespect this lady—"

"Her?" He staggered closer, rubbing his jaw. "A lady?"

"Is this how you treat all your guests?"

"Only the unwelcome ones."

"Colin!" A new voice called. "Leave them."

Anthony turned to see Sir Donald eyeing him with dislike. "I do not expect to see guests treating my home as a boxing saloon."

Anthony inclined his head. "I am sorry for the rumpus—"

"Neither do I expect to be interrupted when I am speaking. Although, considering you are the heir of that Irving fool, one cannot expect proper decency, I suppose."

"You seem to have a very strange idea of proper decency if it permits your son to insult a young lady, sir."

"Be silent!" The elderly man heaved in a deep rasping breath. "Your family has stolen from mine, but I refuse to allow you to steal any more of our dignity. Do not make me regret our hospitality."

With a stiff scowl reminiscent of his son's, he marched away.

Verity met Anthony's gaze. "I'm so sorry."

"You are not to be held responsible for the misguided actions of others."

"I did not envisage what riding today would mean for you, or for the Chisholms." Her chin wobbled. "I hope it has not impaired Helena's prospects."

"Or your own?"

"I . . . I have never had prospects."

Protest bubbled up within. What about James? He'd seen how James had looked at her; had recognized the look as one he shared. "Surely that is not true."

She gave a bitter-sounding laugh. "Oh, if only you knew."

He picked up her cold hands. "Verity, I—"

"I *had* to race. I know it was scandalous, but I had to help James. I hate to see injustice. And I cannot help but own to a sense of satisfaction at seeing their shock and dismay when a mere girl bested them."

"But surely you can understand their dismay when it was discovered it was an *English* girl who bested them. Miss Chisholm said the defeat of the English was the cause of celebration. Surely you can understand that your effort taints their sense of history."

"Oh! I did not think of that." Her shoulders slumped as she turned away. "No wonder they all hate me."

"Hate is a trifle strong."

"Perhaps you do not hear what everyone is saying."

"Not quite everyone."

"Well, I am thankful for your selective hearing, sir."

"An important quality in a friend, is it not?"

"I do not hold my friends to be in the same category as mere mortals, Mr. Jardine." The sparkly smile flickered.

His heart hitched. To have thought a year ago he would crave the affection of a young miss, and now look at him. A glutton for her every smile. He shook his head. What kind of fool was he?

Her face fell. "I suppose you do not wish me to jest about such things." She sighed, then whispered, "I have such a lot to learn about being good."

"I rather suspect you have always known, just chosen not to."

"Perhaps." She turned to face the sea.

The view here was not as good as from Dungally but still could captivate. At least he thought she was captivated—until he noticed her damp cheeks.

"Ah, lass." He pulled her close as she cried silently.

His shirt grew damp, the incessant burn in his chest now overlaid with something infinitely more tender. Verity, his beautiful, spirited Verity, needed comfort and assurance.

"Is there someone I can get for you? Miss Chisholm? Perhaps her mother?"

She shook her head against his chest, then snuggled closer, her arms around his back, as shuddery breath after shuddery breath released. His clasp tightened. He would do all he could to protect her, to provide solace. She sighed, the stiffness in her shoulders easing, and he kissed the top of her head, inhaling her scent. So sweet, so alluring. He cradled her closer, kissed her forehead. He should stop, should release her, but his lips burned for hers . . .

"Well, I never!"

Anthony pulled away, met the outraged stare of Lady Guthrie who gave a loud sniff and marched away. He groaned. "I fear we will receive another scold. I am sorry."

Verity smiled shyly up at him. "I cannot be sorry."

He chuckled despite himself, tugging her closer, Verity's expression so winsome he could not help but lower his head and ensure his lips finally found hers again.

Heat, tenderness, passion ignited within. He tasted the salt of her tears on lips that were so soft, so pliant, so irresistible, he felt his knees tremble. Oh, how he loved—

"Mr. Jardine!" Mrs. Chisholm's voice intruded. "Release Verity this instant."

His arms dropped, he pulled away and turned to face the irate minister's wife.

"Verity, I did not wish to believe the reports of your conduct but I see myself sadly mistaken."

"Mrs. Chisholm, I am not—"

"Lady Guthrie told me the gossip is all over the assembly, that you and the laird were seen alone together."

A smile finally tweaked Verity's lips. "Begging your pardon, ma'am, but one cannot be both alone and with someone else."

"That is enough! Have you forgotten all manner of propriety? I knew you to be a willful madcap kind of girl, but I did not expect you to so utterly sink."

She turned to Anthony. "And you! Do you dare presume?"

Dare presume? He swallowed. "I dare only because I love—"

"Come." She snatched Verity's hand. "Oh, whatever will your mother say?"

"Mrs. Chisholm," he began.

The lady turned, eyes unrelenting, like green stone. "I cannot express how disappointed I am in you, sir. I had hoped—but no. No more. I'm glad to say my duty is nigh done. Unless you are prepared to make Verity an offer you are not to see her again."

Verity reddened. "But Mrs. Chisholm—"

"No! The only way such behavior can be explained without further injury to your reputation is if there is an immediate betrothal."

A coldness, unrelated to the temperature, seeped into his soul. This was not how he wished to propose. Was not how he'd envisaged the night to progress at all!

A dizzying pain pierced his head. His knees swayed. He grasped the pillar for support. Managed to croak, "You may expect my visit tomorrow, ma'am."

"Good." Her eyes softened fractionally. "I'd had such hopes . . ."

She turned, shaking her head, forcing him to trail behind through a gauntlet of hard stares, until he finally found Mac and hurried away, to retire, shivering, into his lonely bed.

CHAPTER TWENTY-EIGHT

THE RECRIMINATIONS OF the previous evening lasted throughout Mr. Jardine's nonappearance on Saturday, through his lack of attendance at services Sunday, right through to this morning's non-visit. The kiss she had felt sure was prelude to something most miraculous had instead become something sordid, as his lack of attendance attested.

Had she just been used? It was hard to equate such an idea with the heat she'd thought she had seen in his eyes, with the comfort she'd found in his arms. But, as Mrs. Chisholm had said after venting her upset, if he did truly care he would come, would offer his hand. Indeed, it almost seemed as though underneath her vented spleen lay a deeper hope, revealed in her murmured, "But only a laird."

"But what should that have to do with anything?"

"A great deal, I should imagine, if you seek your parents' approval for the match."

Verity bit her bottom lip. It was utterly impossible, yet a quivering hope refused to die.

So, she had prayed, pleading with God, dreaming of the magical moment when Mr. Jardine would appear and ask for her hand.

To no avail.

And now it was Monday afternoon. Desperation had all but killed off the last vestiges of hope. Papa's most recent letter put her departure at Wednesday at the latest. Only two days away!

Which left her here, standing outside the walled garden.

She could *not* leave without saying farewell, no matter what Mrs. Chisholm said. It would be cruel to leave without a final goodbye. So she had coerced Helena and Ben into accompanying her on a final visit.

"But I would hate for Mama to find out," Helena whispered as they traipsed through the intricate gardens below the terrace.

"You may blame me if you are." Verity found a smile. They had been in short supply lately. "I am certain she will understand. For as James always says, I am incorrigible."

James had not been backward in sharing his thoughts on the matter, saying the laird's punching of Guthrie (which the assembly had buzzed about) had been the first real sign he possessed enough grit to win his respect. Verity had almost fallen off her chair at that, before proceeding to tell him about all the other good qualities the laird possessed. Qualities that made her certain something must have detained him, a certainty that grew only stronger the longer he kept away. For he could not look at her like that—could not kiss her like that—and not care.

She climbed the stairs, wrapping her shawl closer against the stiff breeze, led the way to the front door, and tapped the heavy brass rapper.

No answer.

"Perhaps no one is at home."

"I don't believe it." It would be cowardly, ungentlemanly behavior, and Mr. Jardine, though not perfect, could not behave so. She lifted it again. Pounded harder this time. Frowned.

"I'm sorry, Verity, but it looks as though nobody is here."

Had he gone away? But would he have taken all the servants, too? Wasn't Mrs. Iverson unwell?

Of course!

She turned the handle. It squeaked open.

"Verity! What are you doing?"

"Shh. Do you hear anything?"

"No." Both Helena and Ben craned their necks, listening. "Wait, is that a cough?"

"Hello?" she called.

Seconds later Mr. McNaughton appeared, eyes bloodshot, looking gray with fatigue. Dougal was whining at his feet.

"Oh, my! What has happened?"

His eyes widened. "Miss Hatherleigh? What are you doing? You should go." He shuffled them back to the door. "This is no place for you."

"Is the laird sick?" At his nod, Verity's heart dropped. "We can help, we can—"

"Miss, ye should nae be here. I be managing well enough."

"On your own?" She narrowed her eyes. "You have been doing this by yourself, haven't you? Mrs. Iverson is sick, as no doubt is her useless husband. What about the maids?"

"They haven't been in since Saturday. Betty was looking peaky then . . ."

"You poor thing!" Verity turned to Helena. "Do you think your mama would mind sending Fiona along? Or even some food from Mrs. Cready? I'm sure her sense of Christian charity would not mind."

"Of course not. Come, Ben, let's see what we can do."

Ben looked from his sister to Verity before nodding and disappearing with his sister.

"Now, tell me what is happening with meals. I admit to a sizeable lack of expertise in domestic arts, despite the best efforts of Haverstock's, but I remember a few basics—"

"Verity, Verity!" Helena rushed back inside. "There is a band of men coming down the drive! The leader is on a big horse, and looks like Colin Guthrie!"

"Guthrie?" McNaughton's sleepy-eyed expression sharpened. "Is he not the fool who caused the rumpus the other day?"

"Aye." Verity nodded, ignoring Helena's quick grin. "What could he want?"

"He looks like he wants trouble," McNaughton growled.

"And poor Mr. Jardine, no doubt."

As the steward closed the door with a thump, Verity rushed into the adjoining room, the library, and peered out the window, thinking, thinking. *Lord, what should I do?*

All at once an idea so outrageous popped fully formed into her head. Either God had given inspiration, or He might need to forgive her, but she could see no other option.

"Helena, go with Ben to the Rose Room and use the tunnel. This does not appear to be a friendly visit, and I fear the animosity may extend to your family. Oh, and give me your betrothal ring!"

"My ring?"

A thump came at the door.

"McNaughton, are you willing to trust me?" The spur rowel pendant, secured on a chain, she plucked from under her bodice.

His brows rose, but all he said was, "Will you be causing the laird strife?"

"I will do my utmost to prevent any harm falling to him or any other."

He gave her a piercing look that she felt to her marrow before jerking a nod. "Aye, lass."

"Then please follow my lead." She hissed after Helena. "Your ring!"

Another thump.

Helena handed Verity her engagement ring and rushed with Ben to the secret passage. Verity stuffed the slim gold band on her finger, squared her shoulders, and opened the door.

Colin Guthrie's face slackened. "You!"

"As you can see." Perhaps seven or eight burly men stood behind him. She looked over the men, noting one whose girth bore strong resemblance to her nemesis at the masquerade. She fixed him with her narrow-eyed stare; his bold gaze lowered. "Can I help you?"

"We've come for the laird."

"I beg your pardon?"

"We have need to speak with Jardine."

She cleared her throat. What had James said the other day? God bless her enormous gift for incorrigibility! "Pray, what business could you have with my husband?"

Beside her, hidden by the door, she heard McNaughton's gasp. Doubtless his expression matched the sagged jaws of the men in front of her, whose eyes glanced at her left hand where she had shoved

Helena's ring. Well, he *would* be her husband if she had any say in the matter! Murmurs filled the air. "Never tell me you be his bride! Ye be an English lass."

"If I cannot tell you, then how will you ever believe me?"

Guthrie drew into himself, brow wrinkling. "You lie. Ye were not married last week." Yet his voice held a trace of uncertainty.

"Surely you did not expect to receive an invitation to our wedding after you called me a doxy?" Several of the men's jaws dropped further. "I'm sure that after last week's *fracas* you can understand why Mr. Jardine took exception to your uncouth manner towards me."

He blustered something about not knowing how things stood.

"Would that have made much difference? I wonder."

He flushed, again muttering about not knowing of Mr. Jardine's nuptials.

"Yes, well, it proved a very sudden thing." She smiled. "But I'm surprised you did not think it likely. After all, it was at your house where the dispute occurred. Did you not hear Mrs. Chisholm insisting on our marriage? How fortunate for us that Mr. Chisholm is a minister and able to perform ceremonies at a moment's notice."

"But—"

"I'm sorry, but if you wish to discuss this further we will need to go inside. I'd prefer to do without this discomforting breeze." She tugged her shawl close, as if to reinforce the chill.

"Er, ah, certainly, ma'am."

She nodded to the other men then closed the door firmly on them before returning to her unexpected guest, who stood, hat in hand, gazing around the Great Hall as if stupefied. "McNaughton here will take your hat." She nodded to him before leading the way to the library. "Pray excuse the mess. We have not had the time, nor, truth be told, much inclination for redecorating in recent times. Now, would you care for some tea? I imagine that after your ride you must be in need of some refreshment."

"Er, yes, thank you . . ."

"Lady Dungally," she prompted.

"Lady Dungally," he repeated, as if pained.

She seated herself and motioned for him to do the same, before ringing a bell, and issuing instructions to the bemused McNaughton. "Ah, there you are. Could you please bring tea? And"—she glanced at Guthrie, brows raised—"perhaps something stronger for the men outside?"

"Certainly, ma'am." He withdrew, eyes twinkling, as if to assure her he knew just which drop should be shared with the men outside.

"Er, thank you."

Verity nodded regally. "I have always believed it to be of the greatest importance to treat one's guests as one would like to be treated. Wouldn't you agree?"

He reddened. She hoped he remembered his decidedly inhospitable actions the other day.

Dougal, as if to counteract her claim, started to growl. Verity laid a hand on his head and felt his hackles ease. "That's enough, Dougal. We don't treat our guests like that."

His little black head tilted up at her, his eyes reproachful.

"Go find Mac, that's a good boy." She waited as he trotted from the room, then turned her attention back to the visitor. "Now, you said you had business with the laird?"

"Y-yes."

"I hesitate to enquire, but unless you tell me, I cannot be of assistance, and I would not like your errand to be wholly fruitless."

"Er, you see . . ."

The door opened. McNaughton reappeared, balancing a tea tray with two cups and a selection of biscuits. The shortbread she recognized as the fruit of Mrs. Cready's labor.

"Thank you."

He nodded, eyes shifting to her guest and back, with the faintest question in his brows. "If I can be of further assistance?"

She smiled reassuringly. "That will be all. Oh, did the little birds escape?" She turned to a frowning Guthrie. "You called at a most inopportune time. I hate to see young creatures trapped, don't you?"

He nodded as McNaughton said gravely, "Yes, m'lady."

"And did the men receive their refreshments?"

"I am about to deliver the special whiskey Iverson rates highly."

"Then that is indeed all. Thank you."

He nodded, exited, leaving the door slightly ajar.

She turned back to her guest. "Now you were saying, Mr.—?" She wrinkled her brow as if forgetting his name, an action she'd seen her grandmother use, whenever "a vulgar mushroom" needed to be put in his place.

"Guthrie, ma'am."

"Mr. Guthrie, of course."

"Well, you see . . ." he paused and wiped his brow, the moment stretching out longer.

"I'm afraid I will never see unless you explain things to me."

"Of course! It's just, well, we've come for the laird."

"Yes, I gathered as much from your first comments. I fail to under-stand whether you mean you have come to speak with him, require his assistance, or perhaps wish to take him away."

"Uh, I'm sorry, miss—"

"Lady Dungally." Oh, it had such a nice ring to it!

"Er, yes, b-but it is the last mentioned for which we need him."

Her fingers gripped the teacup until she feared the handle might snap. "Am I to understand you mean to kidnap him?"

He sighed, slumping in his chair. "That be the sum of things, yes."

"Ah." Verity sipped her tea, heart racing, while she strove to appear calm. "May I ask why you wish to commit such an act?"

He seemed to collect himself, straightening. "Because I refuse to be treated as I was the other day. His actions were humiliating!"

"This does appear to be a predicament." She eyed his empty cup. "Would you like me to refresh your tea?"

"Er, no, thank you."

"Oh. Was it not to your liking?"

"No. I mean, yes. It was very good, but . . ."

"You would have preferred whiskey," she guessed.

"No, miss—my lady. It's just, well, I'm not in the habit of kidnapping—"

"No? I am so pleased to hear it."

"And I really would prefer to get back to the matter at hand, if you don't mind."

She waved an insouciant hand. "Far be it from me to distract you from your purpose."

"So can you please point to where the laird might be?"

"You might wish to rephrase your request. I could point to many locations, such as here"—she pointed to the window—"or there"—she pointed to the empty hall—"or even up there"—she pointed upstairs. "There are numerous locations where he *might* be, but a far more helpful request would be, 'Could you please tell me where he is?'"

"Er, of course. Could you please tell me where he is?"

She smiled her sweetest smile. "No."

He blinked. "But—"

"How could I possibly know for certain? What I do know is that he has a most appalling habit of disappearing without telling me. He did this just the other week! Simply left the estate, without giving me a drop of information. We were not sure if he had gone to Edinburgh, or Glasgow, or if indeed he had changed his mind entirely and gone to London instead. Here was I, forsaken and alone, wondering if the man I loved would ever return."

All true.

"Oh." He looked nonplussed, gazing around the room distractedly.

"I'm so sorry. It's most unfortunate he should not be able to see you."

"Y-yes." He half rose, then resumed his seat. "But what about you?"

"I beg your pardon?"

His eyes brightened. "We'll kidnap you."

Her heart thumped painfully. Had Helena enough time to warn James and Mr. Chisholm about the intruders at Dungally? She poured herself a second cup, willing her hand to remain steady. If the men grew impatient, they might storm inside and discover the poor laird in the sickroom above, and then what would happen?

"I'm afraid the answer is no."

"No?"

"That is correct. I simply cannot allow you to kidnap me. And really, you would find me a most unpleasant companion, I assure you."

A kind of desperation stole over his features. "But you cannot—"

"Allow either myself or Mr. Jardine to be kidnapped, yes, you are correct. You see, I will die before I allow you to touch a hair on his head." Her smile grew brittle. "Now, Mr. Guthrie, if you are finished?"

"But I cannot return empty-handed!"

She studied him thoughtfully. Cleared her throat again. "May I enquire as to the cause of this enmity between your family and the laird's?"

He stared at her, a muscle working in his jaw.

"Mr. Guthrie? Surely you can appreciate the fact that I have a right to know, especially when it leads to threats of kidnapping and such." She raised her brows, settled back in her chair as she had seen her mother do many times, as if she had all the time in the world.

Finally he sighed. "The laird once stole something from my grand-father."

"The laird? You must be mistaken. Anthony"—his name tasted absurdly sweet in her mouth—"has only recently come to these parts, and I'm sure has never had the chance to meet your grandfather."

"Not the current laird. His uncle."

"Do you possibly mean great-uncle?"

He nodded.

"Well, that is understandable. He seemed to be a man of few prin-ciples and even less care. Can you believe he preferred to spend money on his house than attend to his tenants?"

Guthrie flushed.

"I know! Most inconsiderate, hardly befitting his status. Now, you were saying?"

"Er, well, he took something one time at a ball, much like the one the other night."

"Took something? Like a cold? I'm afraid my poor Anthony took quite a cough the other day. He seems to have given it to the servants, poor things, which is why poor McNaughton looks so weary. He's been doing the job of a dozen for far too long."

Guthrie cleared his throat. "Miss . . . ?"

"Lady Dungally, thank you."

"Lady Dungally, if I might continue?"

"Of course."

"It appears a certain object went missing that night. An urn."

"Ah. Was it of great value?"

He flushed. "Well . . . no."

"Yet you go to all this trouble for its return. Does it hold sentimental value?"

"Well, you see, it holds something—"

"Gold doubloons? Rare jewels?" She smiled. Gone were all her earlier fears. This was actually somewhat enjoyable. "Perhaps a letter signed by Bonnie Prince Charlie?"

He shifted uncomfortably.

"I seem to be nearing the mark." She leaned forward. "Come, Mr. Guthrie. Enough playing coy. If you wish for my help, then you simply must be forthright."

He met her gaze, glanced away, sighed loudly, and mumbled something.

"Excuse me, but you must speak more clearly. I cannot understand you."

He returned his attention to her and said desperately, "It is a piece of silk."

She blinked. "You want a piece of silk? What, is it from Queen Mary's robe?"

"It's a long story."

"Well, I am hardly entertaining hundreds of other guests."

So he told her, about the Guthries' support of the Jacobites, the banner they'd kept hidden in a tinware urn, keeping their secret until one day it went missing, and Anthony's Great-Uncle Irving began to look smug and drop hints.

"And you believe he returned it here?"

"Aye."

"I see." She pondered him a moment longer. "Surely you can understand trying to locate something like that in a house this size is next to impossible. Mind you, I do believe in miracles now, but I think something like that is of a magnitude even our good Lord might balk at." She touched the ring on her hand. How pretty it looked, with its small ruby gleaming red in the stream of light from the windows. If only . . .

She pulled her thoughts back to the matter at hand. "May I present an alternative scenario? My dear Anthony, as no doubt you are aware, is quite new to his position, and has never mentioned such things to me, which makes me believe he is entirely in ignorance of the underhanded deeds of which you speak. I can assure you, Mr. Guthrie, that I have a very real appreciation for the difficulties that family pride can lead one into." She drew in a breath, watching the visitor carefully. "Tell me, who else is aware of these matters?"

"My father," he muttered.

"So the men outside? The animosity from the villagers?" She arched a brow.

He shrugged.

"I see. So what you're saying is that they know nothing, and simply support you because they are afraid of what might happen if they do not."

He glanced away, then gave a short nod.

"If it is true that nobody save us and your father is aware of such things, can it not remain that way? I assure you nobody need be any the wiser."

She tilted her head, and when he finally offered a tiny nod, rang the bell again. "Thank you, Mr. Guthrie, for your understanding. I assure you, nobody will ever hear me speak about such matters, and I'm sure I do not have to ask for your assurance that your enmity towards Mr. Jardine will cease. He is but an innocent party in this matter, is he not?"

He nodded, albeit a trifle reluctantly.

The door opened. "Ah, McNaughton. Would you mind filling a sack with the special silver? It seems the men outside have the desire to kidnap the dear laird, and as that is an impossibility, I thought the next best solution is for the men to return with some of the silver."

She turned to Mr. Guthrie and smiled. "That way your mission will not be deemed a failure."

He nodded. "Thank you, my lady."

McNaughton gave her a pointed look, which she returned with slightly raised brows.

"The new silverware should suffice. Anthony mentioned the pieces from the East of which Mrs. Iverson was rather fond. I believe I saw them earlier in the library."

He nodded, the faintest lift of his lips indicating his understanding of her coded instructions. She hoped.

"New?"

"Why, yes, Mr. Guthrie. You would not want the old. It is so tarnished, it's virtually worthless."

"Of course."

McNaughton returned a short time later with the sack filled, with—just as she'd hoped—the gleaming dragon tinplate candelabra on top. He handed the sack to the officer and bowed. "Was there anything else, ma'am?"

"No, thank you, McNaughton. You've been marvelous."

He cleared his throat. "I believe there are more visitors coming from the seafront."

"Oh!" She rose and turned to Mr. Guthrie. "You best be on your way. I suspect those men will not understand why you are making threats against the laird, nor why you are holding the Dungally silver." She ushered him outside, where the men, who had heavily imbibed, judging from the fumes breathed their direction, were muttering slurred protests.

"Where's the laird?"

"Come on," Guthrie muttered. "We best be going." He turned to Verity. "Thank ye, Lady Dungally."

"Thank *you*, Mr. Guthrie, for your understanding of how things should be."

He nodded then mounted his horse, and soon the thunder of hooves echoed up the drive.

She hastened inside then moved unsteadily to clasp the wooden bannister. Heart still racing, she dragged in breath after breath of damp air, but her legs soon failed and she sank onto the step. How things should be. Oh, if only . . .

"Verity!" James rushed through the open door, closely followed by his father. "Are you quite well? Helena arrived home in such a state, with some cock-and-bull story about a gang of rogues. I didn't believe it, but then I saw Guthrie and those men. Are you hurt?"

She drew in a shuddery breath. "I have suffered no injury, thank you."

"But what were they carrying?"

"Merely some tinplate I suggested."

"And some coal," McNaughton's voice added.

She glanced up, met his twinkling eyes, which seemed to instantly melt away her shock. "How clever of you!"

He shook his head. "How clever of you, Miss Hatherleigh, to pretend to be the laird's wife."

"The laird's wife?" James shoved closer again, picking up her hand. "That's Helena's ring."

"Very observant." Verity sighed, drawing her hand away. A creak drew her attention upwards. "Mr. Jardine! Oh, sir, we did not mean to disturb you!"

McNaughton hurried up the stairs, murmuring something, but Mr. Jardine shook his head, coughing as he slowly descended, Dougal barking at his heels.

"You could have been hurt," Mr. Chisholm said.

"But I was not." She kept her eyes fixed on poor Mr. Jardine. He looked so pale, so thin, so weary. "Good evening, Mr. Jardine."

"Good evening," he rasped, coughing again. His gaze traveled from person to person before alighting on her. "To what do we owe the pleasure of so many visitors?"

"A marriage," muttered James.

"A marriage?" He glanced sharply from James back to Verity, his gaze dropping to her hand. "Is this true?"

"No." Oh, what would he think when she owned the truth?

"But you wear a ring?"

"It belongs to Helena."

He stepped closer, gaze serious. "Then why?"

Verity closed her eyes. How had something so nerve-wracking turned into a farce? How had blessed relief turned to tension so quickly? She rubbed her upper arms, trying vainly to control the shivers.

"You are cold."

She looked up into the worried eyes of the laird and her own filled with tears.

"My dear, what has happened?"

"Perhaps I might be of assistance, Mr. Jardine," McNaughton offered quietly. "If we might all step inside to the Rose Room?"

There was a general assent and movement inside to the light and relative warmth of the drawing room, where Mr. Chisholm insisted she took the comfortable seat near the fire. She lowered herself into a chair, and Dougal trotted over, pawing her knee until she lifted him onto her lap.

After being assured she was quite well, James said with wrinkled brow, "I fail to understand why you would say you were married to the laird."

Mr. Jardine's gaze returned to her, questioning, yet with such a look of concern her throat tightened again, forbidding speech.

"It appears," McNaughton's voice came smoothly, "that the young lady has averted a possible tragedy."

"Tragedy?" Mr. Jardine stepped closer. "You were in danger?"

She shook her head. "I was not, but it appears you were."

"I beg your pardon?"

"Guthrie wanted to kidnap you."

"Kidnap me?"

"I could not let them touch you, being so sick, after all."

"Thank you." A smile crossed his lips. "But how did you stop them?"

She glanced pleadingly at his servant, who rose to the occasion. "After pretending the laird was away, the young lady called me in and offered the gentleman tea and whiskey."

"Gentleman?" James choked. "Guthrie? How can you say such a thing?"

A growl came from the bundle of warmth on her lap. Verity hushed the dog, stroking his neck until he relaxed once more.

Mr. Jardine's attention returned to her. "You pretended to be my wife, and offered tea and whiskey?" The frown left his eyes, replaced with a look of bemusement. "What, not crumpets as well?"

She chuckled.

"This is no laughing matter, Verity!" James exclaimed. "You might well have been killed, or kidnapped. Then where would we be?"

"You would most likely be here. The better question is where would *I* be?"

Amid smothered laughter from the others, James snorted and stamped away to the fireplace, savagely kicking a log with his foot, a wince now accompanying his mutterings.

"It may please you, sir, to know it was not the best whiskey that was served."

Mr. Jardine met her gaze and smiled. Her heart fluttered, and she knew her emotions would be on full display.

To cover her confusion, she hastened to explain. "I knew I had to keep them distracted from their business, in order to allow time for Helena and Ben to return to the house and get help." She looked at Mr. Chisholm apologetically. "I wanted them safe."

"Verity." At Mr. Chisholm's solemn voice, the air seemed to suddenly suck from the room. Verity sat motionless. Was he about to reproach her for her deceit? She looked up to meet the cleric's clear gaze. "Thank you for protecting my children."

The back of her eyes burned. She swallowed. Nodded.

James snorted. "Guthrie is a great simpleton and a hothead. What will he do when he realizes his mistake?"

"I . . . I think he will prove unwilling to own such a thing. He strikes me as someone who has allowed family pride to cloud his judgment at times." She added softly, "As for being hotheaded and impulsive, I cannot judge him too harshly for that."

There was a pause, broken only by another of Mr. Jardine's coughs.

"Oh, sir, you really should rest—"

He shook his head, gaze fixed on her. "Not until I've heard the full."

"But that is all." All she was prepared to share, anyway. Not after what she had promised Mr. Guthrie.

"Aye. They be very foolish rogues, wouldn't ye say, Miss Hatherleigh?"

She met McNaughton's smiling gaze. "They definitely were none too sharp."

Mr. Chisholm turned to the laird's servant. "There were more?"

"Aye. The young lass here had the presence of mind to get the others to focus on what profit they could return with, and persuaded Guthrie to return with the silverware. But I understood what the lass meant, so I retrieved the ugly tinware from the library and placed that and a few other worthless trinkets in a sack half filled with coal and we gave that to him."

"You mean to say Guthrie could not tell the difference between tinware and silver?" James asked. "He must be very stupid."

"And very unfortunate to have met with such quick wits," said Mr. Jardine, smiling at Verity, causing another twinge in her chest.

"What I can't understand is why they would want to harm you." Mr. Chisholm's brow creased as he looked from Mr. Jardine to Verity. "Does it stem from the incident the other night?"

"I believe so," she murmured.

"One thing is for sure. Guthrie will be keen to steer clear of any more trouble from *you*, Verity."

For some reason James's reference to her notoriety made her wince inside.

Tiredness washed over her. No good would come of continuing conjecture. "I suppose we should head back. No doubt Mrs. Chisholm is beside herself with worry."

James and his father murmured agreement, and moved to the door.

Verity placed Dougal on the floor and moved to rise, and was offered the hand of Mr. Jardine. "Miss Hatherleigh, a word."

"Of course."

His hand remained clasped with hers. "I cannot express my immense gratitude for all you've done in looking after my interests today." His strong fingers wound round hers more tightly. "I am forever indebted to you, Verity."

Something sweet and indelible burned across her soul. Oh, he made her name sound precious. He lifted her hand, brushed the back with his lips.

Her chest tightened. Would he now make her an offer? Surely after their shared kiss he would know what propriety demanded. It's what a gentleman would do.

He lowered her hand and studied it, thumb caressing her palm, and uttered a deep sigh, as if rent from the innermost depths of his spirit. "I wish . . ."

She held her breath.

His gaze lifted, his eyes meeting hers before dropping to her lips. Anticipation lit within. Would he kiss her again? Oh, how she longed—

His lips pursed, then he gently squeezed her hand, let go and turned away.

Leaving her feeling bereft, and cast aside.

"Verity? Are you coming?"

He did not want her? Eyes blurring, she turned to where McNaughton remained. "Th-thank you, for all your assistance today."

"A pleasure, ma'am."

She swallowed past the boulders in her throat as he escorted her to the door. "I trust the tinplate won't be terribly missed."

"Nor the coal." His eyes softened. "Good night, Miss Hatherleigh."

"Goodbye."

She glanced quickly at Mr. Jardine but he remained mute, so she turned and followed James outside. She turned to say farewell, but the only person who remained in the doorway was a grim looking McNaughton. Verity exhaled, bowed her head, and let James lead her away.

Sometimes, what a man should do was very different from what a man wanted to do. Anthony watched his neighbors depart from the safety of the drawing room's heavily swathed window, his hand gripping the curtain tightly as dizziness begged him to fall. What he *should* do was exactly what he was doing, remaining here, so the beautiful yet obviously weary Verity would not pick up this wretched cold. What he *wanted* to do was kiss her senseless, then insist Mr. Chisholm stay to make Verity's claims true. For her actions today once again proved how wonderful she was, and how dear she was to him.

To have considered the safety of others before her own welfare? To have thought so quickly, maintained calm in such a dangerous situation? Truly, she was a remarkable lass—no, *lady*. He could think of her as a lass no longer, for no mere lass could have maintained such poise, or in fact given the impression she was his dutiful wife.

Wife. His wife. Wearing the family crest spur rowel around her throat. Her beautiful throat he wanted to—

"Sir?"

He turned to the door, tried to cover new light-headedness with a smile. "It appears Miss Hatherleigh has averted tragedy."

"She was quite extraordinary," Mac said warmly. "If she hadn't the presence of mind to act as she did, I'm sure the men would have forced their way inside. Who knows what may have happened?"

"Who knows, indeed." A cough ripped from his throat; fire danced across his chest. The room swam before his eyes.

"Now, sir, you really should return to rest as the lassie suggested. You are not well."

Anthony nodded, obeyed, and moved to his own bedchamber, Dougal's barking adding to the thumping in his head. And spent a considerable amount of time in thanks for the safe outcome of the day's events—and prayers for wisdom and direction regarding the future.

A NIGHT OF rain preceded further damp conditions, where heavy clouds forbade the sun to shine beyond stretches of ten minutes. After a fruitless night's sleep, caught between worry and wracking coughs, his heavy limbs refused any attempt to rise from bed. The highlight of his day was the tasty soup, prepared by Mrs. Cready at the reverend's wife's orders, so Mac said. But beyond that, Mac could provide little of what Anthony truly wanted, as the worries from the night ate into his day.

How was Verity feeling after the previous day's ordeal? Had she missed him? He longed to see her, to thank her, to explain. He had the feeling his words yesterday had not sufficed.

The steady patter of rain on glass continued. By midafternoon, with no sign of her, the questions intensified, along with the downpour. Would she still feel anxious? Did she think his behavior strange? He really should have said something about the future, about what was owed by his kiss. He hadn't explained his absence, although surely she would have realized it was due to his illness . . .

The next morning saw him feeling much stronger. With no sign that the weather was improving, he nevertheless decided to visit the neighboring property. He knocked on the door, which was soon answered by the wide-faced housekeeper. "Yairs?"

"Good afternoon. I was hoping to speak with Miss Hatherleigh."

She blinked. "I'm afraid ye cannae do that."

"Is she out? I can return later if that is more convenient."

"Mrs. Cready? I was—Oh! Mr. Jardine! How are you?"

"Much better, Mrs. Chisholm, thank you. And thank you also for sending the soup. It was greatly appreciated. I was . . . I was hoping to speak with Miss Hatherleigh."

"Oh." She glanced at the housekeeper before gesturing him forward. "Please, come through." He followed her through to the drawing room he'd visited before.

"Mr. Jardine!" Ben jumped up with a huge smile. "I'm so glad you're here. It's been terribly lonely without Verity—"

"Without Verity?" Anthony looked at Helena. "Where is she?"

Her eyes narrowed. "You should have come earlier."

"I beg your pardon?"

She rose from the couch. "If you were a gentleman, you would have come the next day."

"Miss Chisholm, I must beg an explanation. Which day?"

"You made her think—made us all think—that you cared, but you didn't, and now she's gone, and will never return, and it's all your fault!" She rushed from the room, swiping at her eyes.

"Please excuse Helena, Mr. Jardine. She's a little upset."

He turned to Mrs. Chisholm. "Verity has gone?"

Her eyes filled with compassion. "She has gone home."

"Home?"

"Aye. The viscount's carriage came to collect her yesterday," Ben announced. "I've never seen a coach with a crest on it, have you, Mr. Jardine? With the most bang-up horses, too. Four grays. But they didn't stay for long."

"The viscount? Which viscount?"

"Verity's father. He's taken her away." The boy shook his head sadly. "I'm going to miss her."

"Pardon?" His thoughts refused coherence. Had the lad truly said Verity's father was a peer?

"I said I am going to miss her," Ben enunciated loudly. "She's a lot more fun than my sisters—"

"Verity's father has taken her away?"

"Lord Aynsley. He is a viscount."

A viscount's daughter? He had guessed she was gently born, but aristocratic? The pulsing in his temples ricocheted deeper. That settled things. How dare he offer for the daughter of a viscount? No wonder Mrs. Chisholm had talked about presumption! Perhaps Verity herself might hold such matters of title loosely but, depend upon it, her father would not.

"They have a large estate in Somerset."

In Somerset. He could hear her sunny voice now, describing her home as "south of here." He grimaced. It might as well be New South Wales for the distance.

"She is much like others who prefer to be appreciated for more than their name and good fortune," Mrs. Chisholm continued. "You know she is worth fifty thousand pounds."

He blinked.

"I understand it is a shock. But I'm afraid there is something else you should know." Mrs. Chisholm eyed him. "She is betrothed."

Something dark and deep twisted within. For a moment he couldn't speak. He swallowed. Swallowed again. Found something vaguely resembling his voice. "I . . . I . . ." He dragged in a burning lungful of air. "I did not know."

She looked at him with no small degree of pity. "As Helena mentioned, we had hoped to see you earlier, but I understand you've been unwell."

He nodded, throat clamping again. She had gone. She was *betrothed*. All his hopes, his dreams of the future, withered up and died.

"If it is any comfort, we would all much prefer to see her marry you."

"I beg your pardon?"

"You do love her, do you not?"

"I . . ." Oh, what was the point of denying things anymore? "Of course."

"She should marry someone who loves her, not because her parents want to punish her."

"I don't understand."

"I can scarcely comprehend it myself. Helena and Verity have been friends for a long time, but even I did not think such a thing possible. Suffice to say, Lady Aynsley has more pride than all the Guthries and Irvings combined. I am sure the Bromsgroves have a good name and enviable fortune, but those things do not interest Verity. She is a wonderful girl, who just wants to be loved and appreciated. I know at times I have decried her impetuosity, but I fear marriage without love will cause her to lose her spark, the vitality that makes her so engaging. But I am not her mother, so what can I do?"

He nodded. Her position was understandable. He thanked her and took his leave.

He strode back to Dungally House, listening to the wash of the sea, the call of the birds, listening for the still small voice that guided his steps. *Lord, what would You have me do?*

Mrs. Chisholm might not be able to do anything, but he still could.
Couldn't he?

God?

Purpose formed. A path revealed.

And suddenly it was very clear just what he needed to do.

❧ CHAPTER TWENTY-NINE

Aynsley Manor, Somerset
September

"GOOD EVENING, MR. Bromsgrove. As you can see, here is Verity, back from the north, unharmed and unscathed."

Hardly unscathed, Verity thought, pushing down the panic that—along with a cold—had steadily grown since leaving Scotland. Her heart had learned to love, to hope, to dream, only for it to be crushed by a careless man. Nevertheless, she felt God wanted her to atone for past misdemeanors, so she obeyed her mother's gritted smile and murmured a greeting to her future husband, who instantly grew magnanimous in his compliments.

Perhaps it would not be so bad. Charles seemed a somewhat pliable creature, even if his conversation tonight was limited to horses and harvests. His dark eyes slid over her as though she were a prize mare, no doubt calculating just how much her dress cost, no doubt mentally counting the fifty thousand he would soon be able to call his own.

The panic surged again. Soon? After the announcement at tomorrow night's ball she would officially be betrothed to Charles, and the way her parents were talking, it would be a matter of only three Sundays of banns posting before she would be married. Married! Not, of course, like Cecy, with all the pomp and ceremony attending a London wedding, but quietly, as if her parents wished to keep things as hushed as possible, as if they felt embarrassed by her. Such decisions had only enhanced her sense of shame. A netted bird could not feel more trapped.

Of course Mama did not see it that way. And Papa, too, had been more than willing to go along with her demands, especially as Charles had made it clear he was prepared to adopt the Aynsley name, thus providing the means for their ancient family line to continue.

Grandmama had sneered when she'd heard. "Of course he wouldn't mind! The Bromsgroves are nothing compared to the Aynsleys. They should be the ones offering a dowry to your papa for the honor of marrying into this family."

The marriage settlements had been generous, so Mama had told her, the documents wrangled over by half a dozen legal minds for the entirety of Verity's time away. One of her first duties upon returning home was to sign them, a task she had loathed, but one that had proved impossible to escape.

"Bromsgrove! You look at my granddaughter as though she were a piece of meat. Do you have no compunctions?"

He flushed, offering a stuttered apology, which Verity met with narrowed eyes.

Much to Mary's protests, Verity had insisted on being dressed in her least becoming gown. She might be resigned to a future with Mr. Bromsgrove—perhaps this was justly deserved for all her folly—but it didn't mean she had to promote any warmer feelings. The past two weeks had been a whirl of travel, recriminations, prayers, blame, and the thin wavering hope she dared not articulate, hope that had slowly shriveled, leaving her as though with a painful splinter wedged in her chest that throbbed so hard at night it forced tears from her eyes. If only—

"Miss Hatherleigh?" Charles drew near, the tip of his long nose quivering. "Verity?"

She fought a cringe. He did not make her name sound precious.

A bland smile. "Can I say how much I look forward to the years ahead?"

"Apparently you can."

His brow clouded before he offered a reedy laugh, though he eyed her more uncertainly.

"Verity! That is no way to speak to your intended."

Except he was not *her* intended. Verity bit back the remark though; it was useless to argue with her mother, who, since the horror of Verity's Scottish escapades had reached her ears, seemed to have acquired an element of deafness whenever Verity spoke, save for moments like this.

And although Verity could boast years of practicing arguments, it was hard to see how she could justify it any longer, not when the Bible spoke of honoring one's father and mother. She wanted to obey God, but what if her parents were wrong? Was she still supposed to obey?

So she kept herself contained, cool, pushing down her panic, suppressing any passion, all the sweet memories, lest this façade shatter and she break down in aching despair. Because had she not heard it a million times? The daughters of Aynsley simply did not succumb to baser emotions.

She swallowed another sob.

"IT IS A respectable match, to be sure," Caroline said the following night as Verity's maid curtsied and exited the bedchamber. Was she trying to be encouraging? "I know he is not perhaps the man you would have chosen."

"Would you have chosen him?" Verity studied her sisters in the mirror.

"Well, of course not. I have my Gideon, after all." Caroline eyed her large diamond ring, a gift from her husband upon the safe arrival of their new son. "But Bromsgrove is rich, and dresses well, and his parents possess quite a nice house in town. Of course, Birmingham is a little far from London for my liking."

"How fortunate you need not live there," Verity said. Her sisters' presence, and that of their respective families, had only added to the feeling of tension, the pleasure Verity felt at meeting her nephew largely outweighed by his incessant crying. Caroline's and Cecy's astonishment as to why she had so meekly succumbed to her parents' wishes had left her with questions she could not answer. Would they understand she felt submission was what God wanted?

"I am sure Mama will not mind the distance," Cecy murmured.

She exchanged wry looks with Verity. That was probably the truth.

"You're not wearing that, are you?" Caroline said, frowning at Verity's pendant. "You know it does not suit the rest of your ensemble, don't you?"

Verity touched her silver necklace, her throat tight. If she could not wear the ring of the man she loved, she would at least wear his gift.

"A spur *is* a little unusual. Where did you get it from?"

Verity stifled the emotion. Managed to murmur "Scotland"; to not say "from the man I wish I could marry."

Through blurred vision, she noticed her sisters glance at each other, before Cecy said, "It's very striking," and a servant's knock brought the request that she and Caroline attend their mother downstairs.

Verity closed her eyes, willing the tears away, taking a moment to savor the quiet as Mary returned and continued her ministrations. *Dear God, forgive me for my ingratitude. Help me to forget him. Help me to learn to love Charles.*

Mary was pinning the last silver star in Verity's hair when her grandmother was assisted into the room, her bound leg necessitating such attention. Verity greeted her, then gazed at herself critically in the mirror. For once, she looked almost . . . pretty.

"Very nice, m'dear," Grandmama said, a rare smile of approval lighting her face. "I'm sure those Bromsgroves will be astounded by their good fortune." Her eyes glittered, softened. "I wish I could have dragged you off to Switzerland. I would have, save for this fool leg of mine." She gestured to her bound leg, legacy of a recent tumble down steps.

"I know, Grandmama."

"If only there was something we could have done." She sighed, eyeing Verity's reflection. "I must confess, I still do not understand why you are taking things so well."

"I am trying to be an obedient daughter."

"But why? And why *now* at long last?"

"Because . . ." Verity's cheeks heated. "Because I am aware of my past behavior being not as it should be. And the Bible says so, ma'am."

Her grandmother sniffed. "That is all well and good, but I don't suppose God intends us to willingly follow folly."

Verity's chest tightened. Was this folly? *Lord, give me wisdom.*

Later, as Verity stood next to her parents and Charles and his parents at the front of the ballroom, her grandmother's words resurfaced. Was it mere foolishness to obey her parents in this matter? They had been surprised, even shocked, by her meek compliance. God wanted her to obey them—didn't He? She was trying to trust Him, trying to read and obey the Bible, trying to believe His plans were for her good, as Mr. Chisholm had pointed out that last morning before her father's carriage had appeared. Even when she had finally signed the marriage documents, she had hoped for a miracle, a sign that God would reward her attempts to obey Him.

She sucked in a deep breath. Her mother glanced sharply at her. Verity kept her gaze fixed on the gold-inlaid central doorway. If she held still long enough, perhaps her bubble of hope would not be pricked, the crowds would disappear, and this would all prove a bad dream. Indeed, her dreams had taken on such a quality in recent days, where she spent her nights reliving the exquisite anguish of her time in Scotland, thinking of him, dreaming of him. It was useless, of course. She had hoped against hope, prayed every last prayer, but he had not come. He would not come. She knew that now, just as she knew she must resign herself to a life of propriety and loneliness near Birmingham. But oh, how she wished . . .

The sea of faces blurred slightly as Papa continued his long address. She blinked, forcing the emotion away. Forced her lips to remain slightly tilted, so the likes of Lady Heathcote should not think this marriage the punishment it was. Her gaze dipped to the front row, where her sisters' expressions suggested compassion.

Grandmama offered a grim smile, her efforts to prevent tonight as futile as Verity's own. How could either of them have succeeded, when Verity had been a virtual prisoner in her own home? Mama had been adamant this past week: no rides, no excursions, no visits from friends. It was like she expected Verity to run away! Even Mary's services had nearly been terminated; only Verity's desperate pleading had saved her maid's job. Her parents' displeasure had been fixed, as immovable as the foundations Aynsley had stood on for over ten generations.

Beside her, Charles loomed. She could smell something, an odor like that of a fish. For a moment she closed her eyes, willing her nose to conjure the scent of spiced oranges.

". . . and I am sure will be very happy . . ."

Her father's voice rumbled on. Verity's smile felt plastered on, her heart frozen. No. No!

Beside her, Charles shifted. She peeked up. He leaned down, his smile looming closer. At the last moment she turned her head and his hot lips dusted her cheek. She bit the inside of her bottom lip. She would not cry. She would not!

"So I ask you to join me in congratulating Verity and Charles."

She lowered her gaze to the marble floor as the room echoed with congratulations. Her eyes blurred. *God, why have You abandoned me?*

"No."

Verity stilled.

"No! Let me go!"

Her gaze lifted, sifting the crowd. Then she gasped.

He shrugged off the footman's attempt to hold him, eyes steady on her as he negotiated the gawking masses. Finally. He'd started this trip on little more than hope and a dream. The fire in his lungs had healed, but his visit to the Chisholms had only fanned his soul's desperation into flames, one that could countenance no option other than to find and protect her. So with the Chisholms' encouragement and connections, he had sailed to Liverpool, hired a carriage to London, made his necessary visits and purchases, before getting to Aynsley as quickly as possible, all the while pleading with God that he would not be too late.

He swallowed, staring at her, gowned in cream, lustrous in the candlelight spilling from the vast chandelier. She looked so lovely, so elegant, so unlike the dirt-smudged lass who professed a love for his gardens. Could he dare presume? The Chisholms had been so sure he should. But here, surrounded by so much magnificence, by so many diamond-encrusted ladies and gentlemen, the doubts washed in again.

His shock upon realizing the small village of Aynsley was named for her family was superseded by his impressions of the house—*not* the large gatehouse he'd first assumed. No, the long, deeply graveled approach had given way to a small rise, where the Baroque-inspired house, almost half a mile wide, stood self-importantly in the midst of manicured grounds. Somehow its muted honey-gold sandstone made Dungally seem frivolous, more toy castle than the generational statement of intent this building declared. For a moment he'd been tempted to send the carriage back around. Verity had grown up here? A *viscount's* daughter? What right had he to desire her, to wish to marry her? He might be a laird, but he'd grown up in far more humble circumstances. Surely she should become attached to someone of similar rank.

But then the memories arose of her plaintive face that night of the Guthrie ball, the night he should have told her he loved her, should have begged her to marry him . . .

Verity stepped forward, the silver pendant around her throat glistening, alluring.

His heart leapt. She'd worn it. Surely that must mean—

"Sir, I must insist you leave!"

Anthony ignored the footman, turning to the man whose portrait he had recognized from the room the footman had left him in, the same footman who had insisted his lordship was not receiving visitors, to which he'd replied, "The number of carriages outside suggests that isn't true."

He shrugged his arm free. "My lord, I must speak with you."

The small, gray-haired man frowned. "Who are you?"

He bowed. "I apologize for the unconventional introduction. My name is Jardine. I must speak with you concerning your daughter."

"Which daughter? I have three." The viscount gave a bitter-sounding laugh, motioning to the footman. "Take him away."

"What is this?" A woman with faded golden hair pushed forward, her face as querulous as her voice. He recognized enough in her features to see she was the mother of Verity. Her scowl deepened. "Simmons! Remove this person!"

"Sir, my lord—" Words tumbled round in his head. What could he say? What could he do? *God, help me!* "I am not finished—"

"I am."

"If I might just have a moment's private conversation?"

"Young man, this is neither the time nor the place."

The solidly built man next to Verity grasped her elbow, eyeing Anthony with dislike. "You are aware we are celebrating an engagement tonight?"

"I am indeed. But whether it be cause for celebration . . ." Anthony pushed forward and hurried to her, ignoring the fluttering fans and whispers around them. "You left."

"I had to," she murmured. "Papa—"

"So Mrs. Chisholm said."

"Sir! I must ask you to leave!" The footman plucked at his sleeve.

Anthony shook him off, eyes only on Verity. "You were engaged all that time? Why did you say nothing?"

"I know my duty, and . . . I'm obeying my parents' wishes."

"Not your own?"

She bit her lip, glanced away. He followed her gaze to meet an elderly woman's raised brows, the older woman's scrutiny becoming more hawklike when she saw him noticing her.

He stepped closer, saying in a low voice, "Do you love him?"

The silver spur pendant rose, fell, as she whispered, "You know I do not."

The tightness around his heart eased, even as the babble of voices continued around them. "Do you trust me?"

She nodded.

Anthony looked at the gentleman standing beside her. "Excuse me, but I must ask you to unhand Verity."

"Verity?" His eyes widened. "By what right do you address my betrothed so familiarly?"

"Is it not customarily the right of a man to speak so of his wife?"

Gasps filled the room.

God forgive him, but she *would* be his wife as soon as he got her away. He touched the special license in his pocket that promised this could be true.

"Your wife?" Lord Aynsley said. "No. You are being absurd. She is to marry Charles Bromsgrove. *Who* did you say you are?"

Desperation made him reckless, made him bold. "Some would say Verity's husband."

People like Colin Guthrie, for instance.

"Never tell me you—No. She would not. She *could* not—"

"I am sorry, sir, that such matters have not been made fully known to you. I am sure you can understand my reluctance in entering into congratulations when I know such congratulations are not justified. Not to this man, at least." He gestured to a slack-jawed Bromsgrove.

"But—"

"I assure you, sir, that I love your daughter most ardently." Anthony turned to smile at her.

"You do?" she whispered.

"Most ardently."

She gazed at him wonderingly, then finally, slowly, smiled back. Warmth spread through his body.

The older woman limped forward from the front row of guests. "Perhaps this should be discussed somewhere more appropriate."

He looked at the sea of curiosity. A twinge of remorse hit him as the viscount conducted a hasty conference. Oh, the shame her parents would need to live down, for surely tonight would be a talking point for years to come. But he could think of no other way, his sojourn by sea, his miles via coach and carriage, had fueled nothing more than plying Verity's own game, only this time his quick-wittedness would be tested.

Finally Lord Aynsley said, "Please excuse us for a moment. We will return momentarily." He gestured to the orchestra to play, before leading the way through side doors, leaving Anthony, filled with trepidation, to follow in his wake.

CHAPTER THIRTY

VERITY EASED HER elbow from Charles's limp grasp and moved to hurry after her parents and Anthony, but her grandmother restrained her as they entered the hall.

"Verity, lend me your arm, my dear."

"Of course." She held out an arm.

Grandmama leaned on it heavily. "This . . . this Jardine fellow," she said in an undertone. "Tell me the truth. You are not married, are you?"

"No," she whispered. "But I once pretended we were."

As the Bromsgroves strode past, Verity quickly told her the story, her grandmother seeming to age a dozen years before her eyes.

"At the risk of sounding like your mother, I cannot believe it." She sighed. "He truly is your choice?"

"Oh, Grandmama, Anthony is everything that is kind, and good, and courageous."

"He does possess a certain measure of courage, bowling up here as he's done. But is he a man of fortune?"

"He is a man of faith."

Her grandmother's lips pursed, her steps slowing. "I do not like this." Verity's hopes sunk. "He is the laird of Dungally."

"Scottish titles are hardly worth a snap."

What would appeal to her grandmother? "He has a large estate, and the most beautiful gardens at his castle."

"Castle, did you say?"

"It's called Dungally House, but truly, it's more like a castle than anything else. Oh, Grandmama, you would love the roses. And the gardens overlook the sea, just like at Saltings."

"That's all well and good, but why do you want *this* man?"

"Because he understands me better than anyone." Even more than Helena. "And he makes me want to be the best person I can be. And . . . and he loves me, mistakes and all."

"Hmm." She eyed Verity carefully. "Well, I suppose I should speak with him."

"But what will I do?"

"What do you mean? If I approve, you will marry him, of course."

"But what if he is only asking from a sense of obligation?"

Her grandmother snorted. "I had never thought you a foolish gel until this moment. Do you really suppose obligation made him chase you hundreds of miles? Indeed"—she grew thoughtful—"I think I really *would* like to speak to him."

"Miss Hatherleigh," the butler said, "your father requests your immediate attendance in the library."

She nodded, holding up her chin as he opened the door for them both.

Inside was a hubbub of confusion and recrimination. Mama and Mrs. Bromsgrove conducted high-pitched complaints, as Charles and his father plied criticisms upon Papa, who sat in his favorite chair, eyeing Anthony with disfavor. Anthony turned, smiled at Verity, and then hurried to assist her grandmother to a chair.

As the dark red head bent to the white one, Verity moved to the center of the room, the accusations swirling around her.

"I cannot understand—"

"Simply unbelievable!"

"Reprehensible!"

Verity glanced at Anthony to find his gaze fixed on her, his eyes kindly, his expression tender, even as Grandmama spoke in low and urgent tones to him.

"To think my own daughter—"

"I'd like to know how long this has been carrying on for!"

"He must be mad!"

Anthony spoke quickly to her grandmother then lifted his head. "I assure you I am not mad." He moved so she could feel the heat of him next to her. "I love your daughter with all my heart."

"You cannot love Verity," Mama exclaimed. "She might be a little heedless at times, but no daughter of mine would ever sink herself so low. Verity, why did you say nothing?" Her mother's eyes flashed. "I should have known those Chisholms would lead you astray. How could you? How could they?"

"Mother, you cannot blame the Chisholms. They are entirely innocent."

"I refuse to believe it! They must have—No. You *cannot* be married. You have done many a wild thing, but this, this—"

"You are aware that in Scotland the laws of matrimony permit a lady to marry at a younger age," Anthony said. "Gretna Green is not so terribly far from where I live, after all."

"Yes, but you cannot—that is, she *would* not—it is impossible!"

"I cannot tell you that it is impossible for it is perfectly possible. And when one considers the extreme measures undertaken to remove her from such a proceeding, is it that unlikely she would choose an alternative, rather than be thrust into a marriage she does not want?"

"Why you confounded—"

What followed was a string of epithets Verity had never expected Charles's father to know, let alone use. Everything from Anthony's parentage to his presumption was cursed in accents she was sure would cause even a sailor to blush. Anthony stood still, his face impassive, the only sign of his discomfort the clenching then straightening of his fingers.

"I am sorry you feel that way, sir, but it doesn't change the fact that I love Verity."

Charles's father swore, pounded his fist on the desk, then looked at her father. "Well, Aynsley? I demand an explanation!"

Her father met her gaze, brows upraised.

She swallowed. "Papa, I know this is not to your liking, but arranging Mr. Bromsgrove as my husband was not to mine."

"But you signed the papers. How could you do so if you were already married?"

"I felt I was given no choice, nor would anyone have listened to me if I had explained—"

"You are a wretched, wretched girl," Charles's mother declared.

"I do not think the fault lies entirely with Verity," murmured Grandmama.

"Yes, this is all *your* doing," Mama exclaimed. "If you hadn't spirited Verity away, none of this would have happened."

"Sometimes I suspect you really would prefer your daughter to live in misery all her days," Grandmama mused.

Her mother's face mottled, her lip clamping tight.

"As I see it, there is nothing to be done than to halt proceedings and let Verity and Jardine go on. I confess that I deplore the way this situation has unfolded, and feel that a little more forthrightness at the beginning might have saved everyone a great deal of angst, but what's done is done, and cannot be altered." Grandmama waved a hand before her face. "Now, it is growing rather warm in here. I believe I will retire somewhere with less hot air."

And oblivious to the heated stares, she limped through the doors to the hall.

"Verity, your actions have demonstrated a shocking lack of delicacy," Mama said. "I cannot understand how you could embroil us all in such scandal."

"Shocking, simply shocking!" reiterated Mrs. Bromsgrove.

"What I don't understand," Charles said, frowning at Anthony, "was that if you cared so much, how could you let her go?"

"I was unwell," he said. "You can imagine my dismay to discover she had been removed without my knowledge."

"I cannot believe her madcap ideas would extend so far!" Mother's cheeks had mottled.

"Excuse me, ma'am, but why can't you? When all her life Verity has been made to feel like she is a mistake?"

"How dare you!"

Anthony moved beside Verity, his hand finding hers. He threaded his fingers through hers and squeezed gently. "Did you not wish her to be a son?"

Papa blanched. His chest rose, fell. When he spoke he did not look at her. "She . . . she has always been such a tearaway—"

"I suspect she has always been such a compassionate, intelligent, wonderful girl," Anthony said, "who only wanted love."

Her eyes blurred. His grip tightened.

"And you think you offer that, do you?"

"I know I do." He turned to smile at her gently. "I love you."

His words, uttered with such simple assurance, filled the deepest recesses of her heart. Anthony loved her. *Loved* her! His words tonight might be a blend of truth and hope-filled fiction, but she knew he could be trusted. As Grandmama had pointed out, his very actions in following her here, in doing his best to protect her, revealed a sense of honor and chivalry she hadn't known until now that she desired. Suddenly the night felt manageable, that the game where the two of them must outwit their opponents could be won. She squeezed his hand.

"Who knows of this . . . this *marriage?*" Mama's face twisted as if tasting something sour.

"You mean apart from the Kirkcudbright locals?" Verity glanced at Anthony. "Well, I'm sure Colin would have told Lord and Lady Guthrie."

"And I . . . I have been in recent correspondence with various acquaintances throughout Scotland. I called in to see various friends whilst I was in London. As well as the Bishop of—"

"They *all* know?"

Verity clamped her lips so as to not echo her mother.

"I am sorry if you feel hurt, Charles, but would you really want to be saddled with such a hoyden? You sir," Mama sniffed to Anthony, "are just as wretched as she. Shameless, the pair of you!"

Hurt slashed Verity's chest, and she lowered her gaze to hide her mortification.

Anthony turned, tipping up her chin with one finger. "I am not ashamed at all." He smiled. "You look even lovelier than in my dreams, my dearest."

"Mr. Jardine."

He carried on, as if oblivious to her mother's voice. "Your leaving left such a hole in my heart, I scarcely knew whether it was day or night." He picked up her hand, kissed her palm.

Heat trembled through her. "At the time I thought you did not care."

"I had no wish for you to catch my illness, my love."

A knot in her heart eased.

"I know I should have said more, but at that time I could scarcely think straight. And then when you left"—he squeezed her hand—"it was like you'd run away with my heart. I was more desperate than a motherless bairn."

"A motherless bairn?"

"Aye. Your leaving caused such a kerfuffle. Why, Helena looked like she wanted me dead. Frances blamed me, and poor Benjamin seemed like a sad ghost—"

"Who is this Benjamin?" Papa asked.

"Helena's younger brother," she murmured.

"But their pain was nothing compared to mine, when I realized you had gone, without a word of goodbye—"

"I said goodbye that last night."

Mrs. Bromsgrove gasped. "So wanton!"

Anthony stilled for a moment, shooting that lady a narrow-eyed glance before returning his attention to Verity. His expression grew soft. "I cannot believe such a generous, kind soul as yourself would be so cruel as to think a sick man might remember everything that is said in troubling times." He smiled, his eyes creasing in the corners. "All the way here, I could only think of the great poet's words, 'My love is like a red, red rose—'"

"Pretty words," Mrs. Bromsgrove sniffed.

He continued speaking, eyes still intent on her. "'As fair art thou, my bonnie lass, so deep in love am I, and I will love thee still, my dear, till all the sea gang dry.'"

Her heart swelled until it felt she must burst her stays. He thought her bonny? He was deeply in love with her? Oh, how dear he was!

"All this is very touching, but I fail to see how it proves anything," Mama said. "All we have is your word. After Mrs. Chisholm's promise to safeguard you, I have the greatest doubts of anyone from that part of the world being capable of speaking the truth."

Verity secured her bottom lip to prevent its trembling. Mama was right. Despite Anthony being here, despite his sweet words, he could not truly prevent the marriage.

Anthony smiled, reached into his pocket, drew out a ring. "You should be wearing this."

He slipped it on her finger, where the diamonds sparkled in the candlelight. "It . . . it is beautiful."

"Yet not as lovely as its owner," he said, his gaze dropping to Verity's mouth. Then he was leaning close, closer, was drawing her into his arms, was kissing her.

"Verity! That is enough."

Verity ignored her mother, twining her arms around Anthony's neck as his lips pressed hers warmly, firmly, possessively. Amidst the gasps and whispers, she felt her body sway, melt against his, as his arm tightened around her waist. Oh, if only they really *were* married . . .

"Young man! Stop that right now! Simmons! Simmons!"

Verity felt Anthony's chest rumble with laughter, felt his hands gently ease her away so he could whisper in her ear, "I have a special license. We'll marry as soon as we leave here."

"Really?"

"Really."

Joy surged through her chest. "Oh, let's leave now."

"Verity? What is the meaning of this?" She peeked past Anthony's shoulder to see her grandmother reenter the room. "Why are you allowing this young man to embrace you in such an unseemly manner?"

"He is still insisting he is her husband! I for one do not believe it."

"Why do you not? Do you honestly believe my granddaughter could behave so improperly if she were not married? I would sooner believe you the world's greatest simpleton than to think my Verity could behave so dishonorably." Grandmama turned to Anthony. "Tell me, are you a gentleman?"

"I endeavor to be so, ma'am."

"Which is more than can be said for many. I trust you will treat my granddaughter as she deserves?"

"Of course, ma'am."

Grandmama's eyes glinted, her gaze running up and down him before she gave Verity the tiniest of nods. "Seeing as we missed the ceremony, I will expect you to oblige me with another service at the chapel."

"Of course, Grandmama. As soon as it pleases you."

"Good. I believe you will make a good pair."

"But the marriage documents!" Mama said.

"That's right," Mr. Bromsgrove said, with an air of relief. "It doesn't change the fact that the papers have been signed, including by Verity. So in effect we are still legally bound to go ahead."

Papa nodded, striding to the connecting door between the library and his study. "Bromsgrove is correct." He flung open the doors. "The marriage settlements . . ." His voice trailed off.

Beyond him, Verity could see into the room. Could see the fireplace stuffed full of charred paper, pieces of which even now floated around the room.

"What in the world?" Papa hurried to the desk, rifling through papers. "No. How did—"

Beside her, Grandmama made a sound suspiciously like a giggle.

Papa looked up, brow lowering. "Mother, tell me you didn't burn the marriage documents."

Her grandmother's smile grew sly. "It would seem to be a little too late for papers."

Verity smiled.

"Get that smirk off your face, young lady. This, this is catastrophic! You are ruined!"

"Not if I'm married, Mother," she said gently.

"But, but—"

"Stop gaping like a fishwife. You, too," Grandmama snapped at Papa. "What's done is done. And you know you should never have agreed to this."

"But I had to."

"Nonsense. Because your wife insisted on it?" Grandmama sighed. "I am sorry to have raised such a weak-willed son who cannot do what is right."

"But the family line!" Mama said. "Bromsgrove said he would—"

"I'll warrant that family has said many a thing in their time," Grandmama sniffed.

The Bromsgroves' protests went unheeded, their departure from the room equally so.

Papa turned to Anthony. "I cannot like it, but I suppose my mother is correct in saying what is done is done."

"But—"

"Oh, stop, my dear." Papa sighed, waving a hand to cut off Mother's protest. "I cannot but think we were a little precipitous in foisting Verity into something she clearly regarded as anathema. And it must be said"—he studied Verity—"your attitude and behavior have been improved of late, although I certainly did not account it to this."

"My time in Scotland has changed me," Verity agreed cautiously. God had changed her. Love had changed her.

Papa shook his head, his lips tightening as he eyed Anthony, before releasing in a sigh. "Jardine, you say."

"Yes, my lord. The fourteenth Laird of Dungally."

"Laird?" Mother said.

"Yes, my lady. I am well able to provide for your daughter, not being entirely without portion."

"He has a castle, and a fine estate," Grandmama added.

"A castle?"

Verity held her breath. Was her father finally relenting?

He glanced at her, his gaze sliding to Anthony, whose hand she still firmly held. "What say you, Jardine? Care to exchange your last name for mine?"

Verity's hand gripped his more tightly, even as she cringed inwardly.

"Thank you, sir, no." A beat. "But I'd be happy for our second son to bear your name."

"Second son, eh?" Grandmama looked at her. "Sounds like you'll be busy."

The heat in Anthony's smiling gaze drew matching warmth to her cheeks.

"Oh, whatever will we say to our guests?" Mama moaned.

"I suppose I will need to announce a different groom than whom we expected."

Verity laughed, her father's answering smile encouraging her enough to hug him. As his arms slowly eased around her, she closed her eyes, thanking God for this sign of his affection.

"But sir," Anthony interposed. "I feel it only fair to tell you that I cannot guarantee we will always be in England, nor Scotland. I may need to return to New South Wales at some point in the future."

"But Verity! You cannot leave her."

"She will come, too."

"Really?" Verity slipped from her father's embrace, to study her husband-to-be. "Do you really mean that?"

He grinned, drew her close. "I do, *minha querida*."

"Minah what?" Her father frowned.

"*Minha querida*. It means 'my dearest' in Portuguese."

"Portuguese?" Mama said. "Never tell me you plan to live in Portugal?"

"We never will," he agreed, smiling at Verity again. "*Minha querida, carissima, princesa.*"

"But she is not a princess. As the daughter of a viscount she is merely an honorable."

"And sometimes I'm not even that."

And to prove her point, Verity snuggled into Anthony's arms, and covered his lips with her own.

❧ Author's Note

IN 2015 I was blessed with the opportunity to visit my sister who was living in London at the time. What followed was a wonderful few weeks, traveling to visit so many places I had only ever dreamed about from my little Australian town on the opposite side of the globe. One of these places was Scotland. During our time in this glorious part of the world, my sister and I managed to visit a number of Scotland's top scenic destinations, including Edinburgh, Glen Coe, Loch Ness, Urquhart Castle, and the fabulous Ardverikie estate used in the TV series *Monarch of the Glen*. Added to this were a number of less-visited places, including Kirkcudbright, and the castle depicted on the cover, which is Dunrobin Castle, the home of the chiefs of Clan Sutherland.

For the purpose of this story I transplanted this fairy-tale castle to the Lowlands, so if you travel to Kirkcudbrightshire, don't expect to see Anthony's castle there! This area of the Scottish border is, however, where the Jardine and Irving clans have resided for centuries. The spur rowel given to Verity forms part of the Jardine crest.

The Riding of the Marches still occurs in Kirkcudbright, although a great deal of liberty has been taken for the purpose of condensing events for this story.

Resources used include *Recollections of a Tour Made in Scotland* (1803), *Elizabeth Macquarie's Journal* (1809), *The Diary of Lachlan Macquarie* (1821–1822), and *The British Cyclopedia of Literature*,

History, Geography, Law and Politics (1836). Governor Macquarie did send a pair of emus as a gift to the Marquess of Hastings (stationed in India at the time); this was changed to better accommodate the time frame and possible shipping routes of the story. I was excited to discover the connection between England and Portugal, and the fact that the Macquaries had met the Portuguese prince who became King John VI, so it felt entirely possible such a gift might be made to him, too.

Verity's thwarting of the Guthrie attempt to kidnap the laird is based on an attempt by American sailors in 1778 to kidnap a Scottish nobleman, as told in Peter Newman's *The Empire of the Bay* (2000). Verity's quick-witted courage in refusing their demands and instead acting the part of the gracious hostess is similar to Lady Selkirk's experience, and something which proves the old adage that truth can sometimes be stranger than fiction.

The samples of Scottish brogue are from the Scots Glossary, courtesy of the Mudcat Café resource, spelling as depicted there.

For behind-the-book details and a discussion guide, and to sign up for my newsletter, please visit www.carolynmillerauthor.com.

And if you have enjoyed reading this or any of the other books in the three Regency Brides series, please consider leaving a review at Goodreads, Amazon, or your favorite booktalk site.

Finally, thank you, lovely readers, for all your wonderful support of the Regency Brides series. God bless you!

ℛ Acknowledgments

THANK YOU, GOD, for giving this gift of creativity, and the amazing opportunity to express it. Thank You for patiently loving us and offering us hope through Jesus Christ.

Thank you, Joshua, for your love and encouragement. I appreciate all the support you give in so many ways, including reading this manuscript so many moons ago. I love you!

Thank you, Caitlin, Jackson, Asher, and Tim—I love you, I'm so proud of you, and so grateful you understand why I spend so much time in imaginary worlds.

To my family and friends, whose support, encouragement, and prayers I value and have needed—thank you. Big thanks to Roslyn and Jacqueline for being patient in reading through so many of my manuscripts, and for offering suggestions to make my stories sing.

Thank you, Tamela Hancock Murray, my agent, for helping this little Australian negotiate the big, wide American market.

Thank you to the authors and bloggers who have endorsed, and encouraged, and opened doors along the way: you are a blessing! Thanks to my Aussie writer friends, from Australasian Christian Writers, Christian Writers Downunder, and Omega Writers—I appreciate you.

To the Ladies of Influence—your support and encouragement are gold!

To the fabulous team at Kregel: thank you for believing in me, and for making *Misleading Miss Verity* shine. Big thanks to my editors, Janyre and Dawn, for all you've done through these past books of the Regency Brides series.

Finally, thank you to my wonderful readers! Thank you for buying my books and for spreading the love for these Regency romances. Your kind messages of support and lovely reviews are valued more highly than you realize.

I hope you enjoyed Verity's story.

God bless you.